# A Very Naughty Xmas

Cherrie Lynn
Stephanie Julian
Olivia Cunning
Raven Morris
Cari Quinn

Published by Olivia Cunning, Stephanie Julian, Cherrie Lynn, Raven Morris, Cari Quinn
Copyright 2012 Olivia Cunning, Stephanie Julian, Cherrie Lynn, Raven Morris, Cari Quinn
Cover design and Interior layout: www.formatting4U.com

All rights reserved. No part of this book may be reproduced in any form or by any electronic or mechanical means, including information storage and retrieval systems—except in the case of brief quotations embodied in critical articles or reviews—without permission in writing from the authors. This book is a work of fiction. The characters, events, and places portrayed in this book are products of the author's imagination and are either fictitious or are used fictitiously. Any similarity to real persons, living or dead, is purely coincidental and not intended by the author.

***Dedicated to our readers.***

*Thank you for allowing us to do what we love to do.*

*Happy Holidays from
Raven, Cari, Stephanie, Olivia, Cherrie*

# Table of Contents

| | |
|---|---|
| Jingle Ball | 01 |
| Christmas is Coming | 61 |
| Light Me Up | 127 |
| An Indecent Proposition | 175 |
| Share Me | 227 |

# Jingle Ball

## Cari Quinn

*Jingle Ball, by Cari Quinn*

# Chapter I

Wendy Stanton picked up a length of multi-colored garland and sighed. Red, blue and green garland wasn't classy enough for Martin & Warner Real Estate's annual Jingle Ball. The event was the biggest schmoozer they held all year and lots of rich, important guests would attend. They'd already decided the color scheme would be silver and blue, so the decoration she'd picked up on a whim would just have to go.

She wrapped the garland around her neck and turned toward the full wall of glass behind her boss Des's desk. She thrust out a hip and grabbed a long, narrow notepad, using it as a microphone. Then she rocked out, dirty Christmas style. She didn't remember the lyrics to the song on the radio so she fudged them, making them up as she went along. Her husky voice wouldn't win any awards, but she vamped it up, pushing a hand behind her head and wiggling her butt.

Behind her, someone cleared their throat. Wendy spun around and dropped the notebook, her eyes going wide at her boss lounging in the doorway. His hands were tucked in the pockets of his snug, faded jeans, and he wore a gray silk shirt and striped tie that offset his golden skin.

And he was smirking.

"Didn't mean to interrupt your concert, Ms. Stanton." His voice was as warm and rich as the coffee he walked over to dispense from his personal machine. He preferred an expensive Costa Rican blend, the best of the best. Just as he preferred top of the line in everything in his life, from clothes, to office space, to girlfriends. She still wondered how *she'd* slunk into his office almost a year ago when his secretary had quit on short notice. Des desperate was a mouth-watering sight to behold.

Fine, he was mouth-watering regardless. He had the kind of spiky dark hair that always stuck up in all directions and his eyes were a bright blue-green she'd only ever seen in the waters of the Caribbean. And his body?

Not. Going. There.

"Song's over," she said with a shrug, picking up the notebook she'd dropped. Feigning calm around him wasn't anything new,

*A Very Naughty Xmas*

considering she'd had a crush on him pretty much since the first moment she'd stepped into his swanky office. He'd asked her what she considered her strongest skill and she'd been tempted to say sucking cock, just to see if she'd get a chance at his.

Instead she'd gone with the safe answer of her one hundred words per minute typing speed.

That she'd inquired about the job advertised in the window wearing a pair of yoga pants and a tank top, with her hair held back by an assortment of bobby pins and paper clips—hey, she'd been out grocery shopping before she'd wandered past the office—hadn't ruined her chances as she'd feared. He'd called to hire her the next day. They'd had a cordial, utterly frustrating relationship since.

"So it is. But as it's a radio station," Des gestured with his coffee cup at the sleek wall unit currently playing another Christmas classic, "they keep playing them. Keep singing."

If she was anyone else, she'd probably hurry to obey the command in his tone. Though they were both barely thirty, Des and his best friend Cole Warner had one of the most successful real estate businesses in Eugene, New York, a decent-sized city just outside the one that never slept. They'd climbed far and fast, and that meant they weren't strangers to making demands and ensuring they were met.

She suspected that was true in the bedroom too. Not that she knew firsthand. Both men were nothing but professional to their secretaries. Unfortunately.

It wasn't as if she could tell Des she wasn't a lawsuit waiting to happen. Nor was she trying to climb the corporate ladder, unless it led straight up to the eyepopping bulge in his pants. But that was just her fantasies talking. She wasn't that girl.

Those jewel-like blue-green eyes stared her down, and like a fool, she began to sing into the notebook. She had to look ridiculous with her garland and her steno microphone, but he leaned back against the wall and watched her, seemingly riveted.

Yet again she didn't know the words to the song, so she improvised. A smile began at the corners of his mouth, creeping inward until it turned into a full-blown grin. He set aside the coffee and clapped, the width of his hands catching her attention for the umpteenth time before her gaze skipped to his face.

His smirk returned. Did he know what she was thinking?

Forget that, did she know what she was thinking? He was her boss. He signed her paycheck and ponied up for the fancy health benefits that even allowed her to cover her ailing mom too. The extra expense was significant, but Des hadn't blinked when she'd explained her mom's heart condition and her search for affordable health care since her mom wasn't old enough for Medicare. He shelled out a ton of extra dough each month, and she couldn't afford to fuck that up just to…

Fuck.

"You're a very creative lyricist, Wendy." His smirk disappeared behind his coffee cup as he drank.

And yes, she watched his throat move. And yes, she did get wet. Could've been due to her new thong. That satin panel tended to rub her just the right way.

As right as her vibrator would need to rub her after work if she had any hopes of getting through the holidays without making a very big mistake. Otherwise she just might end up using her garland to bind Des to his desk chair so she could have her jolly way with him.

"It's more fun to make up the words." She tugged off her rainbow garland and snatched a couple of strands of blue-and-silver. "Especially when I get drunk. You'd die if you heard some of what I come up with then."

"I'd like to."

She glanced at him, frowning, but he'd turned away to pour more coffee. The guy was a hardcore caffeine junkie, drinking the stuff like some men swigged beer. Though he might do that too. She didn't know him outside of work.

"I don't drink that often." Wincing at the unexpected loudness of her voice, she bit the inside of her cheek and wound the garland strands together to create a thick, glittery rope. She'd finished her dictation early and hoped to decorate a good portion of Des's office before she had to get back on the phones when the other receptionist Vanessa went to lunch.

The big party was tonight and they had a lot to do to make the place festive. The sprawling Victorian that served as the base for Martin & Warner had been remodeled to look like standard office space, but by this evening, the huge conference room would be set up for dancing, and the reception area would contain enough food for a small army. Van had worked there for three years and she'd set up her share of Christmas parties. Apparently Des and Cole spared no expense for the gathering.

Noticing Des hadn't replied, she looked up to find him studying her silently while he mainlined his coffee. It was disconcerting to say the least, and she was tempted to start singing and dancing again to try to alleviate the odd tension in the room.

"I imagine you don't go out partying too often. You're too responsible to leave your mom on her own all night long, aren't you?"

Rather than reply, she examined the garland she'd continued to twist until shards of blue and silver littered his pristine navy carpet.

She'd probably told him too much about her personal life. But she'd only arrived in town last fall and hadn't known a soul outside of Aunt Gert, the relative she and her mom had moved from Chattanooga to be near. After Wendy's dad had died unexpectedly last year, her mom hadn't been the same. Wendy had wanted her surviving parent to be near family, especially considering Noreen's own heart problems.

So they'd uprooted themselves and moved north—and Wendy had found herself confiding in her surprisingly compassionate boss. He'd listened without offering advice she didn't want, and he'd helped as much as he could. Just offering them health insurance had alleviated the bulk of her stress.

Her loneliness…well, that was a different story.

"You're the most responsible twenty-four year old I've ever met," he continued, drawing her from her thoughts. "Are you sure there's not an eighty-year-old woman hiding in there?"

His teasing defrosted her sudden freeze. "In *this* lingerie?" She gestured at herself, though he obviously couldn't see what she meant. "Doubtful."

He chuckled and reached over to open a packet of sugar, stirring it into his coffee. Weird. Hadn't he already drank half of it? Unless he was developing a sweet tooth.

"Did Daniel Jenkins call?" he asked, and just like that, they were back to work.

No more singing, drinking or lingerie talk. A good thing, she mused later on at her desk, giving her jingle bell earrings a twirl as she considered the reception area. The tree in corner was done up in silver and blue as requested, the boughs dripping with icicles and each branch weighed down with unique ornaments. There were four small trees in the place, along with a huge towering real fir in the conference room.

That morning, a grinning Cole had dragged out the box of ornaments from the attic and unveiled them for Van, Des and Wendy. Van and Des had oohed and aahed then rolled their eyes behind his back, but Wendy had been genuinely impressed with the collection. Most were from the multi-pack boxes found at any retail outlet, with a few unusual ones that gave the trees character.

She sighed and played with her earring again. She and her mom had been forced to leave a lot of their ornaments behind in Tennessee due to the cost of moving, though she'd saved some of her favorites. They were still tucked in tissue paper, waiting for her to get over her holiday blues long enough to unpack them and do up their tree right.

Her mom needed that. She needed it.

Until then, she'd vowed to enjoy decorating the office. She and Van had laughed throughout the afternoon, despite this Christmas being a lot different than others in her past. Back when she'd had two healthy parents and a hometown she loved. When she'd had friends and knew interested guys if she wanted to date...or more, if the urge struck.

Something it was doing now. A lot.

"Hey girl." Van popped around the half-wall sectioning off Wendy's area and grinned. "You still here? I thought you'd be home getting ready by now."

Wendy blew out the cinnamon candle flickering on her desk and faked a smile. "Just about to head out. I had a few letters to finish up for Des. You know how he is, the taskmaster."

"Oh, am I?" Des appeared behind Van, his big hands cupping her shoulders. Her short blonde curls bounced around her face as she hurriedly made room for him at her side. "And here the taskmaster dragged himself from his endless piles of work just to make sure you two ladies had gone home. Guess I shouldn't have bothered."

Van immediately transitioned into full-on flirt mode. "Oh, Des. You're the best boss ever."

"Even if he's not technically *your* boss?" Wendy propped her chin on her hand and smiled as widely as she could when jealousy had her around the throat.

Stupid. She knew Van and Des were just friends—at least she was reasonably sure—but whenever Van switched her hardcore flirting from Cole to Des, Wendy's claws sprouted. She liked Van. She just didn't want her crawling all over Des too much, at least not where she could see it.

He slung an arm around Van's waist and tossed Wendy a grin. "Hey, I sign the checks for everybody around here. Including that clown in the office behind you." He strode to the wall behind Wendy's desk and rapped. Cole grunted from the next room.

After the ornament show-and-tell, he'd retreated to work on some big deal he had in the pipeline for an office complex in nearby Jasper. As easygoing as Cole seemed most of the time, he busted his ass night and day to keep the business running smoothly. So did Des. It was amazing either of them found time for a social life.

*Don't need a ton of time to screw.*

Her chin slipped off her hand at that errant thought and she had to grab the desk to keep from tipping out of her chair. Des shot her a look, but she just kept smiling. That was her, perky twenty-four/seven. As perky as the breasts she could state with virtual certainty were waving hello to Des, even if he were oblivious.

She hoped he was oblivious. Jeez.

"Think I better get out of here." She took out her purse from her bottom drawer and rose, smoothing down her pencil skirt while she grabbed her coat. She flashed another smile and turned to her co-workers, her thoughts vanishing at the sight of Des's outstretched hand. "Oh, you don't have to—"

"Let me."

Sure she was flushing, she handed over her coat and allowed him to help her into it. "See you soon?" he asked once she faced him.

"Yes." This time her smile was genuine. To make up for her jealous harpy routine, she made sure it encompassed Van too. "I'll be back shortly, ya'll. I can't wait."

*Jingle Ball, by Cari Quinn*

# Chapter II

Des pulled on his tie and stared out his window, his focus centered on the small figure hurrying up the street in the lightly falling snow. Wendy always insisted on walking the few blocks to and from work, claiming she enjoyed the exercise, but he knew it was because she didn't want to waste gas or put more miles on her beat-up car. She was a penny-pincher in the extreme. Considering the financial toll her father's death had put on her family, he understood.

"Watching to make sure she gets home okay?"

Cole's voice made him grip the windowsill. "I can't see all the way to her house."

"But you keep her in sight for as long as you can."

Admitting what Cole already knew would cause it to be more real somehow, so he just narrowed his eyes until the darkness swallowed her cheerful red coat. Then he let out a long breath. Relief maybe, mixed with a healthy dose of longing.

And lots of fucking frustration.

A loud exhale preceded the unmistakable sound of Cole slumping in the chair opposite Des's desk. "Are you ever going to, you know, do something about it?"

Though he knew very well what Cole meant, he played dumb. And mute.

"What if she meets someone, Des? Then what?"

Des hooked his thumbs in the pockets of his jeans. He'd wondered that many times himself, and he never came up with a good answer. They worked together. She wasn't his in any shape or form. If she found someone, he'd wish her well.

All right, maybe not.

Truth was, if he'd ever met a woman who more deserved to be taken care of and worshipped, he didn't remember it. She was so capable and strong, but she shouldn't have to be. Not every minute. Not when he knew he was the right man to show her the freedom in occasionally giving up control.

Except he wasn't. He couldn't be.

He turned away from the window and studied his best friend, noting he'd already changed into black trousers and a disturbingly green sweater. They lived upstairs in separate wings, occasionally meeting in the kitchen or living room but mostly staying in their own spaces. Living and working together could get old fast, so they made sure to give each other a lot of room.

A memory from last summer—involving a curvaceous redhead and too much tequila—flitted into Des's mind and he smiled. Well, most of the time.

"Does that smile mean you've come up with a plan? Finally?" Cole smoothed away an imaginary wrinkle in his slacks. "A guy's nuts could shrivel up waiting for you to make a goddamn move."

"Actually I was thinking about…" He paused. Shit, what was her name? Tracy? Stacy? "Redhead, triple Ds. Giggled too much." Moaned even more, which hadn't been half-bad.

"I remember." Cole smiled fondly. "Casey. She was sweet. Very creative. Wonder if she's available?"

"Doing a girl you're not serious about at Christmas never turns out well. You know better, Warner."

Cole stroked his cock through his trousers. "Maybe Daisy was my one true love. Or was it Lacey?"

Des snorted out a laugh and scraped a hand through his hair. He needed to take a shower. The girls would be back soon, and not long after, guests would start flowing through the doors as fast as the champagne. Already he could hear the caterers bustling from room to room. "You good to handle things while I run upstairs?"

"Oh, you're not ready? Hard to fucking tell, since those ratty-ass jeans have been your wardrobe for the past week."

"Scoping out my ass again? I'm so flattered." Des grinned and headed out of the office, humming one of the holiday tunes that had played earlier.

He took the back stairs three at a time. In record time, his cock was in his soapy hand, his forehead braced on the arm he folded against the tile wall. Images of Wendy played behind his closed eyes. Dancing when she didn't know he was there, gyrating her hips in maddening circles, bouncing her breasts with each movement. Her shiny pink lips tilted into a smile as she crooned into her makeshift microphone.

She was so motherfucking sexy.

Des sucked in a breath and tightened his grip, working himself viciously. He'd never squeeze his dick hard enough to erase the pictures stored in his head so he used them as fodder, dragging his hand up and

*Jingle Ball, by Cari Quinn*

down until his gasps mingled with the hiss of the scalding water.

He wrenched the water dial hotter, then hotter still. Soon his skin would flay right off his damn bones, and he'd still be here, jerking off with her sweet southern voice tormenting him. Just her accent reminded him of fucking. She could say "pass the paper clips" and he'd envision throwing her legs over his shoulders and sucking on her swollen clit.

*I'll be back shortly, ya'll.*

Christ. He could've come from just that.

Clouds of steam rose around him and he threw his head back, the hot stream of water stabbing his face and chest offering additional sensation. Groaning, he reached down and grabbed his heavy balls, rhythmically pumping, his breath puffing over the tiles until the long white ribbons of his release fountained into the cascading water.

He slumped against the wall, panting. Shuddering. It wasn't enough. He needed her under him, her tight pussy wrapped around his cock. Her seductively prim and proper voice whispering in his ear, her long nails raking down his back. She'd be a scratcher, he just knew it.

Snatching his bottle of shampoo, he dumped way too much on his head and took out his frustration on his scalp. Even knowing it wasn't going to happen—that it couldn't—the disappointment still cut deep.

Thirty minutes later, he was on his way back downstairs. He passed a couple in a clinch on the landing. They let out guilty laughter when he cleared his throat. "Already seeking out the corners, Edwards?" he asked the gray-haired man who shamelessly left his hand on his partner's ass.

Gerald Edwards, esteemed attorney at law, had boffed every secretary he'd ever had. When he ran out of them, he poached the receptionists from the law office next door. And *that* was exactly the kind of guy Des refused to be. He didn't sleep with his employees. Never had, never would.

"Great party, Des," Gerald said, extending a hand.

Des shook Gerald's hand and continued downstairs. Not his problem.

A crowd had already started to form in the lobby. The entrance area contained several groups of laughing couples, and the hallway to the conference room held even more. A few pairs danced to the music of Josh Groban, and he spotted a few clients hanging out by the punch bowl.

It would be a successful night. He could feel it.

A quick detour to his office yielded a tall cup of coffee, with the added bonus of two sugars. He normally drank his coffee black but with Wendy and her sultry jasmine perfume due to arrive at any moment, he couldn't take the chance. Somehow the burst of sugar on his tongue helped distract him from scenting her like a wolf, and he wasn't about to question his coping techniques. They'd helped him keep his dick in his pants for an entire year so they must be working.

An hour passed in a haze of conversation. It didn't take him long to lose the button-down shirt he'd thrown over a T-shirt—yeah, he dressed casually, Cole could fucking suck it—though he dumped it off on his friend's chair rather than his own. There was a heated argument going on in his office, and he figured he'd be nice and not interrupt since they were the dumbasses who'd neglected to lock their rooms.

Fighting was one thing. But he'd make sure no bodily fluid was spilled in his office unless it was his.

"You wish, Martin," he muttered.

The drinks were flowing, the food was delicious, and the entire place smelled of cinnamon, hot cider, and pine. Everyone seemed to be enjoying themselves, some more than others. He'd come upon several couples under the mistletoe that Cole had insisted Van hang up near the exit, though Des knew his partner hoped to lure her there herself before the night ended. Unlike him, Cole had no qualms about sleeping with his assistants, though nothing had happened between them yet.

Luckily Des had a few more brain cells and knew where to draw the line.

Des did several loops of the party, determined to make sure all of his guests were having a good time. So many people grabbed him to talk that he didn't notice Wendy's absence right away. Cole and Van hadn't seen her either.

He rubbed the back of his neck. Had something happened? It wasn't like Wendy to blow off a work function. She was never anything less than diligent.

Just as he pulled out his cell to call her, a soft moan stopped him. His body tensed as he shifted direction. Ah, Jesus, now there was someone in Cole's office. That sealed it. Time to lock up.

Silently, he pushed the door inward. A lone figure sat at the desk, her back to him. It was a woman, judging from the hair tumbling down her shoulders. From her smell, that perfume that tormented his days and haunted his nights.

Then she turned, a flash of white clutched in one hand, the other buried beneath the voluminous skirt draped over the arms of Cole's chair. He registered her sound of surprise, and the shock that emanated from her pores as she realized she'd been caught.

In Cole's office. In his chair. With her hand between her legs.

Anger spurted hot and furious in Des's chest, swamping the relief that she was okay. How could she be in this room, touching herself, when he'd had his dick on a chokechain for the past year? He'd done everything he could to keep his professional distance. For all he knew, all that time she'd wanted Cole.

Fucking Cole Warner.

He slammed a hand against the door and it clattered shut. She gasped and leaped to her feet, the item she held fluttering to the floor. He stalked behind the desk to retrieve it, not sure what he'd find. Not caring.

They were ending this now.

He bent and yanked up the shirt, his brain clearing. His shirt. She'd been holding his shirt, in Cole's office. Moaning. Touching her pussy, making his mouth water from the scent he could've picked up if he'd been surrounded by a dozen other women. Hers would've overridden them all.

Catching it again, he slitted his eyes. She stood next to Cole's chair, her breathing audible in the small space between them. Her chest lifting and falling, her chin swiveling back and forth as if she were debating making a run for the door.

As if she thought she could get away from him.

She lurched forward and he moved, clamping a hand around her wrist. A startled squeak escaped her before he covered her mouth with his hand, hauling her back against him. "Just be quiet. Do you want everyone to know what you've been up to in here?" He allowed himself one illicit brush of his face against her hair. She smelled of her perfume and soap and alcohol, something rich and sweet. Bourbon perhaps, except they weren't serving that at the party.

Maybe that explained everything. His stalwart secretary was drunk.

He dropped his hand from her mouth. "How much have you had to drink?"

"Let me go." She yanked her arm but his grip held fast.

"I asked you a question, Wendy."

"A couple of glasses."

"How many?"

"Just two, before I came here." She half-spun to face him, her face contorted with anger. "Let me go."

"Why?" Ignoring the warning bells clanging in his brain, he gripped her chin. She was trembling faintly, from fury or nerves. Maybe both. "You never drink."

"How do you know? You don't know me. No one does." She broke free of him and released a long, shaky sigh as if she were stunned she'd managed it. Most likely she didn't realize he'd released her. "Just forget you saw me in here, okay, Des? Please."

The plea in her voice struck deep inside him and he shut his eyes.

Opening them, he let out a sigh of his own. "I can't." He pressed his thumb into the shallow indent in her chin. "Go find Cole. Bring him back here."

"Oh God, I didn't mean—"

"Just do it, Wendy." He refused to allow himself to be swayed by her appeal. "Now."

## Chapter III

She did as she was told.

Finding Cole wasn't difficult. He was always at the center of the biggest group, and tonight was no exception. Feeling like an ashamed child, she slipped between people, murmuring excuses, and tapped his shoulder. He turned, a smile creasing his attractive face. He wasn't as tempting as Des, but— Oh God, Des.

Cole's denim blue eyes sobered. "Wen? What's up?"

"Des asked me to come get you. He's in your office."

"Uh, all right. Just let me—"

"He said it needed to be now."

She looked down at her red patent leather heels, bought especially for tonight. Dammit, she'd ruined everything by getting a little tipsy and acting stupid. She never should've come. Not after she'd gone home and seen her mom asleep on the couch. Her bout of walking pneumonia was kicking her ass, and every time she got sick, Wendy worried she'd lose her like she'd lost Dad. It wasn't the first time the weight of her life had crashed down on her shoulders, but now she'd probably end up unemployed.

"I'm sorry, Cole," she added when Cole didn't move.

"Hey, it's okay. Let's go see what the big boss man wants." Hooking an arm around her shoulders, he gestured with his beer bottle to his crowd of sycophants. "We'll be back soon. Office business, you know. Try not to get the cops called, ya hear?"

Laughter followed them as they slipped away from the masses and down the hall to the relative quiet near the back offices. That's why she'd escaped into Cole's in the first place. She'd only wanted to get back her composure. Then she'd found Des's shirt. The smell of his aftershave had been all over the damn thing, and the collar had been wet from a recent shower. Before she'd even thought about it, her hand had been under her skirt, and God, she'd been so ready…

She knew better than to do something so crazy at work. If he'd just let her make it up to him, to *them*, she'd prove she hadn't gone off the rails. Everyone was entitled to one sanity flight per year, right?

Cole opened his office door and ushered her inside. It was empty. He frowned. "I thought you said Des wanted to see me here."

"Yes. He told me to get you."

Footsteps sounded behind them and she whirled, her eyes going wide as Des strode inside and shut the door. The alcohol was making her head a little fuzzy and nausea crept up her throat. Would they fire her?

Des flipped the lock in the doorknob as casually as if he locked the three of them in Cole's office every day. "This won't take long."

"I didn't mean—please, I swear I won't do it again," she pleaded.

Cole set down his beer bottle with an audible *clink*. "Des, what's this all about?"

"Go kneel behind the desk, Wendy. In front of Cole's chair."

She fumbled for one of her jingling earrings, fingers shaking. She'd just drank too much and was imagining this whole thing. "I—what?"

"You heard me." Des gestured impatiently and something shimmery pink flashed in his hand. "Now."

Okay, fine, she'd gone too far, but this was insane. She wasn't five and Des wasn't acting like himself. His blue-green eyes were wild in the moonlight coming through the blinds and his jaw clicked as he waited for her to move.

"What the hell is going on?" Cole sounded as bewildered as she felt.

"This is between me and my secretary, Warner." Even in the shadowy darkness, the weight of Des's stare burned her skin.

"Then why I am here?" Cole snapped.

"Because you're the one who's going to discipline her for touching herself in your chair." Before she could pick her mouth up off the floor, Des stepped forward and wrapped his hand around her jaw, tilting her face up to his. His nostrils flared and she had the wild thought that he could smell her arousal, now trickling hotly onto her thighs. "You have the choice to leave now. If you do, this stops here. Otherwise go kneel where I told you."

Her heartbeat reverberated in her ears. She couldn't process what was happening, especially since she could still hear the animated voices and cheerful Christmas music just outside the door.

Out there, life was still normal. In here, nothing made sense.

"Des, you're scaring her." Cole laid a restraining hand on Des's shoulder, which he promptly shook off. "Perhaps you misunderstood what you saw."

"Did I?" Des asked quietly.

She wanted to lie so badly. To make all of this end. But part of her...didn't. That part of her yearned to see what lurked behind door number two.

"No," she whispered.

"You chose to do that in here, in Cole's chair. You must've wanted to be caught. Was that your plan? For Cole to catch you?"

She averted her eyes to the floor and wished the thick carpet would just swallow her whole.

"Either leave or go kneel by his chair. Now, Wendy." Her boss's voice lashed against her flushed face like a whip. "We don't have much time."

"T-time for what?"

Cole snagged a handful of her hair, gently tipping her head back. "Go kneel by the chair, love."

"But my job—"

"This has nothing to do with that, and you know it." Cole's breath blew warmly over her temple and this time when she shivered, it wasn't from fear. "Go."

She went.

They walked around the desk, one on either side, and she cast her face down to keep from revealing the extent of her excitement. She hadn't read every line in the employee manual, but she was pretty sure their behavior wasn't following protocol.

Even so, she trusted them. They weren't just her bosses, they were her friends. Somehow she'd unleashed *this*.

Des sat in the chair and spread his legs wide, drawing her gaze to the thick bulge at their apex. Even in the moonlight, his girth dried her throat. She wet her lips and startled at the needful sound he made.

"Yes. You're going to use that tongue, and those lips, you tease. But first, you're going to take off your top for me."

When she froze, Cole tugged up her shirt, making his own sound of approval as she willingly lifted her arms. She'd stopped thinking entirely. He set her top on his blotter and hooked his fingers under the straps of her bra, offering more praise while he drew them down her arms.

"Just push down the cups."

She expected Cole to argue. Normally the two men shared a mutual balance of power, though technically Des owned a controlling interest of the business. But Cole didn't hesitate. He flicked his fingers over her nipples and they peaked, seeking his caress. He stroked them without shame, first through the lacy cups then her bare flesh.

Both men made noises at the baring of her breasts, like animals circling bloody meat. "Pull those pretty tits up," Des grated.

*A Very Naughty Xmas*

Cole tugged her breasts by her nipples, plumping them over the tight band of her bra. The swollen tips jutted outward, asking for their mouths. Begging for them.

Des showed her the items he'd hidden in his hands, pink clothespins with heavy teardrop crystals. She cried out in surprise as he clipped them with swift efficiency on her nipples.

Vision blurring, she stared down at the agile fingers now swirling around her areolas. Was this really happening? Did Des really have his hands on her breasts?

Her drenched sex said *hell yes*. So did her soaked thighs and quivering belly. She shifted forward on her knees, squeezing her legs together to try to get some friction where she needed it. "You stole those off the tree."

His trademark grin flashed just long enough to steal her breath. "It's my tree. My ornaments." He shifted the clips, their teeth scraping her stiff nipples, and she closed her eyes from the bite of pain the dangling crystals caused. "I knew you had beautiful tits. How wet is your pussy?"

He didn't frame it as a question. He merely assumed it was so.

She whimpered, not able to reply. She'd fantasized occasionally about a lover dirty talking during sex, but she'd never gotten that explicit even in her own head. Which was pretty pitiful since it turned her on beyond belief.

"I'm wet," she murmured, scandalized by both the admission and the flush stealing over her cheeks. Today aside, she wasn't a blusher, and she wasn't into kinky stuff with ornaments and…whatever the hell this was.

It was Des. *Des*. Finally.

"Stand up and take off your panties, then get on my lap. Quickly," Des added at her stare. "There's a party going on."

"This is really unconventional." She rose unsteadily and slipped off her thong.

She was pretty sure she would've been shrieking about all of this if she'd been fully sober, but her inhibitions had come down just enough for her to follow her hormones. And right now they were aiming straight for the giant gift in Des's pants.

"We're unconventional guys. Not that way, sweetheart," Cole said when she tried to straddle Des, who made no move to help her. "Have you ever been spanked?"

She jolted and Des steadied her. "I'd say that's a no." He chuckled and drew out his thick cock, smiling at her gasp. "Cole's going to help me get the truth out of you while you make me feel good."

Somehow she draped herself partially over his lap with one knee on the floor, ass tipped in the air. Cole shoved up her skirt and air streamed over her bare bottom. To distract herself from Cole's looming presence, she tentatively wrapped her hand around Des's cock, gasping again at the heat of his flesh. He was on fucking fire and so hard she knew her flush had returned. This time it had nothing to do with embarrassment and everything to do with lust.

"You like that, love?" Cole brushed her hair away from her face, the gesture surprisingly tender. She glanced back at him, questions on the tip of her tongue. Questions she couldn't ask Des when he was being so silent and broody.

Des tapped her cheek and inclined his chin, indicating the swollen length she barely managed to grip in her fist. "Suck."

She nodded, leaning forward so eagerly that both men chuckled. As strange as this whole scenario was, she'd wanted Des forever. She'd take him however she could get him.

Slicking her tongue over her lips, she sealed them over the head, moaning at the first salty taste of him. Fluid pulsed out of his slit as she slid her hand up and down. He was so big that she couldn't figure out how to maneuver him at first. Soon she settled into a rhythm that had him gulping air.

God, she loved sucking cock, and it had been so long since she'd done it. She especially loved sucking *Des's* cock.

Cole cupped the cheeks of her ass, rubbing gently, and she startled, biting down. Des hissed and yanked her hair. "Careful."

"Sorry," she said around him, lips curving at his strangled grunt. She dove back down, sucking him deep, not stopping until her nose pressed into the thatch of dense dark curls in his groin. His musky scent caused her to moan and unintentionally take him farther. He snatched a handful of her hair and directed her up and down, forcing her to move faster than she might've on her own.

The wet glugging sounds she was making might've embarrassed her if Cole hadn't been stroking her ass again, his fingers darting between her cheeks and down below to her cleft. She wiggled to try to get him to actually penetrate her, but he slipped back, his damp fingers trailing over her ass before he lifted his hand.

And brought it down hard.

She yelped and drew off Des's cock, managing not to use her teeth. Barely.

"Uh uh. Not of that." Des urged her back down, feeding her his length. "Cole's going to spank you, and you're going to suck."

She pulled away long enough to answer. "I might maim you."

He laughed and rubbed his thumb over her upper lip. "I'd like to see you try."

The edge in his voice took her off-guard and she wasn't prepared when Cole's caresses led to another slap. Then another and another. She buried her face against Des's stomach, drawing in deep breaths of his scent, and he held her head, cradled it even, as Cole peppered her ass with smacks. In between he rubbed her cheeks, stoking the heat higher and higher until her mortification turned into something that burned deep in her belly. She writhed under his hand, craving it, and Des slipped his fingers into her mouth, giving her an outlet for her need to bite and moan.

"You like that? Your ass on fire? Your pussy dripping?" Cole spoke this time, proving the veracity of his question by dragging his fingers down her soaked cleft. All she could do was nod.

"She likes it well enough to be honest. Which is the whole point." Des caught her in his probing stare. "Why were you in Cole's office?"

With her inhibitions ripped away, there was only the truth. "I wanted to get away from the crowd for a minute. I came in the back door. This...this was the closest empty room."

Instead of a slap, she got a stroke, one that made her arch and whimper from the velvety thrill of Cole's hand sliding over her bottom.

Des reached down and unclipped her sore nipples, giving her a moment of gasping relief before he clipped them again. "You didn't come here looking for Cole."

"No." The word was a moan.

"But you thought you held his shirt while you touched yourself."

She'd known exactly whose shirt she held. She recognized Des's aftershave. Heat blasted over her face and she pressed it against his muscled abdomen. More smacks rained on her butt.

"No..." It was all she could get out before Des pushed her back down on his cock.

She worked him hard, making those wet, urgent sounds that seemed to push him closer to the ledge. She cupped his balls, moaning herself at his violent jerk when she squeezed. Holding him, so strong and vulnerable, in her hand, in her mouth, made her eyes smart and her clit ache. She wanted him in her.

Whatever the consequences, he'd taken her this far. He couldn't leave her now.

As soon as she had the thought, he nudged her away. She was staring at him, trying to figure out what she'd done wrong when Cole drew her up and shoved her belly-first on the desk. For a moment, she'd almost forgotten he was there.

And then he was *really* there, sliding his condom-covered cock inside her liquid sex. She cried out, stunned that he'd given her no warning. Stunned she could want him to fuck her when she so craved the man watching them silently. But Cole was sexy too, and she'd always liked him. She definitely appreciated the way he surged inside her as if they'd been lovers for a lifetime.

She swallowed the moans so insistently working their way up her throat and pulled on the dangling crystals on her nipples, inciting an answering echo in her core. He fucked her just right, hitting her G-spot with a precision that made her sob with all the pent-up passion she'd held back for so long.

Somehow he knew when she couldn't take the anticipation anymore. He pushed her down and started ramming in and out, grinding her clit against the desk. She bit her forearm to stifle her scream as she convulsed around Cole's thick, thrusting length.

"That's it, babydoll. Come on me." He slapped her ass almost as an afterthought, then plunged deeper, harder. His orgasm rocked through him, driving him into her so fiercely that she drew blood on her arm in her attempt to stay quiet from the residual aftershocks.

Holy crap, she'd never come like that before. He'd practically split her open with his intensity. And she'd adored every second.

When Cole pulled out, murmuring an apology—for what, she had no clue, maybe that she'd only come twice?—she turned over as he aimed an arrogant grin at Des.

He pointed at Des's unflagging cock. "Want me to take care of that for you?"

She barely registered the scene in front of her. Des shrugging. Cole bending to suck Des's cock, his lips slicking over the head with the kind of skill that suggested lots of practice. Des fisting his best friend's hair much harder than he'd done with hers, yanking him up and down his dick so viciously she feared Cole would choke.

Fascinated, stunned, she reclined on her elbows on the desk and shuddered from the naked lust on the two men's faces. She twisted the clips on her nipples and bowed up at the ache that twanged deep below.

Cole reached down with his free hand, working his cock, still wet from her juices, making it rigid again. She debated crawling between his legs and sucking him off. Before she could move, Des came hard, his ass lifting off the chair as he pumped his cum into Cole's waiting throat.

Wendy bit her lip on a moan, so turned on she couldn't speak. She'd known they were close, but she'd never guessed...*this*.

Des turned his head. His eyes blazed in the faint light. "Break time's over. You have a party to get back to, don't you, Ms. Stanton?"

# Chapter IV

The rest of the party passed in a blur. Wendy did her best to socialize, though she couldn't find her panties. Somehow their loss felt much more shameful than Des and Cole's unusual strategy to get her to tell the truth.

And come like a faucet.

They'd demanded she kneel and give a blowjob and take a spanking and she'd never once felt as if she didn't have a choice. Along with Des's repeated reminders that she could leave, she had no doubts about the kind of men they were. They wouldn't push her into more than she could handle.

So maybe that part was wrong.

But she *wanted* to be pushed. She wanted to be wanted so badly that her lover—or lovers plural, though she'd never considered multiples before—was driven to the edge of sanity. Did that make her depraved? Or maybe she was just lonely and desperate for something that reminded her of all the living she had left to do and not the death in her past.

The entire weekend she plodded around her apartment. Her mother's pneumonia seemed better, and her spirits were too. But Wendy's mood had been fucked as surely as her—

"Say it, wuss." She faced the bathroom mirror at work on Monday morning, long before anyone else arrived. She'd shown up early to have it out with Des. He hadn't called her, hadn't texted. It wasn't as if they were boyfriend and girlfriend now, but they had to be *something*. She'd given him a blowjob.

Then again, so had Cole and they weren't dating.

Oh God, were they? Was that why Des had never made a move on her? She'd chalked it up to professional ethics or maybe even disinterest. But perhaps he and Cole were a couple, though she'd never gotten that vibe from them.

She screwed up her face and shut her eyes. "Pussy. Pussy. Pussy!" The curse words burst out of her just as the door swung open. "Aw, hell."

Van stopped dead in the doorway and blinked. "I know it's Monday, but it ain't bad as all that, sugar."

Wendy sagged against the sink and covered her face with her hand. She couldn't help grinning. "Sorry. I'm trying something new."

"Seeing how swear words sound in that sultry accent of yours?" Van stepped up beside her and bumped hips. "I like it. Pu-u-u-sy. All those extra syllables give it more emphasis. So who's a pussy?"

"No one. I'm just shy, and I'm tired of it." Wendy glowered at the spotless mirror. The bathroom was always sparkling clean, as if invisible elves snuck in every night with brooms and mops. "I didn't think I was. But I am."

"So you're yelling about pussies first thing Monday morning? Better to get over your shyness with some guy's mouth on yours." Van's eyes gleamed as Wendy bit her lip. "So someone got some action this weekend, huh? Tell me."

God, no. "It was nothing."

Van looked genuinely disappointed. "Dud in the sack?"

"Of course not." Wendy's mind whirled. What would make this conversation end the fastest? "I think he's gay. Maybe." Actually she didn't think Des or Cole was gay, since they'd both been into her. Clearly they were bi. But it seemed as good an excuse as any.

"Damn. Bet he was hot too." Van patted her arm and leaned toward the mirror to touch up her flawless lipstick.

This she could answer without lying. "Oh yeah."

"Sucks. Sorry, chica."

"Me too." Wendy picked up her purse and smiled at her friend. "Guess we better get out there."

"Yeah, there's tinsel fucking everywhere. I'm surprised I didn't pick any out of my cooch." Van shook her head and led the way back to their desks.

So much for catching Des in the office alone.

For most of the day, Wendy didn't have a chance to think. Between the seriously sinful architects who marched through for an urgent meeting with Des and Cole and a mix-up with their standard housewarming flower delivery to new homeowners, it was a Monday to end all Mondays. But at least there was hardly any time for awkwardness between her and her bosses.

Then she heard Van giggling with Cole.

Stomach sinking to her ankles, Wendy rolled her chair closer to her cubicle partition in time to hear Van mention Wen's craptastic weekend with a guy who played for the other team. Shit.

She rolled back to her desk and pounded her forehead on her

blotter. Hard.

God, she needed to leave. It was five, right? She shot up in her seat and glanced at the time. Three-flipping-thirteen.

But she hadn't taken a lunch yet. She could sneak out for a sandwich and creep back in when—

Her phone rang and she picked it up, shutting her eyes. She didn't bother to say hello. "Ms. Stanton, my office please. Now." Des sounded completely cool and composed. Totally fuckable.

"Yes, sir." She hung up and stabbed her thumbnail into her palm. Her time of reckoning had come. She'd blown and screwed her way around a firing Friday night, but now she was going to get it.

Was it wrong that she wanted to ask if she could get the other it again before they booted her out the door? Preferably by Des this time? Not that she hadn't enjoyed Cole's nice, thick cock, but he wasn't her boss. Err, he was, but he wasn't Des.

Dammit all to hell, she wanted Des. Even more so now.

So maybe she needed to show him that she didn't mind handling a few extra tasks around the office? Blowing, and filing, and typing, and fucking...

She adjusted her suit. She'd worn power red today, hoping it would give her a boost. That it looked good with her coloring and the snug skirt revealed lots of leg? Absolutely irrelevant.

While she stood there fiddling with her clothes, the phone rang again. She answered, her belly fluttering in anticipation of hearing his deep, sexy voice. "Now, Wendy."

"On my way." She hung up and strode down the hall, determined to project an outward air of confidence. She was a valuable employee. There was no reason at all to think she'd be fired for such small transgressions.

Then she saw Des standing in his doorway and she stumbled.

Instead of moving to help her, he crossed his arms. Ankles too. He made her think of a king, waiting to be served. That he wore a pair of black jeans, crisp white shirt, and formal pinstriped vest—and a smirk, can't forget the smirk—didn't diminish his kingly air.

She slipped past him into the room. The slam of the door made her jump, and quick as a snake, he shoved her against the wall. She bit the inside of her cheek to keep quiet. At least she hadn't pleaded. Yet.

His breath streamed hot against her cheek. "So I'm gay."

Yep, there was no stopping the squeak then. Classy. "Uh, I didn't say you were gay. That the...individual might be gay. The fictional man I slept with, I mean." She shook her head. "I'm just going to stop talking now."

"No, it's fascinating. Tell me more." While he spoke, he gathered her wrists and—bound them. What the hell?

She whirled to face him then wished she hadn't. He was too close to her, and his eyes were barely slits. If this was Des set on mad, she'd happily return the dial to affable Des. Or Des, sex maniac who demanded she pleasure him. Another good option.

"I didn't tell her it was you. Either of you. But come on, do you really think the idea you could be gay is out of left field?"

"Did you think that when your mouth was on my cock?" His question blew over her lips. "Or when I was watching you get fucked by my partner and wishing like hell it was me?"

"It could've been you. It should've been."

He wrapped his hand around her hair, tugging her back until she had no choice but to meet his simmering gaze. "It's not going to be. So just get that thought out of your pretty head."

Disappointment sliced through her, fast and sharp. She clenched her hands. "What's this about then? Just a way for you to show me who's boss?"

That smile, slow and lethal, should've come with a warning label. "You already know who's boss. This is just to make sure you never forget it."

While she stood there caught between shivering and screaming, he went to his desk and pressed the intercom button. Van's perky voice rang over the line. "Yes, Des?"

"Take the rest of the afternoon off. Boss's orders." He flashed his teeth at Wendy and she flexed her fingers, hating that she was at his mercy. Unless she decided to walk out the door, once she figured out how to open it with her mouth. "Send Cole in here on your way out, please."

Oh hell no.

Oh hell *yes*.

"Are you sure?" She'd never heard Van use that particular soft, entreating tone before. "I can stay as long as you need. Or help if there's something you and Cole have to take care of—"

Des pushed a button with one long finger. "What do you say? Do we need Vanessa's assistance?" Sensuously, he licked his lower lip. "Your call, Ms. Stanton."

She couldn't shake her head rapidly enough. He chuckled and pushed the button again. "I think we'll be fine. Thank you, Van."

He stayed on the line for another moment, making small talk. Van obviously didn't want to go. Was there a reason why? Like, oh, had she been the first test subject for Des and Cole's unconventional disciplinary procedures? And maybe she wasn't ready to be pushed aside.

Almost as soon as he ended the call, the door opened. She shifted her back to the wall, oddly embarrassed to be caught with her hands trapped behind her. It made her feel even more powerless, though really, who was she kidding? They weren't playing pattycake. In comparison to her vanilla existence, these men were hardcore.

Even if Cole entered Des's office with a miniature candy cane in his mouth and another longer, thicker one under his arm.

"Wondered when we'd get back on the job," he said cheerfully, flipping the lock in the doorknob. "So you've labeled us gay, hmm?"

She swallowed and twisted her wrists against her binding. Jeez, was that garland? She peeked over her shoulder. Yep, her favorite multi-colored strand. Figured.

Cole's finger along her jaw had her eyes snapping back to his. He cocked his head, studying her while he sucked on his candy. The gesture made him look boyish, especially with that lock of light brown hair that kept dipping into his eyes. Dark blue eyes that saw too deep and exposed all the lies she told the world on a daily basis.

That she was okay. That she didn't hurt. That she didn't need.

"We're open-minded about who we sleep with, sweetness." Cole crunched into his candy. "Sometimes that includes guys. Usually only each other, and usually only when we're sharing a woman. You don't have to worry that you'll come in here someday and find me with my head in jerkwad's lap."

She flushed and hated herself for it. "I didn't mean—"

"Shh. I'm sure you were confused." Cole's finger found the corner of her mouth and pressed inward until her lips gave way. He eased the tip inside, smiling when her tongue curled around him. "No confusion now, is there?"

When she shook her head, he smiled and held out the long, thick candy cane to Des. Someone had brought it to the party the other night. "Hungry? I brought you a present."

Des came around the desk and accepted the candy, eyeing it with an appreciation that caused her panties to dampen even more. None of this should be turning her on, but apparently her body didn't realize that.

"Hmm. I'm not usually a fan of sweets." She thought of his newly developed sugar habit and then clamped her lips together when he looked her way. "What about you, Wendy?"

"I'm not hungry."

Des and Cole glanced at each other, matching predatory smiles crossing their ridiculously sexy faces. Cole had dimples and Des's spiky hair could've hidden devil horns, but for that instant she could tell they were of one very dirty mind.

Des stepped forward and stroked the wrapped cane down her throat. She held his gaze, unwilling to slip into the same submissive role she had last time. There was no alcohol in her bloodstream right now. Lust, yes, but she could control that.

Maybe.

He ran his tongue under her jaw in a long, patient sweep. "Do you want to be here, Wendy?"

She should say no. What she'd wanted with Des—or what she'd believed she wanted anyway—was a chance at a normal relationship. This was not that.

But she wasn't moving away. She was nodding yes and arching as he unbuttoned her jacket and bared the lacy white teddy beneath. The top of it played peekaboo nicely with her suit, and the rest was a series of swirling cutouts and mesh. Her skirt hid what covered her groin—or didn't.

"So businesslike outside." Des's finger skated down the rise of her breasts, detouring over each taut nipple showcased in thin netting. "So not beneath. What's under here?" he asked, tracing her waistband.

She pulled off a shrug though she could feel herself dampening to the point of embarrassment. "See for yourself."

"I think I will." He passed off the candy cane to Cole then tugged on her skirt with both hands, his expression glazing at the sight of her pussy framed in white lace. Garters and sheer stockings completed the outfit. "You test me, Wendy."

"Do I?" She licked her lips with the tip of her tongue, pleased to see the flex of his cock against his trousers. "It's so hard to tell."

He drew his fingers over her slit, scarcely touching her, and she jerked back. His smile was like the sun emerging from behind a cloud, bright and disarming. "I bet you taste like candy. Do you like having a man between your legs?"

Answering seemed like another way to give in. She tried to make her face expressionless, determined to make him work for her reactions if nothing else.

Cole peeled the plastic off the cane before stepping forward and placing the rounded tip against her mouth. "You know you want some."

Caught in the intensity of his eyes, she licked, involuntarily drawing one heel up the wall. Spreading herself open for them.

Des took her silent invitation and dropped to his knees, finding her clit so fast that she swayed. With her balance altered from her bound wrists and her stance, she might've toppled over had he not locked an arm around the back of her thighs. He wasn't letting her go anywhere, that was for damn sure.

"That's it," Cole said when she drew the candy deeper in response to Des's insistent licking. "Get it wet."

Her eyes shot to Cole's. All at once, she knew they weren't simply plying her with treats.

Of course they weren't. *Moron.*

Des prodded her swollen bundle of nerves with his tongue, flattening it while she sucked harder on the peppermint stick. Her thighs trembled and she rocked forward, unintentionally swallowing more of the candy. Nearly choking on it.

God, who knew Des had such powerful suction?

Maybe Van knew.

She shoved that thought away as Cole palmed the back of her head, finally drawing the cane away to kiss her. He snaked his tongue between her lips, flicking upward against the roof of her mouth, somehow mirroring the way Des was devouring her pussy. "You're delicious. I want this mouth on me. So cool and minty."

Cole stepped back to tug off his belt before following suit with his pants and boxers. His already fully erect cock curved out, even more enticing than the candy he still gripped in one fist.

Inexplicably, she dropped her gaze to Des's dark head between her legs. She wished she could touch him, run all that soft hair through her fingers. Wished they were alone, which made her feel instantly guilty.

She liked Cole, she really did. He definitely cranked her gears. But he wasn't Des, and she was stupidly traditional. One woman, one man.

And that was a fantasy. This was her reality.

Des slid back, his chin damp and his gorgeous sea-colored eyes unreadable. He rose and undid his jeans. He wore no boxers, and just a glimpse of his golden skin, so hard and thick, elicited her muffled cry. Muffled because Cole's mouth was back on hers, his tongue thrusting deep while he pressed his hand between her legs, fingering her with a speed that made her dizzy.

"Ah, darling, you're soaked for us. Come. Just come, baby."

She was so close already from Des that it didn't take long at all. As soon as two of Cole's long fingers pumped into her, she exploded. She buried her face between his shoulder and neck while she rode out the climax, both relieved and tense all over again.

Why wouldn't Des ever take her there himself?

She zeroed in on the man in question, leaning against his desk, stroking his cock in long, even pulls. He'd obviously liked the show. Heavy lidded, surly mouthed, he punched her in the chest with one glance and knocked her right on her ass.

*Jingle Ball, by Cari Quinn*

He crooked his finger. "C'mere."

She didn't look at Cole. Couldn't. She moved toward Des like a zombie, trapped in his web though he didn't speak. He caressed her cheek and rubbed his thumb under her eye, his lips softening into a fleeting smile. Then he reached behind her and freed her wrists. He draped the garland around her neck before he pushed her jacket down to her elbows. The pose slightly pulled back her arms.

"I like that." He traced her shoulders. "You're restrained, just enough to make you remember."

"Remember what?"

He nudged her down to her knees, directing his cock between her lips. "Me."

This time she didn't hesitate. If he wouldn't have sex with her—though she didn't know why—at least she could enjoy this much of him. She kept her eyes on his as her lips engulfed his length, as that first erotic taste of him hit her tastebuds. He didn't shove himself deeper, just waited for her to take him. She swirled her tongue around the wide, swollen head, wiping him clean before more of his arousal flowed out to help ease his passage into her throat.

As off-balance as she felt with her arms behind her, she held the stance, concentrating on taking him deeper without her hands. With just her eyes on his to tell him when to push her for more and when to retreat. She moaned around him, the subtle pulse in his length a promise of things to come.

He leaned back on his desk, spreading his body out for her perusal though she couldn't see it through all those damn layers of clothes. But she could see the pleasure contorting his features, shaping them into something even more beautiful as his throat muscles rippled and sweat dotted his temples.

He'd been led to the edge by *her*, not Cole. Not some other random woman who would never stumble or stutter when he got too close.

She was sure he'd urge her back, but when he did, it wasn't for the reason she thought. Cole had taken his place beside him and now indicated his own impatient cock with a wave of his fingers and a questioning smile. She swallowed the frustration that this moment with Des wasn't theirs alone and shifted on her knees to offer the same treatment to Cole's needy erection.

Soon she wasn't thinking about anything but getting him off, about tasting more of that hot fluid that spurted onto her tongue every time he forcefully slid home. He wasn't gentle with her but she didn't care. She didn't want that. Right now she ached to be used, to use them the same way. To forget everything that had ever happened—would ever happen—outside these four walls.

Des moved closer to Cole and together they fed her their cocks, alternating who she had in her mouth. Even with her eyes closed she knew the difference. Cole was longer, his movements sharper. Des stretched her cheeks and made her gasp from his slow, languid strokes. He filled her, burning away any memory of anyone that had come before. Relentless in his pursuit of her throat, of taking her farther than she'd ever gone before.

He plunged into her and held, his hips so close to her face, his grip on her hair punishing her. Freeing her. And buried down deep he came, releasing into her in an endless stream she fought to contain.

Too soon Cole dragged him back and inserted himself inside her abused mouth, barely getting off a couple strokes before he slickened the same path that Des had. He groaned and jerked her down, holding her still while her hollowed cheeks milked him.

Cole threw back his head and inhaled harshly, finally letting out an awed laugh. "Damn, girl, you're good." He lowered his satisfied gaze to where she pressed her saturated thighs together to keep from squirming. "I think Wendy's earned a bonus this Christmas. Don't you agree, Des?"

## Chapter V

Des eyed the pouty lips of Wendy's pussy revealed by her crotchless teddy as he twirled the peppermint stick. Oh, what he could do to her in that getup.

What he *would* do.

He gripped her elbow and helped her to her feet, then escorted her around the desk to his chair. She sat, still looking shell-shocked, and he bent to lay a soft kiss on her lips. He could taste both of them there, him and Cole, along with a hint of mint. As irrational as it was, he wanted to kiss her until Cole's flavor disappeared, until he was the only one he detected on her lips. "Legs up on the arms."

Wendy snapped into action, doing as he asked. She glanced down at herself in wonderment at how fully she was opened to them and up at him with a half-smile that lit her amber eyes. "Your chair is really comfy."

He laughed and pulled the garland off of her neck before winding it around her legs and the chair arms. Luckily it was extra-long and stretched across her belly like a glittery belt. "You look good in it." He tugged her breasts over the scalloped top of her teddy. Her nipples were rosy pink, as flushed as her cheeks. God, it turned him on when she blushed. "You're incredibly gorgeous."

Rather than answer, she rocked her hips. Just that movement sent wetness trickling down her slit and he groaned, mesmerized by the sight. He knew just how good she'd taste too.

She shocked the hell out of him by cupping her breasts in offering as she shifted to encompass Cole with her gaze. "A girl has rights you know." Her voice was as airy as a caress. "I was promised a Christmas bonus and I'll go to my union rep if I don't get it." Another rock of her hips. "Now."

Smiling, he leaned down, making her lean up for his mouth. Their teeth bumped in their urgency, but when her tongue tangled with his, he groaned his delight. He'd happily die right here.

He lifted the candy to her and she sucked on the tip, looking straight at him. His balls pulsed with the memory of exactly how good that felt and he shook his head. She was torturing him intentionally. In another second she'd be deep throating a candy cane, for fuck's sake.

"Look at her go." Cole moved closer, reminding Des of his presence. Not that he'd forgotten he was there exactly, he'd just sort of blocked him out. His best friend sank his finger into her pussy and growled in appreciation. "Ready to ride, baby?"

Though Cole spoke to Wendy, he glanced back at Des. Silently questioning.

She dragged her tongue up the underside of the cane, her lips faintly tinged red. "You know I am."

Des took the candy stick from her and acknowledged her whine with a laugh. Then he slipped it in his own mouth, sliding it up and down before he knelt between her parted legs. She was so pink and wet, so swollen with longing. He wanted her more than he wanted to breathe. But rather than sliding his already insistent cock into that tight, waiting sheath, he circled the candy cane over her, pushing inward while she gasped.

He didn't look up at her until the candy was inside her, sticking out obscenely. Then he bit into the other end, crunching down so that her body gave and it slipped in just that much farther. He ran his tongue around her where the candy met her skin, worrying her opening with his tongue, flicking teasingly as she grew wetter. She drove both hands into his hair, yanking him down to her groin. Unabashedly asking for what she craved. He ate at the peppermint and nuzzled her, sucking her clit, biting the candy. Pressing his cool tongue against her burning flesh.

Her moan announced that Cole had joined the fray. He filled his hands with her tits, squeezing them so roughly that her nipples reddened and stood out like hard little knobs. When her cries crescendoed, Cole kissed her hard, his tongue wetly sliding in and out just like Des worked the candy in her quivering pussy.

Her pants sliced through the din of noise in his ears. Somehow he heard his name, though Cole managed to stifle most of her cries. In no time at all she was coming against Des's lips, pulsing her cream into his waiting mouth.

Jesus, she was delectable. He needed more. He pulled the candy out and slipped in his tongue, thrusting through her incessant aftershocks. She was even sweeter now, chilly and hot both, and her spasms wrenched a groan from him that reverberated all the way through his newly rigid cock.

He didn't move away until she ceased moving entirely. Her sexy body in motion was a lovely thing, and it was just as beautiful still. Her huge eyes were half-closed, and a smug smile lifted the corners of her mouth as Cole tweaked her nipple and whispered in her ear.

His best friend stepped away and dressed quickly, throwing a jaunty wave over his shoulder on his way out. "Best Monday *ever*."

Des looked back at her as she giggled. "Ya'll are crazy."

"And there goes the southern fucking accent." With a mock groan, he set aside what was left of the candy cane—he intended to enjoy eating every damn bit of it later—and clutched his chest. "All I gotta hear is one more Des in that satisfied, I just came voice and I swear I'll ruin my goddamn rug."

She inched her butt forward, loosening her flimsy bonds on the arms of the chair and cupped his face in her hands. "Des," she whispered tenderly.

The amusement on her face vanished as he knelt like a statue, not saying a word. Her palms felt like heaven on his stubbled cheeks and he longed to reach up for them, to hold them there while he moved forward and surged into her sweet body.

Where he belonged.

Screw the candy canes and the ethics that kept him rooted in place as if nails in his heels pinned him to the floor.

He swallowed the grit in his throat and shut his eyes to avoid the look in hers. It was the coward's way out, and he took it gratefully. "Let me give you a ride home tonight," he said instead of everything else he wanted to.

Already she was pulling back. "I can walk."

"Wendy. I'm giving you a ride home."

His eyes opened as she dropped her hands in her lap. "Okay."

\*\*\*\*

For the next couple of weeks, Wendy learned the true meaning of mandatory overtime. She also got up and close and personal with the terms *rate of return*, *high performance* and *I've been fucked so hard my knees are jelly*.

On one hand, she was happier—and more sexually satisfied—than she'd ever been. On the other, she was so conflicted and confused she didn't know what to do.

Her life had turned into a frigging Dickens novel, assuming Dickens had ever let his freak flag fly. Lately she'd hoisted hers into the stratosphere.

But as great as everything was going, as happily boneless as she felt after every one of their "sessions" behind closed doors, she couldn't deny the thing that was bugging her the most. Well, there were several, but one was worse than the rest.

Des refused to fuck her.

He did everything but. He'd explored her body so thoroughly she figured he could play connect the dots with her freckles from memory. He gleefully went down on her and eagerly came in her mouth. Entered her with all manner of interesting implements from candy to sex toys to a cylindrical ornament from the tree that now held a place of honor in his top drawer.

She even asked him to fuck Cole, just in case he had some sort of penetration aversion. That would be a no. He was just averse to *her*.

As the days passed, the boys got bolder about calling her into their offices while Van and sometimes even clients were in the reception area. They seemed to delight in making her chew through her lip to keep from crying out while Cole pounded into her from behind and Des licked them both from below. Or other wickedly inventive things.

And Van was starting to pay attention. She'd called Wendy out for being scatterbrained more than once and seemed entirely too curious about why she was in the guys' offices so much. The time she'd emerged from Cole's with a fresh run in her pantyhose and her high heel unstrapped hadn't helped matters.

Part of Wendy wondered if Van was jealous. If she knew what was going on because she'd experienced it herself—or wanted to.

"Are you really that worried about her?" Des's mouth skated up the side of Wendy's neck to her ear. They were alone in Des's office, and all she wanted was him inside her. Finally. "She won't interfere with us. Van's a long-term, loyal employee."

The door opened. Van and Cole entered, both of them wearing wide grins. Wendy startled and tried to step away, but Des slid his fingers down the placket of her blouse, flicking open the buttons. "You trust us, don't you?"

Right then she didn't trust anything. But she didn't move.

Once she was down to her bra, he popped open the clasp and the cups fell away. He palmed one of her breasts, rubbing his cock in circles against her ass while she fought to look anywhere but at Van. What must her friend think?

Cole shut the door and locked them in together. Both men were already breathing hard. And Van…

Wendy didn't dare look up to see what her friend was doing.

"Isn't her body beautiful?" Des thumbed Wendy's nipples until they beaded. Her clit swelled at his rough cadence. At knowing she was being watched and caressed by the man she cared about so much. "I'll let one of you have her sweet pussy. Who will it be, Ms. Stanton?"

"You," Wendy gasped, jerking up in bed. "*You*, dammit."

*Jingle Ball, by Cari Quinn*

She rubbed her eyes and chanted a silent thank you that she was alone. Van was a good friend, but there were boundaries she had no interest in crossing. Sex with a woman—or any of its variations—was one of them.

Though she didn't doubt one bit that the guys would love to see their secretaries together. At least they'd never mentioned it.

Maybe she should. Even if she couldn't address the whole Des not doing her thing, she could tell them about the underlying tension with Van. If they'd slept with Van too, she'd end their affair effective immediately. She wasn't some office plaything, despite how it might seem.

It wasn't as if she was any closer to actually going out with Des either. All she'd gotten were a few laughs and a lot of orgasms.

Admittedly, not an altogether bad deal.

She went to work that day full of purpose. It was the Friday before Christmas and she figured it was the right time to call a halt to their fuckstrative relationship. The holiday season was about fun and celebrating, but it would soon be January and she wanted to kick the year off on the right foot. Not on her knees or her belly.

Sure she did.

She kept busy throughout the morning, waiting until Van went out to lunch to march into the conference room where Des and Cole were poring over a map. At first she thought they were mapping some hot new property up for sale, but nope, they were looking at Maine. *Maine*?

"I've heard this new lodge has some of the best skiing in the area." Cole jabbed the map. "Dude, seriously, just come. Mom even bought that stupid Tofurky for you. And I hate fuckin' Tofurky. Tastes like ass."

"You're a vegan?" she asked from the doorway, biting her lip as both men glanced her way. This was yet another reason she wasn't comfortable being their lover. The lines at work blurred. They might be easygoing bosses, but they still signed her checks. "Sorry to interrupt," she muttered.

"You didn't." Des rose as he always did when she entered the room. "Van at lunch?" When she nodded, he held out his arm, inviting her closer.

She couldn't help stepping into that hug any more than she could resist sniffing the collar of his shirt. He smelled like soap and spice, sans aftershave since today he was rocking full scruff. Frigging hot.

"To answer your question," he tugged on her braid, "yes, I'm a vegan. Have been since high school when Johnny went out to hunt and came back with a doe on the roof of the car. Never touched another piece of meat since."

Cole grinned. "But you'll notice he still wears his Italian leather shoes."

Des shrugged. "A man's gotta have some vices." He reached down to pat her on the ass. "Though I do have my favorites, I'll admit."

"Who's Johnny?" she asked to avoid commenting on his favorite vices. She wanted to make sure they set the right tone for a serious discussion.

Something flitted across his expression. "The man who raised me."

She wanted to ask more, almost did, but Cole cleared his throat. "Wen, convince him he needs to head north with me this weekend. What else is his sorry ass going to do here alone? Scratch his balls to the tune of *White Christmas*?"

"Don't you have people here to spend the holiday with, Des?"

He gave her another shrug. "I'm not big on holidays in general. Usually I either visit Cole's folks or I...do some stuff here."

Visions of Des engaging in the debauchery she'd already glimpsed up close and personal danced in her brain. "Stuff like what?"

"The usual," Des said before Cole could reply.

Cole rolled his eyes. "Yeah, if the usual includes going to the children's ward at Brookers."

Wendy gripped the back of the chair in front of her. "You're serious?"

Des leaned forward and picked up half the sandwich sitting untouched next to Cole's elbow. "It's ham and swiss. Want some?" he asked Wendy, clearly not interested in discussing his holiday activities any further.

"No, thanks. I already ate." She hadn't, but it was a small lie. "Listen, I need to ask you both something."

Cole gave her a disarming grin as he relaxed in his chair. He was dressed in his professional best as usual today, not counting his blindingly red sweater. "Only if you convince Des to come with me."

"Go with him," she said to Des before crossing her arms over her chest. Best to just get it out quick before her nerve deserted her. "Am I the first woman you've slept with?"

The men looked at each other, twin expressions of amusement tilting their mouths. "Why, yes, Ms. Stanton." Des toyed with her jingle bell bracelet, one of the relics from home she hadn't been able to part with. The tinkling bells tended to annoy people, but the sound made her happy. "We were both virgins until you came along."

"You'd still be one then," Cole pointed out. "Since you've yet to partake of the lovely Wendy's luscious pussy."

Just like that, the scarlet elephant was out in the room. And she wasn't ready to deal with it. Not with Cole there. "That's not what I meant. I mean, have you shared another woman that worked for you?"

Her bosses exchanged a long glance that set off a round of nervous spasms in her belly. "No," Des said. "We've never been about that. This isn't that kind of office."

"So what's so special about me that Van doesn't have? For example," she added hastily at Cole's piercing glance.

His lips twitched. "Do you want to invite her to play with us, Wen?"

"No," she and Des answered simultaneously.

She looked at him, relief saturating her limbs. "Really?"

"Really." He reached over and laced his fingers with hers. Then he frowned, staring down at her hand. "Why do you ask? Does Vanessa suspect something?"

She wanted to say no, that nothing was amiss, but lying about lunch was about as much as she could stand. Other than lying about being in lo—*lust*—with Des, that is. That secret would remain hers.

"She's asking questions."

Cole shrugged and pulled the crust off the half of the sandwich on his plate. Des still held the other in his free hand though he'd made no move to eat it. "So put her off. It's not a big deal."

"I don't want her to find out," she said, trying to hide her disappointment as Des released her hand. "She's my friend, and if she starts thinking I'm getting unfair benefits because I'm with ya'll—I mean, fucking you both—"

"The only benefit you're getting is the use of our extraordinary dicks." Cole tossed aside his crust like a ten year old. "With Des, you're barely even getting that."

Des's brows dipped low over his churning eyes. "No, she's right. Cole, we can't risk Van's suspicions. This is a business, not a damn brothel." At Wendy's flinch, Des stroked her arm. "You know what I mean."

"Yeah, I do. You think I'm bought and paid for."

"Well, aren't you?" Cole bit into his sandwich. "Not the sex part obviously, but we pay you for a service which you perform very well." He chewed and swallowed before giving her one of those grins that could infuriate her or turn her on depending on the day. This was definitely falling into the infuriating category. "You're amazingly skilled, Wen. Believe us, we appreciate it."

"Shut up, dickhead." Des dumped his uneaten sandwich on the plate and gripped her forearms. "Forgive my hasty choice of words. I just meant I don't want us—any of us," he said with a stern glance at his

*A Very Naughty Xmas*

partner, "to lose sight of we're about here. Van shouldn't have to worry that she works in that kind of office."

"An office where people have healthy sex lives? Oh, no, anything but that."

Ignoring Cole, Des traced his thumb over the inside of her wrist. She hoped like hell he couldn't feel her trembling. Even though she knew what she had to do, her body was already registering its objections. "We've loved getting to know you better, but that's not a requirement of your working here. Anytime you say the word, we'll go back to the way things were. No questions asked."

Out of the corner of her eye, she glimpsed Cole's smirk. "I think maybe we should." Great, now her voice was shaking too. She made herself look into Des's eyes and spoke again, more evenly. "It's been fun, but it's almost Christmas and—"

"And you don't want to start a new year like this." Des nodded as if he understood completely, which didn't make any sense.

How could he understand? This setup should've been perfect. They'd shared amazing sex and tons of laughs. They definitely made it harder for her to remember she was lonely. It just wasn't enough. A taste of Des didn't satisfy her hunger. It only made her crave him more.

"Yeah." Absently she freed her arms from Des and rubbed her hip. Yesterday they'd gotten wild on this very conference table and she had the bruise to prove it. "I hope we can still be friends," she added, glancing at Cole as well.

"Sure thing, babydoll." He stood and leaned across the table, tapping her nose before he gave her a chaste kiss on the cheek. "I'm seriously going to miss your sweet pussy. Did I tell you I even named it?"

She sputtered out a giggle. "You did not." It took all her will not to ask what that name was.

"Oh, I bet he did." Though Des grinned, his eyes were uncharacteristically sober as he flicked the end of her braid. "You've certainly brightened my holiday season, Ms. Stanton."

A smile tipped up her mouth despite the lump growing in her throat. Forget lump. It felt like a concrete slab. "Ditto. So, ah, I guess I should get back to work."

He nodded, his hand lingering on her hair. They were standing close to each other, so close she could smell the spearmint from his gum. She wanted to strip off the navy button-down shirt stretched across his taut abs, then peel down his dark jeans until there were no layers between them, only skin. She'd burrow into him until she forgot all about tomorrow.

When Cole cleared his throat, they sprung apart like guilty lovers. Or awkward former fuckees. Pick your poison.

So…this was it.

"One more thing." Giving in to her impulse, Wendy leaned up on her tiptoes to kiss Des a final time. His lips heated and curved under hers. "Go to Maine."

## Chapter VI

It took him until Christmas Eve to decide for certain he wasn't going. It was tempting. He genuinely liked Cole's parents and younger sisters, and there would be enough activity to drown out the noise in his head. But this year, it felt necessary that he stay home. Why, he didn't know.

"Are you sure?" Cole asked from the doorway while Des pulled the pages off his cartoon desk calendar.

He'd forgotten to change the thing since early December. Wendy used to peel off each day for him without fail, but she'd stopped once they became intimate. He wasn't sure if it was an oversight or intentional. Either way, it bothered him.

Lots of things did nowadays.

"Hot, steaming Tofurky with yummy white flour gravy and all the mixed veggies you can eat. C'mon, you know you want some."

He had to laugh, though the sound crackled in his chest. "Thank your mom and dad for inviting me. And don't forget the presents I gave you for them."

Cole rolled his eyes and straightened his reindeer Christmas vest. His mother had knitted it for him and he hated it with a fiery passion. That didn't mean he wouldn't wear it to make her happy, sap that he was. "Yeah, yeah. Already in my trunk."

Des rose and stuck out his hand. "Have a great time."

Cole grunted and walked around the desk then wrapped him in a bear hug. "Call if you need some company. Stubborn motherfucker."

With that, he was gone.

Des sat back in his chair and glanced at the ticking clock above his bookshelves. Only one-sixteen. They'd given Van and Wendy the afternoon off, but only Van had taken them up on it. Wen had insisted she'd be happy to close the office on her own and had just left to get her lunch from the deli down the street. She'd probably be unpleasantly surprised to find Des waiting when she got back, since she'd assumed he'd be leaving with Cole.

To give himself something to do, he walked into the reception area and turned on the Christmas tree. The blue and silver twinkle lights helped beat back the dismal winter's day, as did the little musical globe on the front counter. The nutcracker inside drummed his way through a traditional Christmas classic, stomping up clouds of flaky fake snow.

The door opened and he glanced over his shoulder at Wendy. She stood in the doorway with her hair in twin auburn ponytails, her cheeks flushed bright pink from the cold. Snow dusted the shoulders of her cheery red coat and melted on her rosy lips. "Des. You're still here."

He dipped his hands in his pockets. Even the defiant gleam of her eyes didn't reduce her utter aloneness. "I decided not to go." He helped her offload the paper sacks she juggled. "What is all this?"

"I kinda went overboard. It's my own Christmas feast." She shut the door, her cheeks reddening even more as he unpacked her lunch. "Both kinds of soup sounded good so I got a small of each and half of a turkey and cranberry sandwich. Have you eaten?"

"No." He unwrapped her pickle and bit in. "What kinds of soup?"

"Butternut Squash and Wild Rice with Eggplant."

"Both vegetarian. I think you should share."

She unwound her scarf and tossed it on the back of her chair. "It is Christmas, so I suppose I could. Why didn't you go to Maine?"

He jerked a shoulder. "I wanted to stay here."

"Alone?"

"Maybe I'll come over to your place," he said, surprised when her lips pursed. He wasn't serious, but he also hadn't expected her to look so dismayed at the idea. "Unless you have big plans."

"Nothing special." As she pulled out the plastic utensils and napkins, she frowned at the nutcracker on the counter. "You really like those things? Music boxes?"

"I like them well enough. Why?"

"Those tinny songs always made me sad." She shrugged and sat at her desk.

"Want me to turn it off?" Though she didn't answer, he did it anyway then turned on her radio. "Better?"

She pushed one of the soup cartons his way and offered him a small smile that never reached her eyes. "Much."

He sat down across from her at her desk and reached for his steaming cup of soup. She'd given him the squash. "Smells delicious. Here," he said, scooping up some and holding it out to her with his other hand cupped beneath. "You should get the first sample."

"Such a gentleman."

"I think we both know I'm not." His cock went painfully hard at

## A Very Naughty Xmas

the flare of heat that blossomed across her face as her lips slid over the spoon. "Good?"

Nodding, she made a show of ripping open a packet of crackers. "Want?"

He couldn't stop staring at the subtle undulation of her throat while she swallowed. Good God, he was losing it. "Yes." Her head bobbed up at his low, hungry tone. "I want."

She quickly changed the subject to something safe, and he didn't try to guide them back to more dangerous territory. It was just as well they keep things semi-professional. Or as professional as things could be when he couldn't stand up for fear of revealing his hard-on.

Their lunch lasted all afternoon. The conversational topics ranged from work to friends to holiday traditions to random shit like their favorite TV shows. They were debating the pros and cons of the Giants versus the Bills when the phone rang. Wendy immediately reached for it, but he covered it with his hand. "It's past three on Christmas Eve. Let it go to voicemail."

"But—"

"As your boss, I insist you keep entertaining me with your devoted assurances that the Bills could actually win a Super Bowl someday." He grinned and waved at her to continue. "As you were saying?"

The next time the phone rang it was almost five, and it was pitch black outside. "Shit." She bounced to her feet as if she hadn't realized it was so late. "I should get home."

He nodded. "Your mom will be waiting."

"Oh, she's got her own plans tonight." She fluffed her hair over her scarf and laughed, but he heard the sadness behind the sound. "She's heading to my aunt's. They're going to snuggle in with some movies and eggnog."

"What about you?"

"I'm staying home."

"Alone?"

"I want to. Really." She grabbed her coat and was about to slip it on when he rounded the desk to do the honors. "See?" she asked breathlessly. "Told you that you were a gentleman."

He lingered with his hands on her shoulders longer than he needed to. Damn, her hair smelled as fresh as the inside of an icicle and as sweet as a candy cane.

Oh fuck, he did *not* need to think about candy canes. Not when she was smiling at him in the twinkling glow from the tree, her eyes deep and dark and way too aware of the energy all but pulsating between them.

"I'm not going to argue, because that would just be redundant." He lifted her ponytails over her coat and swallowed at the spill of her red hair. Once, just once, he wanted to see it across his pillow.

Laughing softly, she grabbed the lapels of his shirt and leaned up to press her mouth to his. She tasted of her peach iced tea and moved back way too soon. "Merry Christmas, Des."

"Merry Christmas, Wen."

Once she was gone, he sat at her desk and stared at the tree until the lights blurred. If he'd ever felt more alone, he didn't remember it.

It didn't have to be that way. They could both be alone or they could be together. Fuck the consequences.

He pulled out his phone. He'd have to get his ass in gear if he had any hope of pulling this off.

\*\*\*\*

Christmas Eve and what was she doing? Giving herself a pedicure while crying over *It's A Wonderful Life*. Later she'd give her props to Santa by curling up in her winter's nest with her vibrator.

Fa-la-la-flipping-la.

Wendy wiped her damp cheeks. Van had called to make sure she was okay and she'd lied through her teeth. Sure, she was dandy. So what if she was alone on the worst night of the year? She'd chew up her loneliness with the same zeal she'd disposed of Aunt Gert's fruitcake. No regrets here, baby.

At least her purple passion toenails looked all sparkly. She'd just apply her mini star stickers to the dried polish and—

The doorbell rang and she nearly slid off the couch. The bell didn't exactly ring so much as give a depressed fart of air that passed for music. Maybe Mom had decided to have Aunt Gert drive her back early, but where was her key?

Cursing her toe separators, Wendy hobbled to the door. On the way she cast a glance at herself. Her hair was still in pigtails and she wore ripped leggings and a hot pink sports bra. They kept the apartment at a zillion degrees to make sure her mom didn't get have a relapse with her pneumonia, so the minute she took off, Wendy stripped down.

She peeked out the curtain though the porch light of their two-family house was out yet again. "Who is it?"

No answer, but her mom was hard of hearing. Just in case, she dumped the silk flowers out of the vase on the side table and swung it above her head, ready to strike, as she yanked open the door.

She blinked, almost wishing it was a lunatic intent on robbing her of all three of her worldly goods. Because then she wouldn't have to mentally berate her floppy hair and raggedy clothes and the fact that Des was carrying the world's tiniest Christmas tree and a wrapped gift as if he were bringing joy to the poor and decrepit.

Which he kind of was.

He looked her up and down, not smiling. Not reacting at all until he noticed the vase she still gripped like a weapon. Then he started to laugh.

"Don't hurt me, please. I come bearing gifts." He held out his miniscule tree and the wrapped box, slaying her with a grin that made her hold turn slippery on the vase. "Can I come in?" he prompted when she only stared.

"What are you doing here?"

"It's stupid for us both to be alone on Christmas, don't you think?"

"But—"

"Let me in, Wendy."

She stepped aside and he walked inside, bringing a wave of cold air with him. She shivered as he shut the door, but she didn't let go of the vase. Right then she needed something to hold on to.

"A little chilly for that kind of outfit, isn't it?"

When she didn't speak, he sighed and set down his pathetic little tree—the last from the lot at the end of the street, by the looks of things—and his gift, along with a plastic bag that he'd procured from under his coat. It smelled like Chinese food.

Her belly rumbled and he smiled, arching a brow. "So you don't want me or my tree, but you'll take my eats, huh?"

Smiling weakly, she shoved the silk flowers back in the vase and set it on the table. Her gaze darted from the shabby multicolored rug to the equally threadbare sofa in the living room and the crappy dollar store pictures she'd framed and hung in an attempt to give the place some life.

And Des stood in her hall in his spendy leather coat and pricey sneakers and designer jeans. She wanted to throw up.

"What's wrong?"

"You shouldn't be here." She flung a glance at her boxy old-fashioned TV where little Zuzu was talking about an angel earning her wings. Lines scrolled across the bottom, for God's sake. "I can't do this."

"Why shouldn't I be here? I want to be." He stepped closer and took her suddenly cold hands in his larger warm ones. "I thought you could use a tree, but you don't have to put it up if you don't like it. That's not why I came."

She angled her head. "So why did you?"

His beautiful eyes burned into hers. "Because I couldn't think of anyone else I'd rather spend tonight with than you."

Her wobbly heart plummeted straight to her toes by way of her vagina. Every spot on the way tingled. "Sure you're not just doing your holiday good deed?"

"Actually, I am. I hope to be repaid in blowjobs and eggnog. Sound good to you?"

She couldn't help laughing as she waved at the living room. "Go on, go sit. I'll just change."

"No. You're fine." He rubbed the indent in her chin. "I'm not company. I want you just as you are."

"Do you hear that dripping noise?" she whispered when she could finally speak.

He frowned. "No."

"That's me, melting." His slow grin turned that melting thing she had going on into a total winter thaw. Especially between her legs. "I didn't know you could be romantic, Des."

"It's probably because I'm getting ready to romance a veggie egg roll in extra duck sauce. It's making me feel all lovey dovey."

She laughed and went back into the hall. "I'll serve the food and you can put up the tree." She knelt, noticing the paper bag on top of the gift. She dug through it and shook her head, hoping the motion would discourage her tears. He really had thought of everything. "Mini lights? And ornaments?"

"I forgot the star."

"Gonna dock your pay for that one."

"The drugstore didn't have much left, but I figured those would—"

Before he could finish, she shot to her feet and whirled into his arms, clamping her mouth down on his so hard that he let out an "oomph." Then he was returning her kiss, his lips as cold as the frost that clung to his coat. He streaked his hands up her spine to tug on her hair, using it to pull her head back so he could plunge even deeper into her mouth. He was practically fucking her, just with his tongue instead of his cock.

She broke away and gasped for air. "You're still my boss."

"I don't care about that. It won't change anything." His palms came up to frame her cheeks, and when his face dipped to hers, she realized he was shaking. They both were. "Just let me love you."

Her rundown apartment and her job suddenly didn't factor in anymore. This wasn't about any of that. It wasn't about Cole or quick office fucks with thick ripple icicles from the tree, as amazing as that had been.

There was a world of secrets in his eyes, and she wanted to learn them all.

"Come with me," she murmured.

## Chapter VII

Her bedroom matched the rest of the house. It was sparsely decorated and the overhead light left the corners in shadows. Not counting her desk. That was bathed in a purple and yellow shimmering glow.

He grinned. "You have a lava lamp. You didn't even live through the sixties."

"No, but I loved them just the same. You should've seen my room back in Tennessee. I had a black light and fuzzy posters." Biting her lip, she walked to the full bed. "Sorry, it's kind of small."

"That's okay. We'll just stack up double-decker."

She laughed and flipped one of her ponytails over her shoulder. "Do you want a drink first? I have soda and eggnog. Coffee too."

"I'm fine, thanks." He came up behind her and snagged her full hips in his hands. She was rounded in all the right ways, and his cock wasn't the least bit bashful about showing his appreciation. "I just want you."

She slipped away and opened the nightstand drawer. "I don't think I have any condoms. I haven't bought any since—" She sighed.

"Since when?"

"Since I came here. I thought I might've had some stashed from home, but they'd probably be duds anyway." She sat down heavily on the bed. "I've never had a guy in this room."

"Am I supposed to be disappointed about any of these things? Because I'm not." He sat down beside her and rubbed her thigh. "I have some."

"Of course you do. You and Cole are always prepared."

He didn't miss the note of dejection in her voice. He turned toward her, waiting until she did the same. "I'd like to not use them tonight. I've never..." He blew out a breath. "I've never gone raw in a woman."

"What about in a man?"

"No. There's only been Cole and some dude in college. I just tried it with him to see if I was really bi." He glanced down at his hands. "The experience sucked, so I decided it was just about Cole for me. And only when we're with a woman."

"You've known Cole a long time."

"Yeah. We met in high school in Maine. We came to New York for college and stayed."

"Was he born in England or something?"

"You mean because he uses the word 'love' as an endearment?" At her nod, he chuckled. "He was an exchange student in London for one semester. Personally I think he tries to sound British to get the women going."

"It works for Van. She swoons every time he starts that 'love' stuff." She picked at a loose thread on her comforter. "When did you and he, you know? Start doing it?"

Considering everything she'd done with them, he found it incredibly charming that she could still be shy. "We didn't have sex until we shared a girl at our prom senior year. We've been together sporadically since then. If you're wondering about my sexual history, I've been tested recently. I'm clean."

Wordlessly, she crawled into his lap and wrapped her arms around his neck. Her tongue parted his lips, tasting. Exploring. Giving him back something he hadn't felt for way too long—hope.

They didn't move from that position for what felt like hours. His lips felt bruised by the time he finally dragged her sports bra over her head and bared her beautiful tits. The light from her lava lamp played over her skin, showcasing the dark nipples that beckoned his mouth. He kissed each one in turn, drawing deeply, not stopping until her soft sighs led him to bury his hands in his hair and lift her back onto the heaping pile of pillows. They filled almost half of the bed and cradled her as she extended her arms to him. He stretched out on top of her and tucked his nose against her throat, just breathing in her sultry jasmine scent while she stroked his back and tangled their legs.

Shit, the room was too warm. He quickly shucked his clothes, though all that did was remind him exactly how small the bed was. Still, it was hard to complain when she flashed him a bewitching smile and settled back with her sexy red hair draped over the pillows.

This was finally going to happen.

She shifted against him, lining his still eager cock up with her pussy. He yanked at her leggings, needing that barrier gone. As soon as she was naked, he inched down the bed and threw her legs over his shoulders, wasting no time in opening her for his mouth.

Slowly, he trailed his tongue over her hot, wet slit, sinking into her over and over. Journeying from her engorged clit over her trembling

*A Very Naughty Xmas*

entrance all the way down to the pucker between her cheeks. She was like an erotic version of that kids' doctor game—each destination earned him a new sound. A helpless mewl, a long sigh, an urgent moan. They left no doubt as to what she liked.

Normally he tried to be a little more precise when he was going down on a woman, but the scent of her desire combined with the tightening of her thighs around his head destroyed his finesse. He wanted her taste inside him by any means possible. She arched, shamelessly grinding against his face until she finally gave in to him on a rippling wave that left her sensitive tissues quaking around his tongue.

He slid back up her body to kiss her, wanting her to know how much he loved pleasing her that way. She whimpered, spanning his stubbled jaw with her fingers to hold him still as she licked his tongue clean.

"Fuck, you're hot." Groaning, he cupped her still twitching sex. He pushed two fingers inside her and absorbed the clenching spasms that instantly overtook her again. "I want in you. Bare."

Wendy's drowsy eyes locked on his. Her nod told him she understood he wasn't demanding anything. It would be her choice. "It's okay." As if in silent acquiescence, more of her liquid dampened his palm. "I'm still on the pill."

He didn't wait. Couldn't. He'd spent so long telling himself this couldn't ever happen. That he wouldn't risk their work relationship—or her.

Now she was beneath him, her nails scraping up his back as he circled her with the tip of his cock. Goddamn, he'd known she would use her nails.

She braced her heels on the bed and rose up, engulfing his length in one slow roll of her flesh meeting his. She moaned at the sensation of him bottoming out inside her, then dragging back and forging forward again. He set a punishing rhythm, determined to pay his way in orgasms. It was a shitty penance for taking her like this, but he'd known he would only be able to resist her for so long.

They weren't the typical boss and secretary, and they'd fucking make their own rules. They'd make this work.

She cupped her breasts, thumbing her stiff nipples. The gesture almost seemed unconscious until she coasted her hand down her torso to encircle him where he pumped into her pussy. She gripped him at the base, squeezing him while her wicked eyes danced in the shifting light from her desk lamp. Purple streaks highlighted her hair and added shadows that made her lips look even more plump.

Oh, fuck, those lips.

He surged into her until he couldn't go any farther, brushing her clit with every pass. Crushing her fingers between their bodies, adding an extra layer of friction.

The wilder he stroked into her, the more fiercely the nails on her other hand scored his back. She reached down to grab his ass, hauling him into her so roughly that he couldn't hold back his shout. The bed frame rammed against the wall, likely gouging out the paint, and still he swiveled into her, finding angles that drew her to new heights. He grasped her breast, massaging it while she sucked him balls deep. She was so tight and slick, and she met his thrusts beat for beat. That she was right there with him, her frantic exhales gusting across his face, wrenched him almost as much as the unrelenting grip of her pussy around his length.

Des gazed into her hazy eyes. In them he saw so much more than passion. She was open to him, all the way. Body, soul and heart.

She bowed up, sobbing through her pleasure. Her shudders reverberated through his body, becoming his own. She pumped more wetness over him, prodding him to enter her faster. Harder. Pounding into her so that his sac slapped against her ass. The wet sounds of their lovemaking offset her cries and stole his focus from her manic thrashing. She didn't restrain anything. What she needed from him, she took.

Tonight they both took. And gave.

He pulled back and held, just barely inside her. "Look at me," he whispered, hating that she'd finally closed her eyes. Her lashes rose and her lips fell apart as he drove into her one last time. "Baby, I've never…this has never…Wendy."

Buried within her, the tingling in his spine exploded in an ecstasy that damn near splintered his balls. He shot his release far into her clutching pussy, each drop pulled from his depths. Now she owned this part of him as she owned all the rest.

Gasping, he collapsed on top of her, his mouth at her breast. The flavor of her skin grounded him. And he drowned in it, just as he'd drowned himself in her.

He almost didn't notice as she eased away from him and shimmied down the sheets. Her mouth gloved his spent cock and tore a grunt from him, but she didn't relent. She swirled up and down his length, using all the carnal knowledge she'd gained from him the last couple of weeks. Her cheeks hollowed to suck him and her tongue fucked his tiny slit and holy shit, he was actually getting erect again.

She was a miracle worker. A goddamn dirty angel. *His.*

When she clasped her fingers around his sac, tugging gently, he hissed a curse and fisted her satin pillows. When she deep throated him so damn hard that his ass clenched to stave off his orgasm, he grabbed one of her ponytails and dragged her off.

She smiled up at him, rubbing her breasts so blatantly that his dick gave a pulse in defeat. He grabbed the base, twisting. It didn't help. She pinched her nipples and flexed her hips, letting him see exactly how excited getting him off made her.

"Roll over." He snatched her ponytails, yanking them while he positioned himself behind her. His cock trailed over the crack of her ass, making her moan, before sliding down and powering into her drenched slit.

"Fuck yes. Give me that pussy." He crushed her to the mattress, still stunned he could even do this again so soon. It was a banner frigging night. Seeing that round ass bobbing in front of him, feeling that brush of fingers that let him knowing she was touching herself again, urging them both to that point there was no coming back from—shit, he couldn't take it.

His body went on auto pilot and his hearing dimmed, tuned only to Wendy's keening moans and her moisture bathing his cock. She rocked back to meet him and he gentled his hold on her hair, releasing one of her ponytails to rain a light series of smacks on her ass. Testing to see if she really enjoyed that sort of play or had just tolerated it to please him and Cole.

She cried out and shuddered through a brutal climax, contracting around him so violently that he used her hair to pull her up again to make sure she hadn't passed out. She mumbled unintelligible words, her hips still racing under his, her nails scrabbling over the sheets.

"Oh baby. You're incredible." He plowed into her until the sexy line of her spine and the curve of her ass blurred. Until his life's purpose distilled to emptying himself in her. Giving her all of him, even when he'd been sure there was nothing left. There was always more, with her.

Des shouted as his release jetted deep into her body. There was so much it creamed around his width, which didn't exactly help in bringing him back down. By the time he finished pounding into her, even his damn balls were sore.

He collapsed atop her, knowing he shouldn't. He should move.

Yeah, he should do that. Someday.

"Des?"

Now he was hearing voices. At least they knew his name. "Mmm?"

"Why wouldn't you make love to me before? With Cole?" She rushed ahead. "I thought...God, I thought so many things. But I want to hear the truth from you."

Somehow he summoned the strength to roll over and draw her into his arms. She belonged there. If he hadn't known that before tonight, he was damn certain of it now.

"That guy Johnny who raised me? He was my mom's best friend. After she died, I ended up with him and his wife. They divorced when I was in college and he died a couple of years back."

She stroked his chest. "I'm so sorry. What about your dad?"

"He wasn't really in my life. He had another family, and they took his focus."

This time she didn't say anything.

"They met at work. She was his receptionist, and he used his advantage to get exactly what he demanded from her. I was the unwanted consequence." The words pressed on his chest, imprinted there like a tattoo he'd never wanted. "She never got over their relationship. Over losing him. Then I lost her too soon too."

She was quiet for so long that he craned his neck to take a good look at her. She was staring at him, eyes wide and wet. "You could've told me, Des."

Shaking his head, he let out an abbreviated laugh. "How?"

"Just like this."

"Yeah, after I've been inside you." He gazed at the ceiling. "I tried, Wen. I really did. It was stupid, thinking that with all we'd done I could still pretend I wasn't like him. I did everything I could to make it clear to you it had nothing to do with your job, and I never took advantage all the way—" He pinched his nose, unsurprised it didn't relieve the pressure gathering in his head. "I lied to myself. Worse, I lied to you."

"You did? I must've missed it." She crossed her arms over his chest and leaned forward so that her hair trailed over his skin.

He couldn't stop the shudder. God, he had so many plans for that hair and her mouth before the night was through…

If she didn't tell him to go to hell.

"You didn't lie, Des, you just didn't tell me everything. And that's okay, because I didn't tell you everything either." She pulled back, retreating even further when he pinned her with his stare. "Maybe we should hit pause right here."

His stomach knotted. When she was nervous or upset, the southern in her voice grew more pronounced. Usually he couldn't get enough of it. At the moment, the rich, silky tones only increased his need to command her to tell him every secret she had.

He was no expert, but he figured that meant he was in love with her. Or possibly a burgeoning psycho.

Inhaling deeply, he turned her face toward his. Whatever it was, he'd face it with her. He'd be damned if he gave her up now. "Tell me."

*A Very Naughty Xmas*

She squeezed her eyes shut, blocking him out. "I'm in love with you."

\*\*\*\*

At least he didn't laugh. She supposed she couldn't complain at his lack of response, or how he went as still as a corpse at her side. He was still her boss, after all. They had their working relationship to think about, and despite his revelations, he might not be ready to take things public. Or maybe he just didn't care for her that way.

She could handle it. She'd handled much worse.

"I don't expect you to love me back." Wendy reached for his hand. His skin was hot to the touch. "I just needed you to know. Every time I was with you and Cole, I wanted it to be just us. You and me, like it was tonight." She glanced around her woefully tiny bedroom and sighed. "Though I wish we'd been at your place. This bed is one Des-powered thrust away from collapse."

He laughed, and her tension seeped away. Well, most of it. "I like your house." He kissed her collarbone with little serpentine flicks of his tongue. "We still have a tree to put up, you know, and Chinese to eat. I also might've gotten you a gift."

"I don't have anything for you," she protested.

Grinning, he caressed her still sensitive pussy. "Oh yes, you do. Santa says thank you."

When he rolled away from her and reached for his clothes, she made her peace with her revelation. Whatever happened after tonight, she would be fine. She felt lighter and heavier, all at once. If she hated him just a little for his honor in not even bothering to pretend to love her, she'd get over it eventually.

Getting over stuff was one of her new skills. Along with her speedy typing and her skillful cock sucking, she was on her way to becoming a damn dynamo.

They decorated her tree and scarfed down the Chinese while they watched an all-night Christmas movie fest. He caught her eyeing his gift and plopped it in her lap, making her open it despite her complaints.

"You shouldn't have done this." She pulled on the ribbon and gave into her urge to shake the box. It barely rattled. She thumbed up the lid, biting her lip. "How about I buy you lunch next week—" She fell silent, her mouth rounding. "*Oh.*"

"I know you said you didn't like music boxes, but I wanted to try to change your mind. Or at least maybe improve your opinion." He popped the lid of the carved crystal box, unveiling a small skater on a pond who did figure eights in front of a charmingly decorated house to *I'll Be Home For Christmas*.

God, she was getting misty again. What the heck was going on with her hormones?

She blinked rapidly and smiled. "It doesn't sound tinny."

"No. Took some doing to find one that didn't in a shop that was still open on Christmas Eve. I got lucky." He gripped her fingers and made her look at him. "You don't like it."

"You're right, I don't like it—I love it." She grinned and kissed his scruffy jaw. "Thank you."

"You're welcome."

Maybe it was the way his eyes twinkled or the lateness of the hour, but an explanation tumbled forth before she thought to stop it. "My dad used to buy them for me. He gave me one every Christmas."

"I didn't see them in your room."

She glanced down at the skater, still moving in methodical circles. "They're in boxes, packed away. I haven't been able to stand looking at them for so long."

"If this is too painful for you—"

"No. No," she repeated, rising. "In fact, I want to show you one of the others he gave me. I think you'd like it."

He accepted the hand she extended and stood beside her. "Show me."

They ended up looking at all ten of her music boxes. He didn't seem bored by the accompanying stories and even helped her dust each one off and clear a bookshelf to display them. It was awfully crowded, but at least they weren't in boxes anymore.

No matter what happened between them, she had him to thank for that.

Just before three, they crawled into her bed and took their sweet time tearing up the sheets she'd neatly remade. With her body warm from his, she dropped deeply into sleep, smiling at the weight of his arm on her belly.

The sound of knocking jerked Wendy up on her elbows. Another knock, louder this time. Blearily, she swung her head around to search for the source.

Shit. Fuck. Damn. Someone was out in the hall.

She snatched the sheet and held it over her bare breasts as she shot a glance at Des, who was happily sawing them off.

"Hang on," she called out, scrambling up so fast that she caught her foot in the comforter on her way to the cold hardwood floor. "One more minute."

Too late. The door was already opening.

Just as she glimpsed her mom and aunt's shocked expressions, she realized that her graceless tumble off the bed had bared her lover's impressive morning wood for all to see.

"Merry Christmas," she muttered.

## Chapter VIII

To her mom's credit, she didn't freak out at finding a strange man in her supposedly single daughter's bed. Aunt Gert was a harder sell, wailing about violating the sanctity of marriage and such, but her mom got her settled down and out of the house before she shattered any windows.

Then it was just Mrs. Stanton, Wendy, and Des—who'd yet to stop grinning despite being ogled by two senior citizens before breakfast.

And his secretary. His secretary had definitely done her share of ogling too.

Since her mom was feeling good, she made them a breakfast of whole wheat waffles and turkey sausage. Discovering Des was a vegan made her mom's eyes glint. The one thing she'd disliked about Wendy's dad was his refusal to give up hunting. Des's love of animals definitely erased any lingering effects from finding him naked in Wendy's bed, though once she'd learned who he was she hadn't been too upset. She knew how Wendy felt about him.

Hell, from the way she was glowing that morning, the mailman could've figured it out.

"Wendy never stops talking about you," Mrs. Stanton said, ignoring Wendy's plaintive groan. "You're every bit as handsome as she said."

Des continued sipping his coffee. He didn't seem the least bit embarrassed by that morning's events. "Your daughter's too kind."

"Not too kind. Wendy's just grateful as all get out for everything you've done for us. She's downright effusive about you. You've changed our lives for the better, son. Sweet Mary, you even brought us a beautiful little tree." She shocked the hell out of Wendy by getting up to kiss Des flush on the mouth. "Thank you so much."

Though Des smiled and returned her embrace, his jaw had gone hard and tight. "Wendy's a wonderful secretary and an even better person. You raised a terrific daughter, Mrs. Stanton."

"Call me Noreen." With that, she shuffled away from the table with

## A Very Naughty Xmas

her cup of tea. She probably had no clue about the stink bomb she'd just set off in the center of the kitchen.

From Des's expression, he was already choking on the stench.

"Look, I can explain—" Wendy began the moment they were alone.

"Don't." He tossed his napkin on the table and stalked to the window. It was snowing outside and looked as pretty as a damn postcard. Inside all she could feel was the arctic chill.

She traced her finger over the wet spot on the table from her glass of orange juice. "You knew I feel grateful to you. You can't be *that* surprised."

He didn't speak for what felt like an eternity. "No. I'm not."

"Then?"

The hunch of his shoulders might've convinced her he was cold if the apartment hadn't been as hot as the surface of Venus. "I thought as much, but to have your mom say it is different."

"What are you talking about?"

He turned to face her, his eyes more turbulent than she'd ever seen them. "You're not really in love with me. You just think you are because I helped you out."

Clearly, she was going to have to stand up for this conversation. "Excuse me?"

"You heard me."

"I did, but you're talking nonsense." She walked over to him and skewered her nail in his chest. He didn't even wince. His pain receptors had likely gone into hibernation from all her scratching last night. "Am I grateful for all you've done for me and my mama? Hell yeah. You didn't have to be so sweet to us. To *me*."

His stubborn nod made her want to kick him. "Gratitude and love are easy to mix up."

"Don't make me kick you in the nuts on Christmas morning, Des. Because so help me, Jesus, if you don't let me finish, I will."

He didn't smile, but he did gesture for her to continue.

"None of that made me fall in love with you. I didn't fall for my accountant who got me those extra deductions that saved me a grand last year. I didn't fall for my garbageman when he said he'd take our old dresser even though the guidelines said it was too big. I freaking fell in love with you because you make me laugh without ever making me cry." She swallowed over the rising lump in her throat. "At least not yet."

He stroked her trembling lower lip. She couldn't stand how emotional he made her, though it was possible that was part of the whole love thing. "What about Cole?"

"What about him?"

"Are you grateful to him too?" he asked quietly.

"Of course," she snapped. "But I don't love him. I only love you, you dolt."

Again he didn't speak. But he smiled, so slow and wide that it teased out her own smile in response. "I believe you."

"As you should."

"I do." He pressed his lips to her forehead. "And I love you too."

Before she had a chance to whoop and holler her joy, he drew back and gripped her upper arms. His face was even more serious than before. "Will you start ripping off the days of my calendar again?"

"You noticed I stopped?"

"Of course I did. I had no clue what day was which anymore."

Laughing, she wrapped her arms around his waist. He was so warm and sturdy and God, he made her feel safe. And happy. So very happy. "I didn't want the days to pass so I stopped tearing the pages off. Every one that went by I knew we were closer to being finished."

"We won't ever be finished." He ran his hand down the length of her hair. "In fact, I think we should take this upstairs."

"With my mom in the living room?"

He only grinned. "The TV's on loud. Besides, she's already seen my equipment. Why not hear it at work making you moan too?"

"Ugh!" But she laughed as he dragged her toward the doorway.

At the foot of the stairs, she stopped him with an impish smile. "Wait. I have one more question."

"What's that?"

She leaned close to his ear and spoke in a whisper. "What did Cole name my...pussy?" There, she'd said it. And she hadn't even burst into hysterical giggles.

But Des didn't notice her inner triumph, because he was too busy laughing. "Sorry. He never told me." With a wink, he chucked her chin. "Guess you'll have to ask him first thing on Monday when he gets back."

"Maybe I'll just name your penises instead. Secret names that I'll only share with Van." As soon as she mentioned her friend's name, she frowned. "What are we going to tell her?"

"The truth. We're a couple and that won't change anything at work." His expression softened and her knees literally went weak. "No more hiding, baby."

She fought not to do a booty dance but it was pretty much a lost cause. She added in one of her improvised carols as she jumped from stair to stair.

When he made a grab for her, she squealed and darted ahead with him hot on her heels. They had a ton of celebrating left to do.

This year, Christmas frigging *rocked*.

THE END

## About Cari Quinn

USA Today bestselling author Cari Quinn saves the world one Photoshop file at a time in her job as a graphic designer. At night, she writes sexy romance, drinks a lot of coffee and plays her music way too loud. When she's not scribbling furiously, she's watching men's college basketball, reading excellent books and causing trouble. Sometimes simultaneously.

Visit Cari at http://www.cariquinn.com

## Other Books by Cari Quinn

# Christmas is Coming

## RAVEN MORRIS

*Christmas is Coming, by Raven Morris*

# Chapter 1

Jack had tied her up again.

Debra smiled. This was getting to be a habit on special occasions.

Ah, well, it only made them more special.

"I see you smiling," said the gorgeous hunk of fun she'd married. "You're awake."

"Yep, I'm awake." She glanced at his beautiful naked body standing beside their bed. "Looks like you are, too."

Jack's cock twitched. He was always awake in the morning. Whether or not they had time to take care of it depended on their busy schedules. But today was a day off. December twenty-second. No one did business three days before Christmas.

Well, of the professional kind. She and Jack were definitely about to get down to *some* kind of business.

"What can I say, Deb?" Jack traced a finger over her shoulder and down her arm. "I can't help it when I'm around you. You turn me on, babe."

"Good." She licked her lips, knowing what that did to Jack. "So are we going to do something about these or not?" She tugged on her restraints—and felt an answering tug in her pussy. She'd never get tired of making love with Jack. The man was talented physically. *And* emotionally... They'd connected on that level from the first moment they'd met.

"Nah, I don't think I'll do anything with them." He flicked one of the scarves they now kept in the bedside table and had ever since he'd first put them there a few months ago after her birthday morning "celebration." These scarves had gotten a lot of use since then. Flag Day, Fourth of July, Labor Day, Secretary's Day—both she and Jack had secretaries so it seemed like a reason to celebrate—every major and minor holiday in between. Amazing how many holidays one could find when properly motivated to look.

"So then what are you going to do with them, Jack?" Her voice was husky—an early morning thing usually, but when Jack looked at her like

## A Very Naughty Xmas

that, it was for a whole different reason.

"I'm going to leave them right where they are."

She liked where they were. She loved being at Jack's mercy—he was so merciful. Always putting her out of her agony... well, eventually. "Good because then you'll have to do all the work if you want me to suck you off."

She bit her lip to keep from laughing when his cock came to full attention. She shouldn't laugh. Jack was very secure in himself—with good reason—but a sudden burst of laughter might shake his confidence just a bit, even if she'd only be laughing because of how utterly easy it was to play him. She knew how to push every one of his buttons.

Like this one...

She leaned over and kissed the tip of his dick.

"Ah, jeez, Deb." Jack's indrawn breath was harsh. And aroused. "You always steal my thunder."

"Quiet, big guy. You've got enough thunder to keep this house rocking for two weeks straight. Now get over here and give it all to me."

That was the thing about Jack; he took direction well in bed. Everywhere else, Jack was in command. But in their bedroom, even though he'd tied her up, he liked her to boss him around as much as he liked to do it to her. They were a good match that way. As were their bodies. In particular, her mouth and his cock.

"Come on, Jack, no holding out on me."

"You got that right." He raised her head and stuffed his cock into her mouth.

God, he tasted amazing. He had a certain flavor that could turn her on quicker, faster, harder than anyone else.

"How's that, Deb?"

She grunted around his throbbing shaft. That was one thing they had to work on; talking wasn't really possible while blowing him, but then, Jack didn't really require the words. A few moans, a couple of happy groans, and he was good to go.

And, God, was he. His dick was hard beneath its velvety surface, and he worked it so well between her lips, the smooth head sliding off the roof of her mouth to the back of her throat. It'd taken her a while to be able to take all of him; Jack had been given quite the gift by Mother Nature. One he was more than willing to share with her. And, after all, this *was* the season of giving.

She gave him good head and Jack groaned as he slipped down the back of her throat. She had to relax her throat muscles but it was a skill he greatly appreciated.

And she appreciated his reaction.

*Christmas is Coming*, by Raven Morris

He gripped her hair and held on, relieving the weight on her neck so she wouldn't have to worry about it. She didn't mind the pain, liked it actually. Kept her focused on him rather than what this was doing to her.

But, oh, what it was doing to her.

"That's it, babe. Take all of me."

She would. Anywhere. Anytime.

She ran her tongue along the thick vein, knowing how much he liked that.

He hissed his appreciation and jerked his hips, sending his dick bumping against the roof of her mouth.

She tightened her lips around the base, sucking harder.

He pumped then, his balls sliding on the satin sheets. He loved the sensation so they'd bought them for not only the house overlooking the canyon, but their mountain home, too.

"Aw, that's it, babe. Suck me. Your mouth is amazing."

It certainly felt amazing having him in her. She'd take him anywhere: in her mouth, between her breasts, in her pussy, anally… They'd practiced that last one a lot recently and she had to say that practice *did* make perfect.

Jack slid his hand over her ass.

Debra shivered. She wanted him to fuck her there. Being on her stomach, her legs spread, at his mercy… yeah, she wanted Jack to take her like that.

"Where do you want me, sweetheart?" he whispered, feathering his fingers over the sensitive flesh on her butt. He ran them along her cleft. "Your ass? Or your pussy?"

She mewled something around his dick though Jack didn't needed clarity. He'd fuck her wherever he chose and she'd like it.

Oh how she'd like it.

Her juices slipped from her channel and she pressed her mound into the sheet.

"Ah, impatient are we?"

She ran her tongue along the vein again then around the rim.

"Jesus." He fell forward, planting his palms on the mattress behind her.

His dick pressed down on her tongue like a tongue depressor, and reflexively, Debra swallowed.

"Oh my God, Deb, what is *that*?" He jerked his hips and his dick circled in her mouth. "Keep doing it."

She wasn't quite sure what it was she was doing, but, hey, if Jack wanted it, she'd do her best.

She tilted her chin down and his dick bottomed out on her tongue.

"Yeah, babe, that's amazing."

She flicked the tip of her tongue along the bottom of his shaft and Jack again hissed his appreciation. He gripped her ass with one hand. *Really* gripped it.

She clenched that sensitive flesh. She needed something in her.

"Plug," she said around his dick.

"Huh?" His cock jerked. "Oh. Yeah. Good idea. Hang on."

She certainly wasn't about to let go.

Jack leaned to the right, stretching his rock hard abs to get to the drawer. His cock slid out a little but she only sucked harder.

"Man, Deb, that is amazing."

It so was.

He fumbled with the drawer—gasped when she rubbed the flat of her tongue along the sensitive head—and he pulled out one of their toys, then drew it down her spine. "Oh, baby, you're going to love this."

She shivered. Jack had found the best toys online and he never tired of using them on her.

He slipped it down to her ass, probing her sensitive flesh.

It was the curved one. Oh, God, what that one could do to her…

"You want it?"

She nodded—knowing what her mouth rocking against him would do to him, But yeah, she wanted that toy in her. Now.

She bared her teeth and scraped them gently along his shaft.

She got the reaction she wanted.

He slicked the butt plug along her pussy, coating it with her juices, then slid it into her ass nice and quick, just how she liked *him* to take her, and her pussy flooded with her cream.

Jake's fingers found it.

He probed her lips, sliding his fingers along the sides, tickling her passage, teasing her, but never thrusting inside, making her ache and swell so much that she was moaning around his cock.

"Ah, so impatient, sweetheart. Relax. I'll get you off. You know that."

That was half the problem. She knew just how well Jack could get her off and her body wanted it. It wanted him.

He brought his fingers to his mouth. She could watch him in her peripheral vision and he made a big production of licking her from them.

"God, you taste amazing. I can't wait to bury my face between your legs and drink you dry."

Her pussy flooded again. Jake would do it, too. He'd once eaten her for over two hours. Two hours in which she'd been a writhing, begging, pleading mass of nerve endings who'd been sobbing for release. When he'd finally gotten her off, she'd come so hard she'd thought she'd never come again.

Oh how wrong she'd been.

But that day lived on in their memories. There were a few of those extraordinary lovemaking sessions. Debra was determined that they'd add another one to their mental keeper shelf this Christmas.

She wiggled her butt. Jack was definitely a butt man.

"Keep that up, Deb, and I'm going to have to spank you."

Her pussy swelled again. The sharp sting of his palm, especially when she had a toy in her, could do things to her that were the farthest thing from punishment.

"You want me to do that, don't you?"

She looked up at him, saw the fire in his gaze, the barely controlled passion as sweat dotted his body, his teeth gritted with the control he had to exert to keep from fucking her mouth so hard and long that he'd gag her and still not be able to stop.

She loved when he lost control .

But Jack was all about control. Rarely did he lose it. Usually it took a couple glasses of wine, some porn—their own—and a few tricky maneuvers she'd practiced until she'd gotten them just right to get him to lose it.

She *wanted* him to lose it this Christmas, preferably with the gift she was going to give him...

"Do that again, Deb. Your teeth." He slid his hand to her knee that was closest to him and drew it up.

The scarf tightened around her ankle and she flexed her foot.

"Too tight?"

She shook her head, smiling when Jack sucked in another harsh breath. He liked when she mouthed him like that.

He walked his fingers down her thigh.

She wiggled with anticipation, sucking him more.

"Don't think swallowing me is going to get you off any sooner, sweetheart." He slid his dick out until just the tip was still between her lips. "You have to work for it."

He rammed back in.

God, she loved when he did that. He was so big and so hard that she felt the force of his thrust all through her, and with her pussy spread as it was, she wanted to feel it. *Needed* to.

She better get him off fast, because she wanted his big, thick cock stuffed inside her so fast and hard and far and long, from the back, from the front, standing, sitting, she didn't care. She had to get Jack into her body.

She rimmed his head with her teeth and wriggled her tongue against his slit. Ah, there, his pre-cum. Jack could never resist giving her a taste when she did this to him.

"You . Aren't. Playing. Fair."

That's because she wasn't playing. She was dead serious about getting him off—then getting him *on*—on *her*.

She circled her tongue around his head, thrusting back against it when he tried to push it farther into her mouth.

"Please, Deb."

She pleased.

"Take me in. Let me in."

She would. In her own sweet time.

One half inch at a time.

"Oh."

She sucked in another half inch.

"My."

And another.

"God."

Jack's arms were shaking as he held her head and her leg, his fingers trembling against her cheek. Both sets of them.

She took in more of him. This time, a whole inch.

Seven more to go.

"Deb." Jack's cry was hoarse. Pleading. Her big, strong, manly husband begging for what only she could give him.

She might be the one tied up physically, but she'd tied him up in other ways, gladly tangling herself up with him.

She took in another inch. Jack had been a very good boy.' He deserved that much.

And then maybe some more.

He let go of her leg and brought that hand to her mouth, running his fingers over her lips where they met his cock, and she looked up to see his eyes so darkly brown they could be black. He licked his lips.

"You look so goddammed amazing right now with my cock in your mouth. Your soft pink lips surrounding me. Sucking me."

She sucked some more.

Jack's head fell back and he surged into her mouth. "Oh, my God, Debra, please, baby. Please just suck and suck and don't stop. I want to pour my cum down your throat."

That's what she wanted, too. Jack was delicious in every sense of the word.

She took his next thrust. And the next. His head was thrown back and his back arched and he was holding her head with both hands, fucking her mouth, his balls constricting as his cock grew thicker.

"Yeah, baby, that's it. That's it." His breathing came fast and shallow, his fingers grasping, and he drew her to him. Then pulled her away. Then drew her to him again, over and over, fucking her mouth, her face, her, as if she existed solely for his pleasure.

Right this moment, she so did.

And then he came. Filled her mouth with his hot, salty, amazing flavor, the thick fluid coating her tongue, and she drank in the very essence of her husband.

"Yes, sweetheart." His voice was harsh, the words tortured pleasure. "God, yes."

His balls constricted against her arm, his cock throbbing its goodness into her mouth and Debra couldn't take her eyes off the beauty that was Jack when he came, his abs standing out in stark relief beneath that smooth skin and the soft patch of hair that led right down to where she was just now, his chest—his gorgeous sculpted chest—heaving as he tried to catch the breath she'd stolen from him.

"Ah, baby...." He grimaced as another flick of her tongue jerked more cum from him. "What would I do without you?"

She lapped up the remaining flow then drew back along his length, earning his hiss the entire way. She circled her tongue on the head then released him into the cool air.

Another hiss. She smiled. That switch from hot to cold was its own sort of pleasure/pain.

"Let's hope you never have to find out what you'd do without me, Jack. But I can tell you right now, if you don't *do* me, you just might have to."

He was on her so fast, his face stuffed between her legs, she barely saw him move.

But, oh, did she feel him.

His tongue was everywhere, licking from her clit right up to that plug, probing everywhere in between. His fingers were just as busy, parting her, stroking her, fucking her... Jack had taken that time he'd brought his friend, David, to their bed to heart and tried to be everywhere and everything to her.

She'd told him he already was.

He slid his hands under her hips and tugged her toward the end of the bed, as far as the ties around her wrists would allow, his tongue thrusting up inside of her.

Debra worked her knees under her and managed to push back into him.

He growled against her and the vibration sent pleasure rippling along her lips.

"Eat me, Jack. Make me come."

He growled again and slid his tongue along her clit.

God, when he did that, there was nothing she wouldn't do for him—if she could move, that was. He'd rendered her immobile and she could only focus on the tight, sensitive bundle of nerves between her legs.

He did it again.

Her stomach hitched, that sweet punch-in-the-gut of desire, something so many of her friends had complained they'd lost for their husbands. Not her; Jack did this to her every single time.

She bowed her back, raising her ass so he could have better access, and Jack, clever boy, slid his hand up along her stomach to find her breast. He flattened his palm to it, then squeezed.

Just what she needed.

Debra rubbed against his hand. The friction drove her nuts, one more sensation in a sea of them.

Then he wiggled the plug in her ass.

*Ohmygod.*

Debra felt her orgasm start. That damned curved end did it to her every time, rubbing up against that thin wall between her ass and her pussy, and she couldn't hold back. Jack could get her off just from playing with that sensitive area and he knew it.

He wiggled the plug again. Then he fucked her with it, all the while his tongue licking her clit with hard, quick strokes, never giving her a moment to breathe.

Not that she would've been able to anyway.

She rode his tongue. Clenched her ass around the plug. Grabbed hold of the scarves holding her arms in place to lift up just enough to rub her nipple back and forth over his calloused hand.

"Ah, yes, Jack. That's it, baby." Her words were soft because of her lack of breath, but Jack knew what she said. They understood each other that way.

He slid his thumb down along her slit and pushed it inside her pussy.

He fucked her in both holes, his tongue working her clit and his fingers plucking at her nipple. She was the luckiest woman in the world to have such a talented and dedicated lover.

Then he rubbed the sensitive skin between her pussy and her ass from the inside and pressed down on the plug.

She got off like a rocket. One minute she was riding up to that wave, building the tension, and the next, she was diving over it, every nerve in her body screaming with release as Jack held on to her nipple and pulled, elongating it in that painfully erotic way she loved. He tongued her clit so fast and hard she couldn't tell where one sensation ended and the other began and his fingers rubbed her in the most perfect rhythm that had her pushing back against him and she came.

Jack groaned as he lapped up her juices. She could picture him doing it—he'd eaten her out enough from the front that the image in her head only added to her excitement.

Then he switched to her other breast and the orgasm hit her all over again.

Debra strained against her scarves, thankful for them because they gave her something to hold on to as her world shot off in all different directions, colors bursting behind her eyelids, every pounding beat of her heart centered between her legs where Jack's tongue was relentless, taking her as she came until, finally, she had nothing left. Not an ounce of strength, barely a thought in her head, and she fell onto the bed, utterly replete.

*A Very Naughty Xmas*

## Chapter 2

"So what do you want to do today?" Jack whispered in her ear as if they'd just had their morning coffee while he released the wrist closest to him from its bonds.

"You mean we didn't just do it?"

He kissed the sensitive spot between her shoulder blades. The one guaranteed to make her shiver.

Though, come to think of it, wherever Jack kissed her was guaranteed to make her shiver.

He untied her other wrist. "Sweetheart, you know I could stay here and make love to you all day, but I thought you might have some last-minute shopping to do."

It was a joke with them; she was an event planner and planned dozens of events at the same time, months in advance, but she couldn't seem to apply that same logic and practice to her real life. She was always running behind schedule. She'd said more than once that she was going to have "If she'd only had fifteen more minutes" engraved on her tombstone. If she could find the time to pre-order it.

"Fine." She kept her arms over her head and rolled over, sighing, knowing exactly what that would do to her breasts.

And exactly how Jack would react.

She was right; his eyes flared.

"God, woman, you are gorgeous." He ran his fingers over her breast, pausing on her nipple a little longer than a mere brush-by. "On second thought—"

She sat up and reached down to undo one of her ankles. "Hold that second thought until tonight. You're right. I do have some shopping to do."

"So where are we going?" He undid the other one then handed over her robe. A pointless gesture given that modesty was out the window with what they'd just done, but he'd bought that robe for her on the business trip to Tokyo. Pure silk and the color of her eyes. He liked to see her in it.

*Christmas is Coming*, by Raven Morris

He also liked to peel it off of her.

She cinched up the sash and headed toward the bathroom. "*We* aren't headed anywhere. Amanda and I are. It's a girls' day."

"So Amanda's in town?" Jack followed her into the bathroom.

"Hold on, you." She put her palm on his awesome chest. He still worked out at least four times a week and it showed. "You are not coming in here or I'll never leave on time."

Sometimes her being late wasn't her fault.

"Two minutes ago you didn't care."

"Two minutes ago I couldn't think straight and forgot all about Amanda. I wonder why that was?"

"How can I argue with that logic?" His grin was pure gloating male—as he had every right to be.

"You can't. Now back off, buster. I'm going to take a quick shower and head downtown. You're going to have to keep yourself occupied today."

"As loathsome as that would normally be, David's back in town, too. I'll give him a call."

*David.* Debra's stomach fluttered. The last time David had been in town, he'd been in their bed. In *her*. Jack's birthday present to her. Her first threesome.

But not her last...

"Tell him I said hi." She undid her sash.

Jack's gaze shifted to her waist. "I'm sure your name will come up."

Her name wasn't the only thing that was up—Jack hadn't bothered to put on *his* robe. He rarely did, preferring to stride around their home naked. She never complained.

"Out." She gripped the door—instead of gripping him. It didn't matter that she'd just had two utterly intense and explosive orgasms, the man could instill lust in her like nobody's business. "Once before noon is enough."

"Babe, it's never enough." He leaned in for a quick kiss. "I'll never get enough of you."

He cupped her breasts and planted a kiss right on her cleavage, his thumbs making quick strokes over her nipples.

And then he left her there.

No fair.

She sighed and leaned against the bathroom door after she closed it. Jack McKittrick was the best thing to ever happen to her.

That's why she wanted to show him how much she appreciated him. Bringing David into their bedroom had been the most generous and thoughtful gift he'd ever given her. Which was saying something. Jack was a successful attorney and he liked to share his wealth by showering her with gifts. She didn't need them; Jack was gift enough, but he liked to see her in gold and jewels and pretty clothing—or in gold and jewels and *no* pretty clothing after he'd tossed it all over the house.

But to share her with another man for the sole purpose of giving her pleasure... Jack was an amazing guy.

Who deserved the same kind of amazing gift.

She headed to the shower and turned it to cold. Just the thought of the conversation she was going to have with Amanda was enough to make her hot. She'd never done something like this before; soliciting someone for sex. With her husband.

Amanda was her college roommate. They'd met freshman year and had been together ever since. They'd never experimented with each other as far as that cliché went, but there'd been that drunken night at the frat party when the brothers had double-dog-dared them to make out with each other. Amanda was a good kisser and could definitely feel a girl up as well as a guy, if not better, since she knew exactly what felt good on breasts.

They'd laughed about it the next morning when they'd sobered up, but it'd never happened again. A one-off, though they'd certainly seen each other in action with guys when they'd forgotten to lock the dorm room door. If Debra was going to allow another woman's hands—and mouth and pussy—on Jack, it would only be Amanda.

Her pussy swelled at the thought. Of seeing Jack fucking her friend. Of seeing Amanda riding him, her double-Ds bouncing above him. Of Jack taking her nipples in his mouth and sucking them, Amanda's head thrown back with the sensation Debra knew only too well.

It was interesting, really, how she wasn't jealous. This was for *Jack*; it wasn't as if he were going out looking for someone on his own because he didn't want her. This was a gift for him like the one he'd given her and if he could be fine with another person doing her, so could she.

Some of her juices trickled down her leg. Actually, she was more than fine with it. She *wanted* it. Ever since the idea had come to her, she'd found herself riding the edge of her chair a little bit more during her day.

Leaning up against the washer in the spin cycle.

Fucking her husband twice a night for a week.

Jack had commented on that, wondering if there was something she'd been trying to tell him.

No, there'd been something she'd been trying *not* to tell him. She hadn't wanted to blow the surprise, so she'd ended up blowing him instead, telling him he was so wonderful she couldn't help but want him.

It was true, though. She did love Jack and she was always ready for him.

The cold water was a shock when she stepped beneath it, but just what she needed. She had no idea what Amanda was going to say. Would this ruin their friendship? What would happen if she said no?

*And if she said yes?*

Debra lathered up, her nipples peaked and ultra sensitive to the brush of her hands, residual from their lovemaking probably, but she couldn't deny it was arousal, too. She *wanted* Amanda to agree. She *wanted* her friend to fuck her husband so she could watch. And maybe she'd sit on his face while Amanda rode him.

That'd turn him on, two women at once. It'd been the ultimate fantasy to have Jack and David on her at the same time.

She slicked a hand between her legs. Her lips were pouting, aching to be touched.

Debra touched.

She stroked.

She flicked the hood of her clitoris. Still swollen from Jack's touch, it swelled even more.

She knew what would make it happy. What'd make *her* happy…

She reached for the shower head and turned it to her favorite setting. Jack had brought six shower heads home when they'd remodeled this bathroom and had made her try each one. While he'd watched.

This had been the third one she'd tried. They'd both agreed it got her off the best.

She was counting on it now.

She sat on the ledge Jack had insisted they have installed in the shower. It'd come in handy more than once when he'd joined her in here.

And it was the perfect configuration for her to get herself off, too.

He'd insisted they try that out as well.

She sat down and spread her legs, putting her heels against the raised tiles Jack had had installed for just this reason. Such a thoughtful man, Jack was.

The fact that the seat was facing the glass doors showed just how much thought he *had* given to this. There was a perfectly comfortable chair directly opposite the shower where he liked to sit and watch her do this—and he'd do the same for her.

She closed her eyes and leaned back against the cool tile wall, spreading her pussy lips and aiming the water jets right at her clit. Ah, God, yes. The pressure was intense. It took her zero to sixty in no time flat and she had to keep from crying out with the sensation—because Jack would break that door down to get in on this action. He was thoughtful that way, too.

She smiled, remembering other times Jack had been so thoughtful.

There'd been the time they'd taken the self-guided tour of the vineyard in Napa and had proceeded to get self-guidedly lost. Champagne bursting from its bottle felt as awesome against her clit as the shower, but didn't last anywhere near as long.

But Jack had lapped it up, every drop of champagne and her juices, when she'd come against his face. She could still feel the warmth of the afternoon sun on her breasts that day, the feel of Jack's stubble against her thighs, the slick, probing hardness of his tongue as he'd worked her, the tightness of her skirt ruched up around her waist, the scratchy wool blanket beneath her ass, the feel of her hands on her breasts while he'd given new meaning to the phrase *in vino veritas*. She could never hide anything from Jack.

A heavy throbbing filled her pelvis as she remembered that day. And others. The time he'd phone-sexed her into getting off in her office with her assistant just outside the glass door and the lunch crowd strolling around the lake outside her office window. The time he'd brought her to a client's cocktail party, only to drag her to a storage room and fuck her silly in three minutes. She'd barely been able to keep the grin off her face for the rest of the night.

Jack kept their life exciting both in and out of bed.

He liked to do it out of bed a *lot*. He'd had a more experienced past than she had and, little by little, he was sharing it with her. David was the perfect example. Both Jack and he had participated in threesomes before so Jack had known he could trust David not to get involved with her emotionally.

Physically was a whole other story, and Debra's passage flooded at the memory. Two men inside of her at once… They'd filled her so tight and so utterly hot that she'd found herself thinking about it a lot.

She'd wanted to broach the subject of doing it again with Jack, but didn't know if she should. It'd been a gift. Something special. It'd been *David*. Someone they both felt comfortable with and who had known how it was supposed to play out.

*David was back in town.*

Debra changed the angle of the jets, her breath catching at the sharp flutter in her belly.

No, she couldn't ask Jack about David. First of all, she had no idea if either one of them would even be into another round. Second, if Jack *did* want to, he'd ask David himself. He'd known she'd enjoyed it. And third, she didn't want her desire to overshadow the gift she was going to give him.

*If* Amanda agreed.

Debra pushed that thought away and focused on Amanda agreeing. With the image of her friend's sexy body naked and writhing, working up and down on Jack's cock, her ass flexing against his balls—hell, maybe Debra would watch Jack fuck Amanda's ass.

That thought brought on a gush of her juices, her pussy clenching with lust. Yes, that was it; she'd have Jack fuck Amanda in the ass. She'd tie Amanda to the bed like he'd tied her this morning and then she'd sit at the head of the bed and get herself off while Jack watched. And fucked.

He'd like that.

Debra slid two fingers into her pussy and angled the shower head accordingly. The images were so strong, so erotic, so fantasy-driven, that a couple of pumps with her fingers had her pussy clenching around them and another orgasm spasming through her.

Amanda *had* to agree.

# Chapter 3

Amanda, as it turned out, *did* agree.

"You're sure you want to share that hunk you married with me?" Amanda stuck another French fry in her mouth. "It won't get weird?"

Debra couldn't stop smiling. Amanda was on board. Jack was going to be thrilled.

She was, too. Her damp panties were proof positive of that. "I told you, when he brought David to our bed, it was the hottest thing ever. Our relationship has only gotten better."

"I didn't think that was possible. I thought Jack was Mr. Perfect already."

Debra stole one of Amanda's fries. "Jack *is* wonderful. But he's human like everyone else. Doesn't have the annoying habit of leaving his clothes or towels all over the place, but he's got his idiosyncrasies." Chief among them being his penchant for risqué sex where people could catch them. But Debra had found those were some of the best times and had learned to let her inhibitions down to enjoy them. What she was asking of Amanda showed how far she'd come in that regard.

"So how's this going to play out? I have to be at my sister's by ten Christmas morning."

"Oh you'll make it. You might be a bit tired"—and well-used—"but we have to go to Jack's parents', too."

"So we're doing dinner at your place Christmas Eve, right, then somehow you're going to introduce the idea? You're sure he's going to be up for it?"

Debra smiled and pulled something from her purse. She'd given this part a lot of thought. Well, okay, maybe not as much thought as imagining Amanda fucking Jack, but still... "I want you to wear these."

Amanda took the scraps of red lace. "You bought me lingerie? Ah, Deb, you shouldn't have."

Debra smacked her arm. "They're not for you. They're part of Jack's Christmas present."

Amanda held up the thong. "Flimsy thing."

"It's not supposed to stay on long." Especially since Jack would undo the bows on the side with his teeth.

Amanda held up what was supposed to pass for a bra, which wasn't much more than two pasties and a bunch of satin ribbon that tied together between her breasts. "Another bow."

"He needs to unwrap his gift." David had worn a bow tie—and nothing else—when he'd been in their bed, and it still bugged Debra that she hadn't "unwrapped" him. He'd just been there, on her, when Jack had told her to close her eyes.

She hadn't complained, but the thought of tugging on that bow tie and watching it fall off of David... Symbolic but evocative. Heady. Sensual.

She wanted to give that to Jack.

"I'm not so sure the girls are going to stay in this thing, Deb." Amanda held it up to those breasts which had been the fantasy of more than a few guys in college.

Jack wasn't a boob man, but he certainly wouldn't complain when he had them mashed up against his face. They were beautiful breasts; Debra had seen them enough to know. Had felt them that night at the frat party. And while that had been hot, she didn't bat for that team.

Though if she did, Amanda would be the one to get her to sign on.

And Amanda didn't play for that side either, drunken frat party night notwithstanding. Still, Debra felt the need to clarify the scenario. "Remember, this is about him. I'm not so into the idea of you and I doing anything."

"What if he wants us to?" Amanda said it so nonchalantly, running another French fry over her lips.

Wait... *what*? "You... you don't mean..."

Amanda popped the fry in and sat back, brushing her hands. "I'm not suggesting we go down on each other, no. But what if Jack wants to see us do some stuff? Kissing, fondling... How are you going to respond to that?"

Debra couldn't answer. The thought of touching Amanda again...

She *liked* that idea.

"Come on, Deb. It's not like we haven't done it before. You can't tell me it hasn't crossed your mind that that might become an issue. I mean, you're giving the guy the ultimate male fantasy. Two women on him. Men like a little chick-on-chick action. You can't tell me Jack the Stud is any different."

"Well, no... I just... I hadn't thought about that." It was enough to get over the mental hurdle of bringing someone else—another woman— into their bed at all that'd been her focus. Plus Jack *knew* she didn't swing that way.

*Yeah, but he'd known you'd never had a threesome before and he'd brought David home to initiate you. Who's to say he's not going to want you to try something new with Amanda?*

"Well, you better start thinking about it." Amanda pointed a fry at her. "For what it's worth, I'm into it. Like we did that night in college. I'm not into carpet munching, though. Not my thing. But I could finger fuck you if he pushes the issue. Or, better yet, if you've got some toys, I could use those. We could do each other that way."

Toys would work. She and Jack had a drawer-full. Well, of *their* toys. She'd never bought any to share.

One more stop on her way home. One more gift for Jack.

And for her. She'd be lying if she said the idea didn't turn her on; Jack watching Amanda get her off with a vibrator, some fondling, a few kisses.

She looked at Amanda's mouth. Amanda had been one hell of a kisser.

"You're right. I hadn't thought about it, but, sure, toys will work. I'll have to get some for, uh, you, though."

"Good. I didn't bring mine with me. Last time I did, I got stopped by TSA at the airport. I swear, I think they have some sort of signal that when the guy watching the scan of the conveyor belt finds toys, he lets the others know. They'd just *had to* go through my luggage, and of course, I'd brought the Monster Man dildo. Biggest thing on the market. In both senses of the word. Works well and gets the job done in half the time it takes other brands."

Deb smiled. She didn't need a Monster Man; she had the real one. Jack was perfectly endowed to be the model for the thing.

"So what time do you want me?"

*Now...*

Debra shook her head. Who was this gift for anyway?

"We'll be back from services around four, so say... five? We always have surf and turf delivered on the twenty-fourth. Saves us from having to cook and clean up, and the chef at Mon Martre is amazing. The food will melt in your mouth."

"Mmm, hot sweet butter. We should save some of that and slather it all over your husband. Can you imagine what it'll do to him to have the two of us licking it off?"

Yes, Debra could. As the gush of juices between her legs illustrated.

"So is there anything off limits? Things you don't want me to do to him? We ought to discuss it now because in the heat of the moment, the issue could get cloudy."

"You've done this before, haven't you?" Debra didn't know why she hadn't considered that. Why she'd thought this would be as new to Amanda as it was to her; Amanda had always been the more daring, the more adventurous one. Debra remembered the ménage she'd walked in on in their dorm room. Two guys doing to Amanda what Jack and David had done to her.

It'd been the beginning of the fantasy.

"I don't want you to kiss him on the lips." That would be the one thing she couldn't watch. Couldn't let happen. Like Julia Roberts' character said in *Pretty Woman*, kissing was personal. The rest of it was just body parts, but lips colliding... that was personal. This had to stay *im*personal. As impersonal as it could get, yet still have some depth to it. It's why she'd asked Amanda. Jack had asked David because he could trust him and knew David would make it good for her without making it complicated. Ditto for Amanda.

"Fair enough. Anything else?"

"No. As long as you're comfortable with it, I'm comfortable with it. I mean, we've already set the ground rules for anything we'll do to each other, so I think we're good to go."

"Interesting choice of words, Deb."

"Huh?"

Amanda ran a hand down her body. Quickly, but she'd done enough to peak her nipples through her shirt, and her hand was resting in her lap. Debra couldn't see beneath the table from this angle, but she wouldn't be surprised to see Amanda's hand cupping her sex.

"I'm good to go right now. The thought of wrapping my mouth around your husband's cock... I've heard rumors that he's hung like a horse. Are they true?'

Oh yeah it was true. Debra smiled. "You'll have to wait and see."

"Damn, woman, you're *teasing* me with your husband? You sure things are okay between the two of you?"

It was a valid question; some people used this sort of thing to rekindle their marriage. She and Jack needed no rekindling. That flame was hotter than molten lava.

"I wouldn't be doing this unless everything was wonderful between us. It's just a special present for him."

"And for you."

"Well, yes, of course. A happy, turned-on, getting-off Jack makes me happy."

"And gets you off as well."

Debra shrugged. "What can I say? This is a win-win for all of us."

## Chapter 4

"Did you have a good time with Amanda?" Jack carried the stack of gifts Debra had bought into the house. Good thing she'd paid for gift wrapping; Monster Man was right on top of the pile. If Jack only knew...

She couldn't wait until he did.

"Of course. You know how much I enjoy being with her." And how much *he* was going to enjoy *being* with her. "How about David? Were things... weird?"

Jack set the stack down on the dining room table then unzipped his hoodie, his typical weekend attire, a big change from his weekday suits. "Weird? No. Definitely not weird. More along the lines of something we had to avoid talking about because both of us got so turned on we could've fucked the restaurant table, and the maitre d' probably wouldn't appreciate that."

"Turned on, huh?" She flung a sexy glance over her shoulder as she kicked off her shoes. She'd been turned on since he'd woken her that morning, and it was time for her sodden panties to come off.

Hopefully she wouldn't have to put on another pair to replace them. She wanted *Jack* to replace them—preferably with his lips and his tongue because she loved when he ate her out.

"Turned on like you wouldn't believe, Deb." His eyes darkened the way they always did when he wanted her.

"So show me." She headed back toward their bedroom.

Jack didn't let her get that far.

He tossed his jacket onto a chair, then grabbed her around the waist and scooped her up in his big, strong arms.

"Jack! What are you doing?"

He grinned that sexy sideways grin that was guaranteed to make her wet.

Yep, those panties were definitely coming off.

"Ah, Deb, don't tell me you've forgotten that night in Aspen?"

She shivered at *that* memory. The hot tub and snow and naked skin.

Champagne and strawberries. It'd been a feast for the senses.

"But it's still light out. The neighbors could see us." Their hot tub was built into the floor of the huge, second-floor wraparound deck between their bedroom and the living room. They'd landscaped it for summer months, but in the winter, anyone with a telescope could see through the bare branches.

"If someone wants to watch us that badly, I say, let them. You know what that idea does to me."

Yes, she did. Jack had always gotten off on the thrill as much as the physical contact. Well, *prior* to her he had, he claimed. Ever *since* her, *her* physical contact had been more than enough thrill for him. Still, adding thrills was fun.

"Do you think anyone *will* watch?" Their deck overlooked the canyon, but so did other houses, many of them on the curving canyon rim. Someone would have to be awfully dedicated to get out their telescope and scan the decks, but Deb was sure they weren't the only couple to enjoy making love *al fresco*.

"We can pretend they are, if you want. Will that make it hotter for you?"

"You're more than hot enough for me. I was just thinking about you."

He kissed her then, long, drawn out, and passionate. A completely different kiss from an I-want-to-get-in-your-pants kiss. Oh, he'd given her plenty of those and she was on board with them because there were times when she *did* just want to get into his pants. But in the end, it was all about the love they had for each other.

Like this kiss. He caressed her lips, tasted them, his tongue stroking hers, rubbing it. He wanted to soothe her, make her feel wanted. Loved. And she did. Jack was so good at loving her. He'd made her a better lover for him.

She wanted to tell him what she had planned, give him the sense of anticipation she was feeling for Amanda's arrival. Then again, she didn't want to tell him because she wanted it to be a surprise. A gift he couldn't refuse. Didn't *want* to refuse. He hadn't given *her* much choice—not that she'd needed it because when David had touched her, she'd been so into the moment that the only way she could've stopped would've been if Jack had asked her to.

"I love you," he said, nuzzling her temple. "The day you came into my life was the best day ever."

She'd often said the same thing. "I love you, too."

She tugged his head to hers, claiming his lips, wanting to show him by her kiss everything she was feeling for him. She always wanted to show him, but kissing wasn't enough sometimes. Sometimes even making love wasn't enough. There were times when she wanted to crawl inside his skin, inside his heart, and stay there always, cocooned in his love and the warmth of his embrace. She needed Jack like she needed air to breathe. He was her everything.

"Make love to me."

"Oh, babe, I intend to."

He nudged open the sliding door in the living room—yes, he'd been planning this. That door was usually locked.

The cold air hit her toes and Debra shivered.

Jack pulled her tighter against him, his t-shirt doing nothing to shield her from the definition of his amazing chest and abs. "I'll get you warm again."

"You'll get me hot, you mean."

That crooked grin was back. "Yeah, that, too."

Six steps later, he was beside the bubbling hot tub.

"You turned it on."

He arched an eyebrow, another sexy look designed by the gods to turn her to mush. "Seemed only fair since I was."

"Ha ha." She tugged on the hair that was brushing his collar. He needed to get it cut. Oh, not that she thought so. She loved running her fingers through his thick hair that started to curl when it got this long, but his firm's partners weren't so sensually driven. Jack's office fit the uptight- -lawyerly stereotype to a T. She couldn't complain, though, because Jack looked scrumptious all done up in his lawyer suits. He looked even better out of them, and she so enjoyed going from one extreme to the other.

If the people in his office only knew how extreme Jack could get.

He set her down on the lip of the tub, holding her against him so she had to balance on her tip toes. She wrapped her arms around his neck, loving that he was eight inches taller than her.

There was a lot to be said for eight inches.

"God, you feel so good against me." He ran his hands down her back to cup her butt.

"You got that right, mister. I could stay right here forever."

"I've got a better place for you to be." He lifted her and set her feet down on the seat in the tub. Hot water frothed around her legs.

"My clothes—"

"I'll buy you new ones. I want to see you wet." He kicked off his shoes and stepped in beside her, plastering his jeans to that fine set of abs.

"I'm already wet, Jack, and it has nothing to do with this hot tub."

He growled when he stepped down with her to the bottom of the tub. "Come here, you." He sat down and pulled her onto his lap, sealing his mouth to hers, his tongue thrusting inside in a move so blatantly erotic she had to clamp her thighs together to relieve the ache.

Then he slid his hand under her skirt and between her thighs and the ache ratcheted up.

"Open for me, baby," he muttered against her lips.

She was a slave to her passion. And Jack's. She opened wide and sighed when his fingers slid beneath her panties, unerringly finding her clit as Jack always did. The man had talented fingers.

"God, sweetheart, you're creaming for me already."

She nodded, unable to say a word. He'd found that perfect spot that made her legs quiver and she had to focus so she wouldn't come right then. Jack was the only guy who'd ever been able to render her speechless.

"Like that, do you?" He nipped her nose.

She bit her lip and nodded. She could only nod.

"What about this?"

He replaced his finger with his thumb, the pressure harder, a bit more surface area, and he ran his fingers along her slit. "Want me to finger fuck you?"

She nodded again. Really, that's all she was capable of.

He nipped her bottom lip. "Hang on tight, babe."

And that was all she could do, too, because Jack's touch threatened to shatter her into a million pieces and she needed his arms around her to keep her whole. She needed *Jack* to keep her whole.

Her knees fell back after he removed her panties, then he slid first one then a second finger into her passage. She needed him to fill her physically like he did emotionally. Her skirt slid up her legs and she could open herself more, rolling back on his thighs so her pussy was right there where he could see her. He liked to watch her come. Loved to watch her contract around him.

"Aw, Deb, you're so freaking sexy." He worked his fingers faster. "I'm going to fuck you so hard after you come. I'm going to ram my dick inside this tight little pussy and wring every drop of cream out of you."

Her folds swelled, engorged with arousal, and her head fell back, the bubbles frothing along her neck.

"That's it, babe. Let yourself get lost in the sensations."

She *was* lost. And floating, both metaphorically and physically. Jack's thumb covered her clit, the calloused pad so erotic against her sensitive flesh as the water rocked her.

## A Very Naughty Xmas

She pulled her knees back farther, her stomach hollowing out with the utter sensation of what he was doing to her, and the bubbles flowed in over her belly, sloshing up to her breasts, plastering her shirt against them, her nipples peaking at first the warmth of the water then the cold air as the water receded. It was as if David were here with them again playing so expertly with her breasts like he'd done that last time.

Oh, God, David... Amanda...

Deb's juices flowed out of her, coating Jack's fingers, making his entry so much smoother.

She didn't want smooth. She wanted her pussy worked, to be taken so that she knew she'd been taken. Jack could pound her to perfection, his pelvis thrusting against her, hitting her G-spot every single time—

Like his finger was now doing.

Oh, God, it was starting. Coiling in the back of her uterus, swirling outward, her breath catching as the pressure and the intensity increased, and she groaned.

"That's it, Deb, go with it. Come all over my hand. Let me feel you grab me and hold on."

She did. Oh, God, did she. His words and the sight of him inside her were just so erotic... Deb floated there, spread wide open, knowing he was looking at her, knowing he was enjoying it, and that one spot that he touched...

The sensation built, expanded, rolled back in on itself and grew some more, and Deb had to close her eyes as color exploded behind her eyelids and her blood roared through her veins, her heart pounding as Jack worked his fingers faster... harder... his thumb never letting up its relentless stroking, taking her right up to that precipice. She couldn't breathe, couldn't think, couldn't do anything but ride the wave he created.

And then it crashed over her, a tumbling spiral of heat and wetness, like the water around her, carrying her off to where nothing existed but Jack's hand and his cock pressed against her ass.

Oh, she hadn't realized—

She pulsed around him, clenching his fingers, her butt pressing down onto his cock, and she felt him swell. Felt Jack stroke himself against her cheeks. He wanted in there and she was so going to let him.

Another orgasm crashed over her at that thought. Debra moaned through it, panting, going with the flow of his fingers inside her until the shudders finally receded.

"You, my darling sexy incredible wife, are magnificent."

He leaned down to kiss her, withdrawing his fingers ever so slowly, then gliding them up over the landing strip she'd had a heart shaved into just for him, tickling her belly and dabbling with her belly button, her stomach always so sensitive after orgasm. As he well knew.

She threaded her fingers through his hair and tugged his head back after just a mere brush of his lips—couldn't give him everything he wanted when he wanted it. Where was the fun in that? "Get your clothes off, Jack. I want to touch you."

She didn't even mind that he dunked her when he stood up because he ripped his t-shirt right down the middle.

She loved when he did that. It's why she'd gotten him a dozen for Christmas.

His jeans were a little tougher to get off. She *had* to help him.

Really. She did.

And if her fingers just so happened to brush his treasure trail, well, the jeans *were* on him tightly. *Plastered* to him.

Honest.

Kneeling on the hot tub seat, she worked her hands inside his jeans, running her palms along his obliques. She loved those incredibly cut lines that ran in a diagonal down his stomach.

"You going to take the pants off or just keep rubbing me, babe?" He smiled his lopsided smile.

She rubbed one more time then worked his jeans down until they got hung up on the curve of his ass.

Jack had a great ass.

"Deb. Honey. You're killing me.:"

"Relax, Jack. You worked your magic on me. Let me work mine on you."

"Oh lord, I've created a monster."

She smacked his ass when she pulled the jeans down over it.

"Do that again, sweetheart."

She licked her lips. "Liked it, huh?"

"So much, babe."

She tugged the front of his jeans down until his cock sprang free. Oh, yes, he'd *definitely* liked what she'd done to him.

She cupped his sac. Squeezed just a bit. "You like this, too?"

His eyes closed as he inhaled and when he opened them again, they were that chocolate brown color that turned her insides to mush. "Tease."

"Yup." She squeezed again. "And you love it."

He reached down, pulled her hand from his balls and wrapped it around his shaft, stroking himself with her hand. "Yeah, I do. Now how much longer are you going to make me wait?"

She slid her other hand over the curve of his ass to between his cheeks, then probed his tight flesh. "As long as it takes, Jack."

He turned sideways, offering her easier access, still stroking himself with her hand. "It won't take long, babe."

"That's what I'm afraid of." She took her hand away. "Did you bring any toys out here?"

"What do you think?"

"I think you're always prepared, Jack. You should have been an eagle scout."

"Too busy scouting other things."

Women. Jack had been a player back in the day. Women flocked to him. Still did, but the difference now was that he never looked twice. Ever.

That was going to make her gift even that much hotter.

She looked around. Ah, there. The picnic basket. He always packed such... *tasteful* things in that picnic basket.

Never letting go of his cock, she opened the basket with her free hand. Scarves, plugs, a couple of dildos—including the double penetration one. Hmm, they hadn't used that in a while.

Maybe she should have bought one of those for her and Amanda.

Her pussy swelled once more. She was going to have to do *some*thing with Amanda just to satisfy her own curiosity, for Pete's sake.

And for Jack's.

She rooted around. "Look what I found." She held up the silicone cock ring, the only one that expanded enough to not do serious damage when Jack got fully hard. As he was doing right now in her hand. "Want this?"

His breath was shaky. She loved when it got shaky.

"Whatever you want to do to me, babe."

She rubbed the smooth toy over the head of his dick. "It's more what I want *you* to do to *me*, Jackie boy."

He always smiled when she called him that. She was the only person who *could* call him that and make him smile. Anyone else, he growled.

Though... he was doing that now, too, but for a totally different reason.

"What *do* you want me to do to you?"

She answered with a smile while she slipped the ring over the rim of his dick. Sometimes they could work this around his balls, but he was too aroused for that now. No matter; this way worked just as well for him and allowed his satiny sac to flap against her ass.

She reached back inside the basket.

There was the lube.

Jack's eyes widened when she took it out. "Oh baby."

She released her hold on him. She worked the lube between her palms, warming it. Then she slathered it over his cock.

Jack's head fell back on a long, harsh groan, his cock jerking and thickening before her eyes. That ring was doing its job. So his dick could do its.

"You want to fuck me, Jack?"

He shuddered and some pre-cum dripped from his slit. "I can't wait, babe."

"Then watch me."

She waited until he opened his eyes and looked at her. Then she made a big production of getting to her feet and turning slowly, her ass now level with his face.

Then she wiggled slowly, enticingly, out of her skirt.

"You have the best ass, honey." He reached for it, but she swatted him away.

"Not yet, big guy." And she meant that in *every* sense of the term.

She ran her hands over her cheeks, cupping them, the lube slick upon her skin.

And then she ran her fingers up her cleft.

"Deb…"

She fingered herself, bending over just enough to let him see her do it.

The next thing she knew, his tongue was where her finger had just been.

Good thing he'd packed the flavored lube.

Her sex swelled and she pushed back against him, the stubble on his chin so erotic against her sensitive flesh as she rubbed herself with it.

Jack tongued her ass, his hands gripping her thighs so tightly she'd probably have bruises, but she didn't care. She needed him to hold her tightly. To work that talented tongue inside her and prep her for his big, throbbing cock.

She bent over farther and reached between her legs to find him.

Jack growled against her ass.

"I want this in me, Jack. I want you to fuck me in the ass and rub my clit while you do it."

He dragged her to her knees, bent her forward over the edge of the tub, and worked the head of his dick into her.

"More, Jack. I can take more." She was breathing through this tight possession.

"Not yet, babe. I'm too big. You have to get used to me. I keep telling you that."

And she kept telling him she could take more. She'd started with small plugs last year this time, prepping herself to take him. Jack had always wanted to do her anally, but she'd been uncomfortable. But then she'd seen him use a plug on himself in the shower when he hadn't realized she was home and it'd started her thinking. Wondering.

So she'd started. Then, on her birthday, she'd finally been ready to try it.

They'd worked on it ever since. And while she could take his full length, he never wanted to hurt her by taking her too roughly. He always eased himself inside of her.

So she'd moved on from a plug to dildos. Had even used the double one on herself on one of the few occasions he'd been gone on business.

Now she could take a lot more of Jack a lot faster and a lot harder than before.

She *wanted* to take him fast. And hard. And long. Over and over again.

She leaned back into him.

"Christ, Deb. I can't stop—"

She pushed back even more, seating him to the hilt.

The feeling was intense, so intense it bypassed *pain* as it shot through her, filing every part of her, and went all the way to *amazing*.

She panted as her body adjusted to his complete possession, her muscles adjusting to the breadth of him.

"Are you okay, sweetheart? I told you we shouldn't—"

"Move, Jack."

"Huh?" He pulled out a little. "Yeah. Sure. Okay. We don't have to do this—"

She reached back and clawed at his sides, dragging him back toward her. "Don't *leave*. *Move*. Shove yourself back into me. *Move, Jack, dammit*."

The steam from the hot tub rose in front of her; that had to be why everything was hazy. Or maybe it was a cloud of lust as she waited for—needed—him to fill her again.

He obliged.

"Yes, that's it." She pushed back against him. He felt so good.

Jack withdrew. But only slightly.

Then he pushed back into her.

"That's it, Jack. Take me hard. Rough. You know I like it that way."

"Jesus, Deb. In your pussy, yeah, but this is so much tighter."

"Then you should enjoy it more."

His answer was a couple of quick thrusts. Then he buried himself to the hilt, his sac tight against her pussy. "I don't think it's possible to enjoy this anymore than I already am."

"Sure it is."

She reached for one of his hands on her hips and dragged it around to her poor, aching, lonely, unattended clit. "Rub me, Jack."

He was only too happy to oblige.

Jack had played the drums in a college band for good reason; the man had rhythm, and he put all his years of practice to good use.

He took her ass, quickly, with short fast strokes, not the long hard thrusts she wanted, but this and the clit stimulation were working well for her. The tension built, the pleasure threatening to take her away before she could wrap her brain around what was happening.

And then Jack snaked a hand up her shirt and shoved her bra up over her breasts, pinning them in place, her nipples rubbing against the wet fabric so erotically.

And then against Jake's palm.

"You have the best tits, Deb." He tweaked her nipple as he thrust inside her.

Jack was so very good at multitasking.

Her head fell forward as she braced herself against the edge of the tub, pushing back against hin, tilting her pelvis just enough to get the full contact of his fingers on her clit.

"I want a dildo in me, Jack. I need to be filled more."

His cock jerked at that suggestion. Dear God, the man was so well equipped for a woman's pleasure. And he was hers. All hers.

"Hand me one, then. I picked all your favorites."

Debra dragged the basket over. She didn't care which one it was; she just wanted her pussy filled.

He'd packed the waterproof ones. Such a smart guy, her Jack. Especially since he'd picked her absolute favorite—the one with the butterfly wings and clit stimulator.

"This one." She held it up.

"But I want to be the one playing with your clit."

It was amazing, really, what Jack's words could do to her. She'd never been into dirty talk before Jack, but now... She'd been missing out all those years.

"You can. You and this." She spread her legs a little wider to take the bulbous head of vibrator inside her.

"That's it, babe. Open wider. Clamp down on my dick."

Of course she did. The suggestion alone was making her do so.

The pleasure was making her stay there.

"Now do it, Deb. Shove that thing inside you."

## A Very Naughty Xmas

Jack's voice was strained and she looked in the sliding glass door beside her to see his reflection, the straining muscles in his neck, the rigidity to his shoulders that said he was trying to hold back his own orgasm. Jack was always so thoughtful.

She slid the vibe in.

"Ah, yes, that's it. I can feel it filling you against my dick."

He'd always liked this one. The extra big head stimulated his big head when he was inside her at the same time.

She rubbed the toy in and out.

Jack sucked in a harsh ragged breath behind her and his fingers tightened on her hip.

She did it again.

Jack's cock jerked and he thrust against her like a piston, half a dozen or so short strong bursts that would have knocked her off her feet if he weren't holding her so tightly.

"Get it all the way in, babe, and turn it on. It's not going to take me long."

Jack lied. The man was a master of control. It took him as long as he wanted it to take.

And oh, did he take.

He pressed the butterfly against her clit, holding it there with one finger while he angled his hand to feel the toy as it slipped inside her. Jack had such long, talented fingers.

"Un. Fucking. Believable." He panted with each thrust he made, repeating it over and over like a litany as his thrusts sped up, his grunts a sign that he was losing his sought-after control. Debra loved when she got him to that point because *he* was no longer in control; *she* was.

She clenched her ass around him and fucked herself faster with the toy.

"Deb." He ran his left hand from her hip down to her inner thigh and pulled her back against him even harder. "I..." He thrust again. "Can't." And another. Double time this time. "Hold." His finger slipped in beside the vibe. "On."

She pushed the ON button.

"Fuck!" Jack got off like a shot at the first vibration.

She'd known he would. Had wanted him to.

He pounded her ass now, no finesse—which made it all the better. Control was highly overrated unless he was losing it.

Then it was everything.

Debra shoved herself back against him, bracing herself against the tub, and she fucked herself faster with the vibe, loved that the rotating the head kept Jack from knowing where it'd rub him next when he thrust back inside her.

Control.

*She* had it now.

Jack jerked and thrust into her, his hips gyrating as she fucked herself. God, getting off in both holes had to be one of *the* best pleasures in the world.

The only thing better was to have two men get her off.

That sent her over the edge. The image of David in her ass while she'd been on top of Jack, taking him in her pussy...

Color once more exploded behind her eyelids and she had to clench the vibrator with her pussy so she could catch her weight with both hands

Jack quickly grabbed it and fucked her with it himself, filling her from both ends at the same time.

It was too much. She couldn't take the intensity, and her knees threatened to buckle.

"Ride the wave, sweetheart. You can do it."

Jack kept thrusting.

No, she couldn't do it. Her arms, her strength, was giving out. And she dropped her elbows.

Oh, God the change in the angle...

It was just what she needed. Her orgasm ripped through her with an intensity that rivaled the hot tub's jets, exploding from where Jack and the vibrator worked her and raging through every cell she had.

She didn't know how long they stayed like that once she'd finished. Not that she had, really. Tiny spasms still rippled through her as Jack held her hips and the vibrator *and* himself rigid inside her.

"How are you still hard?" she had to ask.

"The ring, your ass, and you, Deb. A powerful combination." He ran his left hand up her thigh then down her spine, ending at where he joined her body before sliding out.

She moaned out her protest. "Don't leave me, Jack."

"Never." He removed the toy and gathered her in his arms, then twisted them around, so that he was sitting on the tub with her on his lap.

And he kissed her. A full, tongue-filled, melt-her-heart sort of kiss. "I love you, Debra."

She cupped his cheek and she looked deeply into his eyes. She could see forever in their depths. "I love you, too, Jack."

He nipped her nose. "You know, any holiday—any *day*—is special with you in it, sweetheart, but this year, I have a feeling it's going to be the best Christmas ever."

If he only knew how right he was.

They stayed there for a while. Jack had indeed bought strawberries and champagne. Only one glass for her; the hot tub circulated the alcohol through her system too quickly and she didn't want to get drunk and confess her plans.

He had pulled her onto the reclining chair on the inside of the tub so they could see out through the deck railing to the canyon. It was a horseshoe-shaped canyon, designed by Nature just for the effect of being able to watch the winter solstice moon hang in the very center as it cast its light on the rim. It would've been perfect if there was a full moon, but she had perfection wrapping his arms around her, and a person could only take so much perfection.

"You know, I've always loved the story of The Gift of the Magi." They were discussing Christmas traditions and favorite memories. She and Jack were always talking, and she always learned something new about him. Like this, for instance.

"I would've pegged you for *A Christmas Story* sort of guy."

"Well, duh. I mean, who doesn't love that leg lamp?" Jack resettled her on his lap and crossed his arms over her breasts. "But for the pure spirit of the season, nothing beats two people giving each other the ultimate gift."

She nodded, biting her lip against the smile that wanted to come out because Jack would see her reflection in the sliding glass door beside them. "What do you want for Christmas, Jack?"

He tightened his hold on her. "You're asking me now? I thought you were out shopping today for the perfect gift for me?"

She'd found it. "I know, but is there something special you want? Maybe I didn't come up with it."

Again, his arms tightened, but this time, he pressed his palm against her heart. "Sweetheart, I already have everything I could possibly want right here in my arms. What more could a guy want?"

She was going to show him...

## Chapter 5

She replayed Jack's conversation the next day as she got ready to go to his office party. Yes, their life was pretty perfect. Was she taking an unnecessary chance bringing Amanda into the mix?

She hadn't thought about that. What if Jack *wasn't* interested in having two women do him at once? What if the threesome was a memory of those old party days that he'd said he was more than ready to put behind him once he'd found her because he was well and truly satisfied with just her?

But then she remembered David. Jack had enjoyed them all being together. He'd even had lunch with David, so there were obviously no hard feelings.

Nah, Jack would like having Amanda join them.

*One more day.*

"You look stunning." Jack came up behind her and stared at her in the mirror. He always liked her in red, and the high-necked, sleeveless sheath hugged her body in all the places he liked to touch.

"You do, too." Jack in a suit was gorgeous. In a tux? Devastating.

And he was hers.

He kissed the curve of her neck. "You're looking a little bare right there. Don't you have a necklace or something you can wear?"

Since when had he ever commented on her jewelry choices? She'd never been big into jewelry; what pieces she now owned were because of him. But the diamonds would be too much for the dress's neckline and any of the bigger pieces would look clunky on a sleeveless sheath that'd been designed with simple elegance in mind.

"I have my grandmother's locket if you think I should wear something."

He growled in her ear. "You know me; I prefer you not wearing *any*thing. Jewelry or clothing-wise."

She tapped him on the top of that glorious head of hair. "We have to go to this party. It's for *your* office. Don't get me all distracted with your sex talk."

"Is it working?" He waggled his eyebrows as he stood up and looked at her in the mirror.

She twisted out of his embrace. This Christmas party was one they could *not* miss; it was important to his career. And she really didn't want to have to re-do her hair and makeup.

And anyhow, Jack was going to have so much sex tomorrow, they'd be able to take a hiatus from each other.

Right. Like *that* would happen. That was the thing about her relationship with Jack. No matter how much they were together—in bed or out of it—she wanted more.

"Come on, Jack. We don't want to be late."

He arched his eyebrow. "Uh, yeah, I do. And have a very good reason to do so." Her gaze shot to his groin. Yup, he wanted her. She giggled; she'd never get over the chemistry between them.

He glanced down. "You know, if I were insecure, that laugh would have shriveled me up."

"And we both know that will never happen, so keep Mr. Happy inside your boxers and let's get going. I don't want you to have to do any explaining to the partners."

"The partners wouldn't be surprised. You're a knockout, and I'm the luckiest SOB on the face of the earth to have gotten you. Oh, and there *are* no boxers."

Those words kept Debra flying high all night. Whenever she was in the hotel ballroom, she felt Jack's eyes on her, heated with desire. He could look at her from across the room and it was as if no one else existed but them. She knew other people felt it. It made some uncomfortable; others, jealous. Some were amused, but those were usually the older women who were probably remembering what it'd been like for them in their early days of marriage.

"How do you handle him, Debra?" Cleo Jamison, one of the partners' wives, asked her. "If I had a man looking at me like that, I'd never leave the house."

Debra smiled and blushed. It was one thing to be so uninhibited with Jack in the privacy of their home, but quite another for other people to see what was between them.

"Good lord, Cleo, why don't you embarrass the girl?" Margot Prescott took a glass of champagne off the waiter's tray and handed it to her. "Here, Debra. You look like you could use this."

Debra took a sip to be polite. The last thing she needed was alcohol. As the day had gone on, she'd been fidgeting, trying *not* to tell Jack what she had planned. She didn't need any reason to loosen her tongue.

"Embarrassed? The woman ought to be grinning from ear to ear. I sure as hell would be if I had *that* in the bedroom." Cleo glanced over at her husband at the bar. Approaching sixty with a waistline of the same milestone. "Russell certainly isn't lighting my sheets on fire."

"Try satin ones." Debra couldn't believe she'd said that. One sip of champagne and already her tongue was wagging?

And wouldn't *Jack* enjoy a good tongue-wagging...

She drank half her glass.

"Satin? Really? I thought those were just for porn films." Margot took another sip of her champagne as nonchalantly as if they were discussing a charity luncheon. "Though we did have them on our honeymoon, come to think of it. Tom had enjoyed himself quite a bit with those." Margot smiled and looked at her husband next to Russell. "And I do mean enjoyed *himself*."

Debra wanted to *fan* herself. Instead, she finished her drink.

"Well, if you two are saying satin sheets are a good idea, I'll have to get some. Won't Russell be surprised when he opens them Christmas morning?" Cleo giggled and twenty years disappeared from her face. Good sex could definitely keep you young; apparently even the thought of it worked wonders, too.

"Maybe some toys, too. What do you girls think? Too much?" Cleo looked at them.

"Oh, please, Cleo, do you think *he*—" Margot nodded toward Jack—"needs any help in that area? From the look on Debra's face, I'd say not."

Debra grabbed another glass from a passing waiter. In for a penny—or satin sheets—in for a pound. "Oh, I don't know about that. Toys can always make a good time even better."

Apparently this was the Christmas season where she was a veritable font of great gift ideas, and she hoped the partners appreciated the ones they were going to get.

Heck, they ought to make Jack a partner in gratitude.

Maybe if she told the women of the *special* gift she had planned...

She sipped the champagne this time. No. She wouldn't tell them. For all that she liked the idea of sharing the idea, it was too personal. Too intimate. Which was why only someone as intimate a friend as Amanda—or David—could join them.

"Oh, and speak of the devil, look who's heading this way." Margot nudged Debra with her elbow. Jack had just finished shaking hands with Russell and was walking toward her, all his natural athletic, hip-rolling grace in a tux turning heads from every woman in the place. "From the

## A Very Naughty Xmas

looks of him, I'd say this is where we wish you a good night and a Merry Christmas."

Cleo sighed. "I could only *wish* to have a night as good as the one you'll obviously have."

Debra took another sip of her champagne to keep from grinning. Jack had lasted longer at the party this year than he had in the past. Usually they were out of there by ten, and naked in each other's arms by ten-thirty. He was a half hour late.

"Hey, sweetheart." Jack sidled up next to her and planted a kiss on her temple. "We ought to get going; we have a big day tomorrow." He looked at the partners' wives. "Ladies. Have a merry Christmas."

"We will now, thanks to your wife." Cleo's grin was every bit as wolfish as the one Jack had given her earlier.

Lord, Debra had created a monster. She tried not to laugh.

"You want to tell me what she meant by that?" Jack asked as he helped her into her coat.

"Not really."

"Deb…"

She rolled her eyes. "Okay. I might have mentioned the merits of satin sheets."

"You didn't."

Needing some fortification for this conversation, she picked up her champagne glass. "Okay, I didn't."

"Did you?"

"Do you want the truth or not?"

"Deb, they're my bosses' wives."

"But they're women, too, Jack, and well, you came up in conversation and—"

"Hang on. *I* came up in conversation? And you go right to satin sheets? Just what were you saying about me?"

"*I* wasn't saying anything. *They* were. The looks you were giving me weren't exactly subtle, you know. They saw and they commented and, well, one thing led to another and—"

"And you went to satin sheets."

"And toys."

"Toys?" He groaned and pinched the bridge of his nose. "Are you kidding me?"

She drank some more champagne then raised an eyebrow at him. "I never kid about toys, Jack."

"Just how much of that stuff did you have, sweetheart?" He looked at her glass.

So did she. "Not much." *Yet…*

"So you tell all our sex secrets while sober? Remind me never to let you drink in public."

"I didn't think you'd mind. After all, weren't you the one into open-air daylight-sex yesterday?"

"That's different. I don't have to work with those people."

"Just live next door to them."

"The Bechtels are away, and the Friers spent yesterday with their daughter's family. I checked."

"So you weren't *really* into the exhibitionism; you just wanted me to think so."

"It's not that. I was trying to protect our privacy."

So did that mean he'd be squigged out about Amanda? It was one thing for him to spring David on her, but how would he react to her doing the same thing?

She finished her champagne. "This is a new side to you, Jack. I wouldn't have thought it would concern you."

"It doesn't, but I hadn't ever thought about anyone in my job thinking about my sex life. I don't want the partners looking at me any differently when their wives tell them where the idea came from."

"But aren't you going to look at them differently knowing that they're getting satin sheets for Christmas?"

Jack dropped his hand and his eyes almost popped out of his head. "Oh God. That is an image I didn't need."

"And the image of you on satin sheets may just be the one their wives *do* need to make their night all it should be for both of them."

"That doesn't bother you? Other women fantasizing about me?"

She set the glass down then tugged on his tie. "Hey, they can fantasize all they want. You're going home with me. And you want me, not them."

He wrapped his arms around her. "You got that right, babe." He planted a big, smacking, sucking kiss on her neck. "And I can't wait to get you home."

The sad part was, the champagne kicked in about three quarters of the way home and by the time Jack helped her in the door, Debra was in no shape to make all of his fantasies come true.

"You're bugging out on me, aren't you?" He unzipped her gown when she swayed on her feet.

"I'm exhausted, Jack. Can I take a rain check?"

"Always, babe. You know that." He skimmed the dress down her body, his hands doing all sorts of delicious things to her nerves. "I gotta say, though, it's going to be a long night."

She was about to say something about him being long, but the bed beckoned. She'd been running on all cylinders this holiday season—business was piling up—and those two glasses had lulled her to sleep.

She climbed between the sheets—the satin ones—and spooned into him when he crawled in beside her. "I'll make it up to you tomorrow, Jack. I promise."

"I'll hold you to that."

She had no problem with that—Jack was going to get more than he bargained for.

## Chapter 6

Jack wanted her to fulfill that promise first thing the next morning and didn't give her the chance to say no.

Oh, he didn't tie her up with the scarves again; he didn't have to. His mouth on her clit was more than enough to tie her up with. Debra woke to the utterly delicious sensation of him tonguing her. Feather strokes, just enough to wake her nerves up slowly, with her consciousness following along like an eager little puppy.

Make that, eager little *pussy*.

The coiled sensation was unraveling in her belly when she was finally conscious enough to realize what was going on, and then—*wham*!—full-on desire took hold, swelling her folds, creaming her passage, and Debra was moaning and writhing against his mouth.

"Hold still, Deb," he said releasing her aching clit from the suction he'd put on it. "I've got a surprise for you."

"This wasn't it?"

He grinned that sideways smile she adored. "This was just the start. Now hold still or I'll have to tie you up again."

"Promise?"

He dropped his forehead to her mound and exhaled. His hot breath stirred her already sensitive flesh. "God, woman, you're going to kill me."

"What a way to go, Jack. What a way to go."

He looked up at her again with that smile. "You've got that right, babe. Now lay back and let me love you."

She couldn't argue with those words.

But then he got off the bed.

"You're leaving me?" She propped herself up on her elbows.

Jack leaned down and planted a hot, sexy, take-me-I'm-yours kiss on her mouth and ran his palm over her breast, squeezing just enough to ramp up her desire. "I'll never leave you, Deb. I'm just going to grab your surprise. Now lie back down and finger yourself for me, why don't you?"

His eyes shimmered with desire for her. No, he wasn't going anywhere.

She plopped back down on the bed to wait.

"Uh, Deb?" He swirled her nipple with his palm and Debra closed her eyes at the sheer pleasure he was giving her. But when he tweaked it, she had to open her eyes.

"I thought I asked you to finger yourself?"

"Huh?" It took a second for the words to sink in. "Oh, right. Okay."

She slid her right hand to her clit and spread her legs. Wide. There was only one reason for her to have to do this to herself when Jack was so much better at it: so he could watch. Jack liked to watch.

"That's better." He skimmed his hand down her belly and pressed her fingers against that aching part of her. "Get yourself off for me."

She pulled her knees up, changing the tilt of her pelvis so that her engorged lips and clit were right there for his viewing pleasure.

"Jesus, sweetheart." He dropped to his knees beside the bed, his gaze trained on her pussy. "I'm trying to walk across the room."

"I'm not stopping you."

"No?" He ran his palm over the curve of her ass and his fingers slid into her slick folds.

"I thought you were getting me a surprise?" She rubbed her clit and moaned at how good it felt.

"*This* is a surprise," Jack muttered, working a finger inside her.

"Jack." She flicked his hand away. "You owe me a surprise. I'm not going to keep doing this unless you give it to me."

He looked at her, frustration stamped across his face. "I'll give it to you, all right." Then he sighed—exaggeratedly—and climbed back to his feet. "Jesus, woman, you drive a hard bargain."

"And you just drive hard. Now go get me my surprise so you *can* drive that thick, luscious cock inside me."

That thick, luscious cock sprang to life with mouth-watering quickness. She loved making love to Jack.

"Close your eyes," he said with a brush of his hand over her pussy when he came back to the bed, something curled in his fist. "Please."

The word was soft, just a touch agonized, and Debra was powerless to resist Jack's pleading.

*Liked* his pleading actually.

She rubbed her clit again, feeling it become engorged, feeling the pulsing of her blood flowing into her pussy, preparing her for Jack's invasion.

She made long strokes, then short ones, fluttering her clit with her fingernail and pulling her knees back wider, exposing her as he liked.

"That's it, Deb, show me." Jack climbed back on the bed where he'd have the perfect view.

And then he licked her.

Oh, God, the sensation of her hand on herself and Jack's tongue lapping at her juices was enough to take her over the edge. Her legs shuddered and her pussy clenched with the oncoming orgasm.

"Hey, not so fast." Jack stilled her hand, pressing it against her clit. "Let's take this slow, sweetheart."

She didn't want slow; she wanted hard and fast. A decent pounding in the morning to get her up and ready to face the day.

Jack moved her hand and nuzzled her mound. "Let me, okay?"

She'd let him do anything he wanted.

Debra opened her eyes to see him looking up at her, the heart shape in her landing strip right under his nose. She loved seeing him between her legs. Loved watching him eat her out. Jack was so very talented that way.

"Eat me, Jack."

He smiled then, the sexy soft smile that was just for her. Mostly at moments like this, but every so often, he'd look at her somewhere—at a restaurant, at a barbecue, at an office holiday party—and she'd know exactly what he was thinking. Exactly what he wanted to do to her.

He did it then. He licked her, a long stroked right up her center, culminating with the most amazing tongue action on her clit right where it was guaranteed to drive her the most wild.

This morning was no different.

He flicked and he licked, he fluttered, and he pressed. Then he rubbed and sucked and got his fingers in on the action, and all of a sudden, Debra couldn't look. She couldn't keep her eyes on him or their room or anywhere else because the feelings were rising in her like a tidal wave and she had to close her eyes as she fell under its spell.

"Pull your legs back for me, babe," he muttered between the incredible sensations he was wringing from her pussy.

She hooked her arms beneath her knees. He liked having her so open, so exposed. It allowed him free access and, with her arms in place like this, the only movement she could make was to arch into his mouth.

It worked for both of them.

Jack's tongue was everywhere. Not just at her clit, he licked her pussy lips, lapping the juices that were flowing from her as if a dam had burst.

It felt like it was going to. He was increasing her excitement, driving her insane with the need to come against his mouth, but he always pulled back at just the moment she'd go soaring over the edge if he'd let her.

He would eventually, but half the fun was the journey there.

"You want me, don't you?" he whispered, his hot breath and early morning stubble raking over her swollen flesh. He knew it, too. Had done it on purpose. He always said that he loved to see her at his mercy, her lips pouting for him to touch them, her cream coating them.

"I do, Jack. Take me." She panted the plea, she couldn't help it. All that sex talk last night with the women, and then falling asleep before she and Jack could do something about it left a big aching need inside of her.

"I will, Deb. Trust me."

She did. She trusted him with everything she was had and wanted. Forever.

He slid a finger inside her pussy.

"Yes, Jack. More."

"I'll give you more."

And then she felt it. Jack's surprise.

He slipped a strand of tiny balls inside her, working them in one at a time.

"What are they?"

"Shhh." He kissed her clit. "Just feel."

She could do nothing *but* feel. Each one slipped inside her, filling her with the others. Knowing they'd eventually come out left Debra breathless with anticipation. Jack had put Ben Wa balls in her before, but only two at a time and those had been a lot bigger than these.

She liked Jack's surprises. And prayed he'd like hers.

*Amanda.*

Just the image of Jack doing this to Amanda sent shivers up her spine and she clenched her pussy around those tiny hard things.

"Like that, huh?" He slipped another one inside her.

Yes, she liked, but she like the idea of Amanda even more.

Tonight was the night.

Her pussy fluttered at the thought and Jack growled against her clit. "Not yet, Deb," he said between strokes.

He slipped more tiny balls inside her.

His finger followed and then, oh God, he swirled those balls around.

She couldn't tell how many there were, not that it mattered, but it was one continuous sensation of rolling pressure, touching every part of her and it was driving her insane.

"Jack—"

"Sssh, babe, just feel."

She did. She felt those balls, she felt his finger, she felt his tongue—and then the lack thereof when he knelt between her spread legs.

Her eyes flew open. "What are you—"

He ran his other hand up over her mound then along her tummy, up to her nipples—Jack's hand was large enough that he could spread it and reach both at the same time. It was a handy skill—and testament to the size of something else. That old wives' tale was true.

When her nipples were tight points stabbing this hand, making her ache with need, he abandoned them to the cool air to trace his finger up her breastbone, along the column of her throat, right along her jaw to her lips. She latched on and sucked it like she wanted to suck him.

"Ah, yeah, Deb, that's it. Take me in."

She sucked his finger to the back of her throat, wishing it was his cock. She loved getting Jack off with her mouth. Loved swallowing that thick, salty essence of him that stayed on her tongue the rest of the day, a constant reminder of what they'd done together. Of the pleasure they found in each other.

His dick prodded her passage.

Oh, God, those balls were in there…

The head slipped in and it was as if another realm of sensation had been revealed to her. He was so thick her body always had to make adjustments to take all of him in, but with the added things inside her… Good lord the sensation was indescribable.

"How's that?" he asked, circling his dick with his hand. "Feel good?"

"Amazing." She was able to find breath for one word. Just one.

Jack lid in a little more. "Yeah, it is."

And then he seated himself to the hilt and Debra practically screamed out his name as those balls went with his dick up inside her, dragging pleasure the entire way.

"Deb—"

"Move, Jack. Just please move. Fuck me."

He did. Oh did he.

He pistoned inside her, and those balls had to be doing something as erotic to him as they were to her for the speed with which he was moving.

Good. She shouldn't be the only one to enjoy this.

She spread her legs wider, wanting to take him deeper. Jack fell over her, bracing himself on the mattress by her head, his hips rocking into her with a jerking motion she'd never felt before.

"Oh. My. God." Each word was punctuated by his thrust. "This is amazing."

She raised her head and brushed a kiss on his nose, the only part of him she could reach. "*You're* amazing."

His gaze met hers then and she saw not only this incredible desire that was between them in his eyes, but the love. Jack loved her every bit as deeply as she loved him and it was all right there for her to see in his eyes.

Tears filled hers.

"Ah, sweetheart, don't cry." He kissed her and she clung to his lips with a shaky breath.

"I'm crying because this is so beautiful."

"Nothing is more beautiful than you are. Right this moment."

He kissed her again, slowing his thrusts—which only made them more pleasurable.

Those balls rolled up inside her, all over her, as if they were dozens of fingertips touching every nerve ending she had.

"I love you, Deb." Jack groaned as he slid his cock out until just the tip was still inside her.

"More, Jack. Faster. Harder."

He needed no extra encouragement. All of a sudden, Jack was moving in and out so fast, his hips jerking, his moans louder than hers, and Debra could feel it building. The tension coiled, her pussy swelled around him. Whatever these things were, they were going to use them every single time.

And then he rammed one right up against her womb with the very tip of his dick.

"Fuck, yeah," he growled, pounding that same spot with that same tiny ball as if it were caught in his slit.

And that image took her over the edge. Jack continued to pound into her, dragging those balls with him, each one causing its own ripple of desire, but it was that one hitting her G-spot that gave her the most intense orgasm she'd ever had.

"Jack!" she cried as her legs flared open, her knees locking and wave after wave of pure sensation rolled through her, making her throb, surge, clench around him.

"That's it, Deb. Take it. Ride it."

She grasped the sheets beside her hips and dug her nails in, holding on for dear life as her body spasmed around him, as it arched up into his thrusts, needing every stroke, every ounce of pleasure he could give her.

And when she thought she had it all, had come all she could, that there was nothing left, Jack surprised her even more when he came.

That tiny ball exploded against her passage like a pinball bouncing pleasure everywhere it hit as his cum shot into her, mingling with her own cream, giving Jack the most perfect wetness to fuck her with.

"God, Debra!" He pounded and pounded, his breath labored as if running a marathon, and he couldn't seem to stop fucking her.

That was okay, she'd take Jack for as long as she could get him.

Sweat dripped from his forehead, landing on her already sweat-slicked chest, the glide of his wetness along her nipples enhancing the sensation he was creating in her pussy.

"Grab my dick, babe," he said, still fucking her.

She clenched her inner muscles and smiled when he reared back onto his knees and grabbed her hips, now pounding her into him. The headboard banged against the outside wall every time he pulled her off him before impaling her once more, and Debra was glad the Bechtels were away. She didn't need the sly looks Rich Bechtel gave her on occasion after a particularly headboard-banging night.

"Yeah, babe, that's it, grab me some more."

Debra tried to match his rhythm, but he was too fast, so she let herself ride his tempo, clenching when she could and moaning because she had to.

And then Jack buried himself inside her and arched back, his fingers gripping her hips so tightly, and he poured himself into her on one long drawn out utterly primal groan.

"Jesus," he said at last.

"No, *Debra*." Her lips twitched when she said it. "Your wife, remember?"

Jack opened one eye and looked at her. His fingers tightened briefly on her hips. "As if I could forget."

He released his hold then, letting her body sink back onto the mattress and he slipped out of her just a little.

She clenched him again.

"Ah, Deb," he hissed. "You're going to kill me."

"Not for a very long time, I'm not." She wrapped her legs around him. "And certainly not before you do that to me again. That was amazing. What are those things you put in me?"

He wiggled his hips, getting her to unlock her ankles. "They're your surprise."

"They certain were."

"Oh, the surprise isn't over yet."

"Huh?"

Jack pulled out of her body—*that* was a surprise. Usually he didn't like to pull out until she asked him to.

He sat on the bed with her right leg on his shoulder, keeping her open for the finger he slid inside her.

He drew the beads out slowly. One by one.

And gave her another orgasm.

It was different, this one. Almost like a violinist drawing a bow over the strings of his instrument, Debra's body arched with the sensation of those balls slipping out and she didn't stop coming until the last one had been removed.

Her legs fell to the mattress then, her arms to her side, and it was an effort just to keep breathing, never mind opening her eyes when Jack drew those beads up along her pussy lips and over her mound. He coiled them on her stomach, swirling them slowly, her juices making them slick against her skin.

Then he drew them up to her breasts and circled her nipples, the smooth surface feeling incredible, then pooled them in the hollow of her throat before rubbing them against her lips.

"Suck them in, Deb," he whispered.

Debra took them in her mouth rolling them around her tongue. She could taste herself on them. And him. She could taste him.

Jack took the other end in his mouth and did the same thing, their lips meeting in an erotic kiss as they tongued the balls between them, swirling them around each other's mouths, tongues meeting, dancing, stroking each other.

Finally, Jack ended the kiss and pulled the balls from her mouth with his teeth.

They were pearls. A long strand of pink, shimmery pearls.

"Merry Christmas, sweetheart."

"Oh, Jack, they're beautiful."

"And come with one hell of a memory, eh? Whenever you wear them, I want you to remember today."

As if she'd ever forget today. "I love them. Thank you."

"And I love you. So we're even."

They'd never be even. Jack had given her so much she didn't think she'd ever be able to match it. But Jack felt that way, too. They'd talked about it, and had finally realized that they couldn't match each other because they both had different wants and needs, but in the end, they fulfilled them for each other and life was so utterly perfect it'd be foolish to question why.

Was it going to be foolish to bring Amanda into their bed?

## Chapter 7

Jack ruined her surprise.

After showering the heady scent of their lovemaking off this morning—no need to make other people jealous—they'd finished up some last-minute shopping, gone to church, and had returned home in time for the delivery of the meal they always ordered out on Christmas Eve.

She'd spent the entire day trying not to fidget out of her skin with anticipation of Amanda's visit.

Especially when the doorbell rang.

Trying to keep her composure, Debra refrained from running to the door to let her friend in.

Only... it wasn't Amanda.

"Oh. Um, hi, David." This was the first time she'd seen him since he'd been in bed with them and if that weren't already awkward enough, now she had to figure out how to either get him to leave or call off Amanda.

"Hey, Dave." Jack walked up behind her. "I hope you don't mind, Debra, but I invited him for dinner. "

"Uh, no. Of course not. Why would I mind?"

Because David's arrival screwed up her whole plan for Jack's gift? Amanda had to go to her sister's tomorrow and out of town after that; this was the only chance for this to happen.

"Come on in, Dave." Jack opened the door wider. "Drinks are on the bar."

Debra wanted a good stiff one.

Her gaze flew to Jack's cock. It was good and stiff, too.

She blushed then. David's arrival came with some pretty thrilling memories.

"You okay with him being here?" Jack whispered as they headed in after David. "You look, I don't know, a little odd."

"Odd? No, just surprised. You didn't tell me."

"That's because I wanted it to be a surprise."

His last surprise had had her coming six ways to Sunday. Unless he was planning a repeat of her birthday, she didn't think this surprise could compete—

Wait. *Was* he planning a repeat?

Debra's knees threatened to collapse at that thought. *Ohmygod...* Was Jack thinking of a repeat?

Wasn't *she*?

Well, yeah, but that's because she knew what was going to happen tonight as soon as Amanda arrived. Well, not *as* soon as. Debra would like to think she had some semblance of control. She could wait until after dinner before introducing the subject.

But what did she do now that David as here?

She should cancel Amanda. Just end it now.

Except Amanda showed up at the front door then.

"Hey, Deb, you ready?"

Amanda looked ready. She wore a figure-hugging, red velvet cocktail dress with fuck-me pumps that laced with red ribbons up her calves. The perfect Christmas present to unwrap.

Deb kissed her on the cheek—would she be kissing her elsewhere soon?

The thought sent a shiver through her.

"Hey, there's, um, been a slight change in plans."

"Oh?" Amanda arched an eyebrow. "You chickening out?"

"No, it's just that Jack invited his friend David over for dinner."

"*The* David? The one he brought in to fuck you?" That bra Debra had bought her to wear wasn't doing anything to shield the fact that Amanda's nipples were suddenly peaked beneath it.

Debra felt her own nipples tighten. "Yes, that David."

"Are you sure he's just here for dinner? Maybe he's dessert."

"But you're here. He can't be dessert."

Amanda patted her cheek. "Deb, Deb, Deb. Don't you know that you can have more than one dessert? This kind isn't fattening." She walked past her and dropped her coat onto the chair in the foyer, then headed into Debra's living room. "Hey, boys."

Debra drew in a big breath. *Two* desserts? Was Amanda suggesting...?

Yes. She was.

The night had just gotten better.

"You didn't tell me you'd invited Amanda," Jack whispered when they met at the bar to pour drinks for everyone.

"You didn't tell me you invited David."

"I wanted him to be a surprise."

Oh he definitely was. "And I wanted Amanda to be a surprise."

The look he gave her said Amanda was definitely that.

But did he understand *why* she'd asked Amanda?

He tossed back the two fingers of Jack he'd poured himself then poured another two.

Um, yeah. He might have an inkling why Amanda was here. Question was, how did he feel about it?

The fact that he'd need to fortify himself with alcohol didn't bode well.

But then, she could use a drink too, and it wasn't as if that'd put her off the idea. If anything, the alcohol lessened her inhibitions and would make tonight go a lot smoother.

And harder. And rougher.

Oh, God, she creamed her thong. She'd been hoping to make it to at least dessert before that happened.

There were two hot desserts waiting at her dinner table.

"Here you go." Jack placed David's and Amanda's drinks in front of them, then wheeled the delivery cart over. "We're so glad you could join us tonight for dinner."

He lifted the lid off the art. Four meals.

She glanced at him. They'd both added to their order.

"We should eat before this gets cold."

It would be the only thing that was. Debra was getting hot, and Jack looked a little uncomfortable—in a completely good way.

How about David and Amanda, though? Had they figured it out? And how would they feel about going from a threesome to a foursome?

The steak and lobster were delicious, but Debra barely registered that fact. She ought to be paying attention, ought to be enjoying the meal, but all she could see, feel, hear, think about was the two people at her dining table who were about to join she and Jack—if they wanted to—and what they'd all do to each other.

It would be good. Of that, she was certain. She already knew it would be good for her with David, and had to believe that all the moaning she'd heard from Amanda's boyfriends during the time they'd roomed together meant that Amanda could give Jack that same pleasure.

Talk centered around David's travels. He'd been in Asia since they'd last seen him, traveling into a few areas American citizens weren't supposed to go. But that's how David got the big news stories and how he was making a name for himself.

"Wow, that is so cool," said Amanda. "I bet you've had so many different experiences."

"Yeah, I have. My life is just one big new experience from the minute I get off the plane in whatever country I'm in."

"So you like trying new things?" Amanda cocked her head to the side in a pose Debra knew all too well. It was *dessert* time and David didn't have a prayer of resisting her. Few men ever could.

"Sure. I don't want to leave this world regretting not having done something."

"I like that train of thought. Kind of how I live my life."

Not Debra. She was more than happy with the status quo—she and Jack had a nice status quo—but tonight was all about giving Jack the same kind of love and trust and pleasure he'd so thoughtfully given her.

They finished dinner, the talk still a little stilted, with Amanda leaning heavily on innuendo, when it came time for their actual dessert, *crème brûlée*.

What do they do now? Should Jack and Amanda go off into one room and she and David into another?

No. Part of bringing Amanda here was so that Debra could watch Jack have his pleasure. So that she could be a part of it with Amanda.

Amanda finally stood up. "Well, folks, I thank you for dinner, and I really appreciate you inviting me, but this is getting awkward."

The three of them looked at her and Debra wasn't sure what her friend was doing. Amanda had always been a little outrageous, but this...

"Amanda, maybe we—"

Amanda shook her head and held up a hand. "Deb, you're new to this. The guys, I don't think, are. And me? This is old hat but it's about time someone took charge."

Amanda reached behind her back and Debra heard the hiss of a zipper.

The guys were staring at her.

Debra couldn't blame them. Those double-Ds were a sight to behold.

Amanda drew her dress down and pulled her arms out of the sleeves.

"Holy fuck." David took the words out of Debra's mouth.

"Yes, Dave, that's what I want from you." Amanda cupped her breasts in that sexy scrap of lace that was held together with one tiny bow-shaped ribbon at the center, her thumbs playing with her nipples. "While Jack over there sucks on these." She looked at Debra. "Okay with you, Deb?"

Debra looked at Jack. His eyes had fire in them.

"Deb?" he asked.

Debra swallowed then licked her lips. "Merry Christmas, Jack."

## Christmas is Coming, by Raven Morris

He dragged her to him. Put a hand behind her neck and practically dragged her across the table, planting such an erotic kiss on her she could have come just from that.

But she didn't. She was going to need all her strength to get through this night.

"I'm guessing that's a *yes* for everyone." Amanda's laughter broke through the haze of sensuality and got him to stop.

But he didn't move away.

"You're sure, sweetheart?"

Debra nodded. "As sure as I was when you brought David here before."

"I brought him back because you said you wanted to unwrap your gift. He's wearing a bow, you know."

Debra glanced over. David had opened the top two buttons of his shirt. "I don't see one."

"That's because it's not around my neck." David unbuttoned another button and stood.

Jack chuckled when Debra's gaze flew to David's crotch.

David was just as aroused as he'd been last time and if she remembered correctly, quite well endowed. Not quite like Jack—but then, no one was like Jack—but enough that he'd given her pleasure.

"Great. We're all in agreement." Amanda stepped away from the table and dropped the dress into a puddle on the floor.

That tiny little thong with its side bows just begged for attention. As did the long line of red satin ribbons that wound up Amanda's legs, with the pumps that would make an exotic dancer weep with envy.

Debra was already weeping...

Even more so when David dropped to his knees in front of Amanda, grabbed her hips, undid the bows, and shoved his face between her thighs.

"Oh, yeah, Dave, lick me."

"No. Wait." Debra surprised all of them by standing up. David pulled his face out of Amanda's muff to look at her. "Sorry you two, but tonight is all about Jack's Christmas gift. And you, Amanda, are that gift. If anyone's going to be eating you out, it's my husband."

The words sounded surreal coming from her lips, but the image... that was pure fantasy. She wanted to see Jack eating Amanda's pussy. Licking her clit until Amanda lost that cool, hardened façade and turned into a writhing, feeling being, pulsing against her husband's face, coming against his mouth.

"Then let's get to it because I'm dripping with need." Amanda tapped David on the head. "I believe you're here for her." She winked at

Debra while she walked over to Jack and ran a hand over his shoulder and down his chest, rubbing her tits against his back. "So, big guy, how's this going to work? You want us all in one room or just you and me on our own?"

Jack looked at Debra. "Deb?"

"Tonight is your gift, sweetheart. However you want it."

Jack surged to his feet, grabbed Debra around the waist and hauled her up against him, plastering another tongue-filled, knee-shaking kiss to her lips. "Dave and Amanda are our gifts to each other. We're going to unwrap them together."

He picked her up, strapped her legs around his waist, and strode with her to the bedroom. "Come on, you two. Time to get this party started."

And oh what a party it was.

## Chapter 8

Amanda kept her shoes on, David was naked by the time he entered the bedroom except for the cock ring—red with a bow on top—wrapped around his dick, and Jack was peeling off Debra's dress one inch at a time. With his teeth.

And then David joined in. Amanda watched, fondling her tits with one hand and stroking her pussy with the other as she propped one foot on the edge of the bed so Debra could see everything between her legs.

"Jack's going to enjoy eating you." Debra couldn't pull her gaze off Amanda's pussy. She'd never watched another woman get off before, hadn't thought she'd find it arousing... Oh how wrong she'd been.

"You like that, don't you, Deb." Jack's worked her thong off her butt.

"I can smell how much she likes it." David ran his hands up her legs beneath her skirt, taking the thong from Jack and slipping it down her legs.

Jack shoved her skirt down, then parted her folds. "Lick her, Dave."

Debra thought she'd pass out from sheer sensuality as she looked down to see Jack's fingers holding her open and David's tongue licking her.

Her stomach hollowed at the image and it was only Jack's hand there, wrapped around her, that kept her upright.

"How's that, Deb? Feel good?"

She mewled some sort of response because she couldn't talk.

"Suck her, Dave," Jack ordered, the hand on her belly sliding up to cup her breast. He pinched her nipple and Debra felt her clit respond.

David sucked it into his mouth.

Oh God. Stars and lights and colors and fireworks and a zillion other things flashed behind her eyes at the sensation. David's tongue was different than Jack's, which only made this whole situation more erotic.

"Suck her tits, Jack," said Amanda.

Debra opened her eyes to see Amanda's palm circling on her own tits, her hips pushed forward, her hand working quickly between her pussy lips, the slick slosh of moisture an incredible turn-on.

Jack nudged Debra back over his arm, angling her breast just right for his mouth and tilting her hips just right for David's.

Oh, God, David sucked in more of her swollen flesh and ran his tongue alongside it. Heat spiraled out from that spot just as Jack pulled her nipple into his mouth, and then it was almost a tug of war between two pulse points as lust surged between them, and if it weren't for the two men holding her so tightly, she would have melted into a puddle of molten hormones.

"Bring her over to the bed, guys, so I can get in on the action."

Debra's pussy throbbed at Amanda's words. *Get in on the action*? She'd never had a woman go down on her.

Would Amanda be the first?

The satin sheets were cool against Debra's back for all of about twenty seconds before three more bodies joined her, heating the sheets up pretty damn fast.

David rolled her hips to the side so he could lie between them and eat her out her, while Amanda tongued her ass. Oh, God, *Amanda tongued her ass.*

Debra's hole clenched against the sweet invasion and her body shook with the erotic need that surged through her—especially when Jack then knelt over her to suck her breasts, his hand playing with the one that wasn't in his mouth, keeping every part of her stirring with need.

And oh, did she need. She reached between his legs and felt the hard rod she knew so well. "My mouth, Jack. I want you in my mouth."

He drew off his belt while she undid his fly and then—-thank you, God—he was there, hard and smooth with enough pre-cum coating his head to make her yearn for more, and she took him in deep.

"God, yes, Deb. Suck me." Jack muttered it against the breast he then nipped with his teeth.

She loved when he used his teeth. He loved when she did, too, so she scored his dick gently and was rewarded with a long hiss that had him tensing above her.

She ran her fingers between his legs, cupped his balls, then worked a finger into his ass.

He jerked in her mouth and Debra smiled. She could get him off so quickly—

But then David shoved two of his fingers into her pussy and Debra almost came herself. The sensation of him filling her while he ate her, of Amanda kneading her ass cheeks as she tongued her, rimming her, puffing against that so-sensitive area... All of a sudden, Debra couldn't focus. Didn't know who was where or what was what, all she could do was become this feeling, needing machine, taking the dick in her mouth down her throat as far as it could go, working her throat muscles so she wouldn't gag, spreading her legs to give the two people between them the most access as she pulsed against their tongues—oh, God, their tongues—and bore down into the tight, heady sensation of a coiling orgasm.

Then Jack sat back at her head, taking his mouth from her breasts, and she cried out around his cock.

"Shh, sweetheart." His palms circled her nipples fast, almost painfully, the peaks so hard and aching. "I want to watch them work you."

The words made her stomach flutter. Jack liked to watch. Porn, the neighbors, her, himself... Jack was all visual and what a sight he must be seeing.

She wanted to watch, too. Damn, it, they needed to have those windows mirrored before her next birthday so she could see everything that was happening on this bed.

But then Jack reached for something on the bedside and all of a sudden there was a whirring noise.

Debra looked over. Mirrors were sliding down from the ceiling in front of the windows.

"Merry Christmas, Deb."

Holy hell. There they *were*. All four of them. *Four*. Jack on his knees by her head, his body looking as if it'd been sculpted from a block of marble, Amanda's perfect heart-shaped ass with the red fuck-me pumps curled under it as her bright red nails cupped Debra's cheeks and her long brown hair fell onto the bed in a steady rhythm as she slicked her tongue in and out of Debra's ass, and David... Debra could just see the rise and fall of David's head as he ate her.

Jack cupped her chin. "You like?"

She nodded at him, knowing he'd like the sensation, but, really, they needed to discuss his penchant for wanting her to talk when she was blowing him.

"I think you'll like this, too." He tapped Amanda on the head and that sweet stroking stopped.

Debra wasn't sure she liked *that*...

"Come here, Amanda. I want to suck your tits."

Okay, that Debra liked.

She liked it even more when Amanda straddled her face, fingers still working her pussy, and bowed back enough for Jack to suck one of

## A Very Naughty Xmas

those huge tits into his mouth.

Debra didn't know where to look first. She had Jack's cock in her mouth and Amanda's pussy right above her, those red fingernails disappearing into her passage only to return coated in glistening cream and circling her engorged clit, or at the mirror where she could watch her husband enjoying another woman's breasts.

And then there was David. Sweet, sweet David whose tongue was just as talented as Jack's, working her aching, throbbing, pleading clit so expertly, stopping just before she came to tongue her passage and slide a finger inside both her holes.

So she watched all three, mentally thanking Jack for the mirrors.

Jack was moaning against Amanda's tits, and Amanda was making sloppy, stroking noises between her lips, and David was just groaning in pleasure as he ate her.

"Yeah, Jack, suck me. Bite me." Amanda's hand was circling wildly all over Jack's head—in time with the one circling wildly all over her clit. "Now the other. That's it, baby, take the other one. Pinch it. Oh, yeah, harder. Pull it."

Her head fell back, her long brown hair caressing Debra's stomach.

David reached up and tugged it.

Jack caught Amanda before she fell backwards, but the site of her friend arched back over her, her breasts pointing to the ceiling, Jack's mouth covering one, his hand in the small of her back just above her ass—an ass that was brushing against Debra's boobs, as Jack's cock surged with cum in her mouth…

Debra couldn't take it. It was too much. Too erotic. Pure fantasy, and she let the orgasm rip through her, pulsing down onto David's mouth, clenching his fingers inside her, sucking Jack until she heard him gasp and felt the cum surge from his sac.

"Fuck, Deb, I can't take it!" Jack wrenched himself off Amanda's tit and grabbed the base of his cock, squeezing and trying to pull out of her mouth, but Debra wasn't letting go. She wanted every last drop of him and Jack had a lot to give. He was so excited, so big, that she knew what this would be like for him. Occasionally she got him off like this in one explosive burst and he loved it. It wore him out, but he loved it and just because they had hours of pleasure to go didn't mean he wasn't going to get to enjoy this. Amanda would take care of him when he was too tired to move.

"Honey, please, I can't—"

Oh yes, he could. And she knew just how to make him.

She curled her finger in his ass, and stroked the gland, while she bared her teeth around his rim. He couldn't move for what her teeth would do, and he couldn't *not* move for what her finger was doing. Who needed scarves to tie their lover up? All she needed was her tongue.

And then Jack came in one long, explosive burst that locked him in place, his muscles rigid—all his muscles—and it pulsed out of him as she sucked.

And then Jack rammed his dick deep into her mouth, burying it in her throat as he fell forward, bracing himself on the mattress beside her head.

Then David pulled his fingers from her quaking passage and kissed her mound before moving around on the bed. He helped Amanda out of the contortion she was in until Debra lay there naked, aching, exposed, throbbing, with Jack's dick slipping from her lips with a soft *pop* as he fell to his side on the bed.

"My turn." David knelt on all fours above Debra. "You want to suck or fuck?"

She looked up at him, her mouth still filled with her husband's cum, and it was one of the most erotic decisions of her life. "Suck. I want to swallow you, too."

Beside her, Jack groaned. "I gotta see this."

"Then turn around, buddy, because I got a wad I need to blow and it's going right in your pretty little wife."

David plunged his dick into her mouth and Debra groaned when the gel-filled cock ring butted against her lips, that red bow tickling her nose. He was so different from her husband, but still so sexy. And he tasted amazing. Different, but amazing. She ran her tongue along his length as he pushed in and pulled out, tracing the vein as Jack liked her to do.

David apparently liked it, too. "God, yes, Deb. That's awesome."

It certainly was.

"Come here, Amanda." Jack turned on the bed until he was beside Debra. "Sit on my face."

Oh, no fair. Debra wanted to watch *that* and she couldn't with David's leg obstructing her view.

She cut the suction and released him.

"What—"

"Move around, David. Fuck my mouth from the side."

David repositioned himself and shoved his dick back into her mouth quicker than she would have thought humanly possible. But she wasn't about to complain because she could turn her head just enough to watch Amanda lower herself onto Jack's mouth.

Her gaze met Debra's. "He's good, Deb. Really good."

Debra nodded. She knew how good her husband was.

David hissed at the motion. "Jesus, that's amazing

The women smiled at each other then Amanda cupped her breasts, tossed her head back, and rode Jack's mouth.

And when David reached out to tweak Amanda' nipple, she rode that caress, too. "Oh, yeah, that's it, Dave. Touch me. Play with me."

David surged into Debra's mouth while he played with Amanda's breasts. And then he played with Debra's, flicking the pointed tips until they were so hard she couldn't take it.

And then he flicked some more.

Debra didn't know how it was possible, but she felt another orgasm coil inside her.

"Swallow, me, Debra. Take me to the hilt." David kept up the pace, matching it to the flex of Amanda's hips against Jack's mouth, his dick thickening inside the constraint of the ring circling his base.

Debra's hand crept down to her own pussy. She ached. She needed. She wanted.

Amanda reached over and replaced Debra's fingers with hers. "Hold yourself open, Deb. Let me get you off."

Jack arched his hips, moving himself and Amanda closer and suddenly Jack's hand was beneath her ass, squeezing, his fingers finding her cleft. Dear God, she was going to explode.

Amanda rocked with the pleasure Jack was giving her, soft moans giving rise to longer ones as the tempo increased, and she worked Debra's clit accordingly.

David swelled in her mouth and she tasted the first drop of pre-cum when he leaned over to suck Amanda's nipple into his mouth.

"Oh man, yes, Dave. That's it. Suck me." Amanda worked Debra's clit faster, the pressure harder. "Eat me, Jack," she cried as the tempo picked up and Debra could hear the slapping of Jack's balls against his thighs. Amanda's left hand had disappeared behind her; she was probably jerking him off.

Oh, God, that image. Debra loved watching Jack get himself off, the head of his dick so dark it was almost purple before he'd finally let himself go. The surge of liquid that coated his hand and his shaft that tasted so good in her mouth—

David's orgasm started. She could feel his balls tighten against her head, taste the saltiness that came before. Feel the tightness of his breath and the flick of his rod as the cum surged through him, that red bow tickling her chin and bottom lip now.

"Suck harder!" Amanda's fingers were going crazy and Debra had to open her legs. Had to spread herself wide and if she could just get a dick inside her, she'd be happy.

"Ah, yes, that's it, that's it." Amanda rode Jack's face, her hips jerking in a rhythm Debra could relate to.

She sucked David harder, wanting to get him off so she could watch Jack with Amanda. Wanting to sit up and maybe even help out—rubbing Amanda's clit while Jack tongue-fucked her.

She relaxed her throat muscles and let David slip as far down as the cock ring would allow him to go.

"Son of a—!"

He came then, jerking, throbbing, pouring himself into her mouth. She swallowed him, taking every ounce he wanted to give, running her tongue along the vein, milking it, and he groaned his approval. She approved, too. He tasted good.

But he wasn't Jack.

No one was Jack.

Amanda moaned as she jerked up and down on Jack's tongue and Debra knew *exactly* what that felt like. If it were anyone other than her dearest friend, she'd be jealous.

David slipped out of her mouth, his cock still erect in that ring, leaving a trail of salty wetness across her lips as he leaned down to kiss her, his tongue sweeping some of his cum into his mouth.

"That tastes good," he muttered against her lips.

She nodded. "It does. Thank you."

One more sloppy, cum-filled kiss. "No, thank *you*, Debra. It's truly been a gift. Both times."

"You're not leaving?" She grabbed his arm. He'd left too early last time.

"No. After all, you still have to unwrap me."

She looked at the ring still on his cock and smiled at the bow.

She did so love unwrapping presents.

"Yes, that's it, Jack! Harder. Harder!" Amanda was bobbing on Jack, her tits bouncing, her hair falling over her face, yet still she didn't stop rubbing Debra's clit.

Debra removed her hand. "Finish, Amanda. Enjoy what Jack can do to a woman."

It was what Amanda needed. She braced her hands on the bed behind her, arched herself into Jack's mouth, and came with a long, low groan that Debra felt in her pussy.

"Holy fuck!" Amanda's body was flush with her orgasm, the straps of her shoes straining against her tightened thighs, the spiked heels practically digging into Jack's legs as she rode it out.

And then David was there. His cock, still so fucking rigid from that ring, poised to take Amanda if she moved forward just a bit...

She did and David impaled her. In her ass.

Amanda braced her hands on the headboard as David's thrusts tore her from Jack's mouth. But Jack was right there, running his hands over her breasts, moving to suck them while David thrust up into her.

"That's it, Amanda," David grunted. "Take me. You want it. You're so fucking tight."

"Yes. Yes. Yes." Her words were barely coherent, punctuated by moans and gasps, each one getting an answering jerk of Jack's cock.

Jack's cock... It was right there, hard and long and so close to David's ass that Debra was turned on in a way she'd never been.

Would Jack and David...?

She didn't wait to find out, though. So far she'd had two men in her mouth and a woman on her clit, but she hadn't had anyone inside her pussy and Jack's cock was calling to her.

She rolled over, straddled him and sank down on him.

David looked back over his shoulder. "Best holiday party ever."

She laughed and slicked her hand down his back.

And fingered him.

His eyes rolled back and he turned back around, his thrusts harder, quicker, into Amanda.

Debra worked a finger into his ass.

David exploded again.

Amanda was practically shrieking and Jack was groaning and circling his hips and Debra was riding him, still fingering David, until suddenly, like a well-rehearsed orchestra, they all came. Jerks, groans, and a whole lot of thrusting took over until Debra wasn't sure what was her own orgasm and what was others' rippling through her.

Not that it mattered. She and Jack had just given each other the best gift.

## Chapter 9

They needed a bigger bed.

It was the first thought Debra had when she could finally open her eyes the next morning.

Christmas morning. A day of good cheer, good friends, and gifts.

She had all of that with her in this bed. Jack was beside her, his deep, even breaths the most comforting sound in the world. Amanda was across the bottom of the bed, her back to her, the satin ribbons sagging around her knees from the workout they'd taken. Nothing could have stayed up during that group fuck.

Then she felt Jack's dick and had to take that statement back, smiling. Only Jack could go through two women with another guy in the room and still have some *oomph* left in him.

Her *oomph* had left hours ago. She could barely move an eyelid, forget about any other body part.

Jack, however, could. He slid a hand up her thigh.

Which proved her nerves were still working.

"Merry Christmas, sweetheart. You okay?" His breath was hot against her neck.

Ah, he'd moved closer. "I'm so okay that I think I might have died of pleasure." Oooh, and her voice still worked. That was something.

"Amanda?" Jack was always so considerate, making sure their guests had a good time.

"Mmmphh..."

Debra smiled. That was a good Amanda sound.

"Dave?"

"Yeah, I'm here. So I must not be dead."

Debra had enough strength in her hand to stretch it out across the bed toward him. She still hadn't unwrapped him and that red bow beckoned.

But then she stopped. Jack had brought him back to her because she *hadn't* unwrapped him. Maybe she *shouldn't*.

"You're not going to do it, are you?" Jack was resting his cheek against hers as he spooned her.

"No, I don't so."

His sigh was so big it was almost comical. Almost. Because she knew what he was going to say and it filled her with that feeling of being loved.

"I'm going to have to give him to you again, aren't I?"

"And again and again and again."

Jack kissed her then. A hot, wet, sloppy, I-want-to-fuck-you sort of kiss. "Then I guess you and I both know what you're getting for every holiday to come."

"Well, if the holidays get to come, you and I should, too."

Jack and Debra's Christmas—and all the ones that followed—were very merry, indeed.

The End

## About Raven Morris

Raven Morris loves celebrating birthdays. Has she ever received a present like this? Ah, that's for this fiction writer to know and you to wonder... But instead of wondering about her love life, set your imagination to work on your own. And if her books can help those fantasies along, well, there's always a reason to celebrate. You can put all her books on your wish list. Find them on her website: www.RavenMorris.wordpress.com

See her alter ego, Judi Fennell's romantic comedies at www.JudiFennell.com or www.facebook/JudiFennell

# Other Books by Raven Morris

Want to see what all the excitement was about for Debra's birthday and Jack's gift? Check out more stories in the **Tied with a Bow** series:

# Light Me Up

### CHERRIE LYNN

# 1

Candace Andrews was sweating, and it had nothing to do with being wrapped shoulder-to-floor in some green monstrosity her mother had requested she wear to the Andrews' annual Christmas party. It had nothing to do with the champagne clutched in her trembling hand, either, as she feigned an attitude of polite attentiveness in the face of her uncle's blathering.

Well, okay, those things weren't helping the situation. At all. She reached up to touch the bead of sweat at her hairline before it could threaten her foundation, smiling as she pretended only to make sure every hair was in place. Surely someone in the small cluster of people she stood among would soon notice she was flushed bright red beneath her makeup. She'd caught a glimpse of herself a few moments ago in the gigantic mirror hanging in her parents' grand entryway, so she knew.

All Brian Ross's fault, and he wasn't even near her. He stood halfway across the enormous living room, trapped with her dad and some of his business associates. Looking absolutely devastatingly gorgeous in all black...no suit for him, no matter how formal the occasion, but it didn't matter because no one got past that face or those intense blue eyes anyway. She could just see his profile over her aunt's shoulder—she never let him get too far out of sight at one of these things. He hated them, and so did she, so she constantly watched him for the subtle head-tilt toward the door that indicated he was ready to get the hell out. So far, he hadn't given it.

Brian was her...well, she didn't know what label to put on him. "Boyfriend" seemed way too casual. "Fiancé," too premature, as indicated by the longing look she cast toward the bare ring finger on her left hand. "Soulmate"? Too cliché.

He was her world, and that's all that mattered.

His hand drifted into the pocket of his slacks again, and every muscle in her body went on alert. It was another motion she'd constantly been on the lookout for tonight.

*Oh, no, don't. No more. Don't...*

Inside the lacy scrap of a thong she wore, a vibration came to silent life directly on her clit.

Expecting it didn't squelch her reaction. She nearly jumped three feet off the floor, and in her heels, that would be quite the feat.

"Are you all right, hon?" Her aunt Deb, who stood directly across from her, looked at her with concern. It was hard to believe she and Candace's mother Sylvia shared parents. If Sylvia had been standing nearby, she would've given Candace what Brian called her ocular lashing.

Candace mustered what she hoped was a blithe smile as sensation ricocheted through her lower belly and dangerously tightened all her muscles. From wherever she'd dredged up that smile, she found her voice. "I'm fine. Will you excuse me?"

Without waiting for an answer, she broke away from the group, almost collapsing in relief when Brian had mercy on her and the vibration stopped. When had she ever thought this would be a good idea? Well, she hadn't, actually. He had. He got his kicks out of flustering her in front of her insanely conservative family. As if her being with him in the first place wasn't enough to almost give them all a coronary. And God help her, she couldn't say no to him. Didn't want to.

It seemed she loved this as much as he did. But if he was insisting on driving her to orgasm at the celebrated Andrews Christmas party, she had to get out of range before he succeeded—

Like right now. The damn thing buzzed to life again as she cut a path through the guests. Any more and she was going to plunge her hand under her dress and rip it out in front of everyone. Frantically, she looked over at Brian to give him a finger-slash-across-the-throat gesture, but he only smirked at her. No quarter. *Oh shit. Oh God, no, he isn't...*

Her knees weakened as it went on and she grasped an accent table for support, upsetting one of her mother's prized crystal vases and making a grab for it before it could topple over and crash onto the floor. Brian took his finger off the button almost too late for her to recover. She fought the pleasure radiating from her desperately clenching muscles before it could consume her like an inferno.

Candace didn't know whether to kill him because he'd spared her or kill him because he'd stopped.

Who knew how long the reprieve would last, though? She drew a labored breath, looking up...right into the alarmed eyes of Jennifer Rodgers. Her best friend Macy's mother.

"Are you all right?"

"Sure," Candace said brightly, casting a glance around. No one else had seemed to notice her nearly collapse in racking waves of ecstasy.

"Just...stumbled a bit, there. Oh, I *love* your dress."

Distraction. That was the way to go. Not that Mrs. Rodgers's ivory gown wasn't lovely; she'd always had impeccable taste.

"Thank you, but are you sure you're okay? You look really flushed."

"Do I? I think it's...a hot flash or something." She flapped her hand at her own face.

The other woman laughed as she turned to go. "Oh, honey, you're way too young for those."

*Not when Brian Ross is standing across the room remote controlling my orgasm.*

She made for the stairs before he could fire the thing up again.

"Candy!" The voice she heard in her nightmares cut through her distress, and she cringed. Sylvia was summoning, and God help anyone who didn't come running.

Breathing deeply in the hopes of calming her agitated heart rate, she spotted her mother at her station near the fifteen-foot red-and-gold Christmas tree. Only Sylvia Andrews sparkled brighter than that eyesore, dripping with diamonds and gold, her lithe figure shown to its fullest advantage in sleek red satin.

Candace glanced back over her shoulder at Brian, who was watching her now. She could only hope he read the meaning as she narrowed her eyes at him: *Don't you fucking dare.*

The way the corner of his mouth kicked up didn't bode well.

Sylvia broke away from her guests and tilted her head toward the towering doors of the study. Candace obediently headed in that direction, gritting her teeth, marveling at how fast the prospect of dealing with her mother killed any below-waist sensation. Now she'd sweat for an entirely different reason.

The dark paneling of her dad's study was a welcome change from the glitz and glamour outside, and as her mother closed the doors behind them, the light piano rendition of "I'll Be Home for Christmas" faded to a familiar but still awkward silence.

Candace bit her tongue on asking, "*What have I done now?*" She'd worn the dress. Her tattoos were hidden. She'd even colored her hair back to its natural blond—the pink streaks had nearly driven her mother insane. But when Sylvia turned toward her with a smile instead of her usual critical eye, she was taken aback.

"How are things, Candace?"

Candace? Instead of Candy? Instant alert. This must be serious. "Fine."

Her mother strode to the side bar and poured herself a drink;

Candace still white-knuckled her flute of champagne. Sylvia didn't like to drink alcohol in public for some reason. At least not at parties she was hosting. "We haven't really talked for some time, have we?"

*There's a reason for that.* "No, we haven't."

Sylvia turned toward her, now reinforced with a glass of scotch. Her gaze drifted down to Candace's champagne, and for a second she wondered if her mom was about to impose a similar restriction on her. To which she would tell her to bite it. Candace occasionally made goodhearted efforts to make Sylvia happy—hence the dress and the hair—but try as Sylvia might, she didn't rule her daughter with the iron fist that she used to.

Candace took her preemptive battle stance, lifting her chin and softly clearing her throat, preparing for the worst.

"Things are all right with Brian?"

Wow, she'd actually said his name. "Yes, they're great."

"How long have you been together now?"

"A year and a half."

"I have to admit I didn't think you'd make it two months."

"I figured as much. I mean, there had to be some reason you finally gave in and—well, *accepted* him is too strong a word, isn't it? Tolerated, maybe. You didn't think he'd be around for long."

"We welcomed him into our home, and believe me, that's far more than mere toleration."

The woman might have a point there, at least where this family was concerned. "Okay, Mother. I can't figure out what you're getting at, so why don't you just come out with it?"

Sylvia sighed and took a drink. "You always think I have some ulterior motive."

"Don't you?"

"You're my daughter. I'm still interested in your life. And…you do seem to love him very much."

Love him? The very thought of him could make her eyes sting. "I do."

Sylvia straightened her back, inhaling as if trying to give strength to her next words. "I was just wondering when we can start thinking about planning a wedding."

Candace blinked. And blinked again. Her gaze drifted downward, and she realized her mother hadn't been looking at her drink earlier; she'd been looking at her ring finger. Just as she often did herself, dreaming of something actually being there.

She knew Brian meant to marry her someday. But she didn't know how soon "someday" would be, and God, she was getting so ready.

"Well, I... We don't have any plans yet."

"I didn't think so. Do you mean to just go on living together from now on? Because you know your father and I don't approve of that. It's your life," she added quickly, raising one quelling hand as Candace opened her mouth. "You'll do what you want, you've proven as much. But surely you aren't content with that arrangement, are you? Surely you want more than that."

"Are you suggesting *I* propose?" It was an option, even if the thought made her mouth run dry. God, what if he actually said *no*? What if she realized this wasn't as solid and permanent as she believed it was?

No. He loved her. She knew he did.

Sylvia laughed. "Not necessarily. But marriage is a partnership. If you're wanting to go into it, then communication is a must from the start." Her mother frowned, worrying the glass in her hands, turning it around and around. "I just think...and please only take this as my advice...you should try to find out where his head is at."

She wanted to only take it as advice, to think her mom was finally making an effort to be motherly instead of manipulative for a change. Unfortunately, she knew her too well. It was just another machination, playing with her head, trying to get her to broach a discussion with Brian that just might result in their demise if she realized his head wasn't in the same place as hers. Or if the very thought of marriage sent him running. Yet again, the woman was making unsavory assumptions about his character when, even after a year and a half, she didn't know him at all.

"Brian and I are doing just fine. We do communicate. We'll get married when we're both ready. Until then, thanks for your advice and your concern, but with all due respect, we're both adults and we'll figure things out without your input or your *planning*." Sylvia didn't wait for her to finish talking before turning away, her heels clattering across the hardwood floor as she drained her scotch. Candace almost flinched with the force her mother used to slam her glass on the bar, but when she turned back, she'd composed herself. Only the tightness of her smile belied her anger. "We need to get back to the guests."

The Candace of old would have felt bad and apologized. The Candace Brian had introduced her to stepped out of her mom's way without a word. And once Sylvia had passed, she tossed back the rest of her champagne in a single shot that would've made the woman faint. Then she followed her out, plastering a smile on her face. She didn't often drink, but when she did, it was usually because of her parents.

God, let this night end.

The Rosses' Christmas party was last weekend. Such a good time. She adored Brian's family, and although there were occasions he didn't

## A Very Naughty Xmas

feel the same, hanging around her parents and brother for a while always made him appreciate his way more. So that was a silver lining. The Rosses were more laid back, more rambunctious, less hoity-toity though they shared much the same status in the community as the Andrews family. Which was local royalty. But Brian had only thought the Rosses were miserably conservative until he'd met her clan. They'd shown him a thing or two.

Her mother took up her position near the tree again, smile dazzling, giving no indication she'd been near to rage not two minutes earlier. She was the queen of keeping up appearances. Candace looked for Brian among the guests but didn't see him.

Oh, well. She'd look for him in a minute. Right now, she needed a moment away to collect herself—being nowhere near as proficient at hiding her emotions as her mother—and freshen up.

Her old room upstairs had been completely redecorated since she moved out—it was almost as if she'd never been there. Not that she expected her parents to keep a shrine to her. But it would've been nice if her mom hadn't mobilized her army of interior decorators not two weeks after Candace's departure, apparently with orders to make the space where she'd spent her entire childhood virtually unrecognizable to her.

This wasn't home anymore. Brian was home. She skirted around the four-poster bed she doubted anyone had ever slept in and headed for the little attached bathroom. It, at least, was the same as before—seafoam green with a tasteful beach theme. Her reflection in the mirror over the bowl sink was much as she suspected: flushed cheeks, tight jaw, too-bright eyes. If she went out there looking like this, she'd get a ton of concerned questions, but she couldn't even splash water on her face. She could only sit on the edge of the bathtub and breathe. And try not to think.

But it was impossible. Maybe her mother was right in a way—she and Brian often got so caught up in expansion plans for his tattoo parlor, Dermamania, that they neglected to give their relationship much thought. It didn't need thought, really, it just *was*. She certainly wasn't going anywhere, and she didn't think he had plans to, either. And the sex...well, the sex was out of this world. No issue there. They just needed to talk, check in, maybe plan the getaway time they often discussed but never quite achieved.

And they'd be good as new.

Right?

If only Macy were here to commiserate with her. Usually, Candace's best friend always attended the Andrewses' party—and Macy's parents were downstairs right now—but Macy had decided to go with her boyfriend to Oklahoma this weekend to visit his sister for the holidays. Her boyfriend being Seth "Ghost" Warren, Brian's best friend. Candace really was happy for those two, but she missed Macy terribly on nights like these.

A sound came from the bedroom…the soft click of the door closing. Candace sat up straight, then jumped up when the sound of carpet-muffled footsteps reached her. She hadn't shut the bathroom door, and now someone had wandered in—

Brian peeked around the doorjamb. "Hey, babe."

She deflated with relief, reclaiming her seat. "Hey. How'd you know I was in here?"

His dark-clad figure filled the door frame and he shrugged before leaning casually against it. "Let's see. Meeting with Mommie Dearest, immediate disappearing act. Call it an educated guess."

She chuckled at the nickname he'd bestowed upon her mom from the time Candace had first hooked up with him.

"So what cardinal sin did we commit this time?"

Long-term pre-marital co-habitation, she wanted to reply, but that might open a can of worms she wasn't ready for yet. Damn, why did Sylvia Andrews always have to get under her skin like this? "It doesn't matter."

"We can get out of here as soon as you're ready, you know."

God, she loved him. He could express the simplest of ideas—*hey, why don't we get the fuck out of your parents' house?*—and she would fall in love with him all over again.

"I'm sorry," she said, standing and moving over to slide her arms around his waist. "It started out such a good night."

"Oh, yeah?" His mouth captured hers and all the bad feelings began to melt away. She was just about to lose herself in his kiss when his lips curved against hers and a delicious vibration buzzed against her clit.

She squeaked and tried to leap away, or at least get his hand away from his pocket, but he held her fast. "God, Brian." Her knees went weak and his other arm tightened around her to take on her weight. The vibration stopped and she gave a full-body shudder.

He nuzzled her neck, his breath soft and warm against her skin. "I loved watching you light up whenever I did that."

"Wanna light me up some more?"

"You have no idea."

The toys were fun, but damn, he didn't need anything to get her going except his mouth, his fingers…and the thought of a certain piercing he had that he knew how to use with shattering precision. Hell, just the sight of him, the way his eyes darkened when she could tell his thoughts were taking a wicked turn, could have her going zero to sixty in .02 of a second. How could she not love this man with all her heart?

His hands slid around behind her and squeezed her ass through her dress, drawing her close enough to feel the ridge of his erection through his slacks. With a little moan, she rubbed against it, internal muscles squeezing with her need to feel that thick cock sink deep, hot and tight inside her.

"I've been walking around with that most of the night," he said with a husky chuckle.

"Mmm." She reached down and gathered her dress up her thigh, giving him easier access. "Feel what I've been walking around with."

He didn't waste any time in pulling one hand back and stroking a finger over the damp silk of her panties. The move was meant to entice him, but dear God, she almost collapsed at his touch. "Shit, Candace," he groaned.

She raised her thigh along the outside of his, opening herself, and let her head fall back as his fingers pulled aside her thong and explored her wetness with the barest of touches. "I love you," she gasped when one finger slipped almost leisurely into her clenching pussy.

He made the little come-hither motion that curled her toes and ignited the familiar but always welcome liquid ache deep inside her belly. "I love you," he whispered back, looking into her eyes as he said it, as each stroke inside only fueled her longing. "So much."

"Please," she said weakly. *Please fuck me. Please marry me. Please spend the rest of your life with me.*

"You sure about this?"

She knew what he meant. It was her parents' house. It was her old childhood bathroom. But it was everything that had repressed her all her life, until he came along. Hell yes, she was sure about it. "I am." She undulated against his hand, ready to climb him if he didn't do something soon, if he didn't give her more, if he didn't get the hell inside her.

It was the only assurance he needed. His eyes darkened in the way that stole her breath. "You're so goddamn perfect," he rasped, his hand curling hard behind her neck and jerking her mouth to his. "So fucking perfect."

Little whimpers formed and died in her throat. His tongue danced into her mouth and she met it with her own, starving for the taste of him. And all at once, she had to see him. She began to work the buttons of his black shirt, fighting the urge to just rip them off to get to the wildness beneath his clothes. The tattoos—the vibrant ink he covered for formal occasions such as these, the real Brian, her man. Shoving his shirt from his shoulders, she trailed her mouth down his neck and kissed his bared chest, running her tongue along the lines and then sucking his nipple rings, first one then the other. His fingers tangled in her hair as he tensed and groaned, demolishing her updo. She barely cared.

Then it was his turn, strong hands shoving away fabric and strapless bra until her breasts were bared to his hands, his mouth…he returned the favor, sucking the little rings she'd finally relented and let him give her a few months back. She gasped and writhed at the tugging sensation, remembering how it had felt to let him do that—the sharp pierce of pain at odds with the warm and gentle way he'd handled her. The consolatory kiss above the still-stinging site of the piercing, to make it all better. *Do you do that to all the girls?* she'd asked him with a giggle. *Only the ones I want to spend the rest of my life with,* he'd replied.

He'd gotten so laid that night.

Her ass met the edge of the vanity. With hardly any effort, he lifted her onto it, stepping between her knees and working his belt without taking his eyes from hers. Their panting breath mingled in the tiny space between their lips.

"Do you know what it does to me to see you look the way you do tonight?" he asked.

*This*, obviously. But she wanted to hear him say it. "What?"

"When you look like this, dressed up, all fuckin' perfection like a priceless doll, it's like you're theirs again. And I just can't wait to take you back. Make you mine." With jerky, desperate movements, he freed his cock, positioned her and rubbed against her drenched panties with only the tip. She squirmed closer, just as impatient, just as frantic. He built that anticipation with every brush against her pulsing clit. Oh, it was delicious. He was delicious.

"I'm yours," she whispered, clutching both sides of his head. "I'm always yours. Please, baby, *please…*" His fingers found the side of her panties and wrenched. She gasped with the sting of the snapping fabric. Then, with one long, firm push she swore she felt all the way to her throat, he claimed her, the bead of his apadravya piercing dragging over the most sensitive part of her inner walls. She bit her lip on a wail they probably would've heard downstairs.

It didn't matter how long they'd been together. How many times they'd done this. He'd been her first—she hoped to God he'd be her last—and every time felt just like that first time. The overwhelming sensation of his body coming into hers, the emotions spiraling out of control. The love so strong it scared the hell out of her.

She let her heels clatter to the floor behind him and wrapped her legs around his waist, locking her ankles. His hands smoothed up her thighs, bunching up her dress, and the sigh that left him sounded almost relieved. "Finally where I've wanted to be all night," he said, the corner of his mouth tilting up sardonically.

Candace's breath gusted in and out. She was beyond replying, beyond thinking; she could only feel. And she needed to feel him move. He seemed content where he was, holding still deep inside her while her greedy body pulsed and wept and begged for him. He dropped his head to her naked breast, tonguing the ring in her nipple and flicking it until she arched and held his head to her in a grip she doubted he could break. When he sucked it gently, more, then harder, so hard it hurt, then gently again…oh God, the answering contractions in her pussy were going to make her come on him even though he wasn't moving an inch.

Jesus! How was he holding back? Why didn't she have his control? She squeezed her internal muscles tight as she could around him.

"Christ, Candace." The breath from the words cooled her heated flesh.

She knew how to break him.

"Please, Brian, please fuck me. Didn't you want to show me that I'm yours? Make me come. Show me."

One of his hands shot up to grasp her chin. Her heart leaped and began to pound. He stared directly into her eyes, his own an unfathomable blue that became her universe if she stared long enough. He made her do that very thing—stare into the beautiful complexity of his eyes as he began to withdraw, as he inched his piercing ever closer to that spot…that spot…oh, God, *that spot right there.*

"Oh, Brian!" she cried, all four limbs locking tight around him.

"Yeah?" he breathed.

"Right there, right there—" She momentarily lost the capacity for speech as, still holding her chin, he slid his cock back and forth, slowly, slowly, too damn slowly. "Faster!"

"Shh."

"Damn you!"

"Bless you."

Even in the midst of ecstasy, she couldn't help but laugh. A common occurrence with them. But he picked up his pace and soon there was nothing but sensation. The feel of him and the familiar smells and sounds of their sex. His eyes closed; his head dropped to her shoulder. Her fingers sank into his thick black hair, stroking through the silky strands then gripping them when the pleasure tightened and built to blinding proportions. Her panting turned into a chant: "Yes, baby, yes."

Always her answer to everything where he was concerned.

He lifted his mouth to her ear. "Come for me, Candace."

Especially that. Sweet release engulfed her, submerged her, somehow grounding her and flinging her into the heavens at once. She dug her fingernails into his back—until she realized she wasn't going to be able to suppress her cries and had to let him go to cover her mouth. So good, oh so good...

He was there with her, cursing and clutching at her while his cock pulsed against her contractions. As the maelstrom began to ebb, his lips found hers, and she slowly drifted down with his kiss to soothe her. One final, long exhale as their mouths broke apart, and the violent need became peace again.

"Damn," he said, stroking her cheek. She nodded her agreement, then let her forehead fall to his shoulder as he drew her closer. Still she trembled all over, and though he seemed calm in her arms, his heart thudded hard next to hers.

"I have plans for you tonight," he said, and she found it funny he could sound so normal after...that.

"Oh, really? What?"

"You'll see."

Pouting, she leaned back to look at him. "Don't do that to me. Why did you even say anything?"

"Because I *love* doing that to you." He reached up and lifted a strand of her tumbled hair, looking thoughtful as he curled it around his finger. "When we get home, I want you to fix this back like it was. It looked gorgeous." Grinning, he let the curl spring back. "Not that it doesn't look gorgeous right now."

"But what—?"

The soft squeak of the door opening in the adjoining bedroom made her heart leap, then the voice that followed made it nearly come out of her throat. "Candace? Are you in here?"

Her mother.

Brian froze, but instead of the alarm she expected to see flash across his face, his mouth broke into a giant freaking grin. He hadn't locked the bedroom door? She should've asked, sure, but she'd kind of assumed he'd known what would happen with the two of them alone in private. Jesus!

"Hello?" Footsteps came closer, and then she heard Sylvia muttering about the maid leaving the bathroom light on.

"Mom! Uh...don't come in, I'm not feeling well," she called.

Thank God, the approaching steps halted, but the irritation in her mother's voice made her grit her teeth. "Oh, Candace. Jennifer just told me she saw you looking as if you were about to pass out earlier. Have you drank too much?"

Brian's face became a mask of silent laughter. She gave him a little punch in the shoulder. "Um…could be, I guess. Sorry."

Sylvia sighed. "Are you okay?"

"I…yes. I'm okay."

"I'll get Brian and he can take you home. I didn't see him downstairs, though. Do you know where he is?"

He took that moment to give her a little thrust, reminding her exactly where he was. She stuck a warning finger in his face. He promptly bit it. Oh, this was kind of sick. "I'm sure he's…down there somewhere." At that, she was afraid he was going to lose it completely. But somehow he maintained his composure.

"Well, all right. I'll go look. When you leave, don't let everyone see you looking unwell. Go out the back."

"Okay."

"And about the talk we had earlier…I didn't mean to upset you. It's just that I know what he means to you, and whether you believe it or not, I want to see you happy. Whatever that means to you. So you just…do what you feel is best."

Candace suppressed a cringe as Brian's jovial expression smoothed out then pinched into a frown. She watched the transformation with a sinking heart. "Thanks," she said to her mother. A moment later, Sylvia shut the bedroom door, and absolute silence descended.

Brian slipped from her body and stepped away, not speaking at first. Candace licked her lips and eased herself down from the vanity, letting her skirt fall around her shaking legs. Her heart beat a painful rhythm in her chest.

"What exactly is it you're supposed to do?" he asked, trying to sound casual as he zipped himself up. She knew him, though. He couldn't hide the little edge in his voice from her.

Her brain replayed her mother's words and she wondered how he'd taken them. "We just…she was asking me, like, what our…future plans are."

"What did you say?"

She shrugged, turning to check out her reflection and take stock of the damage for the first time. Oh, holy hell. No, she really couldn't let anyone see her looking like this, hair all bedraggled and lipstick smeared liberally around her mouth. "I mean, you and I haven't …discussed anything lately, so I just told her to back off. We don't need her trying to intervene in our lives."

"She doesn't like you being shacked up with me."

As usual, he cut to the heart of the matter. Candace began jerking bobby pins from her hair. Better to just let it tumble down. "I don't care what she likes."

"You do a little, or you wouldn't be yanking half your hair out with those pins."

Sighing, she tossed the pins down and set about fixing her face, sharing glances in the mirror with him every few seconds. He buttoned his shirt and made a few quick adjustments to his own appearance, running his fingers through his thick black hair. Then he moved toward the door. "Guess I'd better go make myself available for her to find, or she might come back."

She hated the uncertainty in his eyes. It shouldn't be there, not about *her*. She reached for his hand before he could go, rubbing it gently between her own. "Hey. I love you."

"I love you too, babe." He pulled away and was gone.

Dammit. She cleaned up the remnants of their pleasure from between her legs, then continued trying to tame her hair into something presentable in case they didn't manage to slip out unnoticed. And what the hell to do with her ruined panties and the tiny vibrator? She couldn't hide them in the empty wastebasket for the housekeepers to find, and she had no pockets.

Maybe she'd just slip them in Brian's when he came back to collect his sloppy-drunk girlfriend.

## 2

The drive home was too quiet. The lighted houses Candace usually enjoyed looking at slipped past the windows of Brian's truck virtually unseen. She focused on him, his every breath, every movement, even when she wasn't looking right at him. He didn't seem upset that he was still a subject of dissension between her and her parents—hell, he was used to it by now. But it shouldn't have to be that way. He didn't deserve it. He was amazing and wonderful and if they would just pull the reindeer antlers out of their asses, they would see that.

Maybe they were making progress, though. At least the word "wedding" had actually dropped from her mother's lips. It was a far better word than some of the others she'd uttered about him in the past.

She reached over and laced her fingers through his. He gave her a smile, but it didn't have its usual spark. For some reason, that more than anything else shredded her heart.

"Brian, she asked when we were getting married. She wanted me to ask *you* that. That's all she meant when she told me to do what I thought was best."

If he'd been still before, now he was frozen. *Oh, shit.*

"Really?"

Swallowing against the dryness in her throat, she stroked his fingers with her thumb. "Really. I don't know if it was one of her ploys or not, though. At first I thought it was, but now…I'm not sure."

"Ploy for what?"

"Maybe to get me to bring it up to you and scare you off? You know how she is. I don't know. We don't have to talk about this."

"Baby, that ain't happening. So put it out of your head."

Relief blazed a trail through her chest. She'd known, she *had*, really, but…to hear him say it was more beautiful than all the Christmas carols in the world. "You're a saint to put up with all this. I swear, Brian, they're my family, but if you say the word—"

"Stop that." He drew her hand to his lips and brushed a kiss across her knuckles. "As long as they stay the fuck away from my business, I can handle them."

She fell silent. He referred to the incident that happened shortly after they got together—her older brother Jameson being so outraged his little sister was sleeping with Brian Ross that he trashed Brian's tattoo parlor. Her family's hatred and animosity toward the man she loved had nearly sent her running, because she didn't see any way out from them—at least not for the foreseeable future—and she didn't want to put Brian through their wrath.

In many ways, she was different now. She'd graduated college. She'd abandoned the career path she'd planned for in deciding to help Brian with his parlor—a decision made solely for herself and for him, not her parents. She didn't live under a roof they paid for. She was free of them financially. If her relationship with them was going to consistently drive wedges between her and Brian, she would just have to free herself from them altogether. The thought was one that had loomed for a long time, and it saddened her, but what else could she do?

"And," he said as he turned into the parking lot of their apartment complex, "as long as you love me and aren't planning to cut and run, then there's nothing at all to worry about."

"I would have to be insane to leave you. God, Brian. Don't you know that?"

There was the spark she'd been missing. The smile from him that lit up her entire world. He lifted her hand and kissed the back of it. "I know it, but I still like to hear you say it."

Of course, she knew just what he meant.

Their apartment—his apartment that she'd moved into not long after they got together—was a sight for sore eyes. Decorated mostly with his art and a few of her girly touches, it was small but she considered it the first real home she'd ever had. Her parents' house was like a museum: gigantic, cold, and while you could look, you could never, ever touch. Her first apartment had been paid for with their money and while she'd decorated it herself, it had been under her mother's critical eye. But Sylvia had never stepped foot here, and probably never would. That was fine with Candace.

She moved around turning on some lamps and then plugging in the lights on their Christmas tree. Brian started some music.

"So ready to get out of this dress," she said, heading for the bathroom to do just that.

"I'm ready too," Brian called after her, giving her a shiver of happiness.

"Want to help?"

"You know it."

*A Very Naughty Xmas*

She flipped on the bathroom light and curled her lip at her appearance. "I suppose that's a part of the plan you have for me tonight?"

"A big part." He appeared behind her, and she smiled at his reflection in the mirror.

"Want to clue me in yet?"

Without giving a reply, he slid his hands up her bare arms, leaving gooseflesh in their wake, then pulled the straps of her dress down. "You'll put your hair back up for me?"

"Of course. You just like messing it up, don't you?"

"I do, but not this time." A tug at the back of her dress, then a loosening as he pulled down the zipper. She stood still as he let the fabric slip down her body and pool at her feet, glad to be rid of it. In short order, her strapless bra followed, leaving her naked since he'd demolished her panties in her old bathroom.

She watched in the mirror as his gaze slowly slid down and up again, seeming to caress her every curve and lingering on his favorite ones: her breasts and nipples with their silver rings. His fingers lightly traced around her waist to her belly, hands forming a V as he moved them down to the bare juncture of her thighs. He watched the slow progression intently, and she loved watching *him*. Before she knew it, her breath was coming in shallow pants as arousal tightened her muscles under his seeking fingers.

"I'm going to draw you like this," he said, and her knees went weak. Again.

"Like...this?"

"With your hair up, that beautiful neck bared. Along with everything else." Gently, he gathered her hair at her nape and lifted it, grazing the side of her neck with his lips.

"Oh my...God."

He'd drawn her before; it was something he loved to do. Right now, a portrait he'd done of her during their turbulent inception as a couple hung over their bed. More than once, she'd been relaxing and watching TV with him while he doodled on his sketch pad, only for him to lift it up later and show her the breathtaking profile of her he'd sketched out while she hadn't even known. But he hadn't done that in a while, and well, he'd never asked to draw her nude.

She closed her eyes as his hands released her hair then traveled all over her body, almost as if he were memorizing her lines and curves to better help him transfer them to paper. "Is that okay, sunshine? Just know if you say no, you spoil all my carefully made plans."

Was he crazy? *No* had never even occurred to her. She was too busy trying not to go up in flames, shove him onto the bed in the next room and ride him to ecstasy. His hands covered both her breasts, kneading lightly. She inhaled to drive them further into his touch. "You know my answer is yes. My answer is always yes to you."

He grinned at her in the mirror, his smile white and beautiful against his olive complexion. Hopefully this would involve him getting naked too, at least before the night was over. "Let's hope so. Now get ready for me." He kissed her cheek, then turned and left her melting, watching him go adoringly.

God, she loved that man.

Repairing her hair wasn't such a chore this time, as she wasn't striving for perfection. For this, she left it soft and a little disarrayed, some tendrils still hanging in loose ringlets. She hoped he would like it. Donning her fuzzy pink robe, she headed toward the living room, where she found him rearranging the throw pillows on their couch.

He'd changed into a pair of ripped, faded jeans, but he'd lost his shirt, for which she'd be eternally grateful since she was more than a little obsessed with his body. His ink, his piercings. Lord. She swallowed thickly.

"How is this?" she asked, more to get his attention than his opinion. She already knew what he would say.

"Gorgeous. Perfect." The way he smiled told her he genuinely thought so.

Candace took a deep breath and moved closer, fingers clenched on her robe. Given her thudding heart and ragged breath, it was almost as if she'd never been naked for him before. "I think this'll work," he said, eyeing the pillow arrangement critically. "Go ahead and lie down and we'll work on pose."

She licked her lips and slipped out of her robe, which he took from her. As soon as the air hit her nipples, they tightened—or maybe it was because his gaze automatically went there. "This may very well be the greatest idea I've ever had," he said as she stretched out on the couch.

She would've laughed if she weren't so damn turned on. Every inch of her body felt incredibly sensitized, and if he'd touched between her legs, he'd have found her slick and swollen. Hell, if he touched between her legs, she'd end up needing to fix her hair again.

He urged her onto her left side and a little more upright, resting her elbow on the arm of the couch and adding another pillow under it to make her more comfortable. "Put your hand here, like this," he said, moving her hand so that it was against her cheek. "Can you hold that?"

"Yeah, it's fine."

As he continued to work, she simply went limp and let him situate her however he wanted. He brought her right leg forward over her left and bent it at the knee so she wasn't showing *everything*, then paused in his task to stroke his hand over the curve of her hip. "Damn. That's hot. This is going to be perfect."

"And for your eyes only, right?" she teased.

He gave her a wry look. "Given that I'd beat the fucking shit out of anyone else who saw you like this, yes."

"You're not going to, like, have it tattooed across your back or anything?"

"There's an idea," he laughed. He moved her right arm so that it lay along her side, not obstructing the view of her breasts. "Are you comfortable? Seriously. It shouldn't take me long but I'd rather you speak now than have to adjust anything."

Without moving anything except her eyes, she looked up at him. "Yes."

He stroked her jaw with his index finger. "You're beautiful. Once you see this you might *want* to show everyone."

"I doubt that!"

"Tell you what. I'll do a quick close-up of your face too. Then you can show whoever you want."

"Okay. Thanks."

He stood back and looked at her from head to toe, giving her a few minor adjustments. Then he dragged his chair over and sat, propping his ankle on his opposite knee and reaching for his large sketchpad. Of course, after that, he moved his chair three times to find just the right angle. All the while she watched him in amusement, falling more in love with him every passing minute if that were possible. He was never satisfied until his work was flawless, and if he needed another hour to make it that way, he would take it.

"Okay," he finally announced. "Ready."

"You know, you've drawn me from memory before. I think you just want to have an excuse to stare at me naked," she said.

"There is that," he agreed, and she giggled when he didn't dispute the accusation.

Now came the hard part—remaining still and quiet while he needed total concentration. But that was okay, because it gave *her* an excuse to look at him and nothing else the entire time he worked. Shirtless, intense, his black hair tousled and his dark blue gaze roving all over her body as his graphite pencil roved the paper…yes, this was the greatest idea he'd ever had. Time crept by, and she became aware of her pulse all over, especially between her thighs, and she squeezed them together trying to assuage the building ache. That felt good though, so she kept doing it. The rhythmic movements only worked to encourage her arousal.

He took that moment to look up at her over his pad. His eyes followed the curve of her hip, and she felt that gaze so acutely it could've been his hands stroking her skin. The damp flesh hidden from his view throbbed and burned. "God, I want you," she blurted.

"Baby, you have no idea," he muttered, now looking down at his pad. "I could break rocks over here right now."

Oh, damn, that didn't help at all. Brian looking so unimaginably hot right now didn't help, either. All that hard male flesh exposed. His bare feet, which never failed to fascinate her—was there anything about him that didn't? She could scarcely see the movement of his hands on his pad. Those hands were works of art—big and graceful, they created beautiful things and they never failed to make her body sing.

Turnabout was fair play. "I'm so wet. I would touch myself, but I can't move."

He completely stopped and looked up at her. He didn't have to say a word; she knew what the thought of her masturbating did to him—it was a thing. A thing the mere mention of was likely to get her fucked senseless, to drive all thought of it out of her head.

She undulated her hips in tiny, subtle circles. "I'm sorry. I can't help it."

"Candace," he said in a warning tone. The most delicious warning she could imagine.

"Okay," she relented with a pout. He winked at her.

"Not much longer, babe."

"Then you'll fuck me?"

"Jesus. You have to ask?"

"No, I just like to."

He didn't look up. "Fair enough. I like to answer. Yes, I'll fuck you."

"Hard?"

"Like you're unbreakable."

Damn. Her eyes closed. Her wetness doubled, almost as if her body understood and stepped up its efforts to prepare her for the rough play he was capable of. "I can't wait," she whispered.

He heard. "I can't either. Trying not to mess up over here." She repressed a laugh as he winced and reached down to adjust himself under his sketch pad.

"How will you do it?"

"How do you want it?"

"I want you right here as soon as you're done. I won't be able to wait."

"Sounds good to me."

"But will you go down on me first?" He was sooooo good at that. *So* good.

"Goddamn, what are you trying to do to me? I can't concentrate."

He tried to appear cool and affected but couldn't quite pull it off. She smiled. Of course, she could sympathize, being seconds away from breaking her pose to attend to needs that were spiraling out of control. "Will you?"

"I'll suck you until you scream, Candace. Until you make that sound." The corner of his mouth kicked up. "You know the one I mean. It's the sexiest, most primal thing I've ever heard."

Sexy and primal. Interesting that he would use those words to describe that high-pitched, wavering, uncontrolled caterwaul she did when he was giving it to her good. That noise was almost embarrassing. "After that," she said, "I want you wherever and however you want me."

His gaze flickered to hers. A spark of danger lit in his eyes. "Then you'll get it."

She didn't have to explain what she meant and neither did he. Her heart jumped and warmth spread in her face, no doubt turning her cheeks bright red. "Okay," she said softly.

Appearing satisfied he'd shut her up, he went back to work with swift, efficient strokes, his expression tense but otherwise unreadable. She just tried to keep breathing, anticipation and anxiety swamping her as she thought back on the times before, letting him take her ass. The overwhelming fullness that fell just a little too much on the pain side of the pleasure/pain dichotomy. But enough on the pleasure side that she couldn't stop. That she wanted more.

"You got quiet," he observed after more time had passed. "If you don't want—"

"No. I do."

"You know I love you, babe."

"I know. I love you too."

"Me and you?" he said, giving the first line of their favorite motto.

"Against the world," she finished. Always.

# 3

"Done?" she asked, hearing the breathless excitement in her own voice.

"For the moment. I'll play around with it more later."

"Can I see?"

After scrutinizing his work while the seconds ticked away on the clock hanging on the wall above his head, he flipped the pad closed and slipped it behind him on the chair. The grin he gave her was full of the mischief she loved about him...one of the hundreds of things she loved about him, anyway.

"Nope," he said, standing without taking his eyes off her.

She frowned and moved to get up. "No?"

"No. Don't move."

Now those were some sweet words. Swallowing, she fell back in her former position. As his hands went to his belt and began to unfasten it while he stared at her like a starving man about to fall on a buffet, she licked her lips in a feeble attempt to replenish the moisture. Oh. God. Yes. She rubbed her thighs together wantonly in front of him, feeling the slickness between them, encouraging her body's perpetual response to him. She let her fingers slide down over her quivering belly muscles, closer and closer, then opened her legs so he could see her wet folds.

"Sonofabitch," he muttered, fingers seeming to fumble a bit as he worked his fly.

She giggled with the heady intoxication of knowing she held this power over him and let her hand slip lower without taking her eyes from his face. Pushing him. "See anything you like?"

"Fuck, yes."

The first brush of her fingertips over her clit caused her to suck in a breath and then sigh his name as if he were the one touching her. She wanted to rub herself to a frantic orgasm, but that was his job tonight. His eyes flared and she quickly moved her hand away, silently letting him know she would push that particular button of his right now.

A few quick adjustments on his part and he was naked, his cock in his hand. Long, thick, beautiful, hard and ready with the silver beads on the top and bottom of the glans—those little beads in just the right place could have her coming within seconds if she was turned on enough. Now definitely qualified. Her own fingers when she dipped them shallowly into her pussy were no comparison to what he could give her. None.

"Then come get it," she said.

She thought he might bust the coffee table to pieces in an effort to get to her; in the end he practically climbed over it. Reaching her, he crushed his mouth to hers, burying her under his weight on the couch, and she loved it, loved being pinned down and helpless under him. The heaviness of his erection rested on her thigh and she tried to wriggle her legs apart to give him space—

Strong hands grasped her wrists and held them down; he pulled back and shook his head at her. "Uh-uh. You asked me to go down first. I'm just following orders."

All the curves he'd stared at while drawing her he touched now, every move swift and impatient, as if he couldn't feel all of her fast enough. And then he was tasting her, his mouth hot on her neck, her breasts, her nipples, oh God yes, sucking the rings into his mouth and flicking them with his tongue until she writhed in desperation.

Just as he drove her to the point of begging, he changed tactics, gained control of himself, slowed down. Threw her off balance in the way he loved to do. Even as she wanted to claw at him and tell him to hurry up and get her off, she managed to bring her own ragged emotions into check. The only thing better than Brian fucking her senseless was Brian making love to her.

He barely left any part of her unkissed as he made his way down the length of her body. Without the burden of his weight on her, she opened her legs, giving him room. He slid his knees down onto the floor and grabbed her hips, pulling her until the backs of her thighs rested on his shoulders.

For a long moment, he simply looked, and the heat in her face roared to an inferno. It didn't matter how many times he'd seen her this way; whenever the most secret part of her was laid bare in front of him, she could scarcely deal with the intimacy. Her hands trembled as she reached for his hair, itching to sink her fingers deep into the silk of it. Mess it up a bit more. His gaze flickered up her body, finally coming to rest on her face.

"I keep trying to think up new and inventive ways to tell you you're the most beautiful thing I've ever seen in my life," he said. "And you get more beautiful with each passing day."

"You don't have to say it. You only have to look at me like you are right now, and I'll know." His lips curved in a smile, and she went on. "If you ever stop doing that, that's when I would start to wonder."

"It's not something you'll ever have to worry about, Candace. I promise you that." His mouth lowered to skim the crease where her right thigh met her abdomen. He followed it down until his breath tickled right where she needed his tongue most, and then he pulled apart her lips with his thumbs. Looking at her. Breathing on her. Oh, Jesus. Her hands left his head—she feared now she'd pull his hair out—and clenched futilely at the couch cushions.

One lick. One tiny lick she barely felt right on her clit, and her hips tried to wrench upward. Ready for the violent reaction, he held her steady and did it again. "Please, Brian, more..."

He didn't give it to her, and he wouldn't until he was ready. She'd learned long ago not to rush him when he was like this; it was useless. His tongue traveled down her slit, thoroughly tasting her wetness and probing gently into her pussy. He licked and sucked her labia, first one side and then the other. He even placed nipping, sucking kisses along the insides of her thighs while her chest heaved and she curled her hands into fists to keep from reaching down and giving herself relief.

"Do you know how fucking crazy I'd go if I didn't have you?" he whispered, breathing the words right on her wet, hot flesh. Wet from her juices and from his skillful mouth.

"Do you know how fucking crazy I'm going to go if I *don't* have you?"

"But you do."

"I know, just... I need to come. So bad."

"After all this time, I still haven't taught you to enjoy drawing this out."

"It's you. I can't help it. When it comes to you, I'm in the red 24/7."

"Well. Can't say I don't enjoy hearing that." He stroked one hand up and down her thigh, then skimmed the same pattern with his fingertips. "But I love it when you need me this much."

Finally, he brought his mouth to her. He sucked her deep and fluttered his tongue over her clit in the way that drove her absolutely batshit crazy. It pulled that fucking sound out of her throat, the one he'd mentioned, the vibrating note she would never be able to produce in ordinary circumstances. She tightened all over and exploded, her entire body gripped with racking pleasure. At the peak, he slid two fingers inside her, manipulating the spot that brought whole new layers of sensation, prolonging her climax until it wrung everything out of her. Every bit of worry and guilt—gone in an instant. It would come back later, but at the moment, her mind was blank and her heart and body ruled. And those? They were his property.

In her post-coital delirium, she found herself being tugged from the couch. "Come to me, baby," he whispered, pulling her into his arms and settling her—*oh, yes*—right over the head of his hard cock. The stretch of him burned deep and squeezed a few remaining whimpers from her. Her internal muscles still clenched weakly from the strength of her orgasm, gripping him, and he groaned as she took him fully.

Candace hoped he had room to work, because she was nothing but a limp rag doll draped over him. But those colorful, rock-hard arms went around her, lifting her so he could position her better between his hips and the couch. She did manage to lift her elbows to the cushions to help him out and give herself a little more support.

He moved, slowly drawing out, holding still, then pushing back in even more slowly. She groaned in ecstasy, her body reawakening for him. He didn't look away from her eyes. It was glorious. Perfection. It was everything she wanted for the rest of her life. "Kiss me," she pleaded softly, and he couldn't move forward to claim her mouth fast enough. His tongue took up the same slow rhythm of his lovemaking, in and out, pause, in again, swirl. The slight rotation of his hips made his piercing rub all her sweetest spots.

"Candace," he whispered against her lips. Fullness welled in her chest, threatening to build up behind her eyes. Her arms would around him and he lifted her up, holding her close as he continued the same agonizingly slow pace.

She'd thought nothing would ever compare to the scary, explosive wildness she'd felt when they first got together. More than once, she'd thought that surely something that strong and volatile would burn itself out with time. To an extent, that part had, but she hadn't expected what replaced it to be even stronger. Steadier. Sometimes even scarier.

"I swear to God you were made for me," he said. She sank her fingers into his hair, pressing her cheek tight to his clean-shaven one. The spice of his aftershave intoxicated her.

"I was." It had to be true. Every part of him stimulated just the right parts of her, both physically and emotionally. From the slow, wet slide of him between her legs to his hard chest rubbing her nipples to the words he spoke and the soft pant of his breath in her ear. She ran her fingers over his biceps, watching the progression of her fingertips over his beautiful ink, smiling a little when goose bumps rose on his skin.

"So good," he groaned. She rotated her hips on him, pushing another sexy growl from his throat. His hands slid down her back to her ass, cupping her firmly and kneading. "I think I made a promise I have to

### Light Me Up, by Cherrie Lynn

keep, though."

*Like you're unbreakable.* Yes, he had. The problem with being with Brian—and damn, wasn't it a good problem to have—was that she never could decide on how she wanted him. Slow was incredible until he suggested fast. Fast was awesome until he slowed and, oh yeah, ecstasy ensued. It was all good, so damn good.

He managed to climb to his feet with her still clinging to him, laughing when he almost dropped her. Holding her ass, he carried her to their bedroom, still buried inside her. Once he'd laid her across the bed, though, he pulled out and urged her onto her stomach. Grasping her hips, he hauled her up on all fours.

"Bring me that sweet ass," he said, voice somewhere between commanding and cajoling.

"Oh, God," she sighed, thrusting back toward him. His hand smoothed up the back of her thigh and over the upraised curve of her cheek. Then the tip of his finger trailed down her cleft, dragging through the shocking amount of wetness he'd drawn from her. Was he going to…? She arched her back and wriggled her knees farther apart, now fired with the need to tempt him.

"Mmm," he said, sliding two fingers deep and hard into her melting center. Again, she was caught between the disappointment that he passed up her anus and the bliss he invoked with his caresses. She turned her face into the mattress and whimpered. Slowly he fucked her with his fingers, rubbing his other hand over the cheeks of her ass. "Beautiful." Knowing he watched her clenching pussy accept his fingers only made her that much hotter. Her face flamed. But she couldn't take much more of this, she needed something faster and more punishing than that gentle rhythm.

She was opening her mouth to ask him for it when she felt him shifting behind her, and giddiness welled in her chest. *Yes, yes, do it, baby.* Her breath hitched at the suddenness at which his fingers disappeared from inside her. Hard thighs came between hers and he kneed her legs wider apart, his hands grasping her hips and jerking them even higher, to his groin. The hot, heavy length of his cock rubbed on her backside, and then he drew it back, positioning it for entry. The broad head with its smooth ball at the tip rubbed through the slick, needy heat between her legs.

It was all she could do not to push back on him. Desperate, she did try, but his grip on her wouldn't allow it. He held the reins here, holding her steady and absolutely still as he slid inside, inch by torturously slow inch. Her body welcomed him, gripping his intruding length, craving more of it. Everything he had. His breathing grew harsh, pleasure curses tumbling from his mouth. His fingers bit hard enough to bruise her tender flesh.

Once he rested deep inside her, unmoving, his hands released their death grip and wandered gently over her the small of her back, her ass, down her thighs. Then his thumbs came to rest near the place of their joining, and he pulled her labia apart. "Jesus," he murmured. "I wish you could see what I'm seeing right now." She tried to twist back to look at him. He was gazing down, watching as he withdrew from her as slowly as he'd entered.

The friction sent tingles to every nerve ending in her body. She wished she could see too. See herself stretched around his retreating girth. As he pulled out, his cock would shimmer with remnants of her clinging moisture in the lamp light, the evidence of her building need for him. Oh, God. She bit down on a bent knuckle to keep from begging…begging…for what, she didn't know. To make her not love him so fucking much it would kill her? To make her love him until it did?

He was content to draw it out, to keep his strokes so slow and deliberate she could feel everything. His piercing massaging her G-spot in just the right way. His broad base stretching her until she couldn't breathe. Slow, it was too slow. She wouldn't get off like this; she would only hover at the precipice and *ache* until she was wrenched in two.

Frantically, she reached back to grab his hip in a fruitless effort to urge him to move faster. "Please, make me come."

He ignored her pathetic pleading. "That hitting your sweet spot, baby?"

"Oh, God, yes."

"So fucking good. Play with your clit, Candace."

She wouldn't survive it, but damn if she wasn't going to try. When her fingers slid down and found her wet, swollen nub, it was so sensitive she uttered a little cry at the tiny orgasmic shudder that rippled through her just from touching it. Brian must have felt it too. He growled. "Do it, baby, rub it. I'm gonna fuck you long and hard, and I want you to come so hard you'll think you're broken."

Only if he'd be there to put her back together again. Yes. Her fingers began to move in earnest, wringing a cry from her lips as they drew out the waiting orgasm. He waited until she was coming down to pick up his pace, giving her what he'd promised. Slow, but hard. A long, leisurely pull-out, a rough shove back in. So hard she bit her knuckle again.

"Faster," she said around her clenched teeth.

His hand came down on her right cheek with a stinging smack she

## Light Me Up, by Cherrie Lynn

felt all the way to her pussy, but he didn't speed up. Gasping, she pushed her hips back at him, disrupting his rhythm on purpose so he would do it again. And he did. She cursed at the effect the tingling remnants of the strike had on her overly sensitive body. Dammit, her legs were giving out, and as much as she loved it like this, she wanted to hold him. See him.

"You want it faster?" he murmured near her ear.

"Yes!" she cried. He hands roamed up to massage her breasts and pluck the rings in her nipples until she moaned.

"Are you sure?"

"*Fuck.* Yes!"

Instead of giving her what she was ready to scream for, he pulled out. When she looked back, he held his cock in his hands, his beautiful blue eyes heavy-lidded and every muscle defined in his taut abdomen. The color of his ink stood out from his flushed skin, lamp light glinted from his silver piercings, and with his messy black hair he was the most fucking gorgeous thing she'd ever seen. Without his having to ask, she turned and attacked him, shoving him back and circling the head of his dick with her tongue, paying special attention to the silver balls at the head that brought her so much pleasure. Tasting herself there.

"If you won't give it to me the way I want it," she told him, pulling back to look up the length of his body, "I'll take it."

He grabbed her under the arms and hauled her up his body. "Do your worst," he said challengingly. Scrambling over him, she slid back home, taking him deep to fill her aching emptiness and churning her hips to find her favorite angle. Once she had it, she lifted slowly, dropped fast. And faster. And faster. Bliss unfurled. Engulfed her. Her muscles began to tighten deliciously, that note only he could invoke from her building in her throat. Just as she began to give in to it, he rolled her beneath him, pinning her wrists to the mattress, holding still.

"No!" she cried, writing to keep up that heavenly rhythm, caught on the edge of absolute madness. Wrapping her legs around his hips, she pumped against him, but couldn't get enough momentum to coax that blessed release any closer. The liquid ache pooled in her belly and he wouldn't agitate it. She writhed in desperation.

"Shh," he soothed with a crooked little smile, and she wanted to smack him.

"Brian, please, *please.*"

"That's real sweet. I like that."

"Yeah? I like orgasms. I want to have this one."

At that, he left her. *Left* her. She opened her mouth to deliver a tirade that would've made him proud, but when she saw what he was doing, she clamped down on it and repressed a whimper. Their toy box was under the bed; he went down on the floor to rummage through it and came back with her favorite vibrator. And lubricant. Anticipation and no small amount of anxiety sparked in her belly, ratcheting up her arousal tenfold, if that were even possible.

"You want it, baby?" he whispered, taking a moment to lean down and brush his lips across hers. She nodded, and closed her eyes. "Turn over for me." Once she obeyed, she simply lay there and watched him, trying to keep breathing. He removed his piercing—it would be too much for her—and rolled on a condom. She resisted the urge to slip her hand between her body and the mattress, to get off this one impending orgasm that loomed over her...

He moved behind her and she lifted her hips for him. For several luxurious minutes, he stroked her, caressed her, brought her back to those amazing heights. He fit two fingers in her pussy, stroking her until she shivered and undulated, dying to be filled with something bigger. As those delectable caresses went on, she suddenly felt the gentle probe of another finger at her anus.

It had taken a while for her to enjoy this. He didn't ask for it often—mainly when he was feeling on edge or possessive and needed her in every way. And she'd always trusted him not to take more than she could give. Now, as his lubed finger gained entry to that passage and he buried it to his knuckle, bliss overwhelmed her.

"Ohhhh, yes," she sighed.

"Christ, do you know what you do to me?"

If it was the same thing he did to her, then yeah, she had a pretty good idea. When he removed his fingers from her pussy and focused on her ass, she clenched the comforter with both hands, holding absolutely still and absorbing the sensation. He snugged two fingers inside her, gently stretching her.

"Ready for me?" he murmured in her ear.

"Yessss," she hissed. His hands left her, and a moment later she heard the vibrator buzz on.

"Turn over."

She obeyed readily, comforted with knowing he would be able to see her face while he took her this way. And vice versa. He gave her the vibrator, but she didn't dare touch her clit with it yet. She'd be done. She needed to balance that sensation with the overwhelming and initially uncomfortable fullness as he entered her.

He sat up straight and she spread her legs over his thighs, then stroked her all over, leaning down to kiss her belly and nipples. She burned for him, ached for him, and he drew it out until she was near begging for him. By the time he prodded her rear with the thick head of his cock, whatever anxiety she'd had before had bled away into pure molten lust to have him in every way possible.

It always reminded her of losing her virginity. Overwhelming. Impossible. Incredible. He stretched her to her very limits as she clawed at his arms, cried his name. Just when it was at the edge of unbearable, she lay the vibrator on her clit, her over-sensitized body nearly wrenching off the bed with the sensation.

"Sweet baby," he groaned, pulling back and causing her to damn near black out with pleasure. "Don't come yet."

"Please hurry, I can't wait long..."

"I know, I know." Slowly, gently, he began to fuck her. She rolled the vibrator around her clit, teasing it, knowing he watched every move. When she slipped a little too close to her climax, she moved it away. His hands roamed up her arms, covered her breasts, stroked her nipples with his thumbs. "Goddamn, you are fucking exquisite. I love you."

The point of no return was seconds away. "I love you...Brian...I'm about to..."

"I got you, babe." He withdrew and took the vibrator from her, tossing it aside. Then he stripped the condom and fell on her, shoving into her with a groan that made her heart skip a beat. And he gave her just what she needed. With the strength he couldn't use to fuck her ass, he plundered her wetness over and over, like he promised, like she was unbreakable, lifting his head to stare into her eyes when her cries began to reach a crescendo. Their neighbors probably fucking hated them.

"Come with me, baby," she begged him, needing that oneness with him, not wanting to go through that shattering pleasure alone.

"I'm with you," he rasped, eyelids falling closed and his rhythm faltering as she felt him jerk inside her and bathe her inner tissues with his come. "Oh, *fuck*." If she hadn't been there already, the sights and sounds of his pleasure alone might have sent her over. Her body milked him, worshiped him, squeezed every last drop from him as he finally gifted her with the climax he'd been denying her. It rolled her under, wave after wave, leaving her spent and trembling and clinging to him helplessly once it receded.

Their breaths rasped in unison. Somewhere she felt a pulse pounding, but couldn't tell where it originated or if it was his or hers. Both together? She wouldn't be surprised, they were so in sync in every other way. His weight was heavy on her but she wouldn't have let him go yet if he dared to move.

She might have passed out for a minute. Before she realized it, he was kissing her. Teasing her lips with just the tip of his tongue, rubbing his mouth sensuously across hers. Slow and sexy and enough to make her body take interest again even though she was damn near exhausted from coming so hard. Gently, he pulled out and rolled to his side, keeping her tight against his chest, her leg still draped over his hip.

There was no safer place in the world than right here.

Just as she thought he might be falling asleep, his eyes opened. There she saw the satiation that only comes from great sex, and it made her smile. Yet again, she was right there with him.

"Love you," she whispered. No, she really couldn't tell him enough.

He stroked her hair, smirking a little, and she could only imagine what her updo must look like by now. "Love you too."

"When do I get to see my drawing?"

"Oh, buttering me up. I see how it is. You'll see it when it's done."

She pouted at him. "You're usually faster than that."

"This one needs to be extra special. Gotta give it all my mojo."

"Oh yeah? Did you draw me bigger boobs?" As he laughed, she gave him a little pinch on the pec. "I'm going to have a set of double-D's, aren't I? I hope you wouldn't give me a bigger ass."

"Baby, your luscious ass is perfect, and I wouldn't change your A-cup for the world."

"*B*-cup, thank you very much," she huffed in mock indignation.

"Oh! My bad. I don't know about these things, you know." He circled her nipple with the tip of his finger, making her shiver happily.

"Yeah, yeah, whatever."

His teasing fingertip moved up to lift her chin, making her look him in the eyes. "I wouldn't change a thing about you. You know that, right?"

Candace nodded. "I know. I do."

"Are you happy with the way things are?"

"Incredibly."

"You seem to be. Is there anything at all you would change?"

She opened her mouth only to quickly close it again. Communication, her mom had said. It should be easy with him, and it usually was; she'd always felt like she could tell him anything. But her heart rate kicked up and her mouth ran dry. There was so much riding on this, and the last thing she wanted was to put pressure on him. He had enough dealing with his business and his own family without throwing hers into the mix. She wanted to be his refuge from the storms, not the cause. She wanted to be the one thing in his life he could count on to not cause him any grief or stress—because God knew she'd caused him enough in the beginning.

It meant denying her own desires, though, something she still struggled with.

"Absolute silence," he observed. "I take that as a yes."

"It's not anything I would change about you."

"Maybe what your mom said hit a little close to home?"

"Maybe. Brian—"

"Sometimes I think, you know, I was your first guy, so I wonder if you wish you'd...explored a little more."

After everything they'd just shared? Was he serious right now? "I hate that something like that would even cross your mind. Have I done anything to make you doubt me?"

"No. You're an angel. All my life I've never given two fucks what anyone thought of me. Then you come along, and it's all I think about: if I've done something to make you realize you've made a mistake yet. If anything I've said or done has pissed you off or made you think 'fuck that clown.'"

"I'd be lying if I said you've never pissed me off." She chuckled. Oh, yeah, they'd had their share of disagreements, and he did have a bit of a temper. But he'd never gotten out of line, and the makeup sex alone was worth the fight. "But it's okay. Because I love you just as you are. You aren't perfect, but neither am I. All that matters is that we're perfect for each other. If I'm where you are, Brian, I don't need anything else." *I want it*, she amended silently. *But I don't need it.*

His expression smoothed out in relief. She stroked his cheek, troubled, wondering what was making him question so much lately. It wasn't just her mother's words tonight. Now that she thought about it, this had been going on for a while.

Maybe he was questioning his feelings for *her*? Oh, hell no, she wouldn't even start to go there. It was bad enough when she stared at her left hand and daydreamed a ring being on her finger. She couldn't start wondering if he was considering leaving her or she'd drive herself truly insane.

"Are *you* happy?" she asked on impulse.

"Couldn't be happier."

"Then we're all good. I'm sorry about earlier tonight."

"Don't worry about it." His lips curled in the wicked little smile she loved. "You know, I don't think I'm quite done with you yet."

Jesus Christ. Maybe her parents should have a party every weekend.

## 4

Christmas morning dawned, but in this part of Texas it would probably never be white. The morning light streamed through the bedroom window, hitting Candace right between the eyes. Brian's chest was warm under her cheek, and she planted a kiss on it before raising her head to look at the clock—a little after nine—and then his peacefully sleeping face. Ordinarily she'd let him snooze, but there were more pressing matters this morning. "Baby?"

His head turned toward her on the pillow, but his eyes didn't open. "Hmm?"

"Can I open my present now?"

Both of his arms came around her and he tugged her back down, snuggling her close. "Impatient."

"That's easy for you to say, I let you open yours last night. Please?" It had been a week since her parents' Christmas party, and he hadn't dropped one hint about what her present might be. She was about to explode.

"In a minute!"

She giggled at his mock-angry tone as he pulled her even closer, so that she could hardly breathe. And how could she complain? Best way to spend Christmas morning ever. But she hadn't been this excited about something since she was a kid. Even so, she managed to doze off again wrapped in his cozy arms. When she woke again, he lay facing her, smiling as he played gently with her hair.

Glancing at her watch, she saw another hour had slipped by. "Now?"

He gave an adorable scoff. "Good morning and merry Christmas to you too."

"I'm sorry." She scooted forward and gave him a kiss. "I'm just excited."

"I'll show you excited." Brian grabbed her hand and attempted to pull it under the covers while she squealed and fought him. Because if they got started, it would be well after noon before they stopped.

Laughing, he gave in and sat up, swinging his legs off the side of the bed. "All right, all right. I'm up. In more ways than one, thank you very fuckin' much."

"Oh, you're always up," she teased, springing up after him. "Where is it?"

He cocked an eyebrow at her while he adjusted himself in his pajama pants, and she gave him an exasperated look. "Not your dick. I know where that is."

"Can't help it. You in those silky pink PJs. Does it to me every time."

"I could wear ratty flannel footie jammies and it would do it to you."

"True." He gave a cursory glance around. "Let's see. Where did I hide it again? Hmm."

"Oh, stop. I've waited long enough!"

"Okay, but go in the kitchen or something. I don't want to give up my hiding place."

Candace couldn't scramble out of the room fast enough, but stopped to give him a kiss along the way. In the living room, she turned on the Christmas tree lights and then headed to the kitchen to make coffee and start breakfast. Her heart pounded the entire time, and though she tried not to get her hopes up, to tell herself it didn't matter what her present was, she couldn't help herself. She'd be the happiest girl in the entire world if she had his ring on her finger.

Checking her cell as she waited for the coffee to brew, she saw Macy and Samantha had both texted her merry Christmas messages and asked what Brian had given her. *I don't know yet, still waiting on him*, she told them both.

*Ghost says he knows what it is!*, Macy sent back. The evil bitch. Why'd she ask, then? The central heat kicked on, and Candace almost went to turn it off. She was burning up. By the time Brian took his dear, sweet time strolling into the kitchen with something hidden behind his back, she struggled not to combust.

"I hope you like it," he said, looking somber.

Now that the moment was here, panic filled her chest. Oh, God! What if this was it? But it probably wasn't. But what if it was? If so, it was a lifetime commitment. She wanted it, she wanted it more than anything, but to know everything you wanted in life was within your grasp... oh, she needed a moment.

"Coffee?" she asked, hearing the high-pitched edge in her own voice as she turned and reached for the cups she'd already pulled down from the cabinet.

*A Very Naughty Xmas*

Brian caught her hand, halting her. "Later." From behind his back, he brought out a flat package wrapped in shiny gold paper. Her breath caught. It wasn't a little box, but...she would love whatever he gave her. Smiling up at him, she took it. Given its shape and weight, it felt like a picture frame.

"Can I open it now?"

He was watching her closely. "Sure."

As she gently began peeling the tape away from the end, he rolled his eyes to the ceiling. "Jesus, woman. You damn sure didn't grow up in the Ross household. Christmas morning was no-holds-barred. Usually involved a foot race and a fist fight. Tear into it."

Eschewing years of ingrained propriety, she dug her fingernails into the paper and ripped. It felt good. She kept ripping until she held in her hands a framed sketch—the close-up of her face he'd done the other night. "Oh!" she breathed, immediately struck nearly speechless by his exquisite work. "It's *beautiful*, Brian."

He grinned. "I wanted to frame the other one, but I thought, you know..."

"Not exactly something I want hanging in the living room," she agreed with a laugh, going up on her tiptoes to give him a kiss. "I love it." Which was absolutely true. He never failed to remind her how lucky she was to have someone so gorgeous, funny, cool *and* awesomely talented in her life. Sure, she'd have loved if this were The Big Day, but it would come.

He still looked at her in that odd, watchful way, though. She felt his gaze even when she looked back down at the drawing and studied it, marveling at the time and effort he'd obviously put in. She traced her fingers along the glass, following the delicate lines. She'd never be able to create something so beautiful, so perfect...

Wait a second.

Her finger paused on one little detail. In the drawing, her cheek rested against her left hand. And there was a ring...

She didn't wear a ring. Not on that finger. She didn't even have a...

"Brian?" Candace lifted her gaze to his, pointing at what appeared to be a diamond ring on her finger in the drawing. "What is that?"

"That? Huh. Where did that come from?"

"What are you doing?"

"Oh, I remember now. *That*..." He turned and walked from the room. She stood frozen to the spot, and just as it occurred to her that maybe she should follow him, he returned holding a little box wrapped in the same shiny gold paper. "...is this."

Her eyes filled with tears. She looked up at his beloved face and opened her mouth, but no sound would come. Her pulse pounded in her ears.

With a tender smile, Brian took her portrait from her shaking hands and laid it aside on the nearby counter. "Do you want to open it?"

Candace nodded. That much she could do. He handed it to her, and this time he didn't have to instruct her on how to appropriately open a Christmas gift. She tore into that thing like her entire future happiness lay inside...which, of course, it did. What she revealed was a typical small velvet jewelry box, and inside...

"Oh, my God, Brian," she breathed, the tears spilling freely. "Oh my *God*."

It was like nothing she'd ever seen but it was everything she wanted. It was *black*. Black gold. A large princess cut black diamond. But around the solitaire, it was frosted with tiny white ones, and the contrast was breathtaking. It was so *him*... and since she'd met him, and he'd saved her from everything she thought she knew or had been told about herself, so her. "It's the most beautiful thing I've ever seen!"

"You're the most beautiful thing I've ever seen," he said.

She threw her arms around his neck, still unable to take her eyes off her ring in its box. Brian squeezed her so tight her feet came off the floor. "Thank you," she said over and over. Thanking him, thanking God for him, she didn't know. Both.

"Let's not forget the most important part," he said, gently setting her back on her feet and releasing her but keeping hold of one hand. With his other, he took the ring box from her. As she stared at him uncomprehendingly, he went down on one knee, the swift movement forcing an exclamation from her lips.

"I'd kind of hoped to do this somewhere more romantic than our kitchen," he said though her gasping and crying. "But it doesn't matter where we are. I love you, Candace."

"I... love... you," she managed, a sob punctuating each word. Too bad that for the rest of his life he would remember her being a blubbering fool at this moment. She scrubbed furiously at one cheek and then the other with her free hand.

"You look gorgeous," he assured her, as if he knew what she was thinking. "In fact, this is how I love you best, I think. PJs, hair up, no makeup...the way only I get to see you."

"Bawling my eyes out?"

"I don't mind that as long as they're happy tears."

Oh, they were. The happiest tears she'd ever shed.

He squeezed her hand. "We've been through a lot together since the first time we met. I think if we can get through all of that, we can get through anything."

"I think so too."

"And there's no one else I'd rather have at my side through whatever life throws at us. You've been so much more to me than my girlfriend. You've been closer to me than my best friend. You've been a partner. I mean, only someone who loves me unconditionally would want to give up everything to work at Dermamania and put up with my bullshit all day every day. Don't think for one second that I don't realize that. I just had a hard time coming to terms with the fact that you do care that much about me. I found it hard to believe."

"Oh, Brian, don't you know—?"

"Shh. Let me say this. I've wanted so much to marry you for the past fucking *year*—hell, longer— that it's sometimes taken everything within me not to just blurt it out. But I wanted to make it special. I wanted it to be right, not just for me but for you. I hope I haven't misjudged the timing, but I don't think I have."

He hadn't. Oh, God, no, he hadn't.

"So if you want to be by my side every day, then I want you here forever. I want you to be my partner not just at the shop but in life. I want you to have my name. I want—I *need* for you to vow in front of me and God and everyone that you'll be only mine for the rest of your life. I'm already used to you being here, but I can't let myself depend on it like I want to. Because I keep thinking, 'One day she could be gone, and then where the fuck would I be?' Right back in the gutter again."

She bit her lip, mesmerized by his eyes and his words. He drew a shaking breath, glancing down, and let go of her hand long enough to pull the ring from its velvet box. Holding it with the tips of his fingers, he back gazed up at her.

"So, Candace Marie Andrews, will you do all that crazy shit I just said and marry me?"

"Brian Lorenzo Ross, yes!" She launched herself down at him, knowing he would catch her. Knowing he would catch her for the rest of their lives.

"What the hell! You had to ruin it by using my middle name," he laughed as she rained kisses on his face.

"Well, you used mine, so there. And I love your middle name." Then he began to try to capture her kisses with his lips, and her mind scrambled again. At some point the ring ended up on her finger, a perfect fit, which was good. Because they ended up on the kitchen floor, rolling around madly making out between laughter and her lingering crying fit. Eventually they moved to the couch, where they sat and kissed and talked and talked, staring at the Christmas tree. It had been a long time since Candace had felt so carefree. Since she'd felt she could breathe. She hadn't realized what a burden her bare ring finger had been until it finally had some weight on it, and she couldn't stop looking at her ring. It was just...perfect. Too perfect for words.

"You know my mother," he warned eventually. "She'll demand grandchildren. And I think she has the ability to make them manifest by sheer force of will."

"Well, that's okay, right?" she asked shyly, feeling a blush rise in her cheeks.

He grinned at her. "It's okay with me. I'd rather not throw caution to the wind just yet or anything, but if it happens...yeah." He trailed his lips down her jaw while he slid his hand under her PJ shirt to stroke her bare belly with the back of his fingers. "I think you'd make a terrific mom. I'd love to make you one."

She shivered. "Keep this up, and I'll beg you to make me one now." Truth was, she couldn't wait. She would love knowing a part of him—of both of them—was growing inside her. "But I'm afraid my mom would work black magic on us if she thought it would stop it from happening."

"Don't worry. Your mom's evil powers are no match for mine's baby-making vibes."

"You're probably right."

"When do you want to tell them?"

"As soon as possible. I want to sing it from the rooftops. I want to call Sam and Macy too—although Macy said she knew what you were giving me. Ghost told her."

"Are you serious? Damn him. I told him not to, just because I figured she might torment you. The pitfalls of our best friends being together, I guess."

"Oh, it's okay. If he were going to propose to her, I would want to know beforehand. He's not, is he?"

Brian shook his head. "Not that I know of. But give him time."

The thought of Ghost and Macy tying the knot made her want to laugh out loud with joy. If most people thought Candace and Brian were an unlikely couple, then those two were damn near impossible to imagine together. But beautiful. No one who saw how much they loved each other could deny that.

Candace caught Brian's face between her hands. "At the risk of sounding extraordinarily sappy, I'm the happiest I've ever been in my entire life. You've given me the best Christmas ever."

"I'm glad, babe. You don't know what I've gone through trying not to let my cover get blown. I could tell your mom got to you at the party, so I debated proposing that night, but I had to try to see it through. I already had this planned before I knew she'd said anything, though. I want you to know that."

That's right, he had. He'd mentioned it in the bathroom before her mother nearly caught them. "So this is why you've been a little weird lately? Were you nervous?"

"I was going apeshit. Ask Ghost."

"I can imagine what he's listened to," she laughed. "You did great. You totally had me going with the drawing."

He gave her an incredulous look. "Seriously? You thought I'd do something that lame? Of course, in some people's opinions, the whole thing was pretty lame."

"Ghost's, I assume?"

"Exactly."

She laughed. "Well, I didn't think it was lame, even if it had only been the drawing and not a ring. It's beautiful."

"I can do a drawing for you anytime. It's not something I'd do for your Christmas present."

"There are lots and lots of things you can do for me anytime, Brian Ross, but that doesn't mean I don't appreciate them every time you do them."

"Oh yeah?" He leaned forward and nuzzled her neck. "Then why don't I carry you into the bedroom and do some of those things? Before we go sing from the rooftops."

"Yes, please and thank you."

He pulled her from the couch and up into his arms. Kissing her all the way, he carried her as if she were feather-light to their bed. Her husband-to-be. Her fiancé. She could hardly believe it, though she'd known all along, in her heart, it would happen.

His hands roamed her body, sliding against her silky pajama top. Teasing her nipples to aching little peaks. She gasped and arched against him. He took the opportunity to slide her pants down a bit, so that the first little red-and-black heart tattoo he'd given her was visible just above her panties.

"Where it all started," he murmured, and ran his fingertips over it before placing a kiss on it.

Candace threaded her fingers through his hair. "Mm-hmm. Where would we be if I'd never come to you for that?"

"I think things have a way of working out the way they're supposed to. We'd have found each other some way or another."

Closing her eyes, she smiled. "I think so too."

## 5

Candace rang the doorbell at her parents' house, huddling close to Brian—she'd scarcely been able to keep her hands off him since they left the apartment. He was wearing the new leather jacket she'd given him for Christmas, and he rocked it. Not that he didn't rock anything he wore, he just looked particularly dangerous in leather. And he smelled incredible.

When she'd called her mother earlier, Sylvia had surprised her by inviting them over for dinner, so she'd put off telling her about their engagement until she and Brian could both be there. This would definitely tell the tale about her mom's intentions. Sylvia could recover fast from anger or shock, but there was no hiding that initial reaction.

The mammoth front door flung open to reveal Sylvia herself, surprisingly casual in slim jeans and a green cashmere sweater. "Merry Christmas!" She gave Candace a peck on the cheek and, shocker of shockers, gave Brian one too. "Come in, come in."

They followed her into the house, shedding their coats. "You seem...festive tonight, Mom."

"Just glad everyone could come."

Everyone? Ugh, she should've known her mom would probably also invite Candace's older brother Jameson and his new girlfriend, whom she inexplicably loved. Her mom and dad and Brian could all tolerate one another pretty peacefully, but Jameson was a different story. The best that could be maintained between him and Brian was a hostile silence. Not that she could blame Brian at all for keeping up his end of it, given what James had done to him in the past.

But there sounded like a lot of people in the dining room, given the chatter coming from that direction. Way more than two couples.

"Who's here, Mom?" It was then that she heard Brian's mother's unmistakable Italian accent, and her vibrant laughter.

"Oh, hell," Brian murmured in Candace's ear.

She glanced at him and whispered, "But this is great, we can tell them all—"

## A Very Naughty Xmas

"When you agreed to come, I decided to invite the Rosses too," Sylvia said, walking ahead of them. "We don't get together enough, don't you agree?"

There was a reason for that. Sylvia Andrews had said some things about Gianna Ross's son in the past that hadn't set well with her. But it looked as if everyone was ready to bury the hatchet in the spirit of Christmas. Of course, the pressure Candace was feeling doubled, though she wasn't as worried about Brian's parents' reaction as she was her own. The Rosses were likely to be overjoyed to hear the news, even if it did mean lifelong ties with the Andrews family.

A chorus of greetings went up as Brian and Candace entered the dining room. She accepted hugs and kisses from her dad and Mr. and Mrs. Ross. Jameson tossed her a "Hey, sis," and she was grateful for that much. When he and Brian exchanged the briefest handshake of all time, she could've scooped her jaw off the floor.

Holy shit, this was real progress. She hoped she and Brian weren't about to tear it all apart with a few simple words.

God, she couldn't stand it. "We have news," she blurted, earning a wide-eyed look from Brian, who'd been in the middle of greeting his dad. She moved beside him and squeezed his hand tight. All eyes turned to them. Gianna and Sylvia, who stood beside each other, looked back and forth between Brian and Candace expectantly. Candace almost wanted to chuckle at the hope in Gianna's eyes. She was probably eager for a grandbaby, marriage be damned. Sylvia would've hit the floor if that had been the news.

"Well?" Brian's mother said. Judging by Sylvia's expression, she was afraid to ask.

Candace looked to her fiancé for support. He smiled at her and put his arm around her shoulders. Together they faced their families.

"I—"

"He—"

Dissolving in laughter as they both tried to speak at once, Candace gestured for him to go ahead, rubbing her engagement ring with her thumb in anticipation of showing it off. Miraculously, no one had noticed it yet.

Brian drew a breath and announced, "I asked Candace to marry me this morning."

All around the room, mouths dropped, and Candace thrust her left hand out for all of them to see. "And I said yes!"

She had no chance to watch Sylvia closely. Brian's mom rushed them, nearly knocking them both backwards with the impact of her embrace. After she'd squeezed the life out of them both, she caught

Brian's head between her hands and kissed both his cheeks repeatedly while he turned bright red. As she was laughing at the display, Candace felt someone lift her left hand. She turned to see her mother scrutinizing her ring.

"That is different," Sylvia said. "I figured it would be."

Immediately, she wanted to bristle and give her mother the same different-isn't-bad lecture she'd been giving for a year and a half now, but tamped it down. Sylvia turned the ring in several different angles, examining it in the light from the chandelier. Candace waited bleakly for the verdict.

"Two carats?"

Candace nodded.

"It's quite striking." Sylvia looked up at her and smiled. "It's beautiful."

"So...you and Dad, you're okay with this?"

"We're more than okay, but it doesn't matter. You're happy. *That's* what matters."

The slow exhale Candace released was practically a lifetime's worth of stress and anxiety. To think it had been Brian Ross's love for her that finally brought about this moment she'd never thought would come. Impulsively, she grabbed her mother in a fierce hug. "I love you, Mom."

Sylvia clung to her, and when she spoke, Candace could swear her mom's voice wavered. "I love you, too." It was the first time she'd heard those words from the woman in a long time, but then, it was the first time she'd uttered them in a long time too. Someone had to break the negativity cycle.

Because she realized now their talk at the Christmas party wasn't just Sylvia being manipulative...at least, not in a bad way. And Candace had flown off the handle, not trusting that maybe her parents were indeed coming around. She would start making more of an effort to get along as long as they continued to make one.

"Sylvia, you must have known about this," Gianna said. "I told Alexander when you called that something special must be happening tonight."

Sylvia released Candace, and she saw that for once her mom couldn't quite hide her emotions. "Actually, your son came over soon after our party and requested our permission to marry Candace. He thought we would appreciate the gesture. And we did, very, very much."

*He did what?* Candace turned to Brian, her mouth hanging open. "You did that?" She looked at Mrs. Ross only to find a similar expression on her face, and then to Brian, who wore his best devil-may-

*A Very Naughty Xmas*

care grin. "You're just full of surprises, aren't you?"

"You know it."

"So, yes," Sylvia said, "we did know it was coming. We were pretty certain what her answer would be too."

Gianna smacked Brian on the arm. "Holding out on me, son?"

"You can cuss me out later," he said.

"Don't think I'll forget it, either. We have a lot of planning to do, don't we?"

"I don't know so much about that," Brian said. Everyone looked at him in obvious consternation. *Oh, hell.* Candace couldn't believe he was bringing this up *now*. He could at least let the mothers have their fantasy of a huge society wedding.

"What do you mean?" his dad asked him.

"You think we're turning you guys loose to plan our wedding? No way. We talked about this on the way over; we're all about spontaneity. We'll probably elope."

Amid the outrage that flared at his bombshell, Candace made out only one thing: Brian's dad chuckling. "Smart kids."

It was like a scene out of a movie, one she'd always wished her life resembled. Everyone sitting along a long dining table, an incredible spread of food, laughter, Christmas music playing faintly in the background. The man she loved more than anything at her side. And her family—whether from resignation or a true desire to make her happy—actually accepted him. Inked, pierced, metal-loving tattoo artist. Who loved her madly, to have put up with so much crap from his future in-laws. Maybe all of that was coming to an end.

She should have known he would make everything right for her. He always did. He always made sacrifices and bit the bullet for her where her family was concerned, and she'd do her best to repay him for the rest of her life. Help him build his business to be the best it could be, help him build their life together so it would be beyond his wildest dreams.

She would ask Brian later to pinch her, because she must be dreaming. He would enjoy that.

Within a few minutes after his elopement announcement, everyone had thought he was joking, thankfully, but she dreaded the fallout when they figured out he'd been dead serious. They had plenty of time to worry about that, though. Right now, it was all a little too much for her to handle emotionally. She whispered to Brian that she was going to the bathroom and then excused herself from the table, heading directly for her old bedroom with its little bathroom—the one they'd steamed up a couple weeks before.

*Light Me Up, by Cherrie Lynn*

There, she allowed herself to have a little freak-out. Not a cry, which had been a frequent occurrence in her life. Not a break to fume or brood so she could compose herself. She had a giddy, dizzy, oh-my-God-is-this-really-happening, genuine jumping-up-and-down-and-twirling outburst of joy.

Then a deep breath and a quick fix in the mirror, during which she noticed a carefree sparkle in her eyes and a brightness to her smile that hadn't been there in a while. Not because Brian didn't make her happy all by himself—he did. It was simply that she'd always thought in the back of her mind that it might come down to having to choose him over her family, and while she'd known she was prepared to do so, it wasn't what she wanted. And his actions had also put to rest the niggling little question that sometimes kept her up at night: Would he finally get tired of her parents' bullshit and cut her loose because of it? There had been so many times she wouldn't have blamed him. But he wanted to stick it out with her. Forever. She grinned down at her ring, the sight of it blurring as tears filled her eyes.

Okay, so maybe she'd cry a little.

Good God, she loved him, so what the hell was she doing up here having a sappy-happy explosion? Just as she turned for the door, however, he appeared, making her jump. She hadn't heard him enter the bedroom.

"Oh! You startled me."

His dark blue eyes glanced over her. "Are you all right?"

"I'm fabulous. I'm *perfect*."

He grinned. "Yeah, you are. My mom just elbowed me and told me to go check on you. Not that I wouldn't have on my own, but I figured you were all right."

Mrs. Ross probably had ulterior motives. The woman wanted grandchildren, and she wanted them now, after all. "Have I told you today that I love you?"

He tilted his head, looking pensive and absolutely gorgeous. "I don't think you have," he lied.

"Well. I love you, Brian Ross."

"And I love you, Candace soon-to-be Ross."

Her heart skipped a beat. She didn't have to see herself in the mirror to know she beamed at him. "I love that too," she said softly, moving to him and sliding her arms around his waist. She went up on her toes to kiss him, but he stopped her by cradling her face in his hands.

"Remember when we were in here before and you told me to light you up? I don't think I've ever seen you as bright as you are right now. I did a good job, right?"

*A Very Naughty Xmas*

"Baby, I can't even tell you what an amazing job you did. I'm still half speechless."

"In that case, to hell with talk. Being in here again is giving me ideas."

She giggled as he leaned down and nibbled her neck, kissing a path up to her ear. "Brian…"

"Hmm?"

"I don't think we should…" His hands moved around to cup her ass and squeeze her against his hardening cock. "Oh…"

"What was that?"

They shouldn't, oh, they shouldn't… but he felt so good and so perfect and smelled so freaking awesome… "Maybe, um, maybe we should…wait…oh, fuck it." She grabbed his head and pressed her mouth to his, succumbing to his expert way of kissing her senseless.

"Don't worry, sunshine," he said against her lips. "I locked the door this time."

The End

# About Cherrie Lynn

Cherrie Lynn has been a CPS caseworker and a juvenile probation officer, but now that she has come to her senses, she writes contemporary and paranormal romance on the steamy side. It's much more fun. She's also an unabashed rock music enthusiast, and loves letting her passion for romance and metal collide on the page.

When she's not writing, you can find her reading, listening to music or playing with her favorite gadget of the moment. She's also fond of hitting the road with her husband to catch their favorite bands live.

Cherrie lives in East Texas with said husband and their two kids, all of whom are the source of much merriment, mischief and mayhem. She loves hearing from readers! You can visit her at

http://www.cherrielynn.com
http://www.facebook.com/cherrielynnauthor
http://www.twitter.com/cherrielynn.

# Other Books by Cherrie Lynn

Find out how it all started with Brian and Candace in *Rock Me* by Cherrie Lynn
Now available in print and ebook

# An Indecent Proposition

## Stephanie Julian

## Chapter One

"Do you honestly think she's going to show up? What woman in her right mind would?"

"She'll show. The money will get her here but it'll be up to you to get her to stay."

"Sure. Thanks for laying that all on me."

"Hey, you know what happens when women see me. They freak."

Keegan Malone set his Seven & Seven aside and rubbed a hand over his aching forehead.

Why the hell did he allow Erik to get him involved in these damn schemes?

The fact that they'd been best friends since boarding school probably had something to do with it.

Erik Riley, second son of the blueblood billionaire Boston Rileys, had always been the one goading Keegan to bigger and better, whether it was pranks or grades or sports. They'd been each other's perfect foil. Erik had pushed Keegan and Keegan had reined in Erik. Together they'd become unstoppable.

The world had been theirs to conquer until Erik had been seriously fucked up in that fire three years ago.

After five reconstructive surgeries, Erik had had enough. Why go through the agony if he'd never look the same? He hadn't gotten over that yet. Maybe he never would. But this…

"Don't you think you're taking this too far? I know you've been infatuated with the girl since the party but why not just introduce yourself in some normal way? You know, call her and ask her to dinner. Or 'accidentally' bump into her on the street and introduce yourself. Oh, wait." He let sarcasm bleed into his words. "You never go out so that won't work, will it?"

Erik gave him the finger, using his uninjured left hand. He could do it perfectly well with his right but that hand was scarred from elbow to fingertips.

"This will work out best for all of us. She needs the money for her mom—"

"And you have the hots for her so you'll use the money to get her here and you'll use me to…"

"Fuck her so I can watch. Yeah, I will."

Sighing, Keegan shook his head.

He and Erik had shared women for years, since one drunken night at Princeton had ended with them waking up in the same bed with a blissfully sated co-ed between them.

Afterward, the girl had sung their praises to her friends and a campus legend had been born. They'd never been without willing bed partners.

They didn't only work well together in bed. TinMan Biometrics was proof of that. After eight years, they'd taken the company from startup to global player. They had played their roles well and grown the company until they'd believed there was nothing they couldn't handle.

Then Erik had nearly died in the explosion and the world had shifted under their feet.

That it should've been Keegan in the lab at the time of the explosion and subsequent fire probably had a lot to do with the fact that he couldn't refuse Erik anything.

Including this incredibly ridiculous scheme.

When Erik had suggested it, Keegan had laughed in his face. Until he'd realized Erik hadn't been kidding.

*And you didn't try very hard to talk him out of it, did you?*

No, he hadn't. Because when he'd seen Julianne Carter at the cocktail party their company had held for potential clients a month ago, he'd wanted her. Desperately.

And because of the earpiece he wore to keep in contact with Erik during these events—which Keegan loathed but Erik refused to attend personally—he'd known Erik had noticed her too.

It'd been the first time in a long time that they'd agreed on a woman. And the first time Erik had shown any interest in a woman since the fire.

Keegan hadn't gotten a chance to talk to her that night but, by the next day, Erik had her entire history.

And this crazy-ass scheme.

Keegan had never thought she'd agree. Had expected her to refuse the offer flat out.

If she had, Keegan would've arranged a meeting. Or manipulated one.

Before the accident, Erik had been the master of the straightforward approach and Keegan the one who worked behind the scenes.

After, their roles had reversed. Neither of them was comfortable in their new world order.

But this—

The distant but distinct sound of a car pulling to a stop in front of the house snapped both of them to attention.

Erik grinned at him, the first time Keegan had seen him smile in days.

Holy shit.

She was here.

\*\*\*

Julianne had been told to expect creepy, but this was beyond strange.

If she didn't have such utter faith in her friend, Carol, she would've turned around and headed home after getting a look at the house.

Hell, if you were smart you wouldn't be here at all.

Sighing, she shook her head. There was one huge reason she was here.

No. Actually, there were five-hundred-thousand good reasons.

And she needed every last one of them.

Steeling her backbone, she turned off the car, listening to it wheeze and moan. It needed new brakes to pass inspection. Hell, it needed a lot more than that but she didn't have the money for the brakes much less a complete overhaul.

But she would…if she went through with this very indecent proposition.

She'd have the money for a car and be able to pay off her mom's medical bills and have money left over to start her own business.

But first she had to get out of the car.

Turning, she looked at the house. If this were a movie, she'd get out of the car and a guy in a mask made of other women's flesh would jump from behind one of the huge trees surrounding the place. He'd drag her off to hang her on a meat hook at the back of the house and skin her.

The house… Well, in the daylight, it probably looked a hell of a lot better.

Now, just after nine on the night before Christmas Eve, it looked pretty damn depressing.

No holiday lights hung from the rafters of the Victorian mansion. The building wouldn't look out of place in Cape May. But stuck out here in the middle-of-nowhere Berks County, Pennsylvania, it looked…

Sad. Lonely. And more than a little creepy. One tiny light shone on the porch, barely enough illumination to make out the front door. At least the house had no broken windows or unhinged shutters. And no sign that said "Beware!"

A new coat of paint would go a long way toward a new lease on life for the place. Which was exactly what Julianne needed. A new lease on life.

And this…whatever the hell this was would be the start of that. Half a million dollars would go a long way toward canceling her and her mom's debt and setting them up in a new life.

Far away from small towns and small-minded people.

Resolve stiffened her spine and she got out of the car. Her heels sank into the gravel driveway but she'd been wearing stilettos since she was fifteen. She could probably run a seven-minute mile in them and not break her ankle.

And her high school guidance counselor had told her she had no life skills.

So there, Mr. Clark.

A cold wind whipped through the trees, making them moan and shake. Gathering the lapels of her coat closer together, she shivered as the wind bit at her naked legs.

Hurrying up the front steps, she walked to the door and knocked before she had second thoughts. Or third or fourth. Or fiftieth.

It's not that she didn't enjoy sex. Some people in this one-stoplight town thought she enjoyed it a little too much.

And even if those same people figured she'd probably sold herself before, it would be a lie.

Sure, she enjoyed sex. Hell, she loved it. And if she met a guy she liked and took him home with her for the night, whose business was it but hers and his?

It wasn't like she went out of her way to find married men to tempt away from their wives. Was it her fault she didn't do background checks on every man she was attracted to?

No, god damn it, it wasn't.

But she'd found out the hard way that, even if the man lied and said he was single and had no kids, she was still the bitch who'd ruined his marriage.

She and her mom really needed to get out of here. Start over. Make her dream of owning her own catering business a reality.

The man inside this house would give her the means. According to Carol, she'd be doing this guy a favor. Her friend had implied that he'd been in an accident and had some "issues" from that.

As long as he didn't want to hurt her or, oh, say, hang her on a meat hook and skin her alive, she'd be on board. Five-hundred-thousand dollars was a great motivator.

Julianne was no slut. She had to like a guy to take him to bed. But she was no princess in an ivory tower either. If she really couldn't stand him, she was out. Money be damned.

"Think of this as a blind date," Carol had said. "If you hit it off, that's great. If you decide to spend the night, you'll be five-hundred-thousand bucks richer. If you want to leave, all you have to do is say the word and you'll be out the door. I give you my word."

She still wasn't sure why the man had gone through Carol to approach her with this unusual request. Carol was an event planner. She didn't typically set up reclusive rich guys with minimum-wage waitresses.

No more stalling. Knock on the damn door.

She reached for the old-fashioned brass knocker before she managed to talk herself out of it.

Seconds later, a lock clicked and the door swung open. She almost expected it to creak. Instead, it barely made a noise.

"Come in, please."

The voice was low, cultured and totally fit the man who opened the door. Had to be in his mid-seventies, at least. He was still handsome even though he had a bit of a paunch and not much hair. What little hair he did have was trimmed neatly around his head. He wore khaki pants and a blue, button-down shirt and...

Jesus, the guy reminded her of her grandfather.

This is so not going to happen.

There was no way in hell she could make herself go to bed with him. "You know—"

"Mr. Smith will see you in the drawing room." The man waved his hand down a dark hall to her left. "It's the last door. Can I take your coat?"

So she wasn't here to see him? She almost breathed a sigh of relief.

But really...Mr. Smith. Gee, how original. "No, I think I'll keep my coat, thank you."

If she wanted to make a fast escape, she wanted to have it close. Besides, she didn't want the grandfather look-a-like to see what she had on underneath.

She'd dressed for the occasion.

The man's slight smile appeared understanding. "Then I'll make myself scarce." He held out a little black disk that looked like a car remote. She took it without thinking. "When you're ready to leave or should you need anything, press this. Have a good night."

*A Very Naughty Xmas*

He nodded, turned on his heel, and disappeared down a hallway on the opposite side of the house.

A panic button? Seriously?

She couldn't decide if she should be relieved or amused.

Okay, girl. It's now or never.

Debt free with enough left over to finance her dream, all for one night in a man's bed? Or back to working for minimum wage and trying to dig out from a mountain of bills for the rest of her life?

She turned and headed down the hall.

## Chapter Two

The strong knock made Erik smile, which pulled at the tight skin of his jaw. The pain was negligible but a reminder of why he'd come up with this plan to get Julianne into bed.

From the first moment he'd seen her, dressed in the buttoned-up, black-and-white uniform of a catering waitress, he'd wanted her.

Julianne Carter had long, dark hair, deep brown eyes, curves that wouldn't quit and a frail mother with a mountain of debt. She could have any man she wanted. And she'd never want him.

As beautiful as she was, she'd take one look at him and run the other way. This was the only way he'd ever get close to her.

He'd gotten used to seeing the shock on a person's face. He didn't want to see it on hers. He'd had so much taken away from him over the past two years. But he wanted her, or at least as much pleasure as he could get from watching Keegan fuck her.

And damn it, he was going to get it, even if it took deception and money. Everyone had their price. He'd learned that the hard way.

Anyway, it wasn't like she wouldn't get something out of the bargain. She needed the money. And she'd get Keegan.

If things worked the way he planned, she'd never get a good look at him.

Getting up, he retreated to the far side of the room, where the shadows would hide him, but where he could see everything in the firelight.

"Go ahead. Let her in."

Keegan scowled at him, his normally easy-going expression nowhere in sight. God damn it, Keegan would screw the whole deal by scaring her off before she ever got in the room.

But Erik would frighten her more. Hell, he frightened his own parents. Keegan was the only one who didn't look at him with horror and pity.

The horror he could take. The pity...not at all.

Keegan knew that, which was why he took a deep breath and let the

*A Very Naughty Xmas*

tension bleed away before he opened the door. The man was a damn good actor. He could've had a huge career on the screen.

Dim light from the hallway spilled into the room, though it didn't reach far enough to expose him.

And then she walked through the door.

Holy hell, she was fucking gorgeous.

He clamped down on the urge to groan. His cock hardened in his jeans, his lust for her so fucking hot, he swore he could taste it.

She made him wanted to walk out of the shadows, throw her naked on a bed and fuck her until she was so sated she couldn't see straight. Scars be damned.

But he couldn't take the chance of scaring her away.

She'd been curious enough to open the proposal he'd sent through Carol, their friend and business manager. When Carol had said Julianne had accepted the offer, he hadn't let himself hope she'd actually show up. And now that she was here, he didn't think he'd be able to keep his hands to himself.

He'd told Keegan he only wanted to watch.

He'd been lying. He wanted to do so much more.

\*\*\*

Julianne recognized the handsome man who opened the door, though she couldn't place the face.

He nodded, no hint of a smile on his face. "Come in. I'm…glad to see you made it."

Wow, nice voice with the hint of an accent. Irish? Scottish? She wasn't sure. Whatever it was, it sounded amazing.

The nervous energy gathering in her gut began to dissipate as her sensual, adventurous side responded to him.

"I wasn't sure I was going to come," she admitted. "But when you offer a girl five-hundred-thousand dollars to have sex with you, it certainly grabs her attention."

She swore she saw the faintest hint of a blush color his cheeks. What the hell? This was his deal. Why would he be embarrassed?

Still, it boosted her confidence. She would carry this off. She needed that damn money.

And this guy certainly wasn't hard on the eyes. His dark brown hair glinted red in the firelight and was a little longer than business casual, with waves that made her want to sink her fingers in them. Blue, blue eyes, a strong nose and beautifully curved mouth. And cheeks covered with absolutely adorable freckles.

He looked about ten years older than her so that made him early thirties. Didn't make a difference. Age meant little to her. Unless he was old enough to be her grandfather. Then, yes, that obviously was a problem.

But why would a guy who looked like him need to bribe a girl to sleep with him?

Waving her into the room, he closed the door behind her. She almost expected to hear the click of a lock. She was surprised when he left the door cracked just enough that she could see it.

Had he done that for her?

"Would you like a drink?" He motioned toward a fully stocked bar on the other side of the room from the roaring fireplace. "And can I take your coat?"

Did she hear a hint of nerves in his voice? Was he afraid she'd leave?

Surprisingly, she really wanted to stay.

"I'll take some white wine if you have it."

As for the coat... Maybe it'd be best just to get this part over with. She'd worn her warmest, a down stadium jacket that covered her from neck to knees. Not only because the temperature outside hovered close to zero but because she wasn't wearing all that much underneath.

As he nodded and turned toward the bar, she unzipped. While he had his back to her, she took a deep breath and let it fall to the floor.

And swore she heard the distinct sound of a man drawing in a sharp breath. But she was pretty sure it hadn't come from the man standing at the bar.

Her gaze searched the darkened corners of the room, which was bigger than she'd first realized. Much bigger. Someone could hide in that darkness and she'd never know they were there. Unless they made a sound.

Was there someone else in the room with them?

"You're beautiful."

Her attention returned to the man she could see. He'd turned back to her and now she saw lust in every line of his face.

His desire emboldened her and she walked toward him with her head high and her gaze pinning him in place.

"Thank you for the wine." She accepted the glass and took a sip before touching her hand to the bare curves of her breasts revealed by the slinky corset. "Do you like? I've had it for a few years. Saw it online and knew I had to have it. I just never had the right occasion. I thought tonight might be time for its debut."

He took a gulp of his drink, his eyes closing for a brief moment before he took a deep breath. "I'm honored you wore it for me."

Honored? Okay, what was wrong with his man that he had to offer women a small fortune to sleep with him?

The mass of conflicting thoughts and emotions running through her made her head spin. This evening was becoming more surreal than it already had been. And she was so turned on right now, her panties were soaking through.

What decent girl would be so aroused under these circumstances?

No, she didn't believe sex between consenting adults was a bad thing. And yes, she was consenting.

For five-hundred-thousand reasons.

But the money... Did taking money to have sex with this man make her a whore?

Did it matter?

She took money for performing a service where people looked through her like she was invisible. Why should it be different to take money for a service she actually enjoyed?

"Obviously you know my name, so I'm at a disadvantage. What's yours?"

He didn't hesitate, like he was trying to decide if he should lie. "Keegan."

Unusual. She liked it. "Have we met before, Keegan?"

His gaze never left hers. "Not formally, no."

"But I do recognize you, don't I?"

There was that hint of a blush again. The one she really liked.

"Probably, yes. You catered an event I...attended a few weeks ago."

She thought for a minute, staring into those blue eyes. "TinMan Biometrics. The reception at their offices."

Finally, the guy smiled. And her doubts melted like chocolate in the sun.

Was she being too trusting? Taken in by a sweet face and her own greed?

Maybe. But was it really greed when the money wasn't all for her? When most of it would go to pay her mom's doctor's bills?

Sure, he could still knock her out cold, drag her into his basement and dismember her for kicks and giggles. And even though the agreement she'd signed had included a non-disclosure clause as well as one that ensured her safety, she'd left a note for her mom just the same.

That same agreement had assured her that her partner for the evening had a clean bill of health. Yes, she was on the pill but she'd still brought condoms.

"So tell me—Oh!"

He wrapped one hand around her neck and kissed the hell out of her.

The shock made her freeze for several seconds before her mouth began to soften.

She stood on her toes to make them fit together better. Even though she was wearing heels, he still had a good three inches on her.

She liked that he was taller than her. Liked the feel of his hand on her neck, the way his lips felt against hers.

Her eyes had snapped shut when their lips touched and she let herself fall headlong into the kiss. Holding her steady with one hand on the back of her neck and the other on her hip, he plastered her body against his.

And damn but the guy could kiss. She felt like she was being devoured. In the best possible way. His mouth sealed over hers, his tongue pressing between her lips, sliding against her tongue and demanding she give herself over to him.

Her pussy went wet, a tight ache building low in her body. A void that needed to be filled.

God, she wanted him to lay her out and fuck her until she screamed. And then to continue until she couldn't scream anymore.

Slut.

No. It'd been too long since she'd gotten laid, that's all.

Her arms slid around his waist, head tilting so she could get a better angle. She sought to assert some dominance, to control some part of this—to control him—but he wasn't going to allow it.

Sliding his hands into her hair, he tugged. It wasn't painful but he wasn't letting go either. She let him direct her movement and his mouth moved. He spread kisses along her jaw to her ear, worrying the lobe between his teeth before he bit his way down her neck. Each sharp nip at her skin made her shiver, made her nipples tighten into points as hard as diamonds. Her breasts were crushed against his chest but she wanted to rub herself against bare male flesh.

His bare male flesh.

She gasped as he lifted her off the ground just as he bit the curve of her neck and shoulder.

"Wrap your legs around my waist. Do it now."

My God, that voice. That accent did things to her that should be illegal. Shouldn't be possible. Every nerve ending in her body tingled with anticipation.

Her clit swelled, her sex tightened into a hot, throbbing ache.

Had he put something in her drink? She didn't feel drugged. She felt…overheated. Overwhelmed. Like a vast pit of sexual need had been tapped deep within her and she needed to be fucked. Now. Right now. Hard and fast. Forced to submit. Forced to give over control.

No.

"Yes, that's right." He spoke as if he'd read her mind. But he was only praising her for following his orders, which she hadn't realized she'd done. "Fucking hell, you're beautiful."

Other men had said the same words to her. She'd believed it from some of them.

Now, as this stranger walked with her toward the fireplace, she wanted to believe him.

When he laid her out on a chaise lounge big enough for two people, she almost did.

"No. Stay there." His voice held a note of command as she moved to sit up, to reach for him.

She stilled, though she couldn't seem to catch her breath and her chest rose and fell so fast she thought she might hyperventilate.

Standing beside the chaise, his groin was just above her eye level and the bulge there made her mouth water.

Big and bold and she couldn't wait to uncover it.

She reached for him—

He grabbed her hand, stopping her short of her prize. "No touching. Not yet. I'll let you know when. Right now, I want you to do exactly what I say. Can you do that for me, Jules?"

She liked the nickname. It sounded exotic, intimate coming from his mouth in that accent.

She nodded, not sure she could form a coherent reply. Not even one word.

How the hell had he done this to her in such a short time?

Probably because when he smiled at her like that, lust pulsed through her body and short-circuited every one of her rational brain cells.

"I want you to play with your breasts. Pull your top down and stroke your nipples."

A flush suddenly burned her cheeks, which was ridiculous. Why should her own hands on her breasts make her embarrassed?

Maybe because it was almost too intimate. And this was not a lover she'd chosen for herself.

He'd bought her.

But she'd had to give her consent so technically, this was her choice.

She shrugged and the corset's spaghetti straps dropped off her shoulders, causing the front to dip.

She reached for the middle and pulled the material beneath her breasts, plumping them into overflowing mounds. She had great tits, full and firm. Men liked them, fixated on them. And she appreciated their appreciation.

Watching Keegan, she saw his chest rise and fall in a faster rhythm, saw his gaze narrow as he followed her hands.

Slowly, she cupped her breasts, massaging them. They felt heavy, sensitive. And when she pinched the nipples between her thumbs and forefingers, she groaned from the pleasure.

As she worked them into even harder points, that pleasure sank through her body.

Straight to her clit.

The heat in Keegan's eyes made that tiny organ between her legs throb. She let one hand fall from her breast to trail down her stomach—

"No. I didn't say you could touch your pussy. Not yet."

Keegan's voice sounded almost an octave deeper now and it resonated through her, causing her thighs to clench. She moved her hand back to her breast. Her lungs labored for air, her heart pounded against her ribs.

Could she make herself come with just her hands on her breasts? She wouldn't have thought it was possible but now...

Her eyes closed as she fondled her nipples harder, pinching the tips with more force. Eliciting more of a response.

She could smell her response, smell the scent of her arousal as it coated her pussy and slicked her thighs.

Did he notice?

He'd retreated to a chair not far from where she lay. He had full view of her.

And so would anyone sitting in the farthest corners of the room, where the shadows hid everything.

Was there someone else in the room? She swore she felt another pair of eyes on her from somewhere.

"Jules, look at me. I don't want you to take your eyes off of me, Beautiful. Good. Now take off your panties."

The panties were actually tap pants but she wouldn't expect a man to know that. She almost didn't want to leave her breasts but, right now, she wanted whatever he wanted.

She disobeyed for several seconds before she dragged her hands down her body to the elastic waistband of the pants. Lifting her ass off the chaise, she shimmied them down her thighs then lowered her ass back down and rolled her torso just enough so she could push the pants past her knees.

When they hung around her ankles, she leaned back into the cushion and worked the pants off with her feet.

Then she tossed them at him.

He caught them in one hand and held them, staring at her for several seconds, before he brought them close to his face and took a deep breath. He didn't actually rub them against his nose but he made sure she knew that he liked what he had in his hand.

After a few seconds, he dropped the pants into his lap, where it draped over the bulge of his erection.

Her mouth dried at the thought of what was beneath.

"Now show me how you get yourself off, Jules. Make yourself come."

"Is that all this will be? You and..." she let her pause drag for a second, wanted him to know she suspected there was other person in the room, but he showed no outward response, "me and no contact between us?"

His mouth pulled up at one corner. Sexy as hell. "Oh, I definitely plan to have contact, Jules. But not yet. Not until you show me what I want to see."

"And what's that?"

"I want to watch you come."

Damn, she wanted that too but she wasn't sure she could do it like this. Usually she needed a vibrator. "I don't know that..."

His eyes narrowed. "What?"

"I need a vibrator."

He didn't respond right away. She thought she might have lost him. Then he leaned forward. "Internal or external?"

"External."

Nodding, he rose and walked into the shadows behind his chair. As her eyes became more adjusted to the light level, she followed him farther into the shadows but then she lost him.

The room was much bigger than she realized.

Seconds later, he returned holding something in his hands.

"Will this work?"

He held out a palm-sized piece of green silicon, shaped like a curved leaf with a circular handle on one end and a rounded tip on the other.

She smiled into his eyes. "Yes."

His gaze held hers for several seconds before he let it wander. Down to her breasts, still naked and heaving from before, to her stomach and, finally, between her legs.

She kept the hair on her mound trimmed close and her pussy waxed bare. The lack of hair made her skin that much more sensitive.

He startled a quick gasp out of her when he reached down to stroke his fingertips over that hair. Her sex clenched, aching to be filled, and heat rolled over her like a wave, searing her from the tips of her toes to the top of her head.

"Use the vibrator, Jules. I want to see you come."

If he stood there the entire time, it wouldn't take her long. She couldn't believe how much she was turned on by all of this.

It didn't make any sense. She'd never been an exhibitionist or a hedonist. She loved sex, loved how it made her feel when she was with the right person. But this...

She didn't know Keegan and yet this was turning into the most intense sexual experience of her life.

And he hadn't done more than watch and let his fingertips brush over her.

Dragging her gaze away from his for a moment, she located the button that activated the vibrator then looked back at him. His gaze had transferred to the toy.

Pressing the button, she felt the subtle buzz ricochet through her body. The sound pricked at her ears and made her chest feel like a two-ton weight lay on it.

His fingers froze for a second before continuing up her leg. Curling his hand around her thigh, he pulled her leg out, opening her.

Slightly cooler air brushed against her exposed pussy, teased and tormented. She automatically tried to close her legs, ease the ache, but he held her open.

"Put it on your clit." Keegan voice sounded almost like a growl.

Her hand moved before her brain made sense of his words and she moaned as the vibrating tip made contact. Sensation ripped through her, sending pulses of ecstasy to her womb. Her eyes closed as she absorbed the sensation, let it course through her body.

Her orgasm gathered strength with each second. She knew it wouldn't be long before it broke and she welcomed it.

Opening her eyes, she saw Keegan's had narrowed to slits, his lips parted and his chest heaving.

His erection straining.

She wanted him to fill her with that thick shaft. From this angle, she could tell the guy was well hung, and damn if she didn't appreciate a man with a huge cock as much as the next girl.

Deliberately backing off the vibrator just a bit, she placed her free hand directly over that bulge.

And smiled when he bit back a groan.

She stroked him through the jeans, squeezed and fondled. Through slitted eyes, she watched his expression tighten into a mask of pure lust. His free hand, the one not gripping her thigh hard enough to leave marks, grabbed her and smashed her palm against his groin.

He ground his cock against her until she thought it had to hurt. And he did look to be in pain. But not the kind that made him want her to stop.

"Ah, fuck me. That's fucking—Christ almighty."

He ripped her hand away, startling her into pulling the vibrator away. Her body missed the stimulation and wanted to curl into a ball in denied lust.

She moaned, already reaching for him again when she realized what he was doing.

Ripping at the top button of his jeans, he dragged the zipper down then shoved his jeans and underwear down his hips, freeing his cock. It was just as wonderful as she'd imagined. Thick and long and standing at attention. The head was a ruddy red nearly two shades darker than the shaft. It pulsed with blood and one pearly drop of liquid sat on the tip.

"Suck me while you get yourself off, Jules. I can't wait any longer. I promise to return the favor."

Hell, yes.

She sat up and wrapped her free hand around the vividly hot shaft. So silky soft. And iron stiff.

Rubbing her thumb against the tip, she spread that little bit of moisture around the head, her mouth watering to taste him.

She repositioned the vibrator, catching her clit at an angle that kept her stimulated but didn't push her over the edge. Then she slid her hand back and forth on his dick.

"Yeah, that's right. Jerk me off."

Using every bit of skill she had, she brought him right to the brink but backed off every time she felt him get too close to coming.

His balls were drawn up so tight, she took pity on them and transferred her attention for several minutes. Rolling them in her hands, stroking one finger between them before dragging the tip back along his perineum.

He groaned, one hand reaching for her. But when she thought he'd pull her close so he could fuck her mouth, he only wove his fingers through her hair and cupped the back of her head. He used his other hand to stroke himself as she played with his balls.

She didn't know how long she watched him, holding onto the edge of her own orgasm by a slim margin.

## An Indecent Proposition, by Stephanie Julian

Finally his eyes reopened. "Suck me now, baby. I want to come in your mouth."

She didn't hesitate. She shot to a seated position on the edge of the chaise. Keeping her legs spread, she repositioned the vibrator as she opened her mouth and let his cock slip between her lips. Sucking him deep, she held him there, letting her tongue rasp against the slickness of his skin. He stilled for several seconds, head thrown back, the sound of his rough breathing scraping the air around them.

But she couldn't wait that long. She moved, pulling back until only the head rested behind her lips, swirling the tip of her tongue over the slit.

He smelled like clean male, tasted salty and hot. She let herself work him with abandon, shoving all reservations aside. She didn't want to rush, she wanted to savor.

She didn't feel like she had to perform. Instead, she let herself revel in the sensations.

And between the vibrator and the powerful sense that she controlled his desire, a raging orgasm built low in her body.

Increasing the action of her mouth on his cock, she sucked him hard, her cheeks hollowing. She shivered as he groaned, his fingers curling into her hair. The slight burn on her scalp heightened her desire.

She wanted him to come harder than he ever had before. He was in her power.

She dipped down on him again, relaxing her throat so she could take him even deeper. Then she swallowed and heard him swear in a guttural tone that tugged low in her pussy.

She tried to smile but couldn't, her mouth stretched around his cock. As she returned to the tip, she used her teeth to scrape against the skin, making his shaft jerk.

His hips began to move, shallow thrusts as he held her head steady. She let him fuck her mouth, content for now to know he enjoyed this. She concentrated on pleasuring herself, teasing her clit until she teetered on the edge but pulling the vibrator away just before she hit completion.

They did that dance for countless minutes, lost in a sexual haze.

Was it the sheer decadence of the situation that made this so much more exciting? And did it matter?

No. All that mattered was the pleasure. Giving. Taking. Making this man come. The power in that.

With a groan, he began to thrust harder. She felt his heightened sense of urgency.

When he growled low in his throat, she swore it reverberated in his cock, against her tongue. Then his hands stilled, holding her steady as his cock jerked in her mouth and he came.

His fluid hit her tongue and she swallowed the salty essence as she tilted the vibrator at just the right angle and let herself explode.

## Chapter Three

Holy Christ.

Erik had to bite his tongue so he didn't make a sound as he came in his hand.

Warm, sticky fluid spurted over his fingers and spattered against the leg of his jeans. His cock twitched for at least a minute, as he tried not to breathe too heavily and give away his presence.

He'd never come that hard by himself before.

But he wasn't alone, was he? What he wouldn't give to get out of the shadows and join them.

She ticked off every item on his fantasy girl list. Beautiful. Stacked. Adventurous. So very sexy.

Before the accident, he wouldn't have hesitated to introduce himself before seducing her into his bed, would've had no problem inviting Keegan along for the ride if she'd been willing.

Together, he and Keegan made for one outstanding fucking experience, one they'd perfected after years of practice.

Since the accident... Well, he didn't get out much. Or at all.

And certainly not to meet women. His libido had taken a nosedive since the fire.

Until he'd seen Julianne, he hadn't much cared. She'd reawakened something inside him that he'd been content to live without since the accident.

Now... Content sucked. Content should be a four letter word.

And it was all her fault.

He wanted to curse, wanted to scream obscenities until he was hoarse.

He wanted out of the damn shadows.

But he wasn't sure the beautiful woman who'd just sucked off his best friend wouldn't run for the front door the second she saw him.

\*\*\*

*A Very Naughty Xmas*

Keegan fell back into the chair across from the chaise, his lungs working overtime.

Holy hell. She'd made his fucking knees weak.

Jules had stretched back out on the chaise, eyes closed, one arm over her head, the other palm-up by her side. Her dark hair looked like an ink stain spreading across the pale fabric of the cushion, the vibrator abandoned by her side.

Had she come as hard as he had? She looked worn out but satisfied if the curve of her lips was anything to go by.

That mouth... Just looking at her made his blood flow south again. He wanted to join her on the chaise, kneel between her thighs and shove himself deep inside her. Then he wanted to take her ass while Erik fucked her pussy.

No chance of that happening, now, is there?

Shit.

At least a minute passed as they both caught their breath. Finally, her eyes opened and stared straight into his.

"Are you going to introduce me to the other person in the room now or are we going to continue to pretend he's not there?"

He didn't feign surprise. From what he'd learned from Carol, Jules was a smart lady. Intelligent, perceptive and sexually adventurous. Fucking perfect in his book.

She didn't seem shocked or morally outraged. She looked curious.

"Why do you think there's another man here?"

"Because I can feel him watching."

He thought about his response, considered simply outing Erik and letting him deal with the consequences. But he wouldn't do that to his friend. Still, he wasn't going to lie to the woman when she'd asked him a straightforward question.

"I'm not going to introduce you. He has to do that himself. But I don't think he will."

Would that taunt be enough to pull Erik out of the shadows? The challenge had been thrown. She knew he was here.

He didn't think Jules would turn out to be one of those women who flinched at the sight of Erik. If she did... well, then she wasn't the person he thought she was.

Sure, she'd be shocked. But he thought she'd be able to see beyond the scars. Maybe even to the person Erik had been before the fire. The one who'd actually enjoyed life. It pissed Keegan off to know Erik had lost not only his looks but also a shitload of confidence.

And that was the hardest part of all this—for both of them.

Jules' gaze narrowed on his just before she looked out into the shadows on the other side of the room. Where Erik sat.

She couldn't see him. Keegan knew that because he knew where Erik was and couldn't see him either.

Jules sat up, no hint of embarrassment about her partial nudity. "Are you going to join us or are you going to hide there are all night?"

Silence.

Damn it, Erik. Just fucking—

"Maybe you won't like what you see."

Erik's terse reply made Keegan's mouth drop open in shock. Maybe there was hope after all. And it all depended on Jules.

Keegan watched her consider her next move. She took her time before her attention returned to him. "Can I have my panties back? I'm feeling a little chilly."

"Of course."

He didn't want to give up the silky bit of fabric but he understood why she wouldn't want to sit here with her pussy on full display. After he'd handed them over, he reached for the chenille blanket lying over the back of his chair and draped it around her shoulders.

She gave him a grateful smile then stood, holding the blanket together between her breasts. Walking forward a few steps, she paused at the side of Keegan's chair.

"Maybe you should let me make that determination."

She spoke again to the shadows, responding to Erik's earlier statement.

Another silence held for several long seconds.

Keegan couldn't sit still any longer. He stood beside Jules and stared into the darkness.

Come on, Erik. Take that first step.

"I'm not a pretty sight for a pretty woman." Erik's voice held a hard edge of self-loathing. "You'll probably be happier if I stay back here while you and Keegan get to know each other better."

"While you watch?"

"Yes." He paused. "Unless you want me to leave."

She didn't hesitate. "I don't want you to leave. I want to see the man who's watching me fuck his friend. At least," she looked at Keegan, "I'm assuming you're friends?"

Keegan couldn't keep his smart-ass comment to himself. "Only if the bastard manages to grow a set and get out here."

A longer silence this time and Keegan's jaw tightened. Son-of-a-bitch. Erik wasn't going to—

The shadows began to move until they solidified into the form of a man.

## Chapter Four

Erik almost couldn't help himself.

He wanted to join Keegan and Jules so bad, he swore he could taste it. Still, he knew there was a high probability his scars would prove too much for her and she'd run.

He wouldn't blame her. He couldn't. There were days he couldn't bear to look in the mirror.

But the need to touch her, to actually participate in fucking her... He couldn't pass it up. With steady strides, he made his way into the dim circle of light from the fireplace. Gaze glued to her face, breath frozen in his chest, he watched her response.

Her head tilted to the side as he came into view, her eyes narrowing as if she couldn't quite make sense of what she was seeing, then widening as she did.

He stopped as her shock became evident, her mouth parting to draw in a sharp breath. He wanted to keep walking straight out of the room.

Fucking hell, he should've stayed in the shadows where he belonged—

Jules stepped forward, hands reaching out to him. She stopped before she touched him but her gaze held his steadily. "May I?"

She wanted to touch his face? Most women couldn't even look at it. The only people who had touched his face since the fire had been doctors and nurses. No one else had asked or even considered it.

"Why?" His voice emerged like a rough bark, revealing way too much about his mental state.

She didn't appear to be put off by his tone. "Because you need to see I'm not afraid of you. Are you in pain?"

Seriously? "The only pain I feel right now is between my legs. But, no, my scars don't hurt."

If he'd thought she'd stammer or be embarrassed by his crude statement, he'd thought wrong. Her expression never changed.

"How long ago were you hurt?"

"It's been two years. When they wanted to do a sixth reconstructive surgery, I said no. I'd had enough."

He was never going to look like he had before the surgery. Why put himself through the agony? The men and women who worked with him had gotten used to his appearance. Well, they no longer stared, at least.

Large crowds were a different story. He hated that everyone seemed to be looking at him, even if they tried not to. The few women he'd met the very few times he'd ventured out into society had practically run screaming. They couldn't look him in the eyes because all they saw were the scars on the right side of his face.

And those who actually could look at him stared with morbid curiosity instead. They wanted to prod at him, ask questions, dig into his psyche. He felt like a damn sideshow freak.

But he didn't get that vibe from Jules—and the lust pumping through his veins had to be ten times as strong because he hadn't felt it in ages.

Except for the night he'd seen her.

"I understand recovery from reconstructive surgery can be brutal."

Her voice held no pity, which would've turned him off more than if she'd gasped at his hideousness and run for the door.

"It had its moments."

"Is your body scarred too?"

"Yes. Both arms and hands and my left leg. Some on my torso." He paused, another thought occurring to him. "Are you asking if everything still functions correctly?"

She didn't respond, just continued to look at them.

He held out his hand. "I have an easy way to prove that to you."

She didn't reach for him right away but kept staring into his eyes as if searching for answers to questions she hadn't asked. He didn't know what else she could possibly want to know. This wasn't a date. It was more of a business transaction than anything else.

Since he was the one paying, he refused to answer any more questions. If she wanted to walk, now was the time. He opened his mouth to say that but before he could get the words out, she reached for him.

She didn't go for his hand, though. She reached for his cock, already hard again and straining against the zipper of his jeans.

"I guess that answers the question then, doesn't it?"

The sexual innuendo infused in her voice made his lungs tighten until he thought he wasn't going to be able to breathe. It'd been ages since a woman had looked at him like Jules was—with passion in her eyes.

Then she squeezed him, not hard, not to hurt, and he had to restrain the urge to grab her like Keegan had before and kiss her. Instead, he held himself still and let her explore him. With her gaze glued to his, she found his shaft and rubbed her palm against it. A slow steady tease that made his breath rasp in his lungs.

"How long has it been?" she asked. "Have you had sex since the accident? Or will this be your first time?"

Shock made him silent. He hadn't believed anyone could do that to him anymore. A flush rose in his cheeks.

God damn, he refused to be embarrassed here but he couldn't get his brain to come up with a reply. Why the hell would she want to know that?

"I only ask because if the first round is…brief…I can plan for a second. Wouldn't want anyone to be left disappointed."

Seriously? He didn't think she could disappoint him if she tried. Especially not when she reached between his legs to fondle his balls, rolling them with her fingers and making his dick throb.

"Then make your plans," he managed to say. "I think seconds are definitely on the menu."

Julianne would've been lying if she'd said she hadn't been shocked when this man first revealed himself.

But she'd taken care of her mom after her surgeries and she'd learned outward appearances didn't matter as much as most people thought.

Or, more specifically, men like her father. He hadn't been able to look at her mom after the double mastectomy. He'd only seen a woman no longer worthy of his time.

Fucking prick bastard. She'd called him that to his face after he'd blown through most their savings, spending the money on prostitutes and blaming his need for them on her mom's inability to see to his needs.

She'd had cancer, had barely made it through chemo and he wanted her to perform in bed.

Luckily, he'd left or someone would've had to call the cops to save his worthless ass from the Taser she kept in her pocketbook. The Taser she would have used on his pride and joy—his dick.

Her mom had survived. She'd beaten the cancer. She'd even managed to get back to work and attempt to pay off her bills. She'd gone through hell and come back.

This man had been through hell but was still stuck there.

Yes, his scars were ugly but he wasn't ugly. At least she didn't think so.

Or maybe that was the money talking.

Still, if she hadn't forced him out of the shadows, she could've fucked Keegan and taken the money. But her mom always told her she was like a dog with a bone. When she got hold of a puzzle or riddle or mystery, she couldn't let it rest until she'd figured it out.

She'd known someone else was in the room with them. She couldn't ignore it. She'd had to know. And now that she'd met Erik, she wasn't going to allow him to sneak back into the dark. She was baring herself in ways she'd never thought possible tonight. It was only fair that he and Keegan do the same.

"Do you and Keegan do this a lot?"

"What? Pay women to come to the house and fuck us? No. You're the first."

Her first instinct was to take offense at the sneer in his voice. She had a kneejerk reaction to slap him. But he was only answering the question she'd asked. And she heard the soul-deep hurt behind the sneer.

Keegan obviously didn't because he shoved Erik so hard, he stumbled backward.

"You utter, fucking bastard! What the fuck are you doing?"

"Keegan, no!"

She grabbed his arm, pulled him away Erik, who'd held his ground.

Glaring at Keegan, Erik let his hands curl into fists at his side but didn't raise them. "She asked the question. I told her the truth."

"You son-of-a-bitch." Keegan's voice had dropped to a vicious, angry growl, his accent thickening even more. "Do you really want me to tell her why you felt you had to pay her?"

Erik's jaw tightened until she thought it might snap and his mouth drew into a thin line.

"Nothing to say?" Keegan taunted when Erik didn't respond. "No, you don't because you're too much of a damn cow—"

"Stop! Now." If Keegan said anything else, she was afraid it would break something between them. "I already know why I'm here."

Both men turned to look at her, Keegan still furious, Erik with the wariness of a trapped animal.

"You think the only reason I would even consider sleeping with you is for the money, don't you?"

Silence fell until the only sound in the room was the crackling fire and the men's heavy breathing.

Erik blinked first, his throat moving as he swallowed. When he turned away from her, she saw the muscles on the undamaged side of his face jump.

He must have been a gorgeous man before the accident. Women had probably fallen at his feet.

Now... he wasn't hideous. Yes, he was scarred but that didn't make him a monster. It didn't make him a charity case either.

"I think we should start over."

Both men looked at her as if they had no idea what she was saying. Maybe they didn't.

If Keegan had tried to pick her up in the traditional way—without paying her hundreds of thousands of dollars to do it—she probably would have let him.

He seemed sweet and, though that didn't usually do it for her, he also made her want to get him dirty. Or at least try.

Erik... Erik had an edge.

She'd always gravitated toward guys with an edge. Guys who didn't always watch what they said around women and rode motorcycles that tore through the streets with ear-splitting roars and worked with their hands. Guys who drank beer and didn't say "Pardon my French" every time they dropped the f-bomb around a woman.

She wanted to see what happened when she pushed Erik past that edge. According to, well, everyone who knew her, she was good at pushing people past their limits.

Crossing her arms under her breasts so they pushed over the top of the corset, she was impressed as hell when neither man's eyes dropped to her chest.

"Start over how?" Erik finally said. "Do you want me to stick out my hand and introduce myself and say how nice it is to meet you when I've already watched you get yourself off?"

If he wanted to make her blush, he was going to have to work a lot harder than that. "Did you enjoy watching? Did you come too?"

Erik's gaze narrowed. "I did. All over my hand."

Smiling at the surly tone of his voice, she took a step closer. He didn't back away, didn't move a muscle. "Next time I want to watch you."

The corners of his mouth curled into the slightest bit of a smile. The sight made her heart beat faster. "Next time, I want to be inside you when I come."

She lifted a challenging brow at him. "Then you're going to have to change your attitude or you'll be relegated to the shadows for the rest of the night."

Erik's chin lifted. "So you're staying?"

She paused and she swore she heard Keegan draw in a deep breath and hold it. Erik flat-out refused to give her the satisfaction.

"I'll stay. For now. But I expect you both to make it worth my while."

"You mean—"

"Shut up, Erik. Just...shut up."

Keegan shoved at Erik's shoulder but Erik didn't budge. He didn't finish the thought either.

"Jules, would you like another drink?"

She gave Keegan a smile and watched him return it slowly.

Heat bloomed again between her legs, already so turned on she wanted to wrap her body around Erik and she how all that aggression translated into sex. And how the two of them would feel taking her at the same time.

And that had nothing at all to do with money.

As Keegan moved toward the bar in the corner, Erik threw himself on the coach by the fireplace.

He tried not to stare as Julianne walked back to the fireplace, hips swaying with mouth-watering grace. He knew she was exaggerating for him. Jesus, the woman could convince the pope to give up his vows.

She had a world-class ass that he wanted to smack while he knelt behind her and fucked her so hard she passed out. Lust boiled through his veins like lava and he forced himself not to squirm like a teenager with a hard-on in the hot teacher's class.

He needed a drink. Maybe more than one.

His cock already at attention, it thickened even more as she sank onto the chaise and laid herself out on her side, one hand holding up her head. She'd dropped the blanket she'd had around her shoulders onto the floor. This close to the fire, she didn't need it.

Long, dark hair fell to the chaise and pooled there. He wanted to wrap the length around his hand as he kissed her. Then he wanted to wind it around his cock.

She looked relaxed, in charge. And so damn sexy, he had the overwhelming urge to go over there and fall on her like a beast.

He managed to restrain himself. But only barely.

"So tell me, Erik. Do you and Keegan usually do one woman together? Is that the only way you can get it up?"

Keegan coughed from the bar area. Bastard. His so-called best friend was enjoying the hell out of watching her tie him in knots.

The corners of her mouth twitched, as if she knew Keegan was laughing.

He considered ignoring her but found he wanted to talk. Wanted her to talk, as well. "No, it's not the only way. But we've learned women can be very...grateful for the pleasure we can give her together."

"And how did you discover this?"

"In college." Keegan answered as he returned with a glass in each hand. He handed one to Julianne and the other to Erik then made a return trip for his own. "And we found we were good at it."

She took a sip of her drink. "Do you two have a thing for each other?"

It was a common question women usually asked because they thought he and Keegan were bisexual. "Nothing sexual, no."

"And Erik's the only one I would ever trust in this situation." Keegan sprawled back into the chair he'd occupied earlier. "We work well together."

And lately, it was the only way he got laid.

"Do you like to watch each other?"

Again, Erik got no sense that she was asking because she found it distasteful. She was simply curious. She wanted to know how they worked. He liked that about her.

Hell, he liked pretty much everything about her.

"It's not that simple." He thought about it for a second then looked to Keegan for help.

Keegan just sipped his drink and let him swing.

After a heavy sigh, Erik continued. "It's not like watching porn. It's more like sharing an orgasm with someone who appreciates it as much as you do."

Not that that made it any clearer. Still, Julianne nodded as if she understood.

"So if I get up," which she did, "and walk over to you," she stopped in front of Erik, staring down at him, "and tell you to take your clothes off so I can fuck you on this couch, Keegan will enjoy it?"

"Fuck yeah."

Erik heard Keegan's muttered response loud and clear. And apparently, so did Julianne.

Her lips curved in a sensuous smile that made it hard for him to breathe.

"Then take off your clothes, Erik. You look a little warm."

Erik had turned the heat up not long after she'd dropped her coat. He hadn't wanted her to be cold. Now the room felt like a sauna. But Erik was pretty sure that had more to do with his internal temperature than the room temperature.

With her hands on her hips, she watched as he leaned to the side to put his glass on the table next to the couch then reached over his head to pull his shirt off. If she was going to fuck him right here and now, he wanted to feel her skin against his.

Her gaze skimmed over the scars on his arms and body but, again, she didn't seem to be affected by them. When he reached for the button on his jeans, she followed his hand. As he lowered the zipper, he heard her take a deep breath as he bared his cock to her.

Most of his body below his waist had been spared from the fire, although there were a few spots on his legs. His cock had been completely unaffected and now jutted up from his groin, ten inches long and three around.

Women had been known to lick their lips when they saw him. Before.

Julianne looked into his eyes and smiled.

"Is that all for me?"

God, yes. "Absolutely. Why don't you climb on and I'll give you a good ride?"

"I think I will."

With a few quick movements of her hands, her panties and her corset dropped to the floor and she stood naked in front of him.

He sucked in a sharp breath, feeling like he'd been kicked in the gut.

Jesus, she was gorgeous. Her breasts were firm and high, at least a C-cup with just enough jiggle to prove they weren't fake. They were tipped with tight, light pink nipples. Her generous hips were curved and he couldn't wait until she turned around so he could see her ass. This woman wasn't anywhere near model skinny and was all the more beautiful for it.

He didn't have a lot of time to admire her, though. She took two steps forward, grabbed his shoulders and planted her knees on either side of his hips. Her pussy hovered inches above his cock and he felt the heat of it sink into his body.

God damn, she made him ache. He tried not to show how affected he was but it was becoming harder to breathe with each passing second. His hands clenched into fists at his sides but he couldn't contain the urge to touch her. He grabbed her hips, her skin hot and smooth as silk.

Tugging her closer, he nearly had her exactly where he wanted her. But she stiffened her arms and held him away. She stared into his eyes, forcing him to hold her gaze. Lifted one hand from his shoulder, she cupped his cheek. The ruined one.

The urge to jerk away flooded through his body, almost overwhelming. But he knew if he did, she'd just reach for him again. Or she'd move away.

He didn't want her to move unless it was onto his dick.

Forcing himself to stay still, his gaze never straying from hers. That connection sank deep inside him and put hooks in places he hadn't allowed anyone to touch in years.

"I'm going to fuck you now."

Her voice rasped against his libido, making it hard for him to breathe. His lips parted but he had no idea what to say. All he could do was swallow hard and keep his hands on her hips so she couldn't get away.

Something fluttered onto the cushion next to them, drawing her attention away.

A condom. She left it there for the moment.

She took her own sweet time. Reaching between them, she grabbed his cock and began to stroke him. A slow, steady pump that had him gasping for air in under a minute.

Christ, he was going to blow too soon. She worked him slow and steady at first, her hand soft after his cock. But soon enough she tightened on him, her pace becoming faster, her grip tighter. Maddening.

His hips wanted to pump but the angle was wrong. If she'd just fucking sit on his cock, take him high and deep inside her, he could relieve some of this building pressure. And when he started to groan every time her palm rubbed over the head of his cock, he'd had enough.

Before she realized what he was doing, he released one hand from her hip and grabbed the condom. She released her grip on him so he could roll it down his shaft. Then holding it at the perfect angle, he grabbed her hips and brought her down.

They both gasped as he plunged inside, her pussy tight and wet around him. So hot. It made him want to fuck her hard and fast until he came, pumping her full of his cum.

He barely managed to hold onto his restraint. He didn't want to hurt her but she looked a little stunned, her lips parted and her eyes dazed.

"Julianne. Tell me you're okay."

Her eyes had closed and, as he watched, her tongue slicked out to lick at her lips. His cock throbbed in response. He heard her suck in a rasping breath then let his gaze drop to watch her breasts as she drew in another and then another.

God damn, she had gorgeous tits. He wanted to taste them.

"Oh, my God."

His gaze flew back to her face as she whispered those words. With his hands back on her hips, he gave her a shake, just enough of one to make her eyes fly open and his cock pulse inside her at the sensation.

"Julianne. You gotta answer me. Are you okay?"

Her lips curved in a slight smile. "I'm fine. More than fine. Just fuck me. Now. Right now."

His entire body tightened as lust made him feel even more feral than normal. Then he took her at her word.

Using his hands to guide her, he lifted her up then let her fall back down. Every movement made her already clenching pussy even tighter.

He felt like she still had him gripped in her hand, milking his every movement. Because of the position, he couldn't thrust as deeply as he wanted but gravity helped. She slid a little farther down his shaft each time until she engulfed him to the base of his cock, her gaze never leaving his.

He hadn't looked a woman in the eyes while he fucked her since the accident. Hell, he hadn't been alone in a bed with one either. Keegan had always been there, too. Keegan and his unmarked face had kept the woman occupied while Erik fucked her from behind.

He hadn't realized how much he'd missed that connection, watching her eyes darken and her lids fall until her gaze was a bare slit. Seeing her lips quiver as she sucked in a shuddering breath each time he let her sink back onto his cock.

Her hands gripped his shoulders, each finger a separate brand as she held him tight. Her sheath rippled around him as he stroked her body closer to orgasm. He saw her fighting it off, holding back, and he wanted to snarl as he pumped into her, each movement becoming harder, tighter.

He wanted her to go over first, wanted to watch her come as he fucked her, knowing he alone had made her break.

Winding one hand into her hair, he tugged, causing her head to tilt back, arching her back until her breasts were within reach of his mouth. Bending forward, he put his lips around one tight nipple and drew it into this mouth. He sucked hard then used his teeth to scrape the hardened pebble.

Her groan rippled through his body, causing his hips to thrust a little harder, a little fiercer.

The sounds she made low in her throat made him feel like a beast conquering his mate as he worked her on his dick.

He tasted the salty sweetness of her skin as he licked a path across her chest to her neglected nipple. When he bit down, her hips rotated in a way that made stars flash behind his eyelids.

Jesus, that felt amazing. His cock responded with a jerk, but he grabbed her hips and held her still.

He didn't want to come now. Not yet. He wanted to savor this moment, draw every drop of pleasure he could from it.

Pulling away from her breast, he released her nipple at the very last second, making her squirm and murmur something that sounded like a complaint.

## A Very Naughty Xmas

"Stop." His voice sounded like ten miles of bad road and her eyes flew open and locked onto his. "Don't move."

She didn't speak and he thought maybe he'd lost her with the caveman routine. But she didn't move, just continued to stare into his eyes.

"I'm not ready to come yet. You feel too fucking good. So fucking tight. When I do come, it's gonna be after a good, long ride. And you're gonna go first. At least once."

Her lips curled into a smile that made his abs clench and his cock dance inside her. "You better hope you can live up to those words. You don't look like you have much control left right now."

Her pussy clamped around him, milking him, tearing at that control. He groaned, biting down on his tongue until he tasted blood, trying to bring his body back under control.

Then he smacked her ass, just hard enough to sting, and watched her expression go slack with pleasure, her lips parting on a gasp.

"I watched you that night at the party." He spoke through gritted teeth. "You never saw me. I watched you try to look inconspicuous but that's not you, is it? That's not the real you." He punctuated his words with another, slightly harder smack. This time she tried to roll her hips. He held her still, forcing his cock higher inside her. "You want someone to see you, really see you. See the sexy woman you really are."

Holding her hips again, he started an excruciatingly slow thrust and retreat that had her eyes closing tight. Every movement made his balls draw up tighter until they felt like solid stone. Not giving into the urge to come was taking a toll on his body he'd gladly pay forever.

He'd never felt so powerful as he watched each expression cross her face. He made her feel this way. He controlled her response and brought that look of sheer carnal lust to her face.

It healed a piece of himself he thought he'd lost forever.

With a groan, he wrapped his arms around her waist and gave himself over to the rhythm beating through his veins. Her head fell to his shoulder, her hair trailing over his chest, heightening each sensation.

Turning her head, she sucked his earlobe between her lips then bit it. The pain lasted only a second but it lit a fuse that'd been primed for weeks. Since the first moment he'd seen her.

Catching the ends of her hair, he tugged until she lifted her head. Blindly, he sought her mouth, sealed her lips with his, and shoved his tongue into her mouth to tangle with hers.

Her pussy felt wetter each time he pushed inside, her moisture soaking his cock and balls. Their skin, damp with sweat, fused together.

She moaned into his mouth as she came, her pussy quivering

around his cock, her arms tighten around his shoulders. He fought against the urge to release, but it was too much for him to take.

Seating her solidly in his lap, he thrust one last time, pouring himself into her until he had nothing more to give.

## Chapter Five

Julianne didn't know how long she lay against Erik, gasping for air. She'd come so hard, she swore her teeth were loose.

She should feel drained, exhausted. At the very least, sleepy. And she did. To a point.

More importantly, she felt energized.

Inside her, she felt Erik's cock still twitching. Her lips curved into a smile against the smooth skin of his neck on the undamaged side of his face.

Realizing her fingers were nearly embedded in his shoulders, she forced herself to flex them so she didn't draw blood with her nails.

He made a low sound of protest, which she soothed by caressing her fingertips over his nape.

He angled his head to the side slightly, exposing more of his neck. She followed his silent request and rubbed her fingers along the tight muscle.

They lay there, breathing, until she felt his cock slacken and moisture begin to drip between them.

"We're going to ruin this couch."

Her voice sounded husky, sexy, and he responded by turning his face and nuzzling his nose into her neck.

"I don't give a fuck about the damn couch. Don't fucking move."

Since she didn't really want to anyway, she figured it couldn't hurt to give into this demand—until she heard movement behind her.

Keegan.

She'd forgotten he was still there.

Which made her feel guilty for neglecting him. Which then made her feel ridiculous, considering the circumstances.

"I put a towel on the arm of the couch." Keegan pitched his voice low. "I'm just going to—"

"Don't go."

Her head popped off Erik's shoulder and she turned toward Keegan, still standing at the side of the couch. Their gazes connected and it felt right to stare into his eyes while trying to hold Erik's softening cock inside her.

Beneath her, Erik stilled, waiting. She didn't know for what. Did he think she didn't want to be alone with him? That she considered him damaged or scary or some other foolish thing?

There were enough undercurrents in this room to make her feel like she was drowning. The scent of sex surrounded her, the gazes of these two men weighed down on her.

She'd had the best sex of her life tonight and she didn't want to that to end yet. She wanted Keegan to stay. She wanted both of them to take her but she didn't know the right words for this exact moment.

Steady fingers gripped her chin and forced her to look at Erik.

"Say it. Whatever you're thinking, just say it."

Erik's voice made her nipples peak and pussy ripple with a fresh surge of desire, so strong it took away her ability to speak. She shook her head, unable to clear her head enough to say what was on her mind.

Erik continued on. "God, you are so fucking beautiful and sexy and brilliant, you make me want to be worthy of your attention. The first time I saw you, I knew we needed you. I swore I had blue balls for a week after that damn reception."

"It's true." Keegan moved closer. "He couldn't stop talking about you. I've never seen him like that before."

Keegan's quiet voice held regret and she grabbed for him, instinctively knowing he was about to back away. She caught his wrist just before he moved out of reach and held on tight.

"No. You're not going anywhere, Keegan." Taking a deep breath, she forced a little more spine into her backbone. As gracefully as she could, she slid off Erik's lap and stood, grateful her knees held her up.

"I'm feeling pretty damn naked all by myself. I want you both to strip. Now."

She held Keegan's gaze as she stroked her hand up his arm, brushing her fingertips through his hair. She'd expected the curls to be wiry. Their softness surprised her. She sank her fingers into those waves and exerted just enough pressure to hold his attention.

Stepping into him until her nipples brushed against his shirt, she tilted her head back and rose onto her toes until their lips were only centimeters apart. When she closed her eyes, she felt his hot breath against her cheek seconds before his lips took hers in a searing kiss.

Keegan kissed her with an underlying sweetness that made her ache low in her gut. Wrapping her arms around his shoulders, she sank into the kiss, giving over to the erotic pull of the sexual tension running between the three of them.

He grabbed her hips, pulled her tight against his fully erect cock. Rubbing her mound against that hard ridge, she wanted to climb him like her own personal Mount Everest.

As if he'd read her mind, he lifted her off her feet, aligning their mouths and bringing her clit into line with the tip of his dick. She wrapped her legs around his waist and lost herself in the carnality of his kiss, tilting her hips until she could get just the right friction on her clit.

She could come again with just a few more—

"No way, Jules." Another set of hands grabbed her hips and Erik's naked chest plastered itself to her back. "You don't come again until I'm deep in your ass and Keegan's fucking your pussy."

She broke off the kiss, gasping for air as his words shocked her. Lust blazed through her, stealing her breath, stealing her sanity. She couldn't believe how close to orgasm she could get from only the sound of Erik's voice. She shivered, tucking her head into Keegan's neck.

"Will you let me have your pussy, Jules?" Keegan's voice threw gasoline on the fire. With her legs spread, her sex felt so damn empty, she knew she'd agree to anything these men wanted.

"God, yes. Please. I need it. Now."

"Oh, no. Not yet." Erik ran a hand down her back, stroking her, petting her. "It's our turn to make you beg."

Yes, that's what she wanted—for these two men to give her what she needed.

She wanted to say yes but all that emerged was a moan because Erik had slipped his hand between her legs. He played his fingers over her labia and up to her clit, barely brushing against that little bundle of nerves but managing to make her shudder.

Shifting against Keegan, she opened her mouth on his neck, sinking her teeth into his skin as Erik began a wicked pattern, flicking her clit then moving back to wiggle one finger between her sex lips, working a little deeper each time.

Just a little more…

She tried to wriggle down onto his finger but Keegan's arms tightened and she couldn't move. She was totally at their mercy.

And Erik had none.

He played her ruthlessly, teasing her clit until she was right on the edge of orgasm then pulling back to knead her ass, leaving her high and dry. Erik used his other hand to wrap around her hair and pull her head back so Keegan could take her mouth again.

As he slid his tongue into her mouth, winding around hers, Erik pressed open-mouthed kisses to her shoulder.

God, she felt shaky, desperate. When Erik's hand returned to her sex, she felt tears form as he worked two fingers into her sex.

Yes. That's what she needed. To be filled, stuffed to capacity.

Two cocks. One man at her back, another man in front of her.

Yes, yes, yes.

"Let me have her a moment."

Erik's voice barely registered but she felt her weight shift as he wrapped one arm around her waist and held her against his chest. Keegan grabbed her ankles and unwound her legs from his waist, his motions jerky as he stripped off his clothes. She saw buttons fly off his shirt, making tiny pings as they landed on the wood floor. He didn't bother to untie his shoes, just toed them off and shoved his pants down his legs.

Arching her back, she reached above and behind her, her hands curving around Erik's neck, encouraging him to lean forward. He understood what she wanted and let her slide down his front until her feet hit the floor. His hands reached around to cup her breasts, kneading them, pinching the tight nipples with his thumbs and forefingers.

His cock pressed against the small of her back, a hot brand that made her sex weep with wanting. He bit and licked his way across her shoulders as she watched Keegan toss his pants to the side, after pulling a condom from the pocket, and step forward. His cock stood stiff and ready, and she reached for him, wrapping one hand around his shaft while the other went to cup his balls.

She rolled them in her hand, watched his eyes narrow to slits. His handsome face tightened into sharp angles and she knew he'd moved past slow and easy and into hard and fast. His gaze flicked to Erik and he made a motion with his head that Erik must have understood.

Swinging her into his arms, Erik took her back to the chaise. Keegan beat them there, throwing himself onto his back, rolling on the condom then reaching for her.

The chaise was wide enough that she could straddle his hips, in no danger of falling off.

She had the brief thought that they'd bought this piece of furniture precisely for this reason but the idea fled the second she positioned her pussy over Keegan's cock and began to sink down.

She got halfway, already feeling that wonderful sense of fulfillment combined with aching need that hit her just before an orgasm.

Opening her eyes, she smiled down at Keegan but his attention was focused on the point where their bodies joined, his expression tight with his desire to fuck her. So easy to read. So wonderful to see.

She couldn't remember the last time she'd seen that look on a man's face. Way too long. Her life lately had been consumed by work, by the grinding need to keep up with her mom's bills.

So much debt. Too—

"Jules." Keegan's hands grabbed her hips, holding her steady. "Look at me."

She hadn't realized she wasn't. Blinking back into focus, she fell into Keegan's gaze, entranced and trembling.

Shifting her weight, she wanted to take him all the way in. Wanted to fill the emptiness inside her with his cock and the warmth of his body and the way he looked at her that made her feel like a beautiful, desirable, special woman.

His hands tightened. "Stop, Jules."

She shook her head. "I don't want to stop."

"If you start to ride me, I'm gonna blow and then you won't have the pleasure of me and Erik taking you at the same time. Trust me, you want that."

Strangely, she did trust him. Both of them.

She turned her head, finding Erik beside her with his hand on his cock, stroking himself as he stared down at her.

Smiling, she crooked her finger at him. When he'd stepped close enough, she leaned slightly and took him in her mouth.

The head of his cock felt silky smooth against her tongue and his deep groan made her pussy clamp around Keegan's cock. Keegan's grunt of satisfaction made her smile.

*Yes, that's right. I'm still in control.*

Concentrating just on the head, she used her tongue to play at the slit and lick all around the spongy tip. Then she sucked hard, her cheeks hollowing. Erik sucked in a sharp hiss, his free hand going to her head. She thought he'd exert pressure, get her to do what he wanted, but he only let it rest there.

His cock felt like heated iron against her tongue, filling her mouth with his taste and her head with decadent thoughts.

She tried to move her hips again, needing more friction, but Keegan held her steady.

She moaned around Erik's cock, her hands tightening on his balls.

"Fuck." Erik's voice was razor sharp, making her pussy ripple in response, which made Keegan groan, his hips jerking, pushing his dick farther inside her.

With a gasp, she pulled away from Erik. "Now."

Her voice was little more than a growl, which made Erik's expression pull into sharp lines. He looked almost cruel but surprisingly, his scars softened his appearance.

She couldn't quite smile, she was in too much need for that but

Erik knew what she wanted.

Keegan's arms wrapped around her, forcing her to lay against his chest as Erik practically threw himself behind her. Keegan's legs spread to accommodate him, spreading her even further, making her pussy fairly burn.

She felt Eric moving behind her then felt a slick coolness dribble between her ass cheeks.

The anticipation was too much. She lifted her head and molded her lips to Keegan's. His groan intensified as she slid her tongue between his lips to taste him. Keegan's hips shifted and his hands pulled her down, keeping his cock buried deep as Erik's fingers spread the lube.

"You've been fucked in the ass before, haven't you, babe?"

One finger penetrated her ass, making her almost desperate for something bigger. More. Now. Clamping down, she felt Keegan's cock twitch in her pussy and he pulled away to gasp in air. Good thing, or she might've passed out too.

"Oh, yeah, you know what to expect, don't you?" Erik's voice sounded almost cruel, taunting, but the way he touched her... He wouldn't hurt her. "I'm going to give it to you, babe. Right now."

Pulling out his finger made all those sensitive areas tingle and quake.

"Fuck. Erik, hurry the fuck up."

She barely heard Keegan's voice over the beating of her heart but she certainly felt the head of Erik's cock as it pressed against that tiny opening. He forged ahead with steady pressure, one hand splayed on her back, the other gripping her hip.

The pressure of those two cocks lodged inside her built to an excruciating level. Erik's slow, steady progress only added to it. She needed that pressure relieved, needed them to move.

Keegan felt like unyielding stone and Erik... God, Erik spread fire.

She was stretched beyond pain, beyond pleasure. She needed—

"Fuck her now, Keegan."

Keegan groaned as he began to move, too slowly to suit her. He controlled his motions so carefully, dragging against the walls of her pussy so slowly, she almost didn't feel like he was moving. Erik stayed locked in place, his cock a red-hot pole that spread her ass past the burning point.

"God damn it, move, Keegan."

She wanted to scream the words but they emerged as a whisper. Even so, they must have affected him because he shoved back in with a hard grunt just as Erik began to move.

They began to move with a wicked coordination that took her

breath away. Jesus, she didn't know if she could take it.

She began to pant as they alternated their strokes. One in, one out. Slow as molasses. Hot as sin. She wanted to move but they had her wedged so tightly between them, she could only manage to shimmy.

And when she did, Erik held her even tighter and spoke into her ear.

"You stay right where you. No moving. We're in charge now."

"But I need you to move."

"Oh, we will. But right now, I want to enjoy the feel of you so tight around my dick."

"Christ, you're so fucking hot." Keegan spoke into her other ear. "I want to fuck you so hard, you scream."

Yes. Exactly.

But still they wouldn't give her what she needed.

They drew out their thrusts and withdrawals until she floated in a state of heightened arousal. She tried to concentrate, to feel each distinct cock inside her but she couldn't. They worked together so well.

Nerve endings snapped with sensation, her abdomen tight with expectation.

She gripped Keegan's shoulders but now she reached behind her with one hand, coming into contact with Erik's hip. Smooth, sleek skin. She grabbed him, dug her nails in and was rewarded with a hard thrust forward.

Erik's hand slid from the middle of her back to her hair, which he wrapped around his hand then pulled. It didn't hurt but was enough to get his point across.

And she totally ignored the warning.

She moved into Keegan's next thrust, making Erik scramble to stay with her. Her lips curved into a smile when she did the same to Erik and forced Keegan to move to stay lodged inside.

Control was hers once again.

She needed to make only tiny motions and the guys would do what she wanted—fuck her harder.

"Do me. Do me hard."

Her voice barely sounded like hers and that was okay. She didn't feel like herself. She felt like a goddess being worshipped.

Her men started to move faster. Sweat began to form, coating them all with a light sheen until their skin clung.

She lapped at Keegan's shoulder, the taste of him intoxicating. His chin lifted and she instinctively knew he wanted her mouth there. She obliged, licking at the hollow of this throat then biting the tendon.

"Fuck yes."

Keegan's hips began to move faster than Erik's, his cock swelling, making her even tighter. Behind her, Erik groaned and began to move faster. Soon they broke ranks, fucking her with their own rhythm.

She could barely stand the sensation, could barely breathe.

Another orgasm built but wouldn't break.

God, if she didn't come soon, she might shatter. She might—

With a groan, Keegan came, flooding her with warmth. His body shook beneath her as he pumped into her, triggering her orgasm.

Yes. Finally.

As she shook with the force of it, Keegan ground against her as Erik lunged forward one final time, burying his cock deep as he pulsed in her ass.

The sensitive tissues absorbed those pulses, prolonging her orgasm, stealing her breath and leaving her a boneless mass between their bodies.

## Chapter Six

Erik sat on the chair across from the fireplace, staring into the flames. But his gaze kept sliding to the door.

Keegan had taken Jules to the shower in the bath attached to Erik's bedroom on the other side of the house.

He should go join them. He wanted to join them.

Then what's stopping you?

Good question.

He could say the bathroom was too well lit but that would be a lie.

The bathroom would be pretty damn bright but the truth was he wanted to join them. Wanted to be with Jules. And that scared the shit out of him.

Which just pissed him off.

He felt like a fucking coward and it sucked.

After everything he'd been through, could a well-lit bathroom really have the power to bring him to his knees?

No. Because he knew damn well it wasn't the bathroom.

It was the woman. And that might be even more terrifying.

He didn't want a woman in his life. Not full-time.

The business was his wife and mistress at the moment. He and Keegan were building something. They had plans for the next five years, big plans. And that wouldn't happen if they split their focus.

Jules had the potential to be one huge focus-splitter. And not just for Erik.

He saw the way Keegan looked at her. His best friend wanted her just as much as Erik did, but Keegan, with his stick-up-the-ass, do-the-right-thing hero complex would step back the minute Erik expressed the slightest bit of interest in Jules that wasn't related solely to the bedroom.

So what the fuck are you going to do?

Damn good question.

If he followed them into the bathroom, Keegan would know exactly how he felt about Jules. He wouldn't be able to hide it because Keegan knew him better than he knew himself lately.

But if he didn't follow them, Jules would think he was an uncaring prick. And that wouldn't be right. At least the uncaring part.

He was a prick. He was driven and stubborn and he didn't typically give up on something until he'd caught it.

He'd thought after he'd had her, the gnawing ache in his groin would be gone. It'd only intensified.

He was on his feet before he realized he'd moved.

Fuck this indecision. He wanted to be with her. He'd blocked out this night—this one night—for her and he'd be damned if he spent part of it whining like a snot-nosed kid.

When he reached the bedroom, he heard water running but didn't hear voices. The door was open so he only had to walk over.

He stopped in the doorway, jaw clenching at the scene in front of him.

Keegan had her pinned to the wall, fucking her in slow, steady strokes. They were out of the flow of water but they were wet, skin glistening. He wanted to lick the droplets off her beautiful skin.

Keegan had his face turned away from the door and Jules' eyes were closed so neither of them noticed him.

Unlike before, when Keegan had been uptight because he'd felt they were deceiving her by keeping Erik's presence a secret, now he had no reservations. His hips worked with a slow, deliberate pace, drawing out the pleasure Jules was feeling, if the look on her face was anything to go by.

Her expression slack with desire, her hands clenched at his back. Keegan's skin had long red lines left by her fingernails. She'd wrapped her legs around his waist, her ankles crossed at the small of his back. Her hips arched forward on each of his thrusts, moving with him.

Erik couldn't believe he could get aroused so quickly just by watching. But his cock stood at full attention, almost painfully so. Still, he was content in the moment to just watch.

If he was watching porn, he'd be watching Keegan's cock fucking into her body, slow and easy. Instead, he watched her face, the subtle changes that signaled her feelings. How her breath hitched each time Keegan slid back inside. How she bit her lip when his hips began to swing harder and faster.

Keegan shifted her weight in his arms, lifting her high, getting a better angle. The muscles in Keegan's arms stood out in stark relief as he took all her weight, bouncing her on his cock like he was a carnival ride.

She appeared to love it, moaning as she arched her back, trying to get a different angle, a better angle.

God damn, they looked amazing together.

His cock ached for friction but he didn't jerk himself off. He wanted to take her one last time.

He didn't know if he groaned or made a noise but her eyes opened and she stared straight at him. Her mouth parted slightly but she didn't say anything, just stared.

She didn't have to say anything.

Stopping to grab a condom from the pile on the counter, he walked to the free-standing shower stall and drew open the door.

Keegan paused when he realized what was happening, his gaze swinging toward him.

Then Keegan smiled, a flat-out grin Erik hadn't seen in months. Not since the fire. It reminded him of the old Keegan. The one who'd come up with wicked schemes to pleasure women. Who'd taken a hell of a lot of pride in make a woman scream when she came.

"I think he wants to join us. Should we let him?"

Keegan spoke as if there was some doubt then rotated his hips, making Jules' eyes flutter shut for several long moments.

Her thighs tightened around Keegan's waist but he'd already started to pull her away.

Setting her on her feet, Keegan turned her so her back was against his chest.

"She's so fucking gorgeous, isn't she?" Keegan's hands wrapped around her waist then slid up until he cupped her breasts in his palms. They overflowed and Erik couldn't wait any longer.

He stepped forward and bent, sucking on one pink nipple into his mouth on a hard draw. Her hands sank into his hair, holding him tight, her gasp of pleasure turning to a moan as he bit her, hard. He didn't temper his actions. He was sick of not giving into his desires.

Jules had taken him, scars and all. Now he wanted to take her the way he knew would give her pleasure.

Dropping to his knees, he felt the water hit his back as he spread her thighs with his hands then put his mouth over her pussy. He licked at her clit, playing with the tight little nub while she cried out. He bit her, hard enough to make her gasp then licked between her lips to find her slit soaking wet and not just from the water.

He lapped up her juices then fucked her with his tongue, getting as deep as he could. Her hands yanked at his hair as he worked a finger into her ass, wriggling it in and out until she gasped his name.

She tasted fucking amazing and he would have eaten her to another orgasm if he hadn't had other plans. He pushed her to brink then pulled back, looking up at her dazed face.

As he stood, rolling on a condom, she maintained eye contact.

Keegan also watched him and now Erik nodded at his friend, who still wore his grin.

Taking her from Keegan's arms, he lifted her against him, on arm under her ass. When she had her arms wrapped around his shoulders, he used one hand to aim his cock. Then he let her sink.

His cock head breached her, her wet heat encompassing him inch by inch. She was so damn tight, her pussy clenching around him, that he had to strangle the urge to come. Once he had his cock entrenched, he nodded to Keegan, not sure he could speak, he was gritting his teeth so hard.

Keegan didn't need to be told what to do. He closed the distance between them, spread her cheeks and worked his cock inside her ass. Keegan didn't go slow. He took what he wanted, making Jules scream with pleasure.

This time, they fucked her hard and fast. No finesse, no stopping them.

He wanted to get her off fast and intense and then he wanted to blow his load. She barely registered as a weight in his arms, only as a pressure around his cock.

His balls tightened and he knew he was close.

Behind her, Keegan kept his own pace and the dueling sensations were enough to light her up.

This time when she came, she flooded him with her juices, pulling her along with him until his cum joined hers. Just as he pulsed one last time, Keegan pulled out, shooting his cum over her ass then rubbing his cock between her cheeks until the last drop had been spilled.

Hanging limply between them, Jules let out a deep breath then laid her head on his shoulder, her lips brushing against his ruined cheek.

He considered it progress that he didn't flinch away.

And he wondered if he'd be able to let her walk away.

Keegan sucked in a couple of deep breaths, made sure he had his legs under him then reached out to take Jules' limp body from Erik.

Erik held on to her, sliding an arm around her legs and holding her against his chest. Keegan's brows raised and, over her head, Erik scowled at him. The guy looked almost embarrassed as he carried her to the other side of the room.

Setting her on her feet, he wrapped her in a towel then gave her another to dry her hair. Jules gave Erik a sated, sexy smile as she sat on the vanity stool. Erik moved to the side but not too far away and Keegan wanted to pump a fist in the air.

Maybe now Erik would make his way back to the world of the

living. He'd been hiding long enough. Too long.

As Keegan grabbed a towel to dry off, he saw Erik do the same just before he excused himself and headed into the other room.

"When was he scarred?"

Keegan barely heard Jules' question, pitched low enough that Erik couldn't hear her from the other room.

He crossed the room to lean against the counter. She deserved the answers Erik would never give her.

"Two years ago. Someone sabotaged our lab. He wasn't supposed to be there that night. The explosion knocked him out. The fire spread fast and he was trapped. But he made it out."

Her eyes glowed with compassion, not pity. "Has he been afraid to go out since then?"

"He's only recently taken to working in the lab again. The scars were worse at first, and sometimes I think he doesn't realize how much they've faded over the past year. Sometimes—"

"You talk too fucking much."

Erik stood in the doorway to the bathroom, a furious look on his face.

Damn it. He'd probably heard everything and would be pissed as hell that Keegan had opened his mouth.

"Erik—"

"Do you always speak to your best friend like that?" Jules cut in, standing between the two of them. "Is that how you've isolated yourself, here, in this house? You use words to cut off everyone else, don't you? Push them away. Make them think you're a prick."

"How do you know I'm not? I did pay you to fuck me and my so-called friend, after all."

They were back to this shit again. God damn Erik. This time Keegan was going to break the bastard's jaw for disrespecting her this way.

Erik was expecting him to do exactly that. He didn't put up a hand to stop him. And neither did Jules.

Keegan's fist connected with Erik's jaw. He hadn't pulled his punch and Erik's head whipped to the side, nearly taking his entire body with it.

Sonofabitch. That fucking hurt. The bastard's jaw was still hard as a rock. Just like his head.

As Keegan cradled his hand to his chest, Jules stepped up next to him, her arms crossed.

"Feel better now?" she asked.

Erik shook his head, as if settling his brain back in the right spot, then rubbed a hand over the bruise Keegan could see developing.

"Yeah, actually, I do." Erik raised a brow at Keegan. "Do you? I know you've wanted to do that for months now."

Keegan grimaced. Yes, what he'd said was true but... "I won't allow you to be a bastard to her."

Erik immediately turned to Jules and bowed, looking slightly ridiculous with only a towel wrapped around his waist. "My most sincere apologies, Julianne. And my most sincere thanks. I would've never gotten him to take that swing if it hadn't been in defense of you."

Keegan's mouth dropped open before he slammed it shut. The bastard. "Why the hell didn't you just ask me to take a swing at you?"

"Because you wouldn't have done it."

He was right. No way would Keegan have ever hurt him, not after what he'd been through.

Keegan was still shaking his head when Jules rose from the stool and placed herself between them. "I think it's time I went home."

"No."

He and Erik spoke in unison and her mouth curved into a beautiful smile. The woman truly could make a dead man come, as the Stones had said so perfectly.

"Yes, it is. My mom and I have plans for tomorrow... Well, I guess I should say for today. It is Christmas Eve."

Neither he nor Erik had a comeback for that one. They hadn't really planned for the holiday. Erik's housekeeper had set up the tree in the living room. Keegan hadn't even bothered with one at his place.

He'd figured he'd spend Christmas Eve at the office then have dinner with Erik. Erik's mother always had them over for Christmas Day dinner because Keegan's family were all still in Ireland. Of course, neither of them really looked forward to that dismally formal affair and Keegan had actually considered feigning a migraine just so he wouldn't have to go. But he never would've left Erik to go alone. Angelica Riley really didn't live up to her name.

Erik and Keegan exchanged a glance, but neither of them had a good reason for her to stay.

Except that they wanted her to.

Keegan had it on the tip of his tongue to offer her a meal before she left, but Erik stepped forward.

"Thank you for coming tonight, Julianne. I'll get your clothes."

*** 

From the window, they watched her drive away in her twelve-year-old Honda Civic. Rust was eating away at the body, the right tail light was out and the engine sounded like a herd of braying donkeys being massacred.

"That damn car is a death trap." Erik's jaw felt so tight, he was afraid it would break. "Make damn sure she cashes that fucking check. If she doesn't, I'm going to deposit the money in her bank account personally."

"She'll cash it. She can't afford not to." Keegan sighed. "I'm starting to think this was a bad idea."

No, Keegan had known this was a bad idea from the moment Erik had proposed it. Erik just hadn't wanted to listen. He'd been so damn sure this was the only way he could get what he wanted and get her to take the money.

So why did he feel like a Grade-A ass now?

"We'll never see her again."

Another brilliant observation. "When did you turn into Eeyore?"

"When did you lose your humanity?"

"Fuck you." Shit, even he could hear the words had no bite. "You've been watching too many soap operas. Melodrama isn't your strong suit."

Keegan turned to him with a narrowed gaze. "And bitchiness isn't yours."

Erik's mouth screwed into a grimace. "She's gone. Time to move on."

"Neither of us wants to and you know it."

Erik admitted, if only to himself, that Keegan had a point. And that he might have fucked up what could have been a very good thing. He wanted to go after her, bring her back to the bedroom.

"So what do you suggest?"

Keegan just stared out the window.

"Let me think about it."

\*\*\*

Her hair still damp, Julianne drove away.

Five-hundred-thousand dollars richer and fighting the urge to turn around every other second.

It was stupid, really. Thinking the three of them had made a connection in any way other than just sex. Neither man had tried to stop her when she left. That in itself should tell her all she needed to know.

And yet...

She didn't think she'd seen the last of Erik and Keegan.

She started to smile.

## About Stephanie Julian

Stephanie Julian writes stories with alpha males—kinky hotel owners, geeky scientists, werewolves, berserkers, elves, Yeti and Bigfoot. Definitely not your average heroes. She blends hot sex, lush fantasy and gut-clenching emotion. There's a little something for everyone in her list, whether you like contemporary, paranormal, romantic suspense or a combination of all of the above. She's a Browncoat, a Whovian and a Trekker, and her captains are Mal, Jack and Kirk (either incarnation). She believes vampires do NOT sparkle, Bigfoot is real and the truth is out there because Giorgio says it is. A good night always includes a good book. And a good hockey game.

# Other Books by Stephanie Julian

See more of Stephanie Julian's books at www.StephanieJulian.com.

# Share Me

## Olivia Cunning

Share Me, by Olivia Cunning

# 1

The heavy bass guitar line that rumbled from the auditorium's loud speakers caused Lindsey's entire body to throb.

She'd been to several Sole Regret concerts at stadiums, so was painfully aware that their local auditorium didn't do Owen Mitchell's skill with four-strings any justice. The intimacy of the small venue made up for the inferior sound system, however. She'd never managed to get this close to the stage before. The anticipation of seeing the five members of Sole Regret from the second row had her rocketing out of her worn velveteen theater seat and leaning against the curved wooden chair back in front of her. She didn't even care that the move earned her several annoyed looks and a loudly hissed, "Sit down!" from someone behind her.

*Sit down?* At a Sole Regret concert? Was it even possible to remain seated when they were on stage?

Lindsey's best friend, Vanessa, grabbed her wrist and forced her to sit in her seat again. "Your boss is here," she whispered harshly. "Try to control yourself."

That was easier said than done. Lindsey squirmed on the edge of her seat. Hearing Owen play, but not yet being able to see him was hell on her girly bits.

When Lindsey caught her first glimpse of the bassist as he strolled casually across the creaky wooden stage, fingering thick strings with a steady cadence, she almost swallowed her tongue. The man was devastatingly gorgeous. His light brown hair was styled into a playful sweep that brushed his forehead. She couldn't see the color of his eyes from this distance but knew from staring at his pictures for hours on end that they were a hypnotic, brilliant blue. Her gaze moved from his perfect profile, down his neck to his body. Her hands clenched as she fought her need to launch herself on stage, tackle him to the ground, and explore every inch of his hard physique. Tonight Owen wore a tight navy blue T-shirt that clung to his nicely muscled chest and shoulders. A set of silver dog tags swayed between his cut pectoral muscles. As he

*A Very Naughty Xmas*

continued his intro, she became fascinated with the masterful movement of his fingers over the thick strings of his bass guitar. Why were guitarists so fucking hot? It simply wasn't fair.

Lindsey groaned aloud as she imagined all the things those strong, skillful fingers could do to her body. What she wouldn't give to be that man's fret board.

"Girl," Vanessa said, "you're seriously crackin' a moisty right now, aren't you?"

Lindsey's panties were decidedly wet. She couldn't deny it. "He's just so..." Her entire body shuddered as she couldn't find words sensual enough to describe the man.

Vanessa rolled her eyes. "Puh-lease. He's cute and all, but I don't think the mere sight of a man can inspire a big O."

Lindsey released a breathless chuckle. "You'd be wrong, Nessi. I'm halfway there already."

Vanessa turned her head in the opposite direction. "T. M. I," she said under her breath.

When the drummer, Gabe Banner, entered the song with a heavy, building progression of bass drum thuds, Lindsey's heart thumped to match his rhythm. She could just make out the red tips of Gabe's mohawk behind the drum kit and the occasional flailing drumstick as he pounded out a wicked progression of beats on the skins. As the tempo built, Owen turned at center stage and rushed forward, halting at the front edge as the rest of the band came into view and joined the song. Adrenaline surged through Lindsey's body. She was such a groupie for these guys. If her prudish boss, who was seated several seats to Lindsey's left, hadn't been sending her disapproving looks from behind her thick rimmed glasses, Lindsey would have already shed her bra and tossed it on stage. Fortunately, Lindsey still had enough self-control to keep from flashing her bare breasts at the band. Maybe.

Owen held a special appeal for Lindsey, but there was something about the band's vocalist, Shade Silverton, that demanded attention. He knew how to work a crowd. Shade encouraged the audience to its feet by holding one hand at waist level and lifting it up and down. Lindsey knew they wouldn't be able to keep to their seats long.

Even the stodgiest of attendees—who normally wouldn't conceive of attending a metal concert—obediently rose from their chairs. It was easier for Lindsey to enjoy herself when the two rather large men beside her blocked her from Mrs. Weston's ever critical glare of death. She was grateful to Mrs. Weston for hiring her to work at her investment firm, but the woman seemed to think she was in charge of every aspect of Lindsey's life—both inside and outside the confines of the office. It was

*Share Me, by Olivia Cunning*

a good thing Mrs. Weston wasn't a mind reader. She'd have been utterly scandalized by the X-rated thoughts racing through Lindsey's mind as she watched Shade sing the chorus of Sole Regret's hit song, "Darker." Tall, dark and mysterious behind his pair of aviator sunglasses, Shade Silverton gave off raw, sexual energy. What was it about the man that made her want to drop to her knees and suck his cock down her throat?

"Now that man makes my pussy quake," Vanessa said, her eyes glued to Shade, who completely dominated the stage with his unquestionable self-confidence. "I just want to…"

"Suck him off?"

Vanessa laughed. "Oh yeah. I'm on my knees already."

The rhythm guitarist, Kellen Jamison, was whispering into Owen's ear. They were both laughing at their lead singer and lead guitarist who seemed to be competing for crowd adulation. Lindsey worshipped the entire band. They didn't need to fight for her attention. But those two—Owen and Kellen—made her entire body hum with pent-up desire.

Where Owen had light eyes and hair, Kellen was a bronze god with shoulder length black hair and almost black eyes that could stare a person into a coma. She praised all deities that the man never wore a shirt on stage. His long, lean body was filled out perfectly with tight muscles beneath taut, tanned skin. Tattoos decorated both arms in colorful sleeves. There was an intensity about Kellen Jamison that she couldn't ignore. She doubted any woman could ignore it. And when he and Owen stood side-by-side, there was nothing more inspiring on the planet. That's why the pair of them were at the top of her fuck-it list. She and Vanessa had constructed their fuck-it lists a few months before when complaining about their concurrent lack of boyfriends.

The list was comprised of the three men on the planet she most wanted to fuck and, if given the opportunity, she was given a free pass to slut it up. It didn't matter if she was currently involved in a relationship, married, eight months pregnant, or had become a cloistered nun. If the man in question was on her fuck-it list, it didn't count against her. Vanessa said so and her friend had never steered her wrong. *Much.*

Number one on Lindsey's list was Owen Mitchell, and number two, Kellen Jamison, was standing right beside him vying for the top position. Luckily, Lindsey wasn't in a relationship or pregnant. And her current sexual dry spell might make her feel like a nun some days, but she hadn't taken vows of chastity. If only she could get close to them. Gain their attention. Offer her body willingly. Then maybe she could have at least one of the three men who made her drool like a recent root-canal-recipient.

In the middle of the song, the lead guitarist of the band, Adam

Taylor, moved to the front of the stage to play the solo. His dark hair was thick and cut in a shaggy style that drew attention to his face. He had the most sensual lips Lindsey had ever seen on a man. And a collection of chains around his neck and at his hip that she wouldn't mind getting tangled up in. Adam's lightning-fast fingers flew over electric guitar strings, churning up images of fingertips brushing against Lindsey's highly attentive body parts. He was about to kick David Beckham from the number three spot of her fuck-it list. Unless Shade wanted the honor.

"God, I'm so horny," Lindsey growled under her breath.

"I can help you out with that," Joe, who worked at her office, said in her ear.

It was like a cold bucket of water over her head. He hadn't been sitting beside her at the start of the concert. He must have weaseled his way through the standing crowd when she hadn't been paying attention. Lindsey shoved him out of her personal space and changed places with Vanessa so she'd have a best friend buffer that no man was likely to cross. The look Vanessa gave Joe—her dark eyes wide, eyebrows threatening her hair line, lips pursed in a harsh line—had him staring at his shoes and running a finger under his collar.

"That's what I thought," Vanessa said and churned her neck for added affect. "Lindsey done told you she wasn't interested. Bye now."

She had. Many times. She'd thought he'd finally given up. Joe hadn't bothered her in weeks. She must be flinging out pheromones like a bitch in heat or something. It wasn't as if she could help it. The members of Sole Regret lit her on fire, but she'd rather sate her lust with her battery operated boyfriend than with Joseph Bainbridge. She was so not attracted to him and never would be. There was nothing wrong with him, but there was nothing *right* about him either.

Joe sidled away and Lindsey returned her attention to the stage. The song came to an end and the crowd cheered, the riotous noise echoing through the auditorium like waves of an angry sea. Shade moved to the center of the stage and spoke to the audience.

"Thanks for coming to our benefit concert on this cold Christmas eve."

The crowd cheered.

"Ellie Carlisle wanted to be here tonight to thank you for helping her family out with her medical expenses. Unfortunately, after a strong dose of radiation therapy yesterday, they wouldn't clear her to leave the hospital. So tonight she's getting a lot of rest so she can wake up tomorrow and see what Santa brings a perfect angel for Christmas."

It might have been the sound system, but Shade's voice sounded a little raw as he talked about the Ellie, a five-year-old girl who was fighting for her life in a local hospital. The town had come together several times to try to help out her family, but pancake breakfasts and silent auctions for afghans only raised so much money. A Sole Regret concert, on the other hand, brought in folks and their money for hundreds of miles.

"Her father is a big fan of ours," Shade continued, "so when he asked us to come out and help them raise some money to help his little girl fight for her life, we couldn't say no."

"Be sure to buy a T-shirt on your way out," Kellen Jamison said in the deepest, sexiest voice Lindsey had ever heard. How could she possibly think about anything but the sound of that voice in her ear when it echoed around her from every direction? "All of the profits from merch sales go to helping the Carlisle family too."

Owen stepped up to his microphone. "You know what? *Fuck* cancer," he bellowed, thrusting a fist in the air.

He soon had the entire auditorium chanting, "fuck cancer, fuck cancer, fuck cancer" over and over again. Even stick-up-her-ass Mrs. Weston was yelling it along with the others.

When the crowd settled again, Shade said, "Thanks for coming out tonight and supporting Ellie's cause. Now we're going to rock your faces off."

Shade started the next song with a battle cry that caused a thrill to streak down Lindsey's spine. Hard to believe this group of bad ass men would be willing to give up their Christmas Eve to help out a little girl they didn't even know. Lindsey was surprised that tears were prickling at the backs of her eyes as she thought of their selfless act. Suddenly, the members of Sole Regret seemed more substantial to her than walking aphrodisiacs. She wondered what kind of men they were. Maybe she could find a way to get to know them. And not just so she could check two tasks off her fuck-it list. She had a powerful need to thank them for being awesome.

*A Very Naughty Xmas*

## II

Owen glanced around the tour bus, looking from one grim face to another.

You'd think his band mates had just come from a funeral, not from a kick-ass benefit concert that would likely save a little girl's life. Owen shifted his Santa hat to the cocked and ready position and reached for the black garbage bag of decorations his mom had sent along with him when she'd learned he wouldn't be able to attend their family's annual Christmas Eve celebration. His brother wouldn't be attending either—Chad had been deployed to Afghanistan in August—so Owen was somewhat glad that he wouldn't have to sit across the table from an empty chair and wondered if his brother was dodging bullets while he was dodging Grandma Ginny's questions about when he was going to settle down and make pretty babies for her to spoil. Though he missed his family as much as the next guy—yes, even Grandma Ginny—Owen wasn't going to lounge here on the bus and sulk all the way from Wherever-the-hell-they-were, Idaho to Wherever-the-hell-they-were-going, Montana. He was going to make the best of their situation and not let his bummed-out band mates ruin his perpetual good time.

Owen's prime target was Kelly. Not because the rhythm guitarist was the most depressed—that honor went to Shade—but because Owen needed a partner in Christmas cheer and Kelly always had his back. He didn't even have to ask Kelly for his assistance. They'd formed a pact of mutual mischief long ago.

Owen dug the snot-green, artificial Christmas tree out of the sack and set it on the end table between the pair of recliners where the band's drummer, Gabe, sat reading of all things and Shade sat glowering at nothing.

Straightening the branches of the tree into something slightly more pine shaped, Owen hummed under his breath and then broke out into song. *"O Christmas tree, O Christmas tree, how plastic are thy branches."*

Shade lifted his head and one dark eyebrow rose above the frame of

*Share Me, by Olivia Cunning*

his aviator sunglasses. "Do you have to be obnoxious right now?"

"Why," Owen said, "is it interrupting your sulking?"

"As a matter of fact, it is." Shade reached for one branch of the hideously fake tree and bent it into a wider angle.

"And why are you sulking? It's Christmas Eve. Are you afraid you'll get nothing but lumps of coal in your stocking?" Owen dove into the sack of decorations and pulled out several strands of lights. His family was of the opinion that it was not possible to have too many lights on a holiday tree. When fully lit, the Mitchell Family Christmas Tree could probably be seen from Mars.

"Julie only has one third Christmas." Shade arranged another branchthen dropping his hand when Gabe turned his attention from his book to watch him try to perfect the unperfectable.

"But she doesn't have to," Owen said. "You can give her another Christmas when we get home next week. She'll love that. I'll even wear my Santa hat and shimmy down the chimney to put a smile on her face."

Shade crossed his arms over his chest, his scowl deepening. "It's not the same."

"At least it isn't my fault he's sulking this time," Adam said. The lead guitarist had his acoustic guitar out and was quietly strumming some riff he was working on for the next Sole Regret album.

"I'm not sulking," Shade said.

"Looks like sulking to me," Kelly said. He rose from the sofa to stand beside Owen. He inserted a long, tattooed arm into the sack and dug out a red rope garland. He lifted his eyebrows at Owen, before flicking his eyes at Shade pointedly.

Owen tried not to grin and give their silently exchanged plan away, but it wasn't easy. He nodded ever-so-slightly.

"You're the one who signed us up to play a benefit concert on Christmas Eve in the first place," Adam said to Shade. "You don't even know that kid."

Owen winced. Did the two of them really need to pick a fight tonight? Surely they could find it in themselves to put aside their differences on Christmas Eve.

"I didn't have to fucking *know* the kid, Adam. She has leukemia. Her family has no insurance, no jobs, no money to pay for her chemotherapy. A few hours out of our busy schedules gives her a chance to see her sixth birthday. Do you always have to be such a selfish prick?"

"I had absolutely no problem with doing the benefit concert. It's not like I have better plans for Christmas anyway and, believe it or fucking not, I do care. But you sitting there looking like your dog just died after you made the decision to do the concert in the first place is pissing me off. I'm not gonna lie," Adam said.

"There's a first time for everything," Shade grumbled.

"All I want for Christmas is a pair of ball gags to shut you both up." Gabe lifted his book until all that was visible of his head was his foot-high red and black mohawk. "I'm trying to concentrate over here."

"Ball gags?" Kelly nodded. "I can probably fulfill that wish." He started to wrap the rope garland in long loops from hand to elbow. Owen knew Kelly could produce two ball gags in a matter of minutes. He also knew exactly where Kelly kept his secret stash of kinky implements if he ever felt the need to borrow something. Recently Kelly had taken up a new hobby—tying knots. It was a perfectly innocent hobby for most people, but not so much for Kelly.

Carefully untangling a strand of lights, Owen pretended to be intensely interested in their drummer, Gabe, to keep attention off Kelly, who was fashioning a loose noose out of one end of the garland. The dragon tattoos on the shaven parts of Gabe's scalp stood in complete contradiction to the colossal, decidedly boring book in his hands. "What are you reading about?" Owen asked, as if he didn't already know he didn't give a shit.

Gabe pushed his reading glasses up his nose and grinned deviously. "Friction."

"And how to reduce it with proper lubrication?" Owen asked. Gabe was the only person he knew who tried to apply the laws of physics to sex.

"You don't want to reduce the friction too much," Gabe said. "You want it slick and wet, but not too juicy."

"I disagree," Shade said with a grin. "The juicier, the better." At least his sulking had diminished.

"Yeah," Kelly agreed. "I like it dripping wet so I can lick it clean."

"The conversation on this bus always turns to pussy," Adam said.

"There's nothing better to talk about, is there?" Owen asked.

"No," his band mates said in unison. They all laughed at the one thing they *always* agreed on.

"And there's definitely nothing better to think about," Gabe said, "so you all need to shut up. I'm *thinking*."

"Who needs this worse, Owen?" Kelly said. "Shade or Gabe?" He was now prepared to act on his plan.

"Personally, I think they both need it," Owen said.

"Need what?" Shade asked.

"Looks like Shade volunteered to be first."

"First at what?"

Kelly moved fast—*like ninja*—and Owen stepped back out of his way, awaiting his opening to assist him.

Shade was bigger than Kelly, but Kelly had the element of surprise on his side. Before Shade could even react to Kelly jumping on him, Kelly had the garland of red rope around Shade's forearms, binding them together from wrists to elbows. Shade might have been able to break free of the garland given time, but the instant Kelly stepped away, Owen went after him with strands of lights, wrapping several strands around Shade's upper arms and chest, crisscrossed in a web of unbreakable art. Kelly had taught Owen all he knew about shibari and Owen had taught Kelly all he knew about calf-roping. Their combination of skill, teamwork and speed ensured that Shade wasn't going anywhere until they decided to free his arms.

As was common for Shade, once he got over his recent, perpetual dour mood—his divorce was to blame—he was happy to join in on their fun and play along. He laughed as a second strand of lights secured him to the chair around the waist. He was in danger of hyperventilating with laughter when Kelly found some sparkly tinsel in the sack and wrapped it around his neck several times.

"Now you have no choice but to be in the Christmas spirit," Owen said. "No more bah humbug out of you."

Chuckling at the spectacle the coolest member of the band made trussed up like an abomination of a Christmas tree, Adam added to the festivities by strumming Christmas carols on his guitar. *"On the first day of Christmas my buddies gave to me, decorations on a Shade tree."*

"Shut up," Shade yelled, but he was snickering too intermittently for anyone to take him seriously.

Kelly found a gaudy tree topper in the sack. Before he could add it to their *tree*, Gabe snatched the tinsel-trimmed star out of Kelly's hand and set it on the pinnacle of their Shade tree. Gabe wrapped the light cord under Shade's chin and then around the star to hold it somewhat upright atop Shade's head. Apparently, Gabe had given up on reading his *The Physics of Fucking and Friction* book or whatever it was called. None of them could resist messing with Shade. He worked so hard at being cool onstage and in public. Sometimes they had to remind him that he could still act like a kid and have some stupid fun when there wasn't anyone important watching.

Gabe found a package of blue glass bulbs in Owen's sack of Christmas cheer and dangled them from the strand of lights near Shade's crotch.

"You did not just give me blue balls, Force," Shade said with the deep, commanding voice that made their road crew scramble for their lives.

Owen laughed.

Adam added to his song, "*On the second day of Christmas my buddies gave to me, two blue balls and decorations on a Shade tree.*"

"I will give you blue balls when I punch you in them," Shade said.

"You shouldn't threaten people when you can't fight back," Adam said.

"Plug him in," Owen said, hoping Shade and Adam didn't actually get into more than a pissing contest.

Kelly located the power cord and plugged it into the outlet behind his chair. Gabe plugged the star into the end of one of the light strands.

When the multicolored lights began to flash and cast brilliant specks of lights all over their tattooed, buffed-out, sunglasses-wearing lead singer, they all burst out laughing. Owen grabbed his cellphone out of his pocket. "Okay, this is going on Facebook."

"Don't you dare," Shade said, his smile fading and mouth opening in exasperation.

Oh, Owen dared. He even gave the candid picture a caption—*All Dressed for Christmas with No Place to Go.*

"Hey, guys?" their driver, Tex, called from the front of the bus. "We're going to have to pull over soon. The snow is coming down so heavily I can't see the road. We better park until it lets up or a snowplow blows through."

Snow! Oh yes. A perfect addition to Shade's festive attire.

"Sweet." Owen grinned at Kelly who quickly caught on to his newest nefarious plan.

"Shade tied down," Kelly said.

"Plus snow," Owen said.

"Equals projectile fun," Gabe said.

"You guys wouldn't fucking dare." Shade tried to lean out of the chair, but found that while he'd been tethered mostly by complacency at first, he now had no choice but to stay put.

Owen grinned and straightened his Santa hat. "Wouldn't we?"

## III

Lindsey squinted at the dark road ahead. The wipers scraped rhythmically across her field of vision to keep the thick snow at bay, but she was fixated on the glowing red taillights of her favorite band's tour bus. Storm or no storm, she wasn't giving up now. It had been a stroke of luck that Sole Regret's bus had turned out in front of her car as she pulled out of the auditorium after the benefit concert. Instead of taking the proper road toward home, she had continued following them eastward out of town, through the wilderness and up into the mountains. It was pitch black out here in the middle of nowhere and what had started out as a few flurries was now becoming a blizzard.

"It's getting really bad out," Vanessa said from the passenger seat. "We should have gone home instead of following their bus. The farther we go, the worse this shit gets. Can you even see the road?"

"Yeah, I'm used to driving in the snow. And they have to stop sometime," Lindsey said. "I want to meet them and thank them for helping out the Carlisle family."

Vanessa chuckled. "Bullshit, girl. You want to bone them."

Lindsey bit her lip. "Yeah, I do—all five of them—but just meeting them will be orgasmic enough."

Her engine roared as her front tires lost their grip and spun in the slick, wet snow. The car skidded slightly, before finding a better patch of pavement and righting itself.

Vanessa was clinging to the dashboard with long red nails. "Girl, you and your horny vagina are gonna get us both killed."

"It's fine," Lindsey said and laughed. "Well the car is fine. The vagina is still horny. God, those guys were hot on stage." She shuddered at the mere memory of their blatant sexuality. Just watching them perform made her wet and achy between her legs.

"That ain't no lie," Vanessa said. "Too bad they's all white boys."

"Once you go white, you think it's all right." She shrugged.

Vanessa laughed. "Girl, you are too much."

"You know you love me," Lindsey said. They'd been best friends since elementary school and twenty years later, still did everything together. Well, almost everything.

"You're lucky I don't jack your car and get us off this damned mountain," Vanessa said.

"You are all talk, Nessi. You know you want to meet them too."

"Maybe a little." Lindsey could hear the smile in Vanessa's voice. They liked to tease each other and pretend they were as different in attitude as they were in looks, but they really did have almost everything in common—including their taste in music and men.

The right blinker on the bus ahead began to flash. Lindsey saw the sign for a scenic turn out and turned on her blinker to follow them. Finally, her chance. Assuming they didn't think she was bat shit crazy for following them over seventy miles through a blizzard and falling at their feet to dry hump their legs.

The bus pulled to a stop and Lindsey parked behind it. She left the car running, the wipers working extra hard to keep the fluffy white flakes off the windshield. Lindsey's heart thudded faster and faster at the thought of getting out of her car, knocking on the tour bus door and offering her body to anyone who would have it.

"You're going to chicken out, aren't you?" Vanessa said.

"No, I'm just thinking about how to approach them."

She could barely make out Vanessa's rolling eyes in the glow of the dash lights. "Whatever. You say *I'm* all talk. You might *think* you've got the guts to raid their tour bus for cock, but sweetie, I know you. You ain't a ho."

"I'm three times the ho you are, beotch."

Vanessa sniggered. "So what you're saying is you're a ho ho ho?"

Lindsey laughed. "Yeah, when it comes to any member of Sole Regret I'm a ho ho ho." Once she got tickled, she couldn't stop laughing for several minutes. She had to wipe tears out of her eyes with her thumbs. "God, we're corny. No wonder we can't snag decent boyfriends."

"What are they doing?" Vanessa asked, her attention now outside the car.

Lindsey's head swiveled and her heart almost stopped. The band's bassist, Owen had just launched himself out of the open bus door and onto the back of rhythm guitarist, Kellen. Kellen, who was inexplicably shirtless in a snow storm, flipped him into a snow bank and scooped up a handful of snow. He began to pack the fluffy flakes into a large ball. Owen retrieved his Santa hat from the snow and dove for cover behind the front of the bus. A battery of snow balls flew from Owen's hiding place and pummeled Kellen in the chest.

She caught a glimpse of a red and black mohawk just above Owen's hat.

"Gabe too?"

"Adam is sneaking around back." Vanessa pointed at the dark shadow at the rear corner of the bus. "The only one missing is the hottest of the bunch."

"Shade?"

"I'm sure he's too cool for this childish bullshit." Vanessa opened her car door. "All right, chicken shit, you brought us all the way up here to make complete asses out of ourselves, we might as well go talk to them."

"What? Wait! We don't have to. Let's just go home."

But Vanessa had already climbed out of the car and closed the door. Lindsey took a deep breath, shut off her car, pocketed the keys and then surged into the uncharted snowstorm. Vanessa always gave her courage. With Vanessa at her side, Lindsey could have slain dragons, swam the Mediterranean Sea, or even talked to a rock star.

Vanessa was already shaking hands with the lead guitarist of the band, Adam. He'd been the closest target, but Lindsey really wanted Owen. Or Kellen. Or Owen *and* Kellen. So she headed into the epic snowball battle. Heart thundering in her chest, stomach a bit queasy, knees quaking, Lindsey stepped up behind Kellen and was about to tap him on the shoulder which was decorated with an amazingly realistic tattoo of a rearing black stallion, when he suddenly ducked. Fast—*like ninja*.

A barrage of snow balls walloped Lindsey in the face, neck and chest, catching her so off-guard that she just stood there and took every last one of them at full force.

"Oh shit," someone said. "Why did you duck, Kelly?"

A very large, wonderfully strong hand began to brush snow out of her face. "Are you okay?"

She was suddenly looking up into the gorgeous, strong-featured face of Kellen Jamison. "I am now," she whispered.

## IV

Kellen winced at the welt under the attractive young woman's right eye. "That had to hurt," he said, gently rubbing the mark with his thumb.

"Um," she said.

He smiled. He could tell she knew who he was. She had that starstruck look on her face he knew so well. "I'm Kellen."

"Yes."

"And you would be?" She had the biggest blue eyes he'd ever encountered. He was a sucker for that wide-eyed innocent look and if her eyes got any wider, they'd likely fall right out of her head.

"Um." She blinked and then scowled as if suffering from amnesia.

"Lindsey!" another woman ran over and began to fling snow from Lindsey's sweater. It hit Kellen in the chest, but she didn't seem to notice. "Oh my God, girl, what were you thinking? You could have been killed."

"I don't think snowballs are lethal," Kellen said. The look Lindsey's friend gave him could have melted the snow off the entire mountain.

"What kind of crazy person pelts a poor, defenseless woman with snowballs?" the woman said, flinging snow from Lindsey's chest like a weapon now.

*Defenseless?* The only thing that got Kellen's blood pumping hotter than that big-eyed innocent look was a defenseless woman. Tied down. Spread wide. Pussy open and exposed for him to feast upon. Kellen's mouth went dry as images of their guest spread across the tour bus bed entered his mind. Would her eyes get wider when she came or would she squeeze them closed? Damn, he hadn't been the least bit horny two minutes ago and now his cock was fully erect and straining against his zipper.

It couldn't be helped. Lindsey was exactly his type.

*Merry Christmas to me.*

Owen jogged over and assisted Lindsey's hot-tempered friend in cleaning the snow off of his accidental target. Rather than helping

*Share Me, by Olivia Cunning*

Lindsey, Owen's hands on her made her shake uncontrollably.

"You must be freezing," he said. "Do you want to come inside and get dried off? We have towels. And I think we have hot chocolate." Owen turned toward the open bus door. "Tex! Make some fucking hot chocolate!"

Lindsey's friend nodded toward the car behind the bus. "We should probably get—" Her words were halted when Lindsey covered the woman's mouth with one hand.

"Yes, thank you," Lindsey said. "I'm liable to freeze to death if I don't get out of this wet sweater." Lindsey glanced back at the small car. Besides the spot of emerald green on the hood over the hot engine, the entire car was already white with a coating of snow. "And I don't think it's safe to drive in this weather."

She blinked up at Kellen, snowflakes clinging to her long lashes and Kellen decided he would have ripped the engine out of her car and tossed it off a cliff to keep her from leaving. And if she wanted Owen, well, he never had a problem with sharing. As long as he got to eat out the juicy delight between her thighs before Owen got down to business, Kellen would be satisfied. He just wanted to taste her. Every woman tasted different and he was a connoisseur of pussy. He couldn't get enough. He could lick it and suck it and kiss it and nibble on it for hours. Or until she begged for mercy.

Owen took Lindsey by the hand and yanked her toward the bus, breaking the spell she had over Kellen. "Let's go get you warmed up," Owen said.

"Yes," Kellen murmured to himself. "Let's do that."

## V

*Oh God. Oh God. Oh God. Oh God.*

Those were the only words that were capable of echoing through Lindsey's mind at the moment. She was really here. *Oh God.* And Kellen really had touched her cheek and looked at her as if he wanted to fuck her brains out. *Oh God.* And Owen really was holding her hand and leading her up the stairs of Sole Regret's tour bus. *Oh God.* And Shade really was tied to a recliner, flashing with multicolored lights, and looking out of sorts.

"Oh God!" she yelled and burst out laughing. Lindsey covered her mouth with one hand as she tried to comprehend what she was seeing. Well, whoever had turned Shade Silverton into a shidari bondage tree was one hundred percent hilarious. And the pair of blue Christmas balls hanging at crotch level? Priceless.

"We have guests," Owen said to Shade as he led Lindsey past him. "Make yourself presentable."

"Fucking untie me," Shade demanded, straining bulging muscles against the intricately crisscrossed strands of lights. A garland rope bound his arms together from wrist to elbow.

"Don't you dare untie him," some man she didn't recognize said from the kitchen area. He was scooping hot chocolate mix into over half-a-dozen mugs. "He needs to get his sense of humor back. That bitch, Tina, sure did a number on him."

"Un-fucking-tie me," Shade growled between clenched teeth.

"Oh my," Vanessa said from the bus entryway. "Heavens."

She probably thought seeing Shade tied to a chair was hot regardless of the flashing multicolored lights and the slightly askew star on his head.

Owen paused at the end of the corridor and opened an oddly narrow door. He pulled out a towel and handed it to Lindsey. She patted at the melting snow around her neck. It was starting to melt and trickle down between her breasts, but the chill had nothing to do with how hard her nipples were. The musky, sweet scent of Owen's cologne and the ornery look in his blue eyes was one hundred percent responsible for that.

A hand settled at the base of her spine and she didn't have to look over her shoulder to know Kellen was standing directly behind her. That gentle but commanding touch was one hundred percent responsible for the pulsating throb in her panties.

"Would you like to change your sweater?" Kellen's deep, quiet voice made Lindsey's eyelids flutter.

She'd like to rip her sweater off and light it on fire was what she'd like to do. That would ensure she'd have a good excuse to be half naked in the presence of strangers. Except they didn't feel like strangers. She felt as if she knew the entire band. And she definitely wanted to get to know them better. Especially the man directly in front of her and the one behind her, who made her feel like the giddiest piece of cheese to be melted between two hot pieces of toasted bread.

"Lindsey?" Kellen's voice brought her out of her fantasy.

And he knew her name. Squeeee! "Um, yeah." She hoped her voice didn't belay her enthusiasm to get naked. "Do you have something I can change into?" *Nothing, for example.*

Owen opened a door at the end of the corridor and entered a bedroom. Lindsey followed him without hesitation. When the door closed behind her, she didn't need to turn around to know Kellen had entered the room too. She could feel his presence behind her.

"You were following us, weren't you?" Owen asked.

Her face flamed. She supposed it was pretty obvious. "My friend Vanessa and I were at the benefit concert and we ended up behind your bus. When we saw you pull over we thought maybe we could meet you." It wasn't a lie.

"And how did you imagine that meeting would go?" Kellen asked. Dear lord, the man had a delicious voice. He was nice to look at too, but the mere timber of his voice was enough to separate her from her panties. She just wanted to obey him, even though he hadn't asked her to do anything.

"Well I didn't think I was going to get attacked with snowballs," she said and laughed. Her laughter died when Kellen's hard body brushed against her from behind. Her breath stalled in her throat and her eyelids fluttered closed. Her body naturally leaned against his. He was so solid. Hard. His skin cool. And she felt the huge ridge of his arousal against her ass. *Oh dear God.*

"Kelly has a thing for your type," Owen said.

"Yes, I do." Kellen's warm breath stirred a few damp strands of hair against her ear and her knees went weak.

One of Kellen's strong hands splayed over her belly to keep her from sliding to the floor.

"What do you want to do to her, Kelly?"

"I want to tie her down and eat her pussy. After I'm finished and she doesn't think it's possible to come another time, I want to watch you fuck her, Owen, and prove her wrong." His hand slid up her ribcage, stopping just short of cupping her breast. "Is that what you had in mind when you followed us up the mountain, Lindsey?"

She tried to draw in air, but she was so lightheaded, her brain wasn't functioning correctly. Did he just say that? Or was she suffering from hypothermia in her car and hallucinating? That bulge against her ass felt real enough.

Kellen nipped her ear and her entire body jerked. "Answer my question."

She opened her eyes. Owen was gnawing his bottom lip awaiting her answer.

"No," she whispered, her voice trembling.

Owen scrunched his face in disappointment and then glanced over her head to look at Kellen. Kellen took a step back and Lindsey reached behind her to tug him against her again.

"That's far more than I bargained for," she said, "but I want you. Both of you. To do exactly that. And more."

"You're sure?" Kellen deep voice did all sorts of tingly things to her spine.

"Yes."

"Once I have you tied, you won't be able to escape."

Her heart thundered in her chest. What would they do to her while she was utterly defenseless? She couldn't wait to find out. "I understand."

"Kellen knows what he's doing. He'll stop if you're in distress," Owen said.

"You'll be at my mercy," Kellen whispered. "I'll be able to do whatever I want to do to you."

She groaned.

"Does knowing that make you afraid?" Kellen asked. "Are you trembling because you're scared that we'll hurt you?"

"No," she whispered. "I'm trembling because I'm so turned on that I'm about to come."

Kellen's cool hands slid under her sweater and lifted it to expose her belly. "Make her quiver, Owen."

Owen bent forward to kiss and suckle and nibble on her belly. Sparks of pleasure danced across her skin. She was instantly reduced to quivering. The man had an amazing mouth.

Lindsey's sweater passed over her head and then Kellen's strong hands covered her breasts. She cursed her bra, wanting his cool palms against her bare nipples. They strained against the cups of her undergarment, seeking the pleasure offered by his hands.

A knock sounded on the door. Lindsey's entire body jerked.

"Hey, Kellen," a voice with a strong Texan accent said on the opposite side of the closed door.

"We'll take a rain check on that hot chocolate, Tex," Kellen said.

"That's not the problem. This chick out here is trying to *help* Shade by untying him and I think she's somehow managed to cut off the circulation to his dick and one of his spare legs."

Kellen released a heavy sigh and dropped his hands. Lindsey stifled a sob of protest as his warmth faded from her back. "I'll be back in a minute," he said. "Owen, I want her ready for me when I get back."

"She'll be ready."

Lindsey wasn't sure what either of them meant but hoped making her ready involved more of Owen's mouth on her skin.

The door closed as Kellen left the room.

Owen grinned at her and she couldn't help but smile back. The man was cute and sexy and evoked a feeling of joy whenever she looked at him. She was pretty sure it wasn't due to the Santa hat he still wore, but she was definitely feeling some Christmas cheer.

"So what did Kellen mean about getting me ready?" Because she was already horny—her sex hot and swollen and seeping. She'd been horny since Owen had entered the stage back in the auditorium a few hours earlier. And as each member of Sole Regret had entered the stage on cue, the intensity of her desire had increased exponentially.

"Once Kellen has a game plan, he doesn't fuck around. He wants you naked, wet and limbered up."

Her jaw dropped and he laughed.

"How flexible are you, Lindsey?" he asked.

Kellen might be the one who seemed to be in control, but she was starting to believe that Owen was the truly wicked one.

## VI

Kellen cringed when he saw what Shade's little helper had done to the intricate weave of knots he and Owen had made to bind their band's vocalist. It had been enough of a challenge to make the pattern work with the little lights getting in the way, but if a person didn't know what they were doing when restraining or releasing a person, a lot of damage could be done to a person's soft tissues. Luckily, Shade was more hard than soft, but there was no way Kellen would be able to undo this mess. The art of untying was almost as practiced as the precise sequence required to bind someone properly.

"Did you make this mess?" Kellen asked the lovely black girl who was ringing her hands together and almost in tears.

"Don't take time to lay blame, just get me out of this," Shade said.

Kellen disconnected the plug from the wall. "Gabe, get me a knife. We're going to have to cut him—"

Before Kellen could finish the thought, the young woman launched herself across Shade's lap and was practically hissing at Kellen to back off. He would have laughed at her attempts to protect such a big, muscular guy, if Shade wasn't in danger of blood clots and tissue damage from lack of blood flow.

"I'll help him," the woman insisted. "Don't cut him."

"He's not going to cut Shade," Gabe said, with an exasperated shake of his head. "He's going to cut the wires. Now get back, Kellen needs to see what he's doing."

Gabe placed a knife in Kellen's hand and as soon as Shade's female savior moved out of the way, Kellen looked for the snag in Owen's original design. He severed one cord near Shade's left shoulder and another just beneath his sternum. The wires loosened and Shade took a relieved breath. Kellen handed the knife back to Gabe. "You could have cut him free."

"How was I supposed to know that?" Gabe said.

"Aren't you the brains of this operation?"

"Not about stuff like that."

*Share Me, by Olivia Cunning*

"Well, see if you can get his arms loose," Kellen said to Gabe. He didn't want to waste any more time out here with these guys when he had exactly what he wanted in the tour bus's bedroom. And she was alone with his charmer of a best friend. "Just start at the last knot and work your way backwards. Think of it as a puzzle."

"I'm not untying him," Gabe said. "You untie him."

"I'll do it," Lindsey's friend offered.

"What's your name?" Kellen asked her.

"Vanessa."

"Vanessa, do you promise you'll be patient and not jerk on the ropes as you untie them?"

"I promise not to jerk any ropes," she said, "but there is something in his pants I'd like to jerk." She burst out laughing when Kellen's eyes opened wide in astonishment.

"I'll leave you to that then," Kellen said. "He has been really cranky. Maybe blowing his load in front of a crowd will cheer him up."

Vanessa's jaw dropped. Kellen decided she wasn't used to men countering her outlandish statements with outlandish statements of their own.

Her dark-eyed gaze flittered to the bedroom door. "You be good to my Lindsey," she said.

"Oh, I'll be good to her," Kellen promised, "but don't be alarmed when she screams."

*A Very Naughty Xmas*

## VII

As soon as Kellen had left to save Shade from his rescuer, Owen shut the door and turned toward Lindsey.

He knew Kellen could be a bit intimidating if one didn't know him. Owen was sort of glad he'd been drawn away for a moment so he could speak to Lindsey on a more personal level. He wanted her to be able to relax. Her elevated breathing rate led him to believe she was far more nervous than she was letting on. He knew from experience how exciting it could be to no-holds-barred fuck a stranger, but it could also be awkward and a little frightening. Especially in a situation where one woman mixed with two rowdy guys.

"I don't want you to feel like you have to do anything you don't want to do," Owen said, scraping the Santa hat off his head and trying to smooth his hair into place. He'd forgotten he was still wearing the festive accessory. And there was nothing Santa-like about the gifts he was about to bestow on sweet Lindsey.

"Are you kidding?" she said, with a laugh. "You have no ideas what sort of dirty thoughts I was having while watching you on stage."

"Yeah, well, we're just a bunch of regular guys who happen to make music that a lot of people enjoy."

"You're also all fuck-hot."

Owen smiled. He never tired of the ego boosts. Sometimes he wondered how he'd ever lived without them before fame had knocked at his door. "You're fuck-hot too, Lindsey."

She inched closer, until she was standing directly in front of him. Her succulent breasts were inches from brushing his chest. He was well aware that Kellen had instructed him to get her ready and was probably anticipating her to be naked and massaged into submission by the time he got back. But Owen needed a few minutes to get to know a girl before he stripped her of her clothes and got down to business. Just a minute. "So, Lindsey, what do you do for a living?"

"Investment banker. Well, I just started, actually. First job out of college. I kind of suck at it so far. I don't have good instincts when it

*Share Me, by Olivia Cunning*

comes to picking stocks."

"I figured with a body like that you'd be a model."

She lifted an eyebrow at him. So she wasn't buying his lines. Moving on to plan B. "Why did you follow the tour bus tonight?"

"I have a fuck-it list. You've always been at the very top of it."

"A fuck-it list?"

"Yeah, my friend, Vanessa, and I made a list of the top three guys we'd most want to fuck. There's you and Kellen, and some soccer player who I can't recall the name of at the moment."

"I'm ahead of Kelly on your list? I know how much he drives the girls wild."

Her cheeks went pink. "He's close second. Almost a tie."

"Well, just so you know what to expect, Kellen won't fuck you," Owen said.

Lindsey's brows drew together. "Isn't that why he invited me here?"

Owen shook his head. "No. I'm not saying he won't touch you, but when it comes to the actual act, he never goes that far." Or he hadn't since Sara had gone. All these girls who got Kelly's blood pumping at first sight had Sara's same blue-eyed, innocent look about them. Owen wondered if Kelly realized how transparent he was.

Lindsey's jaw dropped. "He's a virgin?"

Owen laughed. "Well, I wouldn't call him a virgin. He's very discriminate with where he puts his cock." He grinned at her. "But not his tongue."

Lindsey shuddered.

"I, on the other hand, will totally fuck you."

"Thank God." She giggled. "So are we going to do this now or wait for Kellen?"

"It's a long ritual for him, you know. I thought maybe you'd like to talk for a bit. He gets rather intense."

"It's a ritual?" She glanced at the door. "Like, what do you mean? I'm not a virgin if he's thinking I'd make a good sacrifice to the gods."

Owen shook his head. "No, nothing like that. He thinks sex is some sort of spiritual connection with the earth. That the body is the gateway to a person's soul. That the right connection between two people during sex can become a religious experience. That's why he only goes so far. It's far more personal for him than most guys." Which was partially the truth and partially a way to protect Kellen's still wounded heart from questions Lindsey might ask. "Do you think it's weird?" Because if this woman was critical of Kelly in any way, Owen would show her to her snow-covered car in an instant.

"Not weird," she said. "Interesting. So if a woman was to get him to fuck her..."

"I think he'd love her forever." Owen chuckled. "Don't get your hopes up, doll. He's not ready for love just yet. We will make you feel wonderful though."

Lindsey placed her palms flat on his chest and looked up at him. "I'm ready for whatever you have in store for me."

He circled her back with both arms and tugged her forward to hold her loosely against his chest. Her entire body was quaking. As he'd suspected, she was far more confident in words than in actions. Owen stroked her back gently and brushed gentle kisses against her hairline. When Kellen returned there would be no time for tenderness and, while what he did with Kellen made his balls throb just thinking about it, he liked a little connection with his bed partners before he got naked. Lindsey rubbed her face against his neck, her lips finding the pulse point in his throat. She placed a wet, tugging kiss on that sensitive spot and the sensation shot straight to his balls. Okay, he admitted it. It really didn't take much to seduce him.

Lindsey's soft breasts warmed against his chest.

"Can I take your shirt off?" she asked. "I want to feel your bare skin against mine." She didn't take her eyes off his as she reached for the hem of his T-shirt. "Owen," she whispered. She removed his shirt and released an excited breath as her gaze roamed his inked chest and the barbells in each nipple. "Your body is even hotter than I imagined."

Owen grinned. Unlike Kellen, he wore a shirt most of the time, but he worked out just as hard as his friend to keep his muscles toned and cut for the ladies.

Lindsey plastered herself to his chest. The heat of her skin permeated his thoughts until all he could think about was warm, soft, female flesh and being buried balls-deep inside it. He flattened both palms over her back and tugged her against him so that her full breasts pressed into his chest. Kellen was going to flip out when he saw how endowed she was. He would have turned her body into a work of art no matter her shape or size, but they both liked the way ropes looked when they dug into a full pair of tits.

What was taking Kellen so long anyway?

Owen began to massage Lindsey's back, kneading her muscles until she melted like butter against him. "I think Kellen wants to help me with this part," Owen said.

"With what part?" Lindsey lifted her head to look at him. She looked tranquil. She wouldn't be looking that way for much longer.

"Preparing your body."

"Oh, my body has been prepared since the moment you walked out on stage tonight, Owen."

He chuckled low in his throat. "I honestly doubt that."

The door handle turned and Owen took a step back, drawing Lindsey deeper into the room with him. Kellen smiled when he closed the door behind him.

## VIII

Lindsey had surely died and gone to heaven. Not only was she half naked in the arms of one Owen Mitchell, Kellen Jamison had just entered the room and was looking at her as if she was his Thanksgiving feast. It was sweet of Owen to try to make her feel comfortable with whatever was about to happen between them, but he honestly didn't have to. She had been serious about him being at the top of her fuck-it list. And Kellen really had always been second, but now that they were all together in the bedroom of their tour bus, she realized how shortsighted she'd been. Both of them at once. That was the true pinnacle of sexual delight. Would she survive the mere thought of being with them both? Even if Kellen did have an unusual way of thinking about sex, she was more than willing to see what his ritual entailed.

"I thought you'd be farther along by now." Kellen moved to stand behind Lindsey. When the cool skin of his hard chest pressed against her bare back, she didn't bother stifling her moan of bliss. Sandwiched between the two hottest men she'd ever dared fantasize about, Lindsey was sure she really had died and gone to heaven.

Kellen's hands moved between Lindsey's belly and Owen's. He stroked her skin with long, strong fingers. The same fingers he used to make six-strings sing made her skin tingle with excitement. Owen's hands slid over her back with equal care.

Kellen's hands cupped her breasts and she shuddered. "Beautiful," he whispered. "I can't wait to create art with your body."

"Hmm?" she murmured.

Kellen and Owen moved away at the same instant and she had to take a step to keep from sliding to the floor.

"Take your pants off for us, Lindsey," Kellen said.

Without the slightest hesitation, she unfastened her jeans and slid them off. Struggling to remove her boots and socks while standing, she decided she must be quite a turn-off at the moment as she gracelessly got naked.

"She has the perfect shape for this," Owen said.

"I could tell from the start," Kellen said.

She stood before them in her bra and panties and fought the urge to cover herself. They were both assessing her with keen scrutiny.

"Diamond weave?" Owen asked Kellen.

"Except for her breasts and her ass. We're going to cage them."

"What are you talking about?" Lindsey asked.

"You said you were okay with being tied," Kellen said. "You haven't changed your mind have you?"

She glanced at Owen, who was smiling at her warmly, and then turned to look at Kellen, who was far more intense. He was almost animalistic in the way he looked at her. "No, I haven't changed my mind."

"It won't hurt," Owen said.

"I'm not afraid." A bit confused, yes. Hornier than a desert toad, yes. But not afraid. "Should I take off my underwear?" Though her thighs were quaking at the thought of being entirely naked, entirely exposed before two men she idolized, her voice was surprisingly steady.

"Owen will take care of that for you," Kellen said. "Get the oil," he said to Owen.

"Which one?"

Kellen surprised her by surrounding her in an embrace, which was now quite warm. He inhaled deeply. "Honeysuckle," he said. "You smell amazing," he whispered to her as Owen started rattling around in a cabinet on the other side of the room. "I can't wait to taste your cum."

Lindsey shuddered at the thought of this man with his head between her thighs. She wanted to fist his long, silky hair in both hands and rock her pussy against his face. And she wanted Owen to thrust into her mouth so she could suck him while Kellen ate her out. She wasn't sure if they were up for suggestions, so she just clung to the thought and Kellen's hard chest until Owen returned and unfastened her bra with a practiced flick.

Lindsey moaned as Owen's hands reached around her and began to rub oil into the skin of her belly. He started at the sensitive flesh just above the waistband of her panties and worked his way up, fingers rubbing in small circles, thumbs massaging more deeply into her flesh. An instant later, Kellen dumped some of the sweet-smelling oil on his hands and, standing before her, reached around to rub the oil into the flesh of her lower back. They worked their way upward—both thorough, both meticulous, both gentle in their muscle-loosening technique. Owen took two more handfuls of oil and covered her breasts, massaging them in slow circles. She was tempted to lean back against his chest, but Kellen's hands were working her back just beneath her shoulder blades and she didn't want to interrupt the duel assault on her senses. She couldn't even open her eyes to look at the magnificent specimen of a man before her. She could only concentrate on the sensation of their hands turning her muscles into delighted pools of relaxation.

"She has beautiful breasts," Owen whispered. His breath stirred her hair and, though his body wasn't pressed against her back, she could feel the warmth of his skin behind her.

"They are beautiful," Kellen said. "Every inch of her is beautiful."

Lindsey wanted to deny it. She'd been carrying around a few extra pounds recently and felt decidedly plump most days.

"The give of her flesh will look beautiful in your ropes," Owen said.

So they had noticed she wasn't rail thin.

"I'm getting hard just thinking about it."

Owen's hands slipped under the curves of her breasts and lifted them. "We're going to have to devise a way to keep these pretty pink nipples hard."

Something warm and wet slid over the surface of one straining tip of her breast. Lindsey's eyes flipped open and her mouth dropped open in wonder. She glanced down to find Kellen licking her nipple as if trying to capture the last bit of pudding at the bottom of a parfait glass.

Owen caressed her breast.

Kellen rubbed his lips over its tip.

*Oh God.*

She lifted her arms and threaded her fingers through Kellen's shoulder length hair. It felt like silk against her fingers.

He tilted his head so he could look up at her while his tongue laved her tender nipple. His eyes were so dark, they were almost black in this lighting. His stare drew her in until she couldn't tear her gaze away.

"We definitely need to keep them hard," Kellen said. "So pretty when they're hard." He flicked her other nipple with his tongue and her entire body jerked. "We'll have to set up the rings."

She had no idea what he meant, but rings, ropes, whatever. She wanted every experience these two could offer her body.

Kellen gave her nipple a sharp nip with his teeth before kneeling before her on the floor. After collecting more oil from the bottle on the dresser, he began to massage it into her thighs. His forehead rested against her lower belly and he inhaled deeply through his nose. "God, baby, I can already smell your excitement." He nudged her thighs farther apart, hands working oil into the insides of her legs.

"Do you want me?" Kellen asked.

"Yes."

"And Owen?"

"Yes. Both of you."

"Are you wet?"

"Oh yes," she whispered, her pussy quaking with excitement.

"I bet you're sweet," he whispered. "Are you sweet, Lindsey? Have you ever tasted yourself?"

"You can't taste her until she's ready," Owen interrupted.

"That's why I asked you to prepare her for me, Owen," he said. "What were you doing while I was out untying Shade."

"Talking."

Kellen snorted. "Figures."

"I'm ready," Lindsey insisted. Staring down at the top of Kellen's head, his breath hot against her lower belly, his shoulders broad and bronzed and decorated with colorful tattoos that extended down both arms in beautiful sleeves, Lindsey was more than ready. Her juices had already saturated her panties and were wetting her thighs.

"Not even," Kellen said. "But we'll work quickly."

Owen massaged oil into her neck and shoulders. She wasn't sure how she was still standing. He shifted her back to rest against him while he massaged her arms and as Kellen, who was kneeling at her feet, rubbed oil into her lower legs. He continued to inhale deeply and released hot, gasping breaths that penetrated her panties. Lord, just that sensation was enough to send her spiraling into nirvana.

"Maybe I should work the bottom half, bro. I think you're about to lose control."

"Lindsey," Kellen said calmly. "Go lie on the bed."

Owen released the hand he was massaging so thoroughly and stepped away. Lindsey didn't even consider questioning Kellen, much less disobeying.

"Remove all the bedding except the fitted sheet," Kellen added. "Wait for us."

She did what he instructed, tossing the powder-blue covers on the floor. She spread out on the bed and watched Kellen and Owen explore a tall stack of drawers that were built into one wall. "Blue?" Kellen said as he pulled open a drawer. "Like her eyes?"

Owen pushed the drawer shut. "It's Christmas Eve. Let's do something more festive tonight."

"Red and green?"

He nodded. "And gold."

Kellen glanced over his shoulder at Lindsey. "She'll look spectacular in gold."

She didn't know if she should thank them for the compliment, since she wasn't sure why they were discussing colors. Kellen pulled out several lengths of green and red rope and dropped them on the mattress next to Lindsey.

"This is your last opportunity to back out, Lindsey," Kellen said.

Her heart skipped a beat. She glanced at Owen who was rolling his eyes at Kellen. She was pretty sure he mouthed, *Mr. Drama*. She remembered Owen telling her that Kellen would stop if she asked. He was just trying to add a certain edge to her experience.

"I don't want to back out," she said. "I can't wait to find out what you're going to do to me."

They got to work. They started by forming a mesh out of the red ropes, tying knots to form a circular pattern that very much reminded Lindsey of a dream catcher, with a quarter-sized hole at the center. She had no idea what they planned to do with it until Kellen fit it over her left breast and carefully tightened it so that she'd never been more conscious of her own breast. Her skin was divided into diamond shaped sections by the ropes. Her nipple protruded through the hole in the center of the design. Owen lowered his head to flick his tongue over her nipple. It pebbled beneath his attention as pleasure radiated out in all directions. Kellen cinched the ropes tighter.

Her breath exploded from her lungs as her breast experienced a million simultaneous sensations, centered on the tongue flicking against its tip.

"Owen," she groaned.

He lifted his head and grinned at her. "There's more."

Soon Kellen had both of her breasts bound in the ropes and Owen had her nipples straining for attention.

They paused to admire her body. "Lovely," Kellen said breathlessly. "Arms to sides. I don't want them to block my view of her gorgeous tits."

Lindsey was eased into sitting position. Her arms were soon securely fastened from shoulder to elbow against her sides. The tension of the rope was all concentrated at the center of her lower back as another length of rope was stretched across her shoulders. They'd tied golden rings into the rope every few inches along both sides. She glanced up at the ceiling looking for hooks. "What are the rings for?"

"We aren't going to use them to suspend you," Kellen said. "You'll see what they're for soon."

They eased her onto her back again and even though her hands and legs were free, she wouldn't have been able to fight them off if she needed to. Something about being so utterly defenseless was exciting and terrifying at the same time. Her heart rate had doubled and she couldn't seem to find enough air. She fought the sensation of suffocation as the room seemed to shrink and the ceiling closed in on her.

"Are you okay?" Owen asked. He leaned into her line of sight and brushed her hair from her hot cheeks. The walls receded again as her attention diverted to Owen's concerned eyes. "If you have a panic attack, we can cut you free in an instant."

"And mess up all the beautiful knots you've tied?" She smiled, forcing herself not to pant too excessively. She honestly didn't want them to stop. She liked the way the ropes pressed into her skin. They made her aware of her body. She loved it. Being confined was sort of a head trip, but she would endure.

Kellen's hands on the top elastic of her panties caused her legs to reflexively close.

"If you close your thighs to me, I'm going to spank you," Kellen said.

She was tempted to push him and squeeze her thighs together so he would spank her, but her thighs had other ideas and immediately went slack. He slowly tugged her panties down her thighs and tossed them aside. Kellen worked on her left leg, and Owen carefully mirrored Kellen's collection of knots on her right. They bound her legs so they were bent at the knee and hip—slightly more severe than fetal position. They worked hard to stretch her into a position she didn't know she was capable of attaining. They massaged her muscles and flexed and straightened her joints until it didn't pull painfully to have her legs bound with her heels against the backs of her thighs and her legs wide open. She did feel incredibly exposed as there was no way she could possibly close her legs even an inch.

The pair of gorgeous men stepped away and she struggled to keep her trembling muscles from collapsing.

"Let the ropes hold you, Lindsey," Kellen said gently. "Don't fight them."

"Think of it like a hammock," Owen suggested.

She didn't fight the ropes for long because she didn't have the strength to do so. As soon as she went slack, the ropes supported her weight entirely and she suddenly wished all those rings they had worked into their design would be used to suspend her. She also wished there was a mirror on the ceiling so she could see how she appeared from their vantage point. Lindsey had never felt more beautiful—as if her body was a cherished work of art. She wanted to be put on display. Her limbs felt wonderfully supported by the ropes, as if they were holding her in a comforting embrace. In a cocoon of pleasure and pressure, her muscles had been stretched to their limits as if she were doing some rope-assisted

*A Very Naughty Xmas*

yoga. There was only the slightest hint of ache in her muscles.

"I feel..." She sucked a rapturous breath into her lungs. "Amazing."

Kellen smiled. She wasn't sure if she'd seen him smile before. Owen constantly smiled, but Kellen seemed to reserve them for special occasions.

"We're going to turn you over. Owen won't let you fall." With her face in Owen's lap, her knees in the mattress and her rear end pointing up to the ceiling, she was treated to the most sensual massage of her life. Kellen's huge hands squeezed the globes of her ass until her back entrance was quivering and she was whimpering to be entered.

"Oh," she whispered desperately.

"Try something from Gabe's stash," Owen said.

She rubbed her face over his lap, wishing he'd removed his pants so she could take him into her mouth. She hadn't known what to expect when tied but being rendered helpless made her want to please this man. And that man. Both men. Yet she couldn't. She just had to wait until they did with her as they wanted.

Kellen moved from the bed.

"Owen," she whispered. "Let me suck your cock."

He stroked her hair. "I can't let it out yet. I have a long while to wait before I get my turn."

"You don't have to wait," she assured him.

Something cold and slippery popped into her ass. Her core clenched at the unexpected intrusion and she shuddered in ecstasy. "Oh!"

She couldn't see what Kellen was doing, but she felt the ropes slide and press against the skin of her rump. Whatever he'd put inside her ass was driving her crazy with need.

"Are you almost finished?" she whispered. "I'm on fire."

"God, your ass looks amazing," Owen said. He released his hold on her upper body and she struggled not to tip to the side. He grabbed her ass in both hands and rubbed her cheeks together, making her acutely aware of all the ropes pressing into her skin and pulling at that amazing object in her ass. It only penetrated her an inch, but the shape of it aroused her like nothing in her experience. The way it teased her tight hole made her pussy spasm with unfulfilled need.

"Now for Kelly's added touch," Owen whispered. He sounded oddly proud of his friend.

They turned Lindsey onto her back again and Owen slid away since the ropes easily held her body in a stable position when she was face up. Kellen took a rope of gold satin and tied a knot in it. He then slid one end of the rope through the collection of rings that were projecting upward around the periphery of her torso. He centered the knot directly over her nipple and continued to thread the rope's end through more loops. When the rope passed over her other nipple, he tied a second knot and continued threading rope through rings on the opposite side of her body.

When he was finished, a bit of knotted rope rubbed against each nipple. It drove her nuts. He moved to kneel between her thighs and took one end of each rope in either hand and tugged them back and forth. The rope slid easily through the rings and rubbed those distracting knots against Lindsey's straining nipples until her back arched involuntarily. She pulled against her bindings for a moment before going slack. The pleasure radiating from her nipples coursed in all directions, following the paths of the ropes, blossoming between them. She was near orgasm already.

"Do you like anal pleasure, Lindsey?" Kellen asked. "Would you like a little tug on that plug I put in your ass? It has a loop I can thread the rope through."

The only word that really registered was pleasure. And she wanted more of it. Her body begged for more. "Yes," she gasped.

She couldn't see what the hell Kellen was doing between her thighs, but she felt a tug at her ass as he threaded a rope through something down there too. Her pussy was swollen and achy and dripping. Her clit was so excited it was driving her mad. The tug inside her ass had her shuddering in unfulfilled spasms. They waited until she'd settled again before tugging each end of the rope near her hips, which pulled the plug inside her puckered hole just enough to drive her insane. Her pussy clenched with a less than satisfying orgasm.

"Oh please," she begged. She needed to come much harder than that to be satisfied.

"Almost, Lindsey," Kellen promised gently. "You're almost ready."

He carefully tied the free ends of the knotted ropes to each of her wrists, and then secured those at her hips as well.

"You're in charge of pleasuring your nipples and ass," Kellen told her. He showed her that the slightest movement of her lower arms simultaneously rubbed the knotted ropes against her tender nipples and tugged at the plug inside her quivering hole. She couldn't stimulate one without pleasing the other, and she was perfectly okay with pleasing herself.

"Oh God," she gasped, getting the hang of the movement and moving her wrists in an alternating pattern to stimulate herself until another orgasm was teasing her pussy. Oh God, she was going to explode. She needed fucked and badly. "Please fuck me. Please. Please."

"I think you've outdone yourself this time, Kelly," Owen said.

They joined her on the bed. Owen at her head. Kellen down there. She lifted her head to look at Kelly. He was gazing down at her fully exposed pussy with hunger in his dark eyes. Oh God. She rubbed the knots against her nipples and tugged at her ass faster. She needed to come. Needed to come. Needed. Needed. Now. Oh. Could she come from this kind of stimulation? She was close. So close.

"I'm going to kiss your mouth to try to keep you from getting too loud," Owen said. "Okay?"

She nodded. *Do whatever you want to me*, she thought. *Anything. Just do something.* Owen leaned over her head to take her lips upside down in a long, leisurely kiss. He pulled away gently and whispered, "Kelly's going to make you come real soon. Don't work so hard. Relax, honey."

She watched Kellen tie his long hair back with a leather tie. He stretched out on his belly between her wide open thighs, and then Owen blocked her view by kissing her again. Lord the man had a strong and sensual mouth. She wouldn't mind him taking all that hot, achy flesh between her thighs in a kiss like this.

Warm breath stole across her swollen pussy. She shuddered and called out against Owen's persistent lips. He kissed her more deeply, his tongue teasing hers. His fingers began to trace patterns on the bare flesh of her upper arms between the braids of rope.

A warm, soft tongue traced the empty opening between her thighs and she almost shot straight off the mattress.

Owen trailed open-mouthed kisses along her jaw. "Easy," he whispered. "He'll take your edge off soon."

She whimpered when Kellen began to slowly and methodically trace her entrance with gentle swirls of his tongue. Her hips buckled. She fought the ropes holding her legs open, wanting so badly to press her heels into Kellen's back and writhe her sex against his face, but she was helpless to move.

"I need fucked," she said. "I need fucked." She couldn't believe the words escaping her lips, nor how much she meant them.

"Kelly, have mercy on her," Owen said.

Kellen's little evil chuckle did nothing to ease her mind. His tongue brushed her clit and her entire body strained for release. She could feel his breath against her, but damned if he didn't touch her to send her flying over the edge. He waited until her body relaxed before he tongued her clenching pussy—in and out—with a slow, maddening rhythm. It made her want to be filled with a big, thick cock but kept orgasm just out of reach.

Owen claimed her mouth again. "Concentrate on me," he said against her mouth. "I'll fuck you when he's finished. It's what you want isn't it?"

"Y-yes. Please. Owen, I need it."

"Shh, let him taste you. Do you feel good?"

She nodded, feeling as if she might burst into tears. She did feel good. Every inch of her flesh was aware. It was overwhelming for her to be so aware of her body. Not just her sensitive lips, clinging desperately to Owen's as he continued to kiss her. Not just her nipples and ass, which she continued to stimulate intermittently with tugs of the silken ropes in each hand. Not just the maddening things Kellen was doing to her pussy. Every inch of her was either aware of the ropes or lack of ropes. The braided cords were exerting enough pressure that she couldn't ignore them. The awareness never went away.

Kellen suckled her clit and she went taut, straining to come. God, she needed release, but he pulled away and waited until she went limp before lapping at her center again.

Okay, she was going to die if she didn't have an orgasm soon. But she didn't die. Kellen just continued to pull her closer to the edge and she was sure she'd breech it the next time. He showed her just how wrong she was. Owen kissed her leisurely until she became so distraught that she couldn't catch her breath. He lifted his head to glare at his friend.

"For fuck's sake, Kelly, give her one," Owen said as he stroked her heated cheeks with cool fingertips. "Shit, dude, I think she's having another panic attack."

She heard Kellen's deep voice from down below. "I'll let her fly if you're willing to wait until I can bring her up again before you fuck her."

"I'll wait. I'm fine."

Kellen's mouth latched onto Lindsey's clit and he sucked, working his tongue against the sensitive bud until she sobbed, expecting him to pull away at the last moment. But he didn't. This time. This time, he let her shatter.

Lindsey screamed as her body quaked with release. Her ass clenched at something small and solid; her pussy clenched at devastating emptiness. Oh how she wanted filled. Wanted it even more than the intense orgasm turning her into a writhing, bucking creature of instinct. Perhaps the build-up and withhold orgasm pattern Kellen had been using on her had been for the best. Even after the waves of release dissipated, her body continued to quake uncontrollably.

"Don't cry," Owen whispered to her, kissing the dampness on her cheeks.

She wasn't sure why she was crying. It wasn't sadness or fear or anger or frustration. It wasn't even relief.

"I'm sorry," she sobbed brokenly. "I don't know what's wrong with me."

"We can cut you loose if it's too much," he said, stroking her hair gently.

"Please don't. I want to continue. I'm just…"

"Feeling things you never felt before," Kellen said. "It's okay. Sex is a deeply personal experience." He grinned wickedly. "Even when it's with a stranger, it touches part of your spirit."

Kellen massaged the insteps of her feet while she pulled herself together. She gulped for air and reminded herself to relax into the ropes. Fighting them only served to exhaust her, but they did cut into her flesh in a most delicious manner if she pulled against them just right.

Still above her head, Owen kept his face buried against her neck, holding her loosely just under her breasts.

"Okay," she said, when she returned to Earth. "I'm good now."

Kellen licked his lips. "I'm ready for more too. How are you, Owen?"

He groaned into Lindsey's neck. "Hard as a fucking rock."

"Hey, you said you were okay," Kellen reminded him.

"I was until she came. Her facial expression totally did me in."

Lindsey's face flamed. Had she made a stupid O-face? In front of Owen Mitchell? How embarrassing.

"Take her high again," Owen murmured against her neck. "Just, please hurry this time."

Kellen released Lindsey's feet and stretched out on his belly between her wide open thighs again. "You're just going to have to suffer a while, buddy. This is the sweetest pussy I've ever tasted and I'm going to take my time making it cream for me again."

"If you don't hurry," Owen growled, "I'm going to kick your ass. I've waited long enough."

Kellen chuckled at his misery.

"If you suck on my nipples, it will really get my juices flowing," Lindsey whispered to Owen. She had no idea if it was true. She just really wanted that luscious mouth of his against her tender nipples. The knot on the rope just wasn't cutting it any longer. Even though it flicked over them in a most distracting fashion, she was ready for a different sensation.

Owen inched lower. As his chest came into view, she couldn't help but pull against her bindings so she could kiss the hard-muscled flesh before her. He nudged the knotted rope out of his way with his nose and latched onto her nipple, sucking hard. She caught the glinting barbell in his nipple between her teeth and tugged. He groaned.

"I shouldn't have moved," he said.

The glorious motion of Kellen's tongue against Lindsey's flesh halted as he lifted his head. "That's not part of our ritual, Owen."

"*Your* ritual," Owen said. He sounded a tad testy.

Lindsey tilted her head back and gazed longingly at the hard ridge in Owen's jeans. She could almost feel him inside her, rubbing her inner walls. Stretching her. Filling her.

She squirmed excitedly. Kellen latched onto her clit and sucked in rhythmic pulses. Was he intentionally matching the pull of Owen's mouth on her nipple? The two were in perfect synch.

Lindsey was building again. She gasped and shuddered, fighting release this time. Not wanting to come when she was empty inside.

Kellen lifted his head. "She needs you to do your part now," he said.

Owen moved in a flash. He bounded off the bed, shucked his jeans and was tearing open a condom before Lindsey could comprehend what was happening. Something metallic glinted just beneath the rim of Owen's swollen cockhead. He carefully unrolled the condom down his length and moved to the end of the bed behind Kellen.

Lindsey lifted her head to try to track their motions, but it pulled a rope at her back uncomfortably so she closed her eyes and relished the sensation pulled from her quivering flesh by Kellen's skilled mouth. Without Owen to divide her attention, she was quickly overwhelmed with sensation, mewing in pleasure as another orgasm teased her with promise.

"Yes," she whispered. "I'm coming again. I'm…"

Kellen moved aside and Owen took his place. He found her and slid deep with one hard thrust. Her eyes widened in surprise when she felt there was something inside her other than just flesh. Whatever that metallic bead near his cockhead had been felt amazing.

"What is that?" she asked.

"It's pierced," he said simply and then he slowly withdrew.

His modification rubbed down her front inner wall. He found a particularly sensitive spot a few inches inside her and she gasped brokenly as the piercing rubbed against it. A devilish smile lit Owen's devastatingly handsome face and he thrust quick and shallow, rubbing that little spot inside her until she thought she'd go mad. When the first throes of another orgasm gripped her, he thrust deep and held. She stared up at him unable to comprehend what he was doing. When her breathing stilled somewhat, he pulled back to that special spot again and took her with rapid shallow strokes. Rubbing. Rubbing. Rubbing against that perfect spot.

"Oh God, that feels good."

Owen grinned at her and thrust deep again. She realized he was just as bad as his friend, Kellen. Teasing her within an inch of a mind-blowing orgasm, yet withholding it from her at the last instant. She didn't know whether to curse them or sing their praises.

The mattress beside her sagged as Kellen moved to kneel at her side. He was naked now, having shed his jeans. She watched him, in total awe of his masculine beauty. He seemed so at ease with his nudity. Even with his enormous, engorged cock fully exposed and standing proud and rigid before him. She'd never seen a man so perfectly put together. So silently powerful. So...

She groaned as Owen shifted his hips and the metal ball on the underside of his cock stroked her rear wall as he thrust into her slow and deep.

Lindsey cried out as an orgasm unfurled within her again. She hadn't thought she was capable of coming three times in one night but, dear Lord, she was coming and having Owen's thrusting cock inside her brought her the full satisfaction she craved at last.

"She's getting off hard with you," Kellen said as if commenting on something far less amazing than the pulsing pleasure shattering Lindsey with bliss.

"She's not screaming the way she did with you," Owen said, shifting his hips and grabbing the ropes at her shoulders so he could fuck her harder.

Lindsey was too incoherent to scream. She could scarcely breathe. He had to stop. She couldn't take it. "Please, stop. No more. No."

"I think she's had enough," Kellen said, his fingers tracing the ropes that were digging into her upper arms. "Take it easy on her."

"S-sorry," she whispered. She wanted Owen to finish. Wanted him to take his pleasure while buried deep inside her, but she had reached her limit.

Owen slowed his thrusts and when she stopped shaking, he pulled free with a wet sound. As soon as he was free of her, she wanted him back. But he had already moved to kneel across from Kellen on her opposite side.

Kneeling across from each other on opposite sides of Lindsey's body, the pair of men stared straight ahead, locked in each other's gazes. Kellen's eyes were dark brown and intense, Owen's brilliant blue and

*Share Me, by Olivia Cunning*

glazed. She wasn't sure what they were doing, but it was as if she was no longer in the room, much less bound between them.

Kellen's hand moved to encircle his cock. He stroked himself slowly from base to tip, working slick oil down his length. Owen stripped the condom off his cock and mimicked Kellen's motions on himself. His body tensed and his mouth fell open to emit gasps of pleasure. Lindsey watched them, partially puzzled, partially turned on by the perfect synchronicity they displayed as they stroked their cocks over her lower belly.

Owen's eyes drifted closed after a moment. Kellen smiled that wicked little smile of his and reached forward to take Owen's cock in his hand. Lindsey's gaze darted from their faces to the action below, back to their faces. Owen shuddered in pleasure and shifted his hand from his cock to Kellen's.

They tugged at each other in unison. Eyes closed, Owen was twitching uncontrollably in Kellen's hand. Kellen watched him, gauging his reaction. His hand moved faster. Faster. Skimming over Owen's flesh with practiced eased.

Owen fell forward and Kellen caught him against his shoulder, still stroking him, his long, strong fingers rubbing over the piercing in Owen's cock with each tug.

Lindsey had never seen two guys stroke each other's cocks before. She wasn't sure why it had her so hot and bothered. She was lying to herself. Watching them get off on each other was the hottest fucking thing she'd ever seen in her life, even if she did feel like an intruder in her own threesome.

"Kelly," Owen whispered. "Can I come? Let me come. Kelly?"

"I'm not ready yet."

Owen began to stroke Kellen more persistently, paying extra attention to the head of Kellen's cock.

"I can't, oh God, I can't," Owen panted. "Please hurry."

Lindsey's eyes widened as Owen rubbed his open mouth across Kellen's shoulder, his eyes squeezed shut. She felt the first pulse of hot cum strike her belly. It wasn't Owen's, it was Kellen's.

She couldn't see Kellen's expression, but she could see Owen's and, as he let go, his face contorted in bliss, she was seriously cursing herself for encouraging him to stop fucking her because she was certainly in need of more now.

Owen rubbed his open mouth over Kellen's shoulder in absolute rapture. He was the sexiest thing she'd ever witnessed in her life. After a moment, Owen lifted his head and gazed up at Kellen with questioning eyes. "Was that okay?" he asked.

Kellen lifted both hands to cup Owen's face. "That was perfect. Thank you." He dropped a gentle kiss at the corner of Owen's mouth and again they stared at each other as if Lindsey had left the planet.

"Let's bring her down slowly."

Owen smiled and nodded.

Was she supposed to believe they'd just jacked each other off all over her belly for *her* benefit?

Kellen's strong fingers played over the flesh on one side of her body, while Owen worked the other. They started by massaging their combined fluids into her skin. She'd watched them, trembling, wondering what part she had really played in the act that was obviously something more between them and less about her. She wasn't sure how she felt about being included in something like this. Oh, sure, she'd had an amazing sexual experience, but if the two of them were attracted to each other, why bother bringing a woman into the mix at all?

"I didn't realize you two were lovers when I agreed to this," Lindsey said as Kellen released one of her legs and slowly unwound the rope from around her thigh. He paused and looked at her as if she was a raving lunatic.

"What do you mean?"

"You and Owen. You obviously have a thing for each other."

Both men laughed. "It's not like that," Owen said. "It's part of Kelly's ritual."

*It's Kellen's way of taking advantage of you*, Lindsey thought. She winced as her left leg was slowly extended and Kellen's deft fingers began to massage its length. She hadn't realized that an uncomfortable ache had built in her hips until both legs were straightened and both men were kneading her muscles until she began to relax.

"It's cool," Lindsey said. "Watching you get each other off was hot and all. I just wasn't expecting it."

Kellen didn't comment, but Owen seemed a bit disturbed. His handsome face twisted in confusion and he glanced up at Kellen. "When did we start touching each other in the ritual? We didn't used to do that."

Kellen grinned. "A few months ago. It feels better that way, doesn't it?"

"Yeah, but she's right. It's kind of gay."

Kellen laughed. "What are you talking about? We both know we're not sexually attracted to each other," Kellen said. When Owen was looking the other way he sneaked a glance at him as if he wondered if Owen was buying it.

"You do know how to get me off hard," Owen said. "I completely forget where I am and lose track of what's going on. It's almost like really intense masturbation, since I have a cock in my hand. It's just not my own."

Lindsey chuckled. The guy was so cute. No wonder Kellen manipulated him into being his unsuspecting toy.

"I don't think I can find my connection without you anymore, Owen." Kellen stared at him reflectively and Owen grinned.

"Don't worry," Owen said. "I'll help you out until you find your perfect woman."

Kellen's smile was genuine this time. None of that usual wickedness in him backed it. "Thanks."

"I'll be your perfect woman," Lindsey offered.

"You were great Lindsey," Owen said, "but he has this crazy idea that he'll know his soul mate the instant he meets her. Ridiculous idea, huh?"

"Kind of romantic," Lindsey said.

"You're not supposed to share that with people, remember?" Kellen said.

They were unwinding the ropes around her torso now. Every inch of her body was massaged as they released her bonds one at a time.

Owen shrugged. "She's seen you stroke your best friend's cock until he came so hard he saw stars. I don't think much of what you share with her at this point is going to phaze her."

"You came that hard, did you?" Kellen said, his lips twisted in that wicked grin of his again.

"Can't help it. You have strong hands."

"Kellen came way harder than you did, Owen," Lindsey said. "I think he bruised my belly with the force behind his load."

Owen chuckled. "I did my best to help him get off."

"We rushed it a bit," Kellen commented. "You were over-excited." He caressed Lindsey's breasts gently as they were freed from their bounds. "Which got me overexcited. I'm not sure if she was completely satisfied."

She couldn't lie, even if it did mean she might have more in store for her. "I was more than satisfied. And it feels absolutely amazing to be touched like this after having been confined," she said quietly. She liked it almost as much as the mind blowing orgasm she was still relishing.

"You'll sleep very well," Kellen promised.

"I am sleepy now," she admitted.

She felt the weariness to her very bones.

And despite her best intentions, her eyes drifted closed.

## IX

Kellen continued to unwind ropes and massage flesh long after Lindsey had fallen asleep. He could feel Owen's troubled gaze on him, but he pretended he was still working through his ritual. When had it become a way to be closer to his best friend? And why were the best orgasms of his life always at Owen's hand? He wasn't attracted to Owen. He didn't get aroused when he was around him or anything. It had to be a completely tactile response of his body. Nothing emotional behind it. Should he tell Owen that or just keep those thoughts to himself?

"I want some hot chocolate," Owen said. "Can you finish this on your own?"

Kellen forced himself to look up at Owen. He hoped his smile didn't appear as forced as it felt. "Yeah, I'm fine. Almost finished. Unless you want to retrieve her anal plug for me."

Owen grinned and Kellen took an unlabored breath. He hadn't realized how constricted his chest had become until Owen's easy smile had lifted some of the emotional burden.

"Sounds like a job for Adam," Owen said. "He's the one who loves ass."

Kellen really didn't want to make things weird between himself and Owen. So what if his orgasms were less intense when he finished himself at his own hand. Kellen had to stop encouraging Owen to touch him. Had to stop touching Owen in return. That's all there was too it.

"You can call Adam in here if you want," Kellen said.

Owen shook his head. "You aren't attracted to me. Are you?"

Leave it to Owen to throw it all out there in the open. Kellen shook his head. "No. I honestly never think of you in a sexual capacity."

Owen released a deep breath. "Thank God. I don't think of you that way either. Why then… Why do we both get off so hard that way? I come so hard when you jerk me off."

"Strong hands?"

"I guess," Owen said and nodded. "The other guys don't know

about this, do they?"

"Not unless you told them."

"I can keep a secret if you can."

"Yeah, but can she?"

They both paused in their massage to gaze down at the sleeping girl. She looked so innocent in sleep. So exhausted. Kellen felt a renewed stirring in his groin. One he absolutely did *not* feel when he thought of Owen. It was a relief, yet he felt a little weird about it. Kellen would have probably felt less weird about getting off at his best friend's hand if he *were* attracted to him. At least then it would make sense.

He just couldn't bring himself to let a woman get him off. Not yet. He should probably move on with his life. Find someone to love. Sara would have wanted that for him. She'd told him as much the last time they'd made love. The last time he'd made love, period.

"You're thinking about her again," Owen said.

Kellen swallowed the lump in his throat and returned his attention to massaging Lindsey's hand. She sighed in her sleep and his heart warmed. He wished he could love someone like her. He wished he could love anyone. Six years was long enough to grieve for Sara. It was much longer than the time he'd had with her.

"I think she'll always be there," Kellen said. "Sara."

"I'm pretty sure that's why you can't bring yourself to, you know." Owen's eyes flicked towards Lindsey's shaven mound. "Dam the beaver with your stick."

Kellen's brow crumpled. "That doesn't even make sense, Owen. You don't dam beavers."

Owen chuckled. "I do."

Kellen could still taste Lindsey's sweet pussy and yeah, things were definitely stirring down below at the thought, but he didn't want enter her shapely body. He didn't want to be wrapped in her arms. He didn't want to move inside her and stare down into her big, blue eyes, because even though Lindsey resembled Sara, she wouldn't be Sara. She could never be Sara. Sara was dead.

"I'm all sorts of fucked up in the head," Kellen murmured.

"Hey, it's alright. No one knows but me," Owen said.

Kellen chuckled. "I guess that's some consolation."

"Maybe if you tried again, you could do it this time. Instead of thinking of Sara while you bang the chick, you could think about my hand." Owen lifted his eyebrows suggestively and wriggled his fingers at him. "I know how much it turns you on."

Kellen might have taken offense if he hadn't known Owen was fucking with him. He laughed harder. "What? Are you tired of having to

*A Very Naughty Xmas*

get me off, Owen?"

"Not as long as you reciprocate." Owen's face split into a wide grin. "We are a couple of fucking perverts, aren't we?"

"Hey, whatever feels good and God knows I need the release."

"I'm really ready for some hot chocolate now. Do you want some?"

Kellen shook his head. "I'll be out later. I need a few minutes to get my head on straight."

Owen climbed from the bed and slipped into his jeans. "I'm going to hold you to that. No lying back here, holding some girl you don't know, feeling all depressed and lonely."

Kellen chuckled. The man knew him too well. He didn't know what he would do with himself without Owen in his life, reminding him to keep living. Or try to.

*Share Me, by Olivia Cunning*

# X

Owen left Kelly with Lindsey and entered the main corridor of the bus. Tex was near the driver's seat, cussing at his cell phone for having no service. With a candy cane dangling from his mouth, Gabe was back to reading his physics book, his attention drifting intermittently to Shade-and-company in the chair beside him. Adam was picking at his guitar strings with a distant look on his face. Shade was still seated in the recliner with the red rope still binding his forearms together. The main difference between now and when Owen had last saw him was that Shade's fly was wide open and his stiff cock was down the throat of Lindsey's friend.

When Owen closed the door behind him, the girl looked up from her task and let Shade's cock pop free from her lush lips. "Are you all done with the bed? I'm all sorts of horny right now. I don't think this guy is ever gonna come."

"Not if you stop sucking it, I won't," Shade said.

She glared up at him from her kneeling position on the floor. "If you don't shut your mouth, I'm gonna knock your ass to the floor and sit on your face."

Owen laughed. He loved this chick's attitude. He found several cups of cold cocoa on the counter and popped one in the microwave.

"Is Lindsey okay?" the girl asked.

"She's resting. Kellen's giving her a massage."

"She sure didn't sound like she was getting no massage twenty minutes ago."

"That must have been when I was fucking her," Owen said. "I think she liked my cock piercing. She has a really sensitive G-spot." He grinned. The microwave beeped and he removed his cup. He grabbed a spoon out of the drawer and stirred the contents of his mug before taking a cautious sip of the scalding liquid.

"Vanessa?" Shade murmured.

Vanessa tore her interested gaze from Owen's crotch and looked up at Shade.

"Are you going to finish what you started or talk to Owen?"

She pouted. "My jaw is tired."

"Then mount up and ride it."

She eyed Shade's huge erection with concern. "You don't expect me to take off my pants and do you out here in front of everyone, do you?"

"You didn't seem to have a problem with our presence when you were trying to suck him off," Gabe said without looking up from his book.

"If you untie me, I'll help you out of those pants," Shade said.

"I like you tied," Vanessa said. "That's what got me so hot and bothered in the first place."

"Yeah, well it's keeping me from yanking your pants down around your knees, shoving your face into the sofa and fucking you doggie style," Shade said, his voice tense, almost agonized.

Still sipping his hot chocolate, which was sweet and absolutely delicious, Owen sat on the sofa in question. "You can bury your face in my lap while he fucks you," Owen said. "I won't mind." He patted his thigh with his free hand and took another sip of his cocoa. He was just trying to get a rise out of her. She didn't disappoint him.

"You want my face in your lap after you just did my best friend? Don't even go there." Her eyes flicked to his lap. "Is your cock really pierced?"

Owen nodded and reached for the top button of his fly.

"Don't take it out and show her," Gabe complained. "One cock out in the main cabin is more than enough."

"I'll just put Shade's away then," Vanessa said. Owen saw the teasing grin on her face as she turned to try to force Shade's rock hard cock back into his pants. Owen liked this girl. Anyone who messed with Shade was okay in his book. "Why won't this thing go down?" she complained and licked it from base to tip. "Maybe if I suck your balls…" If her goal was to get Shade to groan and twitch and rock his hips in excitement, then sucking his balls had been the right solution.

Kellen came out of the bedroom. Owen offered him a wave, but he didn't notice because he was gaping at Shade and the woman with Shade's balls between her lush lips.

"Fuck, Shade. Don't you have any shame?" Kellen raked a hand through his long, black hair, which now hung loose around his shoulders. He only tied it back when he was going down on a lady.

"No," Shade gasped. "No shame. But the bedroom's free now, Vanessa. Since you seem to have at least a little shame."

"Just a little," she said and laughed. She climbed to her feet and grabbed the rope between Shade's wrists, hauling him to feet.

His loosened pants got caught on his thighs as he shuffled down the corridor to bedroom. Well, the bedroom was *mostly* free. Lindsey was still in there. She might sleep through the commotion however.

Kellen rolled his eyes as Shade passed him. "I thought Gabe was going to untie you."

"I wouldn't let him," Vanessa said. "I like Shade helpless."

"I'll show you helpless in a minute," Shade said in a low growl.

"Yeah, *you*," she said, "helpless and flat on your back while I take that huge cock for a ride. And you aren't allowed to come until I say you can."

Owen laughed. Yep, he really liked that woman's spunk. He wasn't sure how Shade felt about it however. He was sort of a control freak.

"Untie me," Shade insisted again.

She hauled him into the bedroom, slapped his ass, and then shut the door.

Kellen took one of the spare cups of hot chocolate on the counter and carried it toward the lounge area.

"You gonna heat that up?" Owen asked him.

He shook his head and took a sip. "I like it cool."

"I swear," Tex said, "you five are the only guys I know who can find willing pussy in a deserted mountain pass during a blizzard." Tex sat on the arm of the sofa with his cellphone clutched in one hand. "Still no service. I hope the equipment truck didn't start up the mountain pass after they finished loading it. I tried to call and warn them to stay in the valley."

"They'll close the pass if the roads are treacherous," Gabe said. "The crew is probably more worried about us."

"We're fine," Owen said. "We have hot chocolate, a fake tree and the sounds of Shade fucking in the bedroom. What more could we ask for on Christmas Eve?"

"Presents?" Adam said, setting his guitar aside, and rubbing his face with both hands. It was always tense when Shade and Adam were in the same room, but now that Shade had sojourned to the bedroom, some of the strain had left Adam's body.

Owen wished the two of them would have it out once and for all. But not tonight. Tonight was for celebrating family and love. And he might be stuck in a mountain pass with his band instead of visiting his parents, siblings, grandparents, aunts, uncles and dozens of cousins, but these guys were just as important to him as any blood relative.

"Santa might leave some presents for you douchebags," Owen said. Which reminded him that his Santa hat was trapped in the bedroom with

Shade and the woman who was currently screaming, "tear that pussy up, tear it up, baby, tear it up," and poor Lindsey. She couldn't possibly still be sleeping through all that swearing Shade was doing.

"There'll be a world-wide coal shortage if Santa visits y'all," Tex said and laughed like a demented Canadian goose until Owen shoved him off the arm of the sofa onto the floor.

"I know for a fact that Santa won't bring anyone coal," Owen said. "But good little boys have to get to bed and fall asleep before midnight or Santa might bypass a certain stranded tour bus."

"*Good* little boys," Tex said, rolling around on the floor laughing his ass off. Owen didn't realize people actually did that.

"Owen, did you get us presents?" Gabe asked. "We said we weren't going to exchange gifts this year."

"I didn't get you guys shit," Owen said.

"Good," Adam said, "because we didn't get you shit either."

"But I still believe in Santa," Owen said. "Don't you?"

"I don't know about Santa," Kellen said, "but Shade sure is praising Jesus at the moment."

## XI

Lindsey's eyes snapped open. Was there an earthquake? Why was the bed rocking so hard? And what were all of those rhythmic, wet noises coming from beside her?

She turned her head and her breath immediately stalled in her throat. A pair of chocolate brown thighs belonging to her best friend straddled the hips of some pelvis she didn't recognize. Vanessa was rising and falling over a thick, veined cock as if she were riding bareback broncos in a rodeo. Lindsey was completely engrossed with watching Vanessa's flesh ebb and flow each time she took him deep inside and lifted her hips to slide up his shaft.

"Did we wake you?" a deep voice said beside her.

*Shade*? She lifted up onto one arm and looked down at his sardonic grin. She couldn't see his eyes, because apparently he wore sunglasses even when he fucked. The Christmas lights were gone, but his arms were still bound before him with a red rope in a crisscrossing pattern from wrists to elbow. Lindsey immediately recognized Kellen's handiwork and began to tremble at the memories of what glorious things he and Owen had done to her body earlier.

"Sorry, girl," Vanessa said. "I had to get a piece of this. Damn, this man is fine."

"I understand," Lindsey said wearily and dropped back down on the mattress. Her body was so exhausted, so relaxed, so completely satisfied that she didn't want to move and lose the feeling of tranquility that suffused every inch of her. Unfortunately, she couldn't seem to stop watching Vanessa's pussy working Shade's cock, so the flesh between Lindsey's thighs started to swell and pulsate with renewed need.

"Your friend has a fantastic pussy," Shade said conversationally.

"Is that so?" Lindsey said.

"Soft and lush. Like her sexy lips."

"You ever been with a black girl before?" Vanessa asked him.

"A few," he said. "I've found that fantastic pussy comes in all colors. Speaking of coming, can I come now?"

*A Very Naughty Xmas*

"Not yet. I'm not finished." For which Lindsey was oddly thankful. She was completely mesmerized by what was going on beside her.

"You know what would be really hot," Shade whispered into Lindsey's ear.

"Hmm?" she murmured lethargically.

"If you moved up behind Vanessa, wrapped your arms around her and held her tits while she rides me."

Lindsey's eyes travelled up Vanessa's naked body to her breasts. Lindsey had seen Vanessa nude numerous times in the past, but she'd never thought of her friend's body as erotic. Or arousing. She also never thought she'd be so easily swayed by a man to obey his suggestion.

Vanessa glanced over her shoulder as Lindsey moved to kneel behind her. "Do you want a turn?" Vanessa asked.

Lindsey shook her head and kissed the warm, smooth skin of Vanessa's shoulder. Vanessa's back brushed Lindsey's suddenly hard nipples as she continued to rise and fall over Shade. With trembling hands, Lindsey cupped Vanessa's breasts. They were smaller than her own, their pointed tips pressed into her palms as Vanessa's back arched and her head dropped back on Lindsey's shoulder.

"Is this okay?" she whispered to Vanessa.

"It's okay," Vanessa said.

Lindsey massaged Vanessa's perky breasts, fascinated by the way the soft globes of flesh moved in her hands. How easy it was to make Vanessa moan by stroking her large nipples. How erotic the contrast of their flesh tones looked as she gave pleasure to her friend. Lindsey shifted so Vanessa's soft ass rubbed against her shaven mound each time she rose and fell over Shade. This was definitely getting her hot and bothered again. Lindsey churned her hips to rub her mound more firmly over Vanessa and her hands began to wander—down Vanessa's slightly rounded tummy, over her hips, her thighs.

*What am I doing?* Was she really going to touch her best friend *there*?

Vanessa began to move faster over Shade. Faster. Seeking her climax. Lindsey wanted to help her find it.

Lindsey's fingers slipped between Vanessa's swollen folds. She found Vanessa's clit with two fingertips and rubbed it fast and hard, the way she rubbed herself when she masturbated. Within seconds, Vanessa's body went taut before her, and Vanessa shuddered hard as she screamed through her orgasm.

"This is not okay," Lindsey said and yanked her hand away.

Vanessa grabbed her wrist and buried her hand between her thighs. "Yes, Lindsey. It's okay. It's perfect. Feel him inside me."

### Share Me, by Olivia Cunning

Lightheaded with shock, but for some reason unable to pull away, Lindsey held Vanessa's mound cupped in her palm while Shade's cock brushed rhythmically against her fingertips.

"That was beautiful," Shade said. "Can I come now?"

Vanessa chuckled. "No, stud. Lindsey needs a turn." She lifted her hips until Shade's cock slipped from her body and then took Lindsey's hand and placed it over the very slippery condom covering his shaft. "Have fun, girl. I need a nap."

Lindsey looked up at Shade, wishing she could see his eyes, wondering what he thought of her behavior. Was he as shocked by what she'd just done as she was?

"If you untie me," he said, "I'll make this easy on you."

"What do you mean?" Lindsey asked.

"You know you want to fuck, but you think you shouldn't."

"And how will untying you change those feelings?"

"You can blame your surrender on me, instead of taking what you want."

"I took what I wanted," Vanessa said.

"But she won't," Shade said. "Even though she does want it."

She did want it, but he was right. She'd already had sex with two strangers tonight. She sure wasn't going to go at it with another one. Unless he... forced her to.

"Are you going to force me?" she asked, her heart thudding with excitement.

"Do you want me to force you?"

"It's not really force if she *wants* you to force her." Vanessa rolled her eyes at him.

"I wouldn't really force her if she didn't want me to. That would be called rape, but it's different if she wants to be held down and fucked while she struggles."

"I do," Lindsey blurted.

Her hands moved to the first knot binding his arms together—his strong, very muscular arms. She had a hard time untying the rope as she thought about those strong muscular arms holding her down while he fucked her. Her fingers weren't trembling because she was afraid. They were trembling because she was excited.

"Should I leave?" Vanessa said.

"No, you're going to watch and not interfere. But I would appreciate it if you got me a fresh condom out of the drawer over there."

Lindsey was floored by the gentle smile he offered Vanessa. Surely this big hunk of sardonic muscle didn't have a gentle bone in his body. She was actually hoping he didn't. She especially hoped that the bone he was about to thrust into her throbbing cunt wasn't the least bit gentle.

Once his arms were free, he rubbed them for a moment and flexed his fingers. She watched the movement of his muscles contracting beneath his skin. He was so big. So powerful. So strong.

"I think you'd better run," he said in a deep voice.

Her heart slammed into her ribcage as she leaped from the bed. He pursued her and quickly trapped her against the inside of the bedroom door. She grabbed the doorknob, but his fingers were like steel bands around her wrists and she couldn't turn the knob.

"Let me go," she whispered, "Please."

"Do you know what I do to girls who make me want them as much as I want you?" He fisted a hand in her hair and tugged her head back. And it hurt. It hurt real good. She forced herself not to purr in surrender.

"I don't know," she said. "Just don't hurt me." *Much...*

Hand still clutching her hair, Shade jerked her back against his hard chest and grabbed her breast with his free hand. He pinched her nipple and she gasped in pain.

"I'm not going to hurt you." His teeth scraped against the edge of her ear. "But I am going to fuck you. Spread your legs."

"No," she said breathlessly. Her blood was jetting through her vessels. She was so amped up on adrenaline, she doubted she'd ever come down.

"Spread your legs or I'll spread them for you."

His cock prodded her in the lower back as he forced a knee between her legs from behind.

"No," she said. "I'll never spread them willingly."

There was a knock at the door. "Are you really raping someone in there?" someone said on the other side of the thin piece of wood before Lindsey's face. "Do I need to geld someone with a rusty knife?"

"Go away, Gabe, you're fucking up our scenario," Shade growled at the door.

"I'm not going away until I'm sure it *is* a scenario."

"It is," Lindsey yelled, her face flaming with embarrassment. What must Kellen and Owen be thinking of her? When had she turned into a ho for real? And why wasn't she thinking that the best way to prevent her further mortification was to stop this? She didn't want to stop. Not at all. So what if this made her a ho ho ho. She was having a very merry Christmas Eve.

"It totally is a scenario, drummer boy," Vanessa yelled. "And damn, Shade, watching this is totally turning me on again."

"If you're sure," Gabe said, still in the corridor outside.

"We're sure," the three in the bedroom yelled in unison.

*Share Me, by Olivia Cunning*

"Then you kids have fun, but keep it down. We're going to bed." There was a short pause. "*Alone* un-fucking-fortunately. Let's hope the generator holds out so we don't all freeze to death."

"Way to spoil the mood," Shade grumbled.

Lindsey grabbed Shade's wrist and yanked, trying to dislodge his fist from her hair. "I said let me go," she said and ground her ass into his cock as she tried to twist out of his grasp.

Shade groaned into her ear. "I am not going to last much longer," he whispered. "Vanessa got me too worked up."

Lindsey bumped her heel into his shin and, caught off-guard, Shade actually loosened his grip. She managed one step, before his fist tightened in her hair again.

"You'll pay for that, darlin'," he said.

*Oh yes, make me pay.*

In an instant, he had her face down on the edge of the bed, his big, strong hand pressing down in the center of her back so she couldn't rise. And it wasn't as if she wasn't legitimately trying, but he was so much stronger than her and no amount of trying to push upward with her spaghetti-noodle arms could dislodge him. Breathing hard, she turned her head so she could draw air. As soon as she stopped struggling to rise, his free hand delved between her legs from behind, no doubt discovering how hot and wet she was down there.

Shade removed his hand from her back and she launched forward, trying to scramble away. He grabbed her by the thighs, yanking them apart and pulling her toward him until she felt his cockhead against her opening. Her core clenched with the tease of an orgasm.

"You want it, don't you?"

*Yes, yes, I want it.*

"No," she forced herself to say. She shook her head vigorously.

"Then why are you so wet?"

"I'm not," she denied.

He thrust into her, sliding to the hilt in one, hard motion.

She cried out. Lord, he was huge. She couldn't help but rock back to meet his deep, punishing penetration stroke for stroke.

"Do you like that?"

"No," she forced herself to say.

"She does like it, doesn't she, Vanessa?"

"I think she does," Vanessa said.

"Do you know what else she likes?"

"Your finger in her ass?"

"I didn't think of that," he said. His firm grip released from one thigh and before she could use that advantage to pretend to fight him, his

## A Very Naughty Xmas

finger slipped in her ass and she exploded with an earth-shattering orgasm. He didn't give her time to recover. He spread her legs wider and fucked her harder.

"Oh please," she begged as she rubbed her face over the bedclothes in blinding ecstasy.

"What were you thinking Lindsey likes?" Vanessa asked.

"I think she likes to eat pussy."

"I hope so. My fingers aren't doing the trick over here."

Lindsey lifted her head and it took a moment for her eyes to focus on her friend, who was indeed trying to get off at her own hand.

"You want to lick Vanessa's cum, don't you, Lindsey?"

"N- no." She swallowed hard. He wouldn't make her, would he?

"I saw how turned on you were when you made her come. She was turned on by you too, Lindsey. I doubt she's ever come that hard before in her life. Her pussy gripped my cock so hard, I almost lost it. She came for you. You want to taste it."

"No, I don't." She honestly didn't want to taste anyone's cum, but would they believe her while she was playing this game of false denial with them?

"Come here, Vanessa," he demanded. "Let her taste you."

"Wait," Lindsey whispered.

Shade grabbed a fistful of Lindsey's hair and lifted her face off the mattress so Vanessa could position herself in front of Lindsey with her legs spread wide. Lindsey had never been this up close and personal to a vagina since birth. Shade released Lindsey's hair, but she didn't lower her head to do what they wanted her to do. She closed her eyes and concentrated on the feel of Shade's powerful thrusts. Damn, the man was a good fuck.

Lindsey could smell Vanessa's excitement now and eventually had to admit it was enticing. Her mouth watered. She wanted to taste it. She did. But she'd never done anything like this. She was afraid of where her own desire might take her.

Vanessa placed a gentle hand on the back of her head. "It's okay, Lindsey," she whispered, stroking her hair tenderly while Shade continued to pound into her.

"Are you sure, Nessi?" she asked.

"I'm sure, baby."

Lindsey lowered her head and drew her tongue oh-so-slowly over Vanessa's quivering clit. Vanessa collapsed back onto the bed with a startled outrush of breath. Lindsey licked Vanessa's inner folds, using the orgasmic, teasing technique Kellen had used on her earlier that night. Vanessa's cum was sweet and tangy and Lindsey couldn't get enough of it. She licked Vanessa's opening until her tongue got tired and then she sucked her clit until her friend came. Lindsey was scarcely aware of Shade thrusting deep one last time or his shouting and shuddering as he took his release. When he let go of her thighs and pulled out, she shifted her arm between Vanessa's legs so she could slide two fingers into Vanessa's sweet, silky pussy. Lindsey loved making her friend moan and writhe in ecstasy. When Vanessa found another orgasm minutes later, Lindsey gasped at the sensation of Vanessa's flesh clenching in hard spasms around her exploring fingers. When her friend had settled, Lindsey kissed Vanessa's shaven mound affectionately and slid her fingers free.

She lifted her head to find that Shade had left the room while she'd been otherwise occupied eating out her best friend. What. The. Fuck?

Vanessa grabbed Lindsey and drew her against her in a warm embrace. "Damn, girl, where did you learn to do that with your tongue?"

"Um." Lindsey flushed. "Kellen Jamison?"

Vanessa laughed. "That man just landed himself at number one on my fuck-it list."

Lindsey lifted her head to look down into the familiar face of her best friend. She loved this woman, she did, but she didn't *ever* want to eat her pussy again. "Nessi?"

"Yeah, sugar."

"Does this mean I'm gay?"

"Naw, baby. We was just caught up in the moment and got a little bi-curious."

"Okay," she said and laid her head on Vanessa's shoulder.

"I don't know what it is about rock stars that makes us act all crazy."

Lindsey knew. "They're walking aphrodisiacs."

Vanessa chuckled and gave her an affectionate squeeze. "You said it, girlfriend. You said it."

Lindsey's mind soon wandered to the remaining two rock stars in on the tour bus.

"Hmm, I wonder if Gabe and Adam are cold and lonely."

"We could go check," Vanessa said.

## XII

Owen hopped out of his bunk and winced when his bare foot landed on a used condom. He was pretty sure it wasn't his, but who the hell knew after the orgy that had gone down the night before.

He peeled the sticky prophylactic off the bottom of his foot and tossed it into the garbage can under the sink. He was always the first to wake up, but this morning, it was important, because *Santa* had been too busy screwing the night before to dig his presents out of their hiding place.

Owen stepped over Tex, who was sprawled in the aisle wearing nothing but his cowboy boots, and for some inexplicable reason, his belt and prized rodeo buckle. Owen's toe connected with an empty whiskey bottle and it rolled across the floor to get lost under the dining room table, which had been used for a different kind of feast the night before. It had been fun while it lasted, but now his tongue would never work properly again and his lower back and hips were calling his insatiable cock every sort of a son-of-a-bitch.

Or maybe he'd dreamt it all. His band members were all stark naked and passed out in various uncomfortable positions around the cabin, but there wasn't a woman in sight.

He found the pair of female friends curled up together on the bed in the back of the bus. When the generous ladies had come out of the bedroom the night before, the only one who hadn't taken a turn at one or the other of them—or *both* of them in Owen's case—had been Kelly. He was still saving his love for a dead girl. Owen hoped his gift helped him get over her a little. If for no other reason, Kelly seriously needed to find something better than Owen's hand to get him off.

Owen donned a pair of discarded jeans he found on the bedroom floor—which turned out not to be his because they were several sizes too big—and his Santa hat. He flopped down on the floor, rolled onto his back, and shimmied his shoulders under the bed. He tugged out the velvet sack he'd stuffed way back under the headboard a few nights before.

A foot stomped right in the middle of his stomach.

"Umph!"

"Oh my God," Lindsey said as she pulled her foot back. "I'm so sorry. Are you okay?"

"You don't need a spleen to live," he said breathlessly and after some scooting around, rose into sitting position.

"Did we really have a sex orgy last night?" she whispered, her innocent-looking blue eyes wide in disbelief.

"Nope. What happens on the Sole Regret tour bus, stays on the Sole Regret tour bus." He winked at her and rose to his feet.

Owen slung his sack of presents over one shoulder and grinned at Lindsey. "Santa already gave you your present last night. You are now permanently on his naughty list."

She flushed and lowered her eyes to her clenched hands.

He leaned over and kissed her temple. "I meant what I said about every sinfully delicious thing that happens on this bus doesn't leave it."

"Okay," she said breathlessly, but didn't look at him.

She really was a doll. He might have considered calling her if she hadn't slept with every last one of his band mates. Oh, and his bus driver.

"You had fun, right?" Owen asked.

She nodded earnestly and then her eyes rolled up in her head as whatever erotic memories were teasing her thoughts.

"Then don't let it bother you."

He tripped over what had to be Gabe's overlong pant legs as he left her to mull over her misdeeds. He should probably find his own jeans, before he started waking people. He found them in the shower and had no idea how they'd gotten there. He took the time to use the john before changing into his own pants.

"Merry Christmas," he bellowed from the end of the corridor.

Tex sat bolt upright in the middle of the aisle. "What the fuck?" He covered his head with both hands and winced in pain. He then noticed his state of undress and shifted his hands to cover his crotch. "Who gave me whiskey?"

Owen chuckled. He wouldn't remember a thing from the night before. He never did when he drank too much whiskey.

"Ah God." He tried to stand but ended up crawling to the bathroom and locking himself inside.

"I said, Merry Christmas, assholes," Owen yelled. "It's time to wake up. Santa came."

"I remember him coming at least four times," Adam said from his bunk. Well, he was mostly in his bunk. One hand and foot were dragging the floor. "I can't feel my arm."

"That sucks for a lead guitarist, doesn't it?" Shade grumbled from the sofa. He had a pair of pink panties stuck to his forehead. Owen grinned, wondering how long it would take him to notice.

Adam rolled onto his back and used his functional arm to try to rub the circulation back into his temporarily frozen one. "I'd flip you off if you were worth the trouble."

"Here's what Santa brought you, Adam."

"Let me guess. Another chain."

Owen laughed. "How did you know?"

"You buy me a chain every year. That's why I have like ten of them."

"Well, now you have eleven. You're welcome."

Adam smiled at him—he really didn't do that enough these days. "Thanks, man. It's exactly what I wanted. And I really didn't get you shit."

"That's not from me, it's from Santa."

"Yeah okay. What are you—five years old?"

"On Christmas, I am."

Gabe hadn't stirred from his upside down sprawl in the recliner. His mohawked head was on the extended foot rest, legs spread and draped over each chair arm. After seeing where Gabe's balls were currently situated, Owen vowed to never sit in that chair again.

"Gabe, are you awake? It's Christmas."

"I just wanna sleep," he said in a slurred voice.

"I guess you don't want this boring ass book that Santa brought you." Owen dropped the heavy book on Gabe's chest, which definitely got his attention. Clutching the book in both hands, he lifted his head and glanced around in confusion. "Um," he said. "How in the fuck did I wind up sleeping like this? It defies all logic."

"Sort of like your hairstyle."

Gabe lifted the book and blinked his eyes until they focused well enough to read the title. "Theories in Antigravity? Now there's a thought. Imagine sex in space."

"Enjoy," Owen said.

He handed Shade a long flat box. "Sunglasses? For me? Good thing. Vanessa broke my last pair when she sat on my face."

"Nope, sorry. Had he known you would be without your precious sunglasses on Christmas morning, Santa would have gone with the usual, but he was a little more creative this year."

Shade opened the box and lifted the flat cross that dangled from a silver chain. He lifted an eyebrow at him. "Trying to keep me out of trouble?"

"Wear it over your heart," Owen said. "And read the inscription on the back while you're at it."

"Your angel," Shade read haltingly. "...is always." He scowled at the words.

"Close to your heart," Owen finished for him, knowing how the guy struggled with written language.

Shade bit his lip. "I wonder if she's awake yet. I need to call her. Do we have phone service yet?" He slipped the chain over his head and patted it into his chest, before peeling the panties off of his forehead and seeking clothes to make himself decent before he talked to his three-year old daughter on Christmas morning.

"Yeah, we have service," Tex yelled from the back of the bus. "I just called the crew. The equipment truck didn't attempt the pass, so they're all fine. A snow plow is trying to clear the roads and they're sending up a tow truck to help stranded vehicles."

Not quite a Christmas miracle, but definitely good news.

Owen found Kelly in the driver's seat. He was wide awake, wrapped in a red plaid flannel blanket staring out at the bleak white landscape outside the bus. The snow had stopped during the night, but the wind had piled it into huge drifts. The sky was gray with dense clouds, making the sunlight dim. Like Kelly's mood. Owen couldn't stand to see him depressed. Especially on Christmas. He stood beside his chair and stared at Kelly's reflection in the windshield for a long moment. Kelly had that familiar far-off, pained look in his eyes. He didn't seem to realize that Owen was standing at his side.

"You're thinking about her again," Owen said.

Kelly sucked a startled breath through his nose and then released it slowly. "Christmas is tough," he said quietly, though his gaze never moved from whatever point in the distance held his attention. He was seeing the past. Still living in the past.

"Why's that?" Owen asked.

"She said she wanted me to take her to see the Christmas tree in Times Square before she died."

Owen knew Sara had died in January, so the opportunity had been there. "Did you go?"

He shook his head almost unperceptively. "I refused to take her. I wanted her to stay in bed. All those little things she wanted to do before she went, I wouldn't let her do them. I was so afraid of her dying that I didn't let her live."

"Are you going to let yourself start living soon?" Owen asked.

Kelly turned his head to look up at him. "You can't help but stick your nose in other people's business, can you?"

"Nope."

"And you can't let people wallow in their misery."

"Nope."

"You know why?"

"Nope."

"Nothing truly horrible has ever happened to you."

Owen smiled. "And I plan to keep it that way." He pulled the last gift from his bag and tossed it on Kelly's lap. "Santa got you something. When you wear it, Sara will know you're still bound to her. When you take it off, it's because you're finally ready to do what she wanted you to do and move on."

Owen hoped Kelly didn't wear the leather wrist cuff for too awfully long. He wanted it to be a constant reminder to him that Sara would want him to find someone to love. Or at least to someone to screw properly.

He patted Kelly's shoulder and turned to go. Kelly grabbed Owen's wrist and stuffed a small box in his hand. "Santa got you something too."

Excitement flowing through him, Owen opened the box and found a set of dog tags on a chain. He ran his fingers over his brother's name—Chad—and then donned them. He'd worn dog tags for years—even before his brother had joined the military—to symbolize how he loved his country. These tags meant something even more to him. He clutched the flat pieces of metal in one hand and sent a silent prayer to keep his brother safe in Afghanistan. He hoped Chad was able to have some sort of celebration. Maybe he could talk the guys into visiting the troops and putting on a concert for them someday. Or maybe he could fool Shade into thinking that he'd come up with the idea and he'd insist the band go overseas.

"Thanks," Owen said, "but don't you think it's kind of lame to give your buddy jewelry for Christmas?" He knew damned well he'd given three out of four of his bandmates some sort of jewelry, but couldn't help but mess with Kellen. He was entirely too gloomy this morning.

"That's from Santa," Kelly said. "Don't tell me you stopped believing."

"Of course I haven't. It's Christmas."

He turned to find Shade talking on his cell phone and grinning like a loon. "Did you open all your presents already?" Shade laughed at whatever his daughter said on the other end of the line. "What did Santa bring you?" He interjected a "wow!" and a "that's awesome!" every now and then, but otherwise just listened to her rattle on about her apparently huge pile of gifts. After several minutes, his smile faltered. "No, angel, I can't come see you today." He put on a pair of horribly bent sunglass to hide his suddenly watery eyes, but he couldn't disguise the breathless quality of his voice as he spoke to her. "I'm stuck in the snow." He chuckled. "Yes, I know it doesn't snow lots in Texas, but I'm in Idaho. It snows lots in Idaho." He bit his lip. "You'd make a perfect snow angel."

Owen pointed at his Santa hat to remind him that they were going to give little Julie a second Christmas this year.

"When daddy gets home..." He paused as she interrupted him again. "Eight more sleeps. I know that's a long time, honey. When daddy gets home in eight more sleeps, we'll have another Christmas with just you and me."

Owen crossed his arms over his chest and cleared his throat pointedly. He totally wanted in on the fun. He loved Christmas just as much as any three-year-old.

"And Owen is going to get himself stuck in the chimney just for you." Shade laughed. "Yep, he does have a flying reindeer as a matter of fact." And then apparently his ex-wife got on the phone because his expression changed from his "melted daddy" look to his "oh my god, what does this bitch want now" look. "Maybe he does have a fucking flying reindeer," Shade shouted.

Really? She was going to yell at him about *that*? Owen normally didn't interfere in Shade's drama with his ex-wife, but he wasn't letting Tina ruin Shade's entire day. He was miserable enough about not getting to see his daughter today.

He lifted the phone to his ear, not really paying attention to her caterwauling. "Tina," Owen said, "he'll be there to pick Julie up a week from tomorrow. Have a Merry Christmas."

He hung up and handed the phone back to Shade.

"Thanks," Shade said, "I can't seem to control my temper when I have to interact with her."

"No problem," Owen said. "I love hanging up on her."

"How about a nice Christmas breakfast?" Shade said.

"Are you cooking?" Owen asked.

"Yep."

"Pancakes?"

"What else?"

"I'm in."

"Me too," Gabe said, setting his new book aside.

"Me three," Adam said.

"Kelly?" Owen called. "You want breakfast?"

"Does Gabe have pants on yet?"

"I'm on it," Gabe promised.

"Then yeah." Kelly shed his blanket, his new leather cuff on his wrist.

It brought Owen no joy to see Kellen wearing the gift he'd given him. He looked forward to the day that he took it off permanently.

Lindsey and Vanessa slinked out of the bedroom at the back of the bus.

"Can we join you?" Vanessa asked.

"Shade tugged a pair of panties out of his pocket and passed them discretely to Owen.

"Did you ever find your panties, Vanessa?" Shade asked.

"No," she said, crossing her arms over her chest. "I think some fool stole them."

Owen tucked her panties into his back pocket."

"I hope they turn up," Shade said. "We have a no panties-no breakfast policy on this tour bus."

"Whatever," Vanessa said.

"It's true," Gabe said. "Why do you think I decided to get dressed?"

"You wear panties?" Vanessa asked.

"Only on special occasions."

Lindsey grinned. "I found my panties. What's for breakfast?"

"Shade's famous melt-in-your-mouth pancakes."

"Sounds great." She moved to sit in the booth at the dining table.

When Vanessa tried to follow her, Adam reached out of his bunk with his now fully functional arm and grabbed her leg. "Panty inspection required."

"I said some fool done *stole* my panties."

"Then no breakfast for you."

Vanessa looked to her friend for assistance. "Girl, you aren't going to desert me, are you?"

"Sorry, Nessi, but I'm starving."

"Some friend you are." Vanessa eventually resorted to wearing a pair of Adam's boxer shorts so she could join them at breakfast.

It wasn't exactly the kind of Christmas morning Owen was accustomed to, but everyone was smiling and happy. That's all that really mattered to him.

*Share Me, by Olivia Cunning*

## XIII

It was a few hours before the snow plow and a tow truck made it up the mountain pass to clear the road and pull Lindsey's car out of a snow drift. She'd had one hell of a crazy night with the boys in the band but was surprised by how normal they were as they had breakfast and joked around with each other and played a game of hide Vanessa's panties. Owen especially liked to get Vanessa riled up. Lindsey was pretty sure Vanessa was overstating her exasperation with the five of them, but it was difficult to tell with Vanessa.

Lindsey almost didn't want to say good-bye to them when her car was deemed drivable and was ready to make the journey back home.

"Later, guys," Vanessa said. "Thanks for the multiple orgasms!"

The tow truck driver literally fell on his ass at this proclamation. He somehow managed to scrape himself off the pavement and climb into the cab of his truck.

Lindsey wasn't quite so bawdy in her farewell, though she was equally thankful for the multiple orgasms. She smiled and waved at them, knowing she'd never see any of them in person again, wondering why that made her a little sad. What they'd shared had just been sex—a hell of a lot of mind-blowingly awesome sex—but it hadn't meant anything.

Lindsey climbed in the car and watched the tour bus pull away, heading in the opposite direction from her boring hometown.

"That was fun," Vanessa said as Lindsey maneuvered her car cautiously down the steep grade.

"Yeah," Lindsey agreed. "Great guys."

"I can't remember ever having a better Christmas."

Lindsey chuckled. "That was very memorable."

Vanessa examined her fingernails. "You know, if you turned around right now and followed them, I bet we could have a very happy New Year as well."

"Vanessa! Damn girl, you and your horny vagina are gonna get us both killed." She said that, but it didn't stop her from contemplating a highly illegal U-turn.

"I'm about to jack this car and take off after them."

Vanessa pursed her lips together to try to stifle a laugh. She lasted almost three seconds before she bust a gut. Lindsey couldn't help but get caught up in the hilarity of their situation.

When the two of them stopped laughing, they exchanged a look of longing, but ultimately continued toward home.

"Merry Christmas, Lindsey," Vanessa said.

"Merry Christmas, Nessi."

The End

## About Olivia Cunning

Olivia Cunning is a NYTimes and USA Today best-selling author of the wildly popular Sinners on Tour and One Night with Sole Regret series. Combining her three favorite topics sex, love, and rock and roll, Olivia writes primarily erotic romance about rock stars.

www.OliviaCunning.com

# Other Books by Olivia Cunning

*Share Me* is a prequel to the One Night with Sole Regret novellas by Olivia Cunning. Read more about the band's drummer, Gabe Banner, in *Try Me*; guitarist, Adam Taylor, in *Tempt Me*; and vocalist, Shade Silverton, in *Take Me*. Bassist Owen Mitchell's first novella in the series, *Touch Me*, will be released soon, followed by *Tie Me*, featuring rhythm guitarist Kellen Jamison!

Made in the USA
Lexington, KY
13 December 2012